FMB ✗

✦ HARLEQUIN® BESTSELLING AUTHOR COLLECTION

In our Bestselling Author Collection,
Harlequin Books is proud to offer
classic novels from today's superstars
of women's fiction. These authors have
captured the hearts of millions of readers
around the world, and earned their place
on the bestseller lists with every release.

As a bonus, each volume also includes a
full-length novel from a rising star of series
romance. Bestselling authors in their own right,
these talented writers have captured the qualities
Harlequin is famous for—heart-racing passion,
edge-of-your-seat entertainment
and a satisfying happily-ever-after.

Don't miss any of the books in the collection!

New York Times and *USA TODAY* Bestselling Author

SHERRYL WOODS

Tea and Destiny

H **HARLEQUIN**®BESTSELLING AUTHOR COLLECTION

ISBN-13: 978-0-373-18494-1

TEA AND DESTINY

Copyright © 2011 by Harlequin Books S.A.

The publisher acknowledges the copyright holders
of the individual works as follows:

TEA AND DESTINY
Copyright © 1990 by Sherryl Woods

LIGHT THE STARS
Copyright © 2006 by RaeAnne Thayne

This edition published by arrangement with Harlequin Books S.A.

For questions and comments about the quality of this book,
please contact us at CustomerService@Harlequin.com.

Printed in U.S.A.

CONTENTS

TEA AND DESTINY

New York Times and *USA TODAY* Bestselling Author

Sherryl Woods

SHERRYL WOODS

With her roots firmly planted in the South, Sherryl Woods has written many of her more than one hundred books in that distinctive setting, whether it's her home state of Virginia, her adopted state, Florida, or her much-adored South Carolina. She's also especially partial to small towns, wherever they may be.

A member of Novelists Inc. and Sisters in Crime, Sherryl divides her time between her childhood summer home overlooking the Potomac River in Colonial Beach, Virginia, and her oceanfront home with its lighthouse view in Key Biscayne, Florida. "Wherever I am, if there's no water in sight, I get a little antsy," she says.

Sherryl also loves hearing from readers. You can join her at her blog, www.justbetweenfriendsblog.com, visit her website at www.sherrylwoods.com or contact her directly at Sherryl703@gmail.com.

Chapter 1

It was already late Sunday afternoon when Hank pulled his pickup truck to the side of the narrow road, turned off the engine and stared. His gaze turned not to the spectacular red-tinted sunset in the west, but east, with a sort of fascinated horror, toward the worst-designed house he'd ever seen. As an engineer with a healthy respect for architecture, that house offended his sense of style, his sense of proportion, even his sense of color.

What had once been a small and probably quite pleasant waterfront cottage now lurched improbably across a tiny spit of land that poked into the Atlantic. Additions had been tacked on willy-nilly, adjusting to whatever natural obstacle had been in the way. One wing took a left turn away from the abrupt curve in the beach. Another detoured around a banyan tree. Although it was all one story high, the rooftops were

not level, as if the specifications for the additions had
been dreamed up without paying the slightest attention
to the original.

The color scheme... He shook his head in wonder.
Was it possible that there had been only one can each
of the salmon-pink, dusty blue and canary-yellow paint
in the local paint store? The effect was jarring when it
should have been soothing. The house reminded him
of the owner.

Hank had met Ann Davies during the three days
of festivities surrounding his best friend's wedding.
Her effect on his system had been about as soothing
as rubbing sandpaper across metal. Ann was a tall,
rawboned woman with short black hair that he was
convinced had been sheared off by a lawn mower.
Her idea of makeup was apparently limited to a slash
of lipstick across a generous mouth that was always
in motion. The woman talked more than any other
human being he'd ever met. She had opinions—strong
opinions—on everything from football to mush-
rooms. She thought the former too brutal, the latter
unappetizing. Hank loved them both.

So why, in the name of all that was holy, was he
parked at the edge of her property? More to the point,
what had possessed him to listen to his friends Todd
and Liz when they'd suggested he come here? They
had actually managed to persuade him—even before
he'd finished the six-pack of his favorite beer they had
settled in front of him—that he could survive in the
same house with this irritating woman for the next few
months while he supervised construction of a shopping
center being built in nearby Marathon. They were crazy.
He was crazier.

He was also desperate, he reminded himself with stark realism. It was early January in the Florida Keys, the worst possible time to be starting a construction job. Condos, houses and hotels were filled to overflowing with tourists. Those accommodations that were still available cost an arm and a leg. The company could have written off the expense, of course, but the few places still sitting empty weren't available long-term. They'd already been booked for scattered weeks of the season.

Even so, he'd looked at every one of them, hoping to find something that would do even short-term. Most consisted of nothing more than a tiny room and a shower. They were all too cramped by far for his big frame. He would have felt claustrophobic after a single night. He'd actually stepped into the shower stall in one and come close to being wedged in.

The remaining alternative, to commute from Miami, while not impossible, would have driven him nuts inside of a week. Traffic this time of the year required the patience of a saint. Hank recognized his limitations. He was no saint. Just the prospect of being locked bumper to bumper with a bunch of sight-seeing tourists made the muscles in the back of his neck knot.

Then Ann had offered, via Liz, to let him have a room in her spacious home at no charge. She'd even volunteered to throw in meals, if he'd pick up his share of the groceries. He couldn't imagine what sort of blackmail Liz had held over her to convince her to invite him.

"Why's she doing it?" he'd asked Liz suspiciously. "I didn't exactly charm the socks off her at the wedding."

He'd meant it quite literally. He'd never before known

a woman who wore bright yellow socks and blue tennis shoes with a green skirt and hot-pink T-shirt. Not even to the movies, much less to a wedding rehearsal. He shuddered at the memory. He should have known right then what this house would look like.

Liz had given him one of her serene smiles and said blithely, "Oh, you know how Ann is."

He didn't know. He didn't even want to. Yet the fact remained, here he was, a couple of suitcases in the back of the truck along with three bags of groceries he'd picked up at the supermarket. Actually it was two bags of food and one of beer and sodas. After a hot day on the job, nothing was better than lying peacefully in a hammock sipping an ice-cold can of beer. The soda was for breakfast. The carbonation and caffeine got his blood circulating. The sugar content of the jelly doughnuts he ate along with it gave him energy. He could have used both right now.

With one last fortifying breath, he turned on the ignition and drove into a driveway with ruts so deep they jarred his teeth. He pulled the truck around to the side of the house. He'd climbed out and was in the process of trying to adjust all three bags of groceries in his arms when he was slammed broadside by something that hit him about knee-high. The bags went flying. Hank grabbed for the beer the way a dying man reaches for a lifeline. He knew in his gut he was going to need that beer, probably before the night was out.

When he and the bag of beer were upright—the groceries were strewn across the lawn—he looked down and saw a child of about three staring solemnly up at him. She had a thumb poked in her mouth and a frayed blanket dangling from her other hand. He only barely resisted the urge to moan. He had forgotten about the kids. More likely, he'd conveniently blocked them right out of his mind.

Hank really hated kids. They made him nervous. They aroused all sorts of odd feelings of inadequacy. They were noisy, demanding and messy. They asked endless, unanswerable questions. They caused nothing but worry for their parents, aside from turning perfectly enjoyable lifestyles upside down and inside out. Girls were even more of a mystery to him than boys. At least he'd been a boy once himself.

Still, he had to admit there was something appealing about this little girl. With her silver-blond hair curling in a wispy halo, she looked placid and innocent, as if she'd had absolutely nothing to do with virtually upending a man six times her size.

"Hi," he said cautiously. It had been a long time since Todd's son—his godson—had been this age, and he'd vowed to avoid Todd's new baby until she could speak intelligently. He'd figured that was another twelve to fourteen years away. He stared at the child in front of him. Beyond hello, what else did you say to a three-year-old, especially one who still had a thumb tucked in her mouth and showed no inclination to communicate?

"Where's your mommy?" he tried finally.

To his horror, tears welled up in the wide, blue eyes and the child took off at a run, dragging her thumb from her mouth long enough to let out a wail that would have wakened the dead.

Hank was just considering getting straight back into the pickup and bolting to the most expensive, tiniest condo he could find when a screen door slammed. The woman who'd loomed in his memory rounded a corner of the house at a run, her ankle-length purple skirt flapping, a butcher knife clutched threateningly in her raised hand. She skidded to a stop at the sight of him and slowly lowered the knife. Her furious expression calmed slightly.

There was nothing at all calm about his own reaction to the sight of her. His heart lurched with an astonishing thump. He dismissed the sensation at once as delayed panic. He'd rarely been confronted at the door by knife-wielding women. Surely that explained the surge of adrenaline that had his blood pumping fast and hard through his veins.

And yet… He took a good long look at her. Somehow all those uneven features he'd recalled had been rearranged into a face that was interesting, rather than plain, especially now with her color high. The tall, gaunt body, still dressed in an utterly absurd combination of colors and styles, seemed, for some peculiar reason, more appealing than he'd remembered. Her hair, still cropped short, suddenly seemed to suit her face with its feathery softness. It emphasized her eyes and those thick, sooty lashes. She looked…good. Damned good. Even with a knife in her hand.

He'd obviously lost his mind.

"Well, here you are," Ann said briskly as she put down the knife and began methodically to gather up the groceries. It gave her something to do to cover the nervous, fluttery feeling that had suddenly assailed her without warning. Nabbing a box of jelly doughnuts, she regarded them disapprovingly, then stuffed them in the bag along with assorted snack foods that she absolutely refused to have within a five-mile radius of the kids except on special occasions. She would deal with Hank Riley's dietary habits later, after she'd reconciled her memory of the obnoxious, arrogant man with the disconcertingly appealing sight of him.

"Sorry about Melissa," she apologized distractedly, fingering a head of lettuce. Lettuce was good. The choke hold this bearded giant of a man seemed to have over her senses was not. She swallowed hard. "I gather she's responsible for this."

"If she's about so high and partial to her thumb, she's the one," he acknowledged with a smile that made her stomach do an unexpected flip. "Did I frighten her or something? I asked where her mommy was and she let out a war cry that would have straightened the hair on Hitler's head."

Ann struggled with the unfamiliar sensations that continued to rampage through her, decided her panic at Melissa's scream was to blame and reclaimed a bit of control.

"So that's it," she said, satisfied with the explanation for her nervousness and oblivious to Hank's confusion.

He was regarding her oddly. "That's what?"

She tried frantically to recall what he'd just said. Something about Melissa's mother and Hitler? She wasn't sure what the Nazi connection was, but she understood precisely what had happened when Hank had mentioned the child's mother.

"I wondered what brought on all the tears. She came in crying about some man."

"Which explains the butcher knife."

She glanced down at the weapon she'd grabbed on her way out the door. It was lying at her feet. "Oh, sorry."

"Don't be. In this day and age, I don't suppose a

woman can be too careful," he said, reaching down to pick it up. "Since you didn't use it on me, I gather you've decided I'm harmless."

Harmless? No less than a pit of vipers. How had she forgotten that he had this strange effect on her? All she'd recalled after the wedding had been his infuriating habit of contradicting every opinion she held.

"Maybe I'd better explain about Melissa's mother," she said, clinging to a neutral topic. "The woman abandoned her a year ago, just took off without a word to anyone. A neighbor found Melissa all alone the next day. They say children adjust pretty easily, but Melissa hasn't. She still wakes up in the middle of the night crying for her mother. Any reminder tends to set her off."

Professional training kept her tone matter-of-fact, but she still seethed inside when she thought about it. "It's beyond me how a mother could leave a child all alone like that. Anything could have happened to her. What if there'd been a fire? Good God, can you imagine?" she said, shuddering visibly. "Even waking up and being all alone would be enough to terrify a baby. When the social worker told me about it, I felt like going after the woman myself. No wonder Melissa's not adjusting."

Hank muttered what sounded like an indignant curse under his breath, then said, "I'm sorry. I had no idea. I guess I was just thinking of you as her mother."

"We don't do a lot of swearing around here," she warned automatically. "The kids, well, some of them anyway, are at that impressionable age. As for Melissa, she calls me Ann. Some of the kids refer to me as Mother. It all depends on what they're comfortable with. Since you're going to be here awhile, I'll give you a rundown on each of them, so you'll understand how they ended up here. The older ones are pretty open about things, but the little ones are still a little sensitive." She fingered a package of cupcakes, regarded them distastefully and sighed. "Then there's Jason. He rarely talks at all."

Hank didn't seem to notice the fact that she couldn't shut up. In fact, he looked decidedly uneasy. "How many are there?" he asked, as if he were inquiring about enemy troops just beyond a strategic hill.

"Five. Six. It depends on whether Tracy stays with friends after her classes at the junior college in Key West. Tonight they're all here. Occasionally one of the kids who used to live here comes back for a visit."

Hank, a man who struck her as big enough and tough enough to fear nothing, seemed to take a panicky step closer to his truck. He looked as though he wanted to escape. She could relate to the feeling. She'd felt that way since the instant she'd spotted him standing in the yard in faded jeans, a body-hugging T-shirt and sneakers. He hadn't seemed nearly as devastating in the suits he'd worn the weekend of the wedding.

"I probably won't see all that much of them," he said, an edge of desperation in his voice. "I'll be working pretty long hours."

She waved aside the objection. "Nonetheless, it'll be better if you know. Come on in now and I'll show you around."

She led him in through the kitchen, simply because it was closest. It was also a mess, as it always was by Sunday night after a weekend of having everyone at home. She saw Hank's eyes widen at the sight of dishes stacked all over the counter and tried to view the clutter

from the perspective of a bachelor who probably paid a
maid to do his housework.

Toys were scattered all over the floor and her papers
were strewn across the round oak table that could seat
ten easily and usually was surrounded by that many
or more, all trying to talk at once. It was chaotic, but
she loved the happy confusion. She could understand,
though, how it might seem daunting and disorganized
to an outsider. She shrugged. He'd just have to get used
to it.

"We have cleanup in another hour," she said, stepping
over a toy tank and rolling a tricycle out of their path as
she plopped the groceries on top of the stove. "It's hard
to imagine now, but by the time we sit down to dinner,
this room will be spotless. Look quick, though, because
it'll only be that way about twenty minutes."

Hank was still standing uncertainly in the doorway.
"Are you sure I'm not putting you out? I know you told
Liz it would be okay, but…" He waved a hand around
the room. "You seem to have enough on your hands."

"Can you do your own laundry?"

"Yes, but…"

"Make your own bed?"

"Of course, but…"

"Are you any good at making coffee?"

"Yes, but…"

"Then it's no problem."

Almost as soon as the words were out of her mouth,
Ann regretted them. If he wanted to run for his life, she
should have let him. She should have encouraged him.

When Liz had first approached her about helping
Hank out, she'd been adamantly against it. The man
was the epitome of everything she disliked in the male

of the species. He was handsome in some indefinable way that made him all the more dangerous. He had the powerful shoulders and chest of a lumberjack. He managed to have a light tan on slightly freckled skin that by all rights should only turn beet-red in the sun. His hair and beard were a golden shade just shy of red. He had laughing blue eyes that could undress a woman in ten seconds flat, usually before the introductions were completed. He was bold and brash and irritating. His treatment of women had all the finesse of the caveman's, yet they flocked to do his bidding. With a reaction that was part astonishment, part dismay, she'd observed his effect on them at the wedding.

To top it off, his opinions on most subjects were diametrically opposed to her own. At the rehearsal dinner they'd been barely civil to each other. Their introduction had quickly escalated from hello into an argument about something so inane she couldn't even recall it now. It might have had something to do with the hors d'oeuvres. Liz had witnessed the clashes with interest, which made her plea to Ann for help all the more unbelievable. Ann realized later it should have made her suspicious at once.

"Think of him as a project," Liz had challenged. "You'll have weeks to work on him."

"I have six kids staying with me, plus a full-time career. I don't need a project. I need a maid."

"You need a man."

"Oh, no, you don't," Ann said, just catching on to the direction of her friend's devious thoughts. "Just because you're crazy in love and radiantly happy doesn't mean that everyone aspires to the same state of marital bliss.

I do not need a man. I especially do not need a man who thinks that watching wrestling is cultural."

Liz had laughed. "Hank does not watch wrestling."

"Okay, maybe it was tractor pulls."

"You're just a coward."

"Hardly. I just don't have time to waste trying to rehabilitate a thirty-seven-year-old man. It's too late."

"You're a psychologist. You know perfectly well it's never too late to reform someone."

"If they want to be reformed. What gives you the idea that Hank Riley has any desire to change?"

"Think of it as an experiment. You could probably get a great research paper out of it."

"You're stretching, Liz."

"I'm desperate," Liz had admitted finally. "I already told him you'd do it."

"Why on earth would you do that?"

"It was a calculated risk. When have you ever turned down a stray?"

"Hank Riley has a home to go to. From everything you've told me and my own observations, he has more women to look after him than Hugh Hefner. He does not need me."

Liz merely smiled. Ann found the reaction irritating. And, unfortunately, challenging.

"Maybe you're the one I should be trying to reform," Ann had finally said with a sigh of resignation. "Send him on. I suppose it won't kill Jason and Paul to share a room for a couple of weeks. I'll put Hank in Jason's room. It'll probably give him nightmares with all those awful sci-fi posters on the walls." That thought had cheered her considerably.

Liz, however, had looked very guilty. It had left her virtually tongue-tied for just long enough to panic Ann.

"Okay, Liz. What is it you're not telling me?"

"Now don't be upset," Liz pleaded. "You can still back out if you really want to."

She buried her face in her hands. "Oh, Lord. It must be even worse than I thought." She peeked. "Okay. Out with the rest of it."

"It's just that it's more like a couple of months, actually. Maybe three or four."

Ann had protested loudly at that, but she'd known she was beaten. There were moments when she'd even convinced herself it would be just fine. It would be good for the boys to have a male role model around. Not that Hank was the one she would have chosen, of course, but a little of that macho nature of his might be okay for them for a short time. He could take them fishing, play baseball. She could do those things perfectly well herself, but she knew in her heart it probably wasn't the same. Whole textbooks had been written on a boy's need for male bonding.

Now that Hank was actually here in the kitchen, though, she wondered. He seemed a little overwhelming somehow. At the wedding, he had infuriated her with such frequency that she'd barely noticed that he had an interesting effect on her pulse. She'd assumed that it had been part of her constant exasperation with him, but he'd done nothing in the past five minutes to flat out annoy her and her heart was reacting peculiarly just the same. Maybe it was the sight of all those empty calories—doughnuts, potato chips, corn curls.

"These have to go," she said, taking a handful of packages and reaching for the garbage can.

Hank snatched them away from her, an expression of horror on his face. Indignation radiated from every considerable inch of him. "Are you out of your everlovin' mind, woman? Liz said you wanted groceries. I brought groceries."

"You brought junk. The kids will all be hyperactive if they eat that."

"So tell 'em not to touch the stuff. I'll sacrifice. I'll eat every last chip myself."

"You can't tell children not to eat foods like that, then put them right smack in front of them."

"I'll hide every bit of it in my room."

"See," she said, waving a finger under his nose. "That is exactly what I mean. You're addicted to that junk. That's what it does to you."

His blue eyes took on a challenging glint. "I enjoy it. I am not addicted to it. There's a difference."

"Smokers enjoy their cigarettes, too. That doesn't mean they're any less addicted."

He took one step toward her, which put them toe-to-toe. Close enough for her to smell the minty freshness of his breath and the clean, masculine scent of his soap. Near enough to kiss. Oh, dear heaven.

"The food stays," he said softly.

That gleam in his eyes turned dangerous. It might have been a warning about those damn corn curls, but she had a feeling it was something else entirely. She wasn't particularly crazy about the alternative. She took a step backward, then lifted her chin to counter any impression of retreat.

"Keep them out of sight of the children."

He grinned. "Yes, ma'am."

The response was polite enough, but the bold and

brash tone made her want to slap him. Hard. She was shocked by the intensity of her desire to strike that smug, unrepentant expression off his face. She was a trained psychologist, a woman who believed in rational thought and the importance of calm communication. She did not believe in spankings for childish misbehavior, much less in beating up on people just because they infuriated her.

"Anything else?" he inquired.

She bit back a whole string of charges about his attitude. He was Liz's friend. Well, more precisely he was Todd's friend, but she would tolerate him just the same. He was only a temporary boarder, after all. With any luck he'd chafe at the restrictions of living with them and be gone by the following weekend.

"Dinner's at seven. We all help. House rule."

"No problem."

"There are others. Rules are important, especially for kids who aren't used to having anyone around who cares enough to enforce them. I'll explain them as the occasions arise." She tried her best to make it sound as though the household adhered to strict military discipline.

"Whatever you say."

She hadn't expected him to be quite so agreeable. For some reason, it increased her irritation. She nodded curtly. "Then I'll show you to your room."

Before they could even gather up his suitcases, though, there was another of those bloodcurdling yelps from the far side of the house. Ann dropped the bag she was holding and took off at a run.

"Does everyone in this house do that?" Hank said, sprinting after her.

"Only when disaster strikes." She hoped that sounded sufficiently ominous to terrify him.

"Does it strike often?" he inquired with what sounded more like curiosity than panic.

"If it makes you nervous—" she began.

"It does not make me nervous. I'm just worried it might be bad for their lungs."

"Their lungs are very healthy, except maybe for Paul's. He's had a few too many colds this winter." She paused in midstep. "I wonder why that is?"

Hank looked confused. "Why what is?"

"Why Paul was the only one to get so many colds?"

"Is this something you really need to figure out now? Shouldn't we find out why someone screamed?"

"Right." She turned a corner into the west wing of the house. "My guess is that the tub is overflowing. Sometimes the faucet leaks and the drain stops up. When both things happen together, well, you can imagine."

As if to prove her point, her sneaker-clad feet hit a wet patch of floor and shot out from under her. Hank grabbed her from behind and held her upright. She enjoyed the sensation of his hands on her waist far too much. She was almost disappointed when he released her. It was not a good sign.

"Stay here," he ordered in the tone of a man used to taking charge. That tone snapped her back to reality. She immediately bristled when he added, "I'll take care of it."

As if she needed him to, she thought with well-honed defensiveness. "I can handle it," she said, stepping past him and immediately skidding again.

"Stay put before you break your neck."

Leaving her sputtering indignantly, he waded off through water that was already soaking the hallway rugs. She glared after him. She could either make an utter ass of herself by arguing or she could do the pragmatic thing and help. Life had taught her the importance of being pragmatic.

She grabbed up the rugs and took them outside, then ran back for a mop. She was trying to stem the flow of water when Hank emerged from the bathroom with Melissa and Tommy wrapped in towels and tucked awkwardly under his arms like a couple of sacks of grain. He looked decidedly nervous. He handed them over as if he couldn't get rid of them fast enough.

"I'm going to get a couple of tools out of the truck. You might want to find some dry clothes for these two."

"Where's Tracy?"

"I left her figuratively holding her finger in the dike. Other than her hysterical scream, she keeps a pretty cool head in a crisis. This could have been a lot worse."

"She's used to it. The tub overflows about twice a week."

Melissa and Tommy, who'd seemed tongue-tied until now, began chattering enthusiastically about splashing through the water. Unfortunately it had become their favorite form of recreation. Ann had a suspicion they were secretly delighted every time the blasted tub overflowed. Hank listened to their excited stories and shook his head.

"Hasn't it occurred to you to call a plumber?"

It had. She'd dismissed it as too costly. She was not about to admit that to him. "The thought has crossed my mind, but I thought I could handle it myself."

"If you handle it any more effectively, you'll have to replace all these wooden floors."

His sarcasm set her teeth on edge. "Mr. Riley, may I remind you that you are a guest in this house. I do not need you to come in here and start telling me how to run my life or fix my house."

"Any more than I need you telling me what to eat," he retorted, matching her hands-on-hips stance. She had to admit he was better at it than she was. He was also grinning, which was not one bit like what she felt like doing.

"Okay," she snapped back. "Eat what you darn well please."

"I will."

"And I'll fix my own darn tub."

His smile widened. Then to her amazement, he backed down so fast it left her head reeling. "As you like," he said pleasantly. He waded off through the water, leaving her gaping after him. She was left with a throatful of angry words and no target at which to spew them.

"Where are you going?" she shouted at his retreating back.

He turned around and shot her a lazy, carefree grin. "I thought I'd have a beer. What about you? Want one? I could pour it while you're working on the tub."

"Go to…"

He halted her in midsentence by gesturing toward the suddenly silent, wide-eyed children standing beside her. "Tsk, tsk, Annie. No swearing in front of the children. Isn't that what you told me?"

As he disappeared from view, she wondered exactly how traumatic it would be for the kids to watch her take a shotgun to their houseguest.

Chapter 2

Ann was horrified. The serene, in-control woman she had always thought herself to be did not yell at the top of her lungs in anger. She did not consider using a shotgun to settle an argument. For that matter, until this afternoon, she'd never lifted a butcher knife except to slice a turkey. What was Hank Riley doing to her?

Bewildered and still fuming, she felt a tug on her skirt and looked down into Tommy's dark, troubled eyes. She was promptly overcome by guilt on top of everything else. She knew how much violence Tommy had endured in his first three years in war-torn Afghanistan. For the two years that he'd been with her, she'd tried very hard to protect him from irrational outbursts. Even with seven very different people in the house, she'd been able to maintain an atmosphere of relative calm. Her own temper was blessedly even.

Until today, she reminded herself. In less than an hour Hank Riley had shaken her normal aplomb to its very foundations. That made her very nervous. She knew perfectly well that any man who aroused that much fury could probably arouse an equal amount of passion.

When hell freezes over, she declared, just as Tommy tugged again and asked in his softly accented voice, "Is he the plumber?"

"No, he is not the damn plumber," she snapped irritably, then immediately felt contrite. She hugged the dark-haired boy who was watching her with eyes that were far too serious.

"Sorry, baby," she said to Tommy as Melissa happily singsonged, "Bad word. Bad word."

Ann considered uttering a whole string of them. Instead she patted the child on her blond head and admitted, "That's right. That is a bad word and I don't ever want to hear any of you using it. You two go on to your rooms and put on some dry clothes."

"Want to swim," Melissa protested, her face screwing up in readiness for a good cry.

"You will not swim for an entire week if you two are not in your rooms by the time I count to three," Ann said very quietly.

They recognized the no-nonsense tone. Melissa's pout faded at once. Tommy was already scampering down the hall, favoring the leg that had been shattered two years ago by guerrilla gunfire. Ann sighed as she watched them go. Another crisis averted. Barely.

"Ann." Tracy's plaintive voice reached her. "I can't stay like this much longer."

"Oh, good heavens!" She ran into the bathroom

and found Tracy exactly as Hank had left her, with her finger stuck at an awkward angle in the leaking faucet.

"Didn't the man even have sense enough to cut off the water?" she grumbled, turning back toward the door. The man in question was standing in her way, arms folded across a chest that could have blocked for offense on the Miami Dolphins.

"The water's off," he said, apparently unperturbed by her scowl or her denigrating comment.

"Oh."

She glanced at Tracy. "You can let go now."

Tracy shook her head. "That's just it. I can't. My finger's stuck."

With an impatient, you-should-have-known glance in Ann's direction, Hank stepped through the remaining puddles and sat down next to Tracy on the edge of the tub. Using a bar of soap, he worked Tracy's finger loose from the faucet. Ann was astounded by his teasing reassurances. She was even more startled by his gentleness. When Tracy's swollen finger was freed at last, he wiped it with a damp cloth, inspected it for cuts, then thanked her.

"You did a great job. Without your quick thinking, this could have been a lot worse."

Tracy beamed. Ann felt an odd fluttering in her chest. She hadn't seen a smile like that on the girl's face in all the years she'd lived there. Usually Tracy was far too quiet and unresponsive, except when she was taking care of the littlest kids. Her inability to get through to Tracy worried her. The ease with which Hank had astonished her.

"Honey, are you okay?" Ann asked, kneeling down

in front of her, oblivious to the fact that her skirt was dragging in the puddles.

Tracy turned the radiant smile on her. "Sure." She held out her hand. "Not even a scratch."

"Great. Would you go check on Melissa and Tommy for me? After that try to get Paul and David to start cleaning up the kitchen. It's almost time to start dinner. I'll be there in a minute."

"Sure, Ann." She looked hesitantly at Hank. "Are you sticking around?"

"Yep." He shot a challenging look at Ann. "At least through dinner."

When Tracy had gone, Ann got to her feet and quickly began mopping up the floor, her soaked skirt slapping soggily against her legs. She couldn't quite bring herself to look at Hank, who was still perched on the edge of the tub fiddling with the faucet.

"You were very good with her," she finally conceded. "Thanks."

He didn't look up. "She seems like a good kid," he murmured, then began working a snakelike device down into the drain.

"Beware of calling an eighteen-year-old a kid. That's an offense considered on a par with listening to phone calls or denying use of the car."

"Umm." He gave a tug on his probe, which emerged with a small plastic dinosaur. Ann recognized it as one of Tommy's collection from the zoo. Hank shook his head, tossed the toy aside and went back to poking around. "Sounds like you know her pretty well."

"I know teenagers pretty well. I'm not so sure about Tracy."

"She's not yours?"

Ann shook her head, instantly feeling a familiar defensiveness steal over her. "None of them are mine, not in the biological sense. I thought Liz explained."

"Only in the vaguest terms. She said you had several children you'd taken in. I assumed that some of the others might be yours."

"No. I've never been married."

That brought his head up, eyes twinkling. He gave her a grin that was only one quirk of the lips short of being a leer. "From what I hear that's not a requirement."

"It is for me," she said stiffly.

He studied her intently. "I see."

"I doubt it."

"Is your sexual hang-up something we should explore?" he inquired in a tone that teased and infuriated.

"I do not have a sexual hang-up," she said with slow emphasis, her temper reaching an immediate boil again. "And don't try playing psychologist with me, Mr. Riley. I'm the expert, remember?"

The grin faded. "How could I forget."

She listened for an edge of sarcasm, but couldn't detect one. An irrational part of her wished that grin were back, though.

"Tell me about Tracy," he said.

The ease with which he switched from provocative teasing to less dangerous turf irritated her almost as much as the teasing itself. Okay, she'd be the first to admit that she'd gotten out of the habit of taking sexual banter in stride, but she wasn't exactly the prude he'd implied. She was inclined to tell him just that, but reminded herself that she owed him no explanations. Instead she took the safe out he'd offered and said succinctly, "Tracy had some problems at home."

That was like saying World War II had been a small military skirmish. At the memory of the psychological and physical pain Tracy had suffered at the hands of an abusive father and a lousy system, Ann felt a familiar weariness steal through her. Apparently Hank caught her shift in mood.

"Bad, huh?" he said with quick understanding and a level of compassion that surprised her.

She stared into eyes that invited confidences and offered strength. "Lousy," she admitted. "Though I confess at times I forget just how bad it was for her. She tends to keep it all bottled up under a tough facade. Nothing I've done seems to get through to her."

"Was she a runaway?"

"I never thought I'd say this, but I wish she had been. Maybe there would have been fewer scars."

"You know that's not true," he said, glancing up. Blue eyes rebuked her. "All you have to do is ride around a few areas in Miami to see what happens to kids on their own too young."

She sighed. "I know you're right. Loss of innocence is pretty crummy at any age, but I doubt if Tracy ever had any innocence. She had a father who…well, I'm sure you get the idea. He wasn't fit to raise pigs. He cast a long shadow. She's been away from there for nearly five years now and she's still not very trusting around men. In fact, she's pretty wary of all adults, probably because she thinks we all failed her."

"Can you blame her?"

"Not for a minute. That doesn't make it any easier when she's treating me like I'm the enemy, when all I want to do is help. Occasionally it wears me down."

"She's stuck around, hasn't she? You must be doing something right."

"Maybe," she said, though she was pleased by his observation. If he could see it, maybe she had been slowly winning Tracy's trust, after all. Though the girl often stormed out with a chip on her shoulder, she always returned and she always abided by the rules. Of all of them, in fact, Tracy was the one who seemed most in need of the reassurance that someone cared what she did—or didn't do. How odd that it had taken this virtual stranger with the penetrating gaze and quicksilver mood changes to make her realize that.

Suddenly the bathroom seemed too confining. Or perhaps it was simply that Hank's body seemed too masculine, too overwhelming, in the intimate space. It reminded Ann in an unrelenting way that she was a woman, something she all too often allowed herself to forget during jam-packed days of counseling and surrogate mothering.

"Why don't you go on and get settled?" she suggested, feeling a sudden need to reclaim some of her own space. "I'll finish cleaning up in here."

"I want to check out these pipes first."

"Don't bother. I'll call the plumber in the morning."

"Why should you do that? I'm here now."

"Then I'll pay you."

"You will not."

Ann's temper flared irrationally at his stubborn insistence. "Dammit, I will not have you coming in here challenging my independence!"

To her chagrin, Hank laughed. The sound echoed off the tile walls. "Is that what I'm doing? It must be on shaky ground."

Fury teased at her insides before she, too, finally chuckled. The tension in her shoulders eased. "Okay. That's a slight overstatement. But you do need to understand that I'm used to being on my own. It's important to me."

"I'll try not to trample on your pride, but you need to understand that for as long as I'm here I want to do my share. The kids have chores. Why shouldn't I?"

She lifted her chin to a defiant tilt. "The kids are staying," she pointed out. "You're not."

The words were spoken flatly, with absolutely no hint of feeling, but Hank took one look at Ann's expression and realized that a whole world of emotion was behind them. In the depths of her eyes he saw stark evidence of feelings he couldn't possibly begin to comprehend. Abandonment. Hurt. Betrayal. Had they been her own? Or had she just seen too much in her life, too many innocent children wronged, too many hearts trampled on? Being a psychologist might equip her with a depth of understanding of human foibles, but the nonstop listening and advising had to take its toll. As he watched, she visibly withdrew, gathering her strength, shrouding her vulnerabilities.

The ease with which she did it saddened him. For a fraction of a second Hank wanted to take the tall, stoic woman in his arms. He wanted to comfort her. He wanted to challenge her easy acceptance of the fact that he was here today, but very likely gone tomorrow. He wanted to promise her a life filled with warmth and love and commitment. He wanted to tell her that the world really wasn't such a lousy place. Ironically, he wasn't sure he believed that himself. Maybe, in the end, he and Ann Davies were two of a kind, both too cynical to believe in happily ever after.

So he didn't argue. He didn't hold her. He didn't do a damn thing, except what he did best: he ran. He turned away from her emotional needs and tackled the practical ones. He went to work on the drain again.

After several minutes of thick, increasingly awkward silence, she left the room. Hank didn't look up. He said nothing.

When she'd gone, the faintest scent of strawberries lingered. It taunted his senses in a way that expensive French perfumes never had. He wondered if the taste of strawberries was on her lips. The possibility was provocative. Maddening. He had the oddest feeling, now that she was out of reach, that he'd made a terrible mistake in not acting on impulse and kissing the woman senseless. Maybe once he'd done it, her odd grip on him would loosen.

His hand slipped and his knuckles scraped along the jagged inside edge of the drain. He cursed as blood welled slowly. He ransacked the medicine cabinet for antiseptic and dumped it on, grateful for the pain. For an instant, anyway, it blocked out his unexpected, inexplicable sense of loss.

It was going to be a very long couple of months.

It was a very long evening. There was absolutely no gracious way Hank could think of to get out of joining the whole unorthodox, noisy family for dinner on his very first night. He figured it was a test contrived by an irritated Maker. He barely passed. His nerves were so tightly wound by the time they finished saying

grace and passed the heaping platters of food that his
shoulders felt as if he'd been lifting weights for an hour.

He discovered that there was no such thing as
conversation, much less seductive intimacy, at a table
with six children. There were pokes. There were
grumbled complaints about vegetables. There were
muttered gripes about the choice of baked rather than
fried chicken. There were threats of banishment if
one single spoonful of mashed potatoes was actually
flung across the table. There were promises of dessert
for those who finished their glazed carrots. And there
was intense bargaining over dishwashing duties. Ann
presided over it all with Madonna-like serenity.

Hank watched her and marveled. While his muscles
knotted at the confusion, she seemed to thrive on it. Her
cheeks glowed. Her blue eyes sparkled with laughter.
She was as adept as an experienced referee in the midst
of a goal-line pileup. She knew exactly what everyone
needed at any given second and provided it. Platters and
bowls came and went with the precision of a banquet
caterer. No argument was allowed to erupt into anger.
She teased. She soothed. She tolerated spilled milk and
gravy stains with equanimity, but drew the line at food
fights.

"Enough," she said, unable to hide a grin as David—
or was it Jason? Nope, Jason was the one who never
talked—promised to stuff cold potatoes down Tracy's
throat if she dared to reveal some secret he'd entrusted
her with. Ann moved the potatoes safely out of reach.

"You are such a jerk," Tracy countered with a look
of supreme disgust for the red-haired boy beside her.
"Why would I want to tell anyone that you—"

"Tracy!" he threatened, stretching to try to get a grip

on the bowl that Ann had just moved. An embarrassed flush spread beneath his freckles.

Tracy grinned back. "Gotcha."

"Mom, make her promise," David implored.

"Not me," Ann said, getting up and beginning to clear the table. "You two work it out or leave the table."

David moved his chair with a thump. Tracy propped her elbow on the table and settled her chin in her hand. Her expression of exaggerated innocence amused Hank. He waited for David's next move.

"What'll it cost me?" he said resignedly, sinking back in his chair.

Tracy reacted indignantly. "I am not blackmailing you, you little twerp. Jeez, what's wrong with you? I was only teasing."

Ann paused behind Tracy's chair and put a warning hand on her shoulder. Hank watched as the girl struggled with her anger. "I'm sorry," she muttered finally.

David blinked at the apology, then stared at the table. "Yeah, me, too," he mumbled.

"Now how about dessert?" Ann said cheerfully, ending the brief moment of tension. "Who wants strawberries with ice cream?"

"Me."

"Me."

The chorus came from around the table. Hank found himself chiming in, though the thought of strawberries brought all sorts of dangerous memories to mind. "I'll help," he said, feeling a sudden need to move, a surprising desire to be an active participant, rather than an observer.

"Not tonight," Ann said, her gaze pinning him where he was.

"You told me everyone helped," he reminded her, wondering if this was yet another attempt to set him apart, to remind him that he wasn't a permanent fixture.

She grinned. "We have another rule. No one helps on the first night here."

"Yeah, but after tonight, watch out," Jason warned in a sullen tone. They were the only words he'd spoken since the start of the meal. "Mom's schedules make the army look like summer camp."

"Who'd like Jason's share of dessert?" Ann queried lightly.

Though he'd been slouched down in his chair, feigning disinterest, Jason immediately scrambled to his feet and reached for the bowl.

"Hey, hand it over."

A grin on her face, Ann held the bowl just beyond his reach. Wiry and swift, he tried to grab it, but she made a move as smooth as any quarterback could have performed and passed it over to David at the table. Jason didn't waste time bemoaning the loss. He simply nabbed the one remaining bowl on the counter, and clutching it securely to his chest, went back to his place at the table. The lightening of his mood surprised Hank.

"That's mine," Ann said.

"Oh, really," Jason said with exaggerated innocence.

"Give that back this minute."

"Gee, Mom, are you sure you should be eating all this rich food? There's gotta be cholesterol in this stuff, right? We wouldn't want to watch you die of clogged arteries or something," he said in a way that brought a laugh bubbling up from deep inside Hank. She glared at the two of them, though he was sure he detected a hint of delight as she watched Jason interacting like the rest of them.

"It's really frozen yogurt," she admitted with a look of supreme satisfaction.

"Oh, yuck." David groaned.

"What do you mean, 'oh, yuck'?" Ann retorted. "You ate every bit of it."

"I wouldn't have, if I'd known."

"Which is exactly why I didn't tell you. Next time I take you all out for frozen yogurt, I expect a few less protests." She scowled at Hank and Jason, who were still laughing. "As for you guys, tomorrow the two of you are on KP and I expect something healthier than hot dogs."

"Hamburgers," Hank suggested hopefully.

She gave him a wilting look that relegated hamburgers to the same junk heap that contained corn curls and potato chips.

"I will not fix steamed vegetables," Hank said staunchly.

That drew a chorus of cheers. He turned to Jason and said impulsively, "Think we can catch some fish tomorrow?"

Jason regarded him hesitantly, his brown eyes suddenly hooded and suspicious. There was an instant's tension before he finally said, "Yeah, I guess."

Ann ignored the hesitation and regarded the two of them with pointed skepticism, then turned to Tracy. "If they're not back here with the fish by five-thirty, you might defrost that chicken in the freezer."

"Oh, ye of little faith," Hank said.

"I'd be delighted to have you prove me wrong," she

retorted cheerfully as she began clearing the dessert plates.

Hank felt his blood stir at the challenge in her voice and the look in her eyes. It was a look that taunted and teased like a delicate spring breeze. No other woman should dare a look like that unless she meant it, but Hank knew beyond a shadow of a doubt that Ann didn't. In fact, he seriously questioned whether she was even aware of its effect on him. He'd never met a woman less interested in using her femininity to lure a man.

Acting on an irresistible impulse, his arm circled her waist and he pulled her down until their eyes were even. Hers were startled and definitely wary.

"You're playing with fire, lady," he warned in a low voice, not meant to be overheard, though of course it was. He released her slowly, watching as the color heightened in her cheeks, enjoying the sudden, sharp catch of her breath as giggles erupted around the table.

And, then, he felt like a heel. The woman had done nothing but welcome him into her home, and here he was blatantly taunting her right smack in front of her family. He was deliberately trying to seduce her, when he knew perfectly well they were about as suited as a porcupine and an armadillo. When would he learn that not every challenge had to be taken, not every bet won? When, he thought in disgust, would he learn to walk away before someone got hurt?

This time, he promised, glancing around at six expectant young faces. Definitely this time.

Then he made the mistake of looking into those blue, blue eyes again and his pulse ran wild. Common sense and decency fled, chased by something much more primitive.

Oh, hell. Maybe not this time after all.

Chapter 3

As exhausted as if she'd never once closed her eyes, Ann dragged herself out of bed when the alarm went off at six and stumbled into the bathroom. Bleary-eyed, she stared at her pale reflection in the merciless mirror. She looked like hell and felt ten times worse. What was wrong with her? She usually enjoyed getting up early. It gave her an hour to herself before the house filled with noise and her day became guided by other people's demands. Today, though, she felt like crawling back into bed, pulling the covers up over her head and staying there until Hank Riley moved out. Unfortunately that was impossible.

Splashing ice-cold water on her face revived her somewhat. She ran her fingers through her hair in lieu of combing it, then pulled on a pair of running shorts and a shapeless sweatshirt. When she'd added her socks and sneakers, she wandered into the kitchen, put the decaf into the coffeemaker and then began a series of warm-up exercises. She groaned with every single stretch.

Her body was tight as a drum, probably due entirely to the tension set off by that look in Hank's eyes when he'd wrapped his muscular arm around her waist and deliberately taunted her at dinner the night before. Most men did not look at her as if she were a tasty morsel of prime rib and they'd been on a starvation diet. Knowing that Hank probably never looked at any woman in any other way didn't seem to stop the palpitations.

A long, strenuous run was just what she needed to take her mind off the man's invasion of her home. She stepped outside and took a deep, reviving breath of the salty air. The sun was just beginning to lift over the edge of the horizon. It would be another hour before it began to burn off the morning fog. For now it was like being all alone in the world. A sense of peacefulness stole over her.

"You're up early." Hank's voice, low and seductive, emerged eerily from the mist. Ann's just-loosened muscles immediately went taut again. She just barely resisted the desire to curse.

"I'm going running," she replied briskly instead, stepping off the porch. Waving in the general direction of the house, she added, "Help yourself to whatever you want for breakfast, if you don't have time to wait for the rest of us."

She took off at a slow jog. Instead of taking the hint, however, Hank fell into step beside her. She heard the clank of a can as he tossed it in the direction of the porch. Soda? For breakfast? Good God, the man would be dead before his fortieth birthday.

"Mind if I join you?" he asked.

"Would it matter if I did?"

"It might. Try me."

"Stay," she ordered as authoritatively as if he were a resistant puppy. He'd obviously had no obedience training. He stayed right beside her.

"I guess that answers that," she said with a sigh. She glanced sideways and noted that he was wearing a University of Miami Hurricanes sweatshirt that had clearly been through several seasons. The neckline had been stretched, the sleeves cut out. His cutoff jeans revealed powerful legs, corded with muscles. For a man who ate garbage, he looked awfully solid. And strong. And tempting. She dragged her gaze away.

"How far do you usually run?" Hank asked.

"Five miles."

He uttered a choking sound. Ann grinned. Despite his awesome physique, she doubted if Hank Riley ever ran farther than the corner grocery to grab another six-pack. She deliberately picked up her pace. He easily lengthened his stride to match hers.

"Do you do this every morning?" he asked.

"Just about."

"Ever do a marathon?"

"I used to. Now I don't have the time to train properly."

Hank muttered something that sounded like, "Thank God."

"What about you?"

"I don't run," he said, confirming her suspicion. She figured that gave him maybe another mile before he started huffing and puffing.

"I do work out at the gym every day, though," he said, sending her hopes plummeting. "I was going to look for a place down here, but maybe I'll just go running with you instead. I hate to exercise alone, don't you?"

Actually Ann had always considered the solitude the height of heaven. To declare that now, though, would only lead to all sorts of speculation on Hank's part. She could tell he was grinning at her. She glanced over. Yep, the smirk was in place all right. There was also a disconcerting gleam in his eyes as he surveyed her from head to toe, lingering an unnecessarily long time on her bare legs.

"You have great legs," he observed with the authoritative tone of a connoisseur.

Ann could feel the heat begin to rise and it had nothing to do with the exercise. If he expected her to thank him for the compliment, he could wait from now till she won the Boston Marathon.

"Why do you always cover them up with those long skirts?" he persisted.

She frowned at the implied criticism. "I happen to like long skirts."

"Why?"

"Do I need to have a reason?"

"In the overall scheme of life, probably not. As a psychologist, though, I'd think you'd be a little curious about your motivations."

"Long skirts are comfortable."

"And concealing."

"I am not trying to conceal anything," she said adamantly.

"I hope not. With legs like yours…"

"I do not want to talk about my legs."

"So it does make you uncomfortable when men find them attractive?"

"It does not!"

He was laughing at her again. "I thought so," he said with that infuriatingly self-satisfied tone that made her want to rip the hairs of his beard out one by one.

Ann finished her run ten minutes faster than usual. She'd run, in fact, as though she were being chased by the devil himself. All in all, she figured it was an apt analogy.

Hank was late. In fact, he'd been running late ever since he'd gone jogging with Ann. He'd skipped breakfast to try to catch up, but that lost half hour in the morning plagued him the rest of the day.

It had been worth it, though. The discovery that the woman had an absolutely knockout body under all those layers of clothes had practically taken his breath away. He hadn't been able to get the image of those slender, well-shaped legs, the smooth white skin and the subtle bounce of her breasts out of his mind. He'd lost a good ten minutes of every hour daydreaming about her. He'd wasted another five cursing himself because of it.

Now he was running behind for his fishing date with Jason. He'd promised to meet him at four, but at three-thirty the construction crew started balking over the quality of some of the materials that had been delivered that morning. Hank went with them to check up on the complaints and found they were valid. The materials were obviously an inferior grade. Whether it was a simple mistake or an outright attempt to defraud the company, it meant a waste of time and money to correct.

Had it not been caught, it could have been disastrous down the line. It was the sort of corner-cutting he and Todd had never tolerated on one of their jobs.

Furious, he spent the next hour on the phone trying to reach the supplier, whose assistant was amazingly adept at evasion. No doubt she'd had a lot of practice. He slammed the phone down for the fifth time, then glanced at the clock. It was already four-thirty. He picked up the phone again and called Miami, this time for Todd.

"Do me a favor, would you, and see if you can straighten this mess out," he requested when he reached his partner.

"I'll try, but you've dealt with this guy before. Can't you get anywhere with him?"

"I might be able to if I spent the next hour hanging around waiting for him to get back to me, but I have an appointment."

"One that's more important than this?"

Hank hesitated. He could understand Todd's amazement. In all the years they'd known each other, Hank had never walked out in the middle of a fight. He actually enjoyed sparring with the more difficult personalities.

Before he could think of an adequate response, Todd demanded, "Okay, buddy, what's up down there?"

Hank evaded. "Nothing."

"Let me guess. You've got a heavy date at five in the afternoon."

"Not exactly," he mumbled. He was used to the teasing about his active social life, but today it made him even more irritable than usual. He'd have hung up if he hadn't known that Todd would only call back with more amused taunts. As a recently reformed ladies' man himself, Todd's wit could be particularly barbed and uncannily accurate.

"What, then?" he was asking now.

"I'm going fishing."

Todd's hoot of laughter could have been heard clear to Marathon without benefit of the phone line. Hank bristled. "What's so damn funny about that?" he growled.

"The last time you went fishing, you got seasick. You swore you'd never go near a boat again unless it was the size of the biggest liner in Carnival's fleet."

"I'm not going in a boat. I'm going to stand on a dock."

"Ah-ha," Todd said slowly. "It's all beginning to make sense. As I recall, Ann loves to fish. Did she talk you into this?"

"Why would you think that?"

"Because you would never decide to spend the evening this way on your own, but with a woman involved, now that's another story entirely."

"Actually, it was not Ann's idea. Not exactly anyway. I'm in charge of dinner tonight. Since she turned down hamburgers and we had chicken last night, that left fish and if I don't get out of here in the next ten minutes, it's going to be too dark for me to see to bait the damn hook."

"You could stop at the fish market."

"It wouldn't be the same. Besides, I promised Jason."

"Jason?"

"One of the kids."

"I see. Sounds domestic."

"Cut it out, Todd. Will you call the supplier back or not?"

"I'll call him."

"Thanks."

"Hank?"

"Yes?"

"The fish market's right on the highway. You can't miss it."

"Go to hell, buddy." He slammed the phone down on another hoot of laughter. He was still muttering about Todd's uncalled-for glee when he pulled into the driveway at the house. Tracy was sitting on the steps watching Tommy and Melissa play on the swings that hung from the branches of the banyan tree.

"You're late," she announced.

"I know. Where's Jason?"

She shrugged. "He got tired of waiting."

"Damn." For some reason, Jason's attitude the night before had made him nervous. He'd been counting on this time alone with him to see if his uneasiness was justified.

"He took a fishing pole with him, though. Try across the street. There's a dock over there."

"Any more poles around here?"

"Ann's is by the kitchen door. Right over there," she said, pointing behind her.

"Thanks." He found the pole and was halfway around the house when he looked back and saw Tracy staring dejectedly at the ground. He realized then that she'd looked just as down when he'd driven up. With Ann not due home for quite a while, he couldn't bring himself to walk off and leave her that way.

He came back, dug around in the tackle box for a minute and asked casually, "You okay?"

She glanced up, looking surprised by the question. Then her gaze shifted down again. "Yeah, sure."

"No school today?"

"Yeah. I went."

There was an odd, flat note in her voice. He couldn't quite recognize it, but it disturbed him. He sat down beside her. Uncomfortable at being cast in the role of confidant, he searched for the right question to ask a sensitive teenager who was practically a stranger. He opted for being direct. "Did something happen?"

She shook her head. "Not really."

He recognized the evasion. "Which means something did, but you don't want to talk about it?"

That drew a slight smile. "I guess."

"Okay, fair enough," he said, respecting her need for privacy, even though her mood worried him. "Sometimes things don't seem quite so awful once you've talked them out. Keep that in mind, okay? Ann's a pretty good listener from all I hear and I'm willing to give it a shot, too, if you need somebody as a sounding board."

"Okay. Thanks."

Reluctant to leave her and still hoping that she might unburden herself, he sat there for another couple of minutes watching as Paul came racing out of the house and started shooting baskets. David hovered in the doorway.

"Hey, David," he called out. "Why don't you get out there and challenge him? I'll bet you're every bit as good at basketball as he is."

David shook his head.

"He doesn't play much," Tracy explained. "Ann says it's because he got kicked out of so many foster homes for being too much trouble. He was always getting hurt and stuff."

Hank was shocked. "But that's what boys do."

"I know, but some foster parents don't want to be bothered. Now I guess he's scared Ann will make him leave, too."

"That's..." He couldn't even think of a word to describe an adult who'd beat down a child's spirit that way.

"Awful," Tracy supplied. "I know. Sometimes Jason can get him to do stuff, but most of the time he doesn't bother, either. Ann figures we just have to keep trying. Sooner or later David's gonna realize that it's different here."

Hank's respect for the challenges Ann faced with these kids increased tenfold as he studied the wistful expression on David's face. His heart ached for him. While he was trying to figure out if there was something he could do, Tracy cast a sidelong look at him. "You'd better go catch those fish. Ann will be home soon. She'll never let you forget it if she has to cook that chicken tonight."

Reluctantly he got to his feet. "Never fear," he said, then leaned down to whisper, "I know where the fish market is."

Tracy giggled at that and, for an instant anyway, her somber expression vanished, replaced by that glorious smile that would turn her into a heartbreaker in another couple of years. An unfamiliar stirring of tenderness welled up inside him and he got the first inkling why some adults got so hooked on parenting. It was the first time he'd experienced the impact that youthful, carefree laughter could have on a jaded heart.

The water was calmer on the gulf side of the key. The setting sun was hovering at the edge of the horizon, a huge orange ball ready to dip below the endless sea of blue. Already there was a chill in the air, which made Hank glad he'd thought to grab his jacket from the truck on the way over. When he spotted Jason, however, the teenager was huddled at the end of the dock wearing jeans and a T-shirt. He could practically see the goose bumps standing out on his skinny arms.

Hank walked to the end of the dock and put down his gear. Jason didn't acknowledge his presence with so much as a glance. Only a slight stiffening of his shoulders indicated that he was even aware that Hank had joined him.

"Catch anything?" Hank asked.

Jason said nothing.

"Sorry I'm late. I got held up at work."

The apology was met with silence. Hank's earlier feelings of guilt were rapidly changing to impatience. "Jason, I'm talking to you."

The boy turned a sullen gaze on him. "So?"

"I expect you to answer me."

"Why should I?"

"Because it's polite."

"It's polite to keep your promises, too. Ain't that right?"

Hank held on to his temper. He recalled what Ann had said about these kids having been mistreated by far too many adults along the way. "Yes, that is right. I've explained, though. I am sorry I got held up."

"Right." He sounded skeptical and angry. Years of rejection had obviously taken their toll.

Hank tried again with a more neutral topic. "I understand I'm borrowing your room."

"It's Mom's house. She can do what she wants."

"But it's your room and I appreciate your letting me use it. I like the posters."

Jason ignored him. Hank had no idea what else to say in the face of all that pent-up hostility, so they sat on the dock in silence until Jason reeled in a good-size snapper.

"That's a beauty," Hank said. Jason almost managed a smile as he unhooked the fish and plopped it into a bucket of seawater. "You're good at this."

Jason shrugged, dismissing the success. "There's not much to it."

"I don't know about that. I haven't caught anything yet."

After another instant of suspicious silence, Jason suggested grudgingly, "Maybe it's your bait. What'd you bring?"

"Shrimp."

"That should be good."

"You fish a lot?"

"Some."

"Who taught you?"

"I just did it. All the guys in Key West did."

"That's where you're from? Key West?"

Jason nodded, then said, "Why don't you just say what's on your mind?"

"What?"

"Don't you want to know how I got here?"

Hank knew at once he was treading on treacherous

ground. As he had earlier with Tracy, he felt out of his depth. "If you want to tell me," he said finally.

"I was in jail," Jason said bluntly. His expression was defiant, daring Hank to react badly.

"Mom bailed me out," Jason added. "Then she brought me here."

Hank had to swallow his shock. He didn't want Jason to see how troubled he was by his belligerent announcement. Was Ann out of her mind, though? What on earth had possessed her to take in some kid who was in trouble with the law?

"What did you do?"

Jason glared at him. "Who says I did anything?"

"There usually aren't too many innocent people in jail, at least not for long."

"Okay, so maybe you're right."

"And?"

"I stole a car. So what? It was no big deal."

"Grand theft sounds like a big deal to me. Why'd you do it?"

"I needed to get to the store."

His sarcasm set Hank's teeth on edge. Again he swallowed his irritation and repeated, "Why'd you do it?"

"My old man needed the money."

The flat tone sent a chill through Hank. "Bad enough to make you steal?"

"When you need a fix bad enough, you don't worry about how you get it. It wasn't the first thing I did. It was just the first time I got caught." Jason made it sound as though *that* were the crime.

Hank felt his stomach churn. Anger and pity welled

up deep inside him. "What you did was wrong," he reminded Jason.

Jason regarded him defiantly, then retorted with youthful bitterness, "Where I come from you're taught to mind your parents."

Hank could see the twisted logic at work. What worried him, though, was how much it was still affecting Jason's thinking. Was the boy ready to break the law again at any provocation? What kind of influence could he possibly be on all those other kids Ann had taken under her wing? He tried telling himself it was none of his business. He tried telling himself she'd be furious at his meddling. He looked again at the tense, angry kid beside him and decided he had no choice. There was no way in hell he could remain uninvolved. He would talk to Ann the minute they were alone.

Getting Ann alone, however, was no easy task with six children underfoot. It was after nine by the time the little ones were in bed and the older kids were settled down doing their homework. Hank took a beer from the refrigerator, popped it open and held it out toward Ann. She shook her head.

"You want something else?"

"No."

"Feel like taking a walk by the water? It's a nice night."

She regarded him warily. Hank grinned. "Don't panic. I'm not planning to rip off your clothes and have my way with you."

Ironically, as soon as the denial was out of his mouth, Hank realized it was a blatant lie. He did want to strip away the layered T-shirts, the too-long skirt and those ridiculous socks. Those socks were orange tonight. With a blue skirt and yellow and green shirts. She reminded him of a particularly colorful parrot.

She also smelled like strawberries again, which made him want to taste the creamy white skin of her neck. Which made him achingly hard. Which would have made the lie obvious if she'd looked anywhere other than straight past him as she said stiffly, "I never thought you were."

Hank held the screen door open. As she marched past him, he wondered what perversity made him want a woman who was all sharp angles and tart tongue, a woman who clearly regarded him as a nuisance. There were a dozen other less complicated women he could have called for a date. Unfortunately, the only woman he seemed interested in spending time with tonight was this one.

They walked in silence. It was Ann who finally broke it.

"Was there something you wanted to talk about?"

"Can't a man just enjoy the night and your charming company without wanting something?"

She regarded him skeptically. "It's possible, but you don't strike me as the type."

"How do I strike you?" he asked, suddenly curious about her impression. She was a psychologist. The possibility that she might be able to read between the lines and detect things about him that even he didn't admit was troublesome.

"As a man used to getting what he wants, women included."

He laughed, relieved. There were no uncanny revelations in that analysis. "I can't deny that. Is there something wrong with going after the things that are important to you? Isn't that what life is all about?"

"It depends on who gets trampled in the process."

"Do you think I'm trying to trample on you, Annie?"

"You've only been here two days."

"Exactly." He grinned. "And I've been on my best behavior."

"Why doesn't that reassure me?"

"You're the psychologist. You tell me."

She suddenly hugged her arms protectively around her waist. Hank had an urgent desire to push them away, to draw them around his own waist so that he could feel her slender body pressed into his. He figured she'd slug him if he tried. He decided he'd better change the subject.

"I wanted to talk to you about Jason."

Her gaze shot to his, her nervousness apparent. "What about him?"

"I think you're taking a bad risk having him here."

She stopped in midstep and her hands went at once to her hips. Challenging. Defiant. Mother-hen protective. "Why on earth would you say something like that? You don't even know him."

"Simmer down," he soothed. "I know he's had problems with the police. He doesn't seem especially remorseful about it, either."

Her expression changed to one of astonishment. "He told you that?"

"More or less."

Her face lit up as if he'd just announced that the kid had been accepted at Harvard. "Don't you see how wonderful that is?"

"Wonderful? It was scary sitting there with this

skinny kid talking about stealing cars and taking dope as if it were perfectly ordinary stuff."

"In his life, it was."

"And that's the kind of influence you want around the others?"

"Jason doesn't try to influence the others. He practically says nothing at all. The fact that he opened up to you means he's beginning to trust adults again. He was obviously anxious for your approval."

"It sounded to me more like bragging. I think he was more interested in shocking me. The boy could be dangerous."

She waved off his fears. "He's not dangerous. He's scared."

Deep in his gut Hank wanted to believe Ann was right. He'd seen for himself the evidence of vulnerable kid behind the tough, grown-up facade. He'd known a lot of kids just like that in his time. Some of them grew up and made something of themselves. Some of them didn't. Those were the ones who scared the hell out of him. He reached out and gently touched Ann's uptilted chin. "What if you're wrong?" he asked gently.

"I am not wrong," she said stubbornly. "With the right environment, the right sort of support and a little unconditional love, Jason will do just fine."

He sighed with impatience at the Pollyanna viewpoint. "You're too trusting, Annie."

"And you're too cynical."

"Being a liberal do-gooder is just fine, as long as it doesn't endanger anyone else."

"I'd rather be a liberal do-gooder than a self-centered jerk."

"It is not self-centered to worry about you and those

kids," he retorted angrily, though he was surprised himself at the depth of his concern. That she dismissed his fears so lightly made him indignant. The fact that he wanted her anyway stunned him. His blood pounded. When Ann parted her lips to counter his last furious comment, he settled his mouth over hers. It was the only way he could think of to silence her.

It was also the only way he could think of to still the demanding throb that had his entire body quivering with the irrational, uncontrollable need to know her touch. He expected a fight, perhaps even hoped for one to prove how foolish the attraction was. Instead her lips were velvet soft and trembling beneath his. And, after an instant's startled stiffening, she relaxed against him. Her arms drifted around his neck. Her hips tilted into his, a perfect fit. Pleasure shot through him. Hot, searing desire replaced casual curiosity.

And Hank knew he was in more trouble than Jason had ever dreamed of.

Chapter 4

Ann heard the music the instant she turned into the driveway. Beethoven? At full blast? She had to be hearing things. She was used to being greeted by rock and roll at best. She listened more closely. The familiar classical strains swelled, carrying on the turbulent wind. It was definitely Beethoven. The night air was suddenly filled with violins and the sound of waves crashing against the shore. She felt as if she'd stumbled into the midst of an outdoor concert in which man and nature combined to stir the soul.

Exhausted and drained by a nerve-racking series of sessions, to say nothing of the residual impact of Hank Riley's totally unexpected and thoroughly devastating kiss the previous night, she leaned back in the front seat of the car. The music flowed over her, soothing, working its magic. Her eyes drifted closed. Hank's provocative

image appeared at once. She opened her eyes to banish
him, but the image lingered just as plainly. She gave
up the pointless battle and shut her eyes again. Her lips
curved in a smile at the pleasantly surprising sensation
of peace after so many hours of jarring dissonance.

"Annie?"

Dazed, she blinked at the sound of Hank's voice.

"You okay?" he asked, leaning down beside the
car and peering in at her. His blue eyes were filled
with tender concern. Recognizing it, her heart tapped
a new and surprisingly sensual rhythm. It had been
years since anyone had ever worried about her, even
fleetingly. She was the strong, clear-thinking one. She
was the one others came to to pour out their troubles.
Whether privately or professionally, she was expected
to cope, to endure. The fact that this man thought she
might occasionally need help in doing that made her
feel cherished somehow, even as it sometimes irritated
her. *Sometimes?* It almost always irritated her. But not
tonight. Tonight she basked in the unfamiliar warmth
of the sensation.

"I'm fine," she told him now. "I was just enjoying
the concert."

He grinned ruefully. "Sorry if it was too loud. The
kids haven't complained, so I didn't realize how far the
sound carried."

"Don't apologize. It was wonderful to come home
to that. Just what I needed."

"Bad day?"

"No worse than most others. I just seemed to have
less patience with it." Probably because she'd been up
half the night for the second night in a row trying to
make sense of the astonishing effect this man had on

her. Her entire body—and her common sense—had melted in his arms. She hadn't been able to come up with a single, logical explanation for it and she was a woman addicted to logic. Logic made sense of life, brought order out of chaos. And it was tidier by far than being prey to erratic emotions. Even though she knew all that, she looked into his eyes and felt the irrational tug of desire starting all over again.

"Have you eaten?" he said.

She shook her head.

"Then come sit on the porch and let me bring you something. Tracy made vegetable soup. With this chill in the air, it seemed like a good night for it."

Beethoven? Homemade soup? What was going on here? "Who's idea was all this?"

"All what?"

"The music and the soup."

"Tracy had the recipe book out and the soup on when I came in from work. She said something about experimenting. It sounded dangerous to me, but it turned out to be edible. Paul and David actually finished every bite. Melissa picked out all the carrots and Tommy threw them across the room, but I think we found the last of them. It's safe to come in now."

She regarded him oddly. He actually sounded as though he'd enjoyed the evening. He was adapting far more readily than she'd anticipated. It sounded as though the children were, too. That pleased her, even as it made her uneasy. How long would it last? How long before he vanished from their lives?

"After all that," he was saying, "I felt like listening to some music. I hope you don't mind that I went through your iPod."

"Not at all. I must admit I'm a little surprised by your choice."

He turned a knowing grin on her. "I'm sure you expected a preference for twanging guitars over violin concertos."

"Something like that," she conceded.

"Loretta Lynn and Tammy Wynette have their places. So do Beethoven and Mozart. I'll have you know I can even manage a little Chopin on the piano."

"You?"

"Three years of piano lessons," he boasted.

"Your mother must have been very strong-willed to manage that."

"My mother had nothing to do with it," he said with an unmistakable edge in his voice. "I took the lessons a few years ago."

Intrigued by his tone, she was more astounded by his announcement. She stared at him in wonder. "You took piano lessons when you were—"

"Thirty-four," he supplied, chuckling as he held up hands that looked far too large, far too strong, to be used in such a gentle pursuit. Those hands playing Chopin? Those hands caressing...

She brought herself up short just as he said, "Hard to imagine, isn't it? I'd always wanted to play, though. There was no money for lessons when I was a kid. Besides, I probably would have been laughed off the football team. At thirty-four I had no excuses left."

"Good for you."

He winked at her. "Be careful, Annie. You may just discover that I'm full of surprises."

Her pulse skipped at the teasing challenge in his voice. All at once she recalled every second that she'd spent in his arms, every sensation that had been aroused by his lips on hers. There was a subtle stirring low in her abdomen. An irrational yearning filled her heart. Wild, magical nights like this were meant to be shared with someone special and she'd been alone far too long. Why couldn't she put aside her doubts and her tendency to analyze things to death? When had she stopped taking risks and turned her life into a predictable routine or as predictable as any life could be with children around? Why couldn't she accept for just this one night the possibility that Hank Riley could be that someone, that he wasn't just an impertinent rogue on the make, that he genuinely cared about her?

Her gaze met his, caught and held. Hers was tentative. His was daring and bold, almost hypnotic in its unwavering intensity. Without taking his eyes from hers, he slowly opened the car door and waited for her to step out. He left just enough room for her to exit without touching him—if she chose. Heart thudding in her chest, she stood, but she couldn't bring herself to take the one tiny step that would put her back into his arms for another of those inhibition-melting kisses. She wanted to. Dear Lord, how she wanted to. But tonight years of restraint and common sense held her back.

Hank's smile was slow and gentle and knowing. "It'll happen, Annie," he promised in a low voice that sizzled down her spine. "Count on it."

The vow eased her instant of regret. It also set her blood on fire in a way she'd never dreamed possible. Trembling, she brushed past him and went inside. She fumbled with the ladle for the soup until Hank finally took it from her and poured a steaming bowlful. He put it in front of her at the table, touched her shoulder with tantalizing tenderness and then he left her to her thoughts.

They were in turmoil.

It was the damn Beethoven, she told herself. And the Chopin.

It was the kiss, she finally confessed with more honesty. One stupid, meaningless kiss and the man had her feeling like a teenager whose hormones were newly rampaging out of control. She'd taken enough courses, handled enough cases to recognize good old-fashioned lust when it hit her in the gut. Forget his tenderness. Forget the concern. What she was feeling had nothing to do with those gentler qualities. What she was feeling was heart-tumbling, spine-tingling desire for the man's body. Recognizing it was half the battle. Now all she had to do was ignore it and sooner or later it would wear off.

Or cause her to do something incredibly stupid. The list of possibilities there was enough to make her choke on her soup. It began with falling into bed with him. It ended with falling in love.

"It'll never happen," she muttered adamantly.

"What won't happen?" Hank inquired curiously.

Her gaze shot up. He was standing in the doorway, watching her again, Melissa cradled contentedly against his shoulder. How could a man the size of a truck move so stealthily? Maybe she ought to insist he wear a bell around his neck. She could use the warning in order to get her defenses into place. Right now he was probably seeing naked longing in her eyes. Terrific, she thought with disgust. Just great!

"Hi," Melissa said with a sleepy smile. She held out her arms. Ann took her.

"Did you have a good day, pumpkin?"

Melissa nodded. "Hank and me built a sand castle. Wanna see?"

"It's a little dark to see it now. We'll look in the morning."

"Hanks says it'll be all gone by then." She gave him a beguiling grin. "We do it again, okay?"

He laughed. "Okay, squirt. Now remember what we talked about."

She nodded. "I go to bed now."

"That's right. Ann will come tuck you in."

"You, too?"

"Me, too."

"Okay."

When she had toddled off, Hank pulled out a chair, turned it around and sat down straddling it.

"I never thought I'd see the day," he said, his eyes filled with amusement.

"What's that supposed to mean?" she said.

"You, tongue-tied. Makes me wonder what you really were thinking about when Melissa and I arrived."

"A case," she improvised hastily. "It's a tough one. It really has me stymied."

"Oh, really."

"Yes. This couple, they, um, they can't seem to figure out what they want."

He looked immediately interested. "So, what'd you tell 'em?"

Gathering her defenses, she met his gaze evenly. "I told them if they couldn't make up their minds about each other, then getting together was probably the wrong decision."

"But aren't doubts normal, especially when a relation-ship is new?"

"Some doubts, yes. But if the love's not powerful enough to overshadow them, then perhaps it's not strong enough to survive, either."

"Perhaps," he echoed, reaching out to pick her hand up off the table. His thumb rubbed across her knuckles. "No guarantees?"

Ann felt an incredible tension begin to build inside just from the brush of his callused thumb across her hand. Her voice was shaky when she said, "There are never any guarantees, with or without doubts."

He turned her hand over, lifted it up and kissed the palm. A current of electricity jolted through her as he said solemnly, "So you might as well play the hand out and see where it leads, right?"

She shook her head and nervously snatched her hand away. "Sometimes it's better just to cut your losses."

"When?" He asked the question very seriously, but she caught the desire to laugh lurking in his eyes.

She swallowed hard and tried to think straight. "When what?"

"When do you know it's time to cut your losses?"

Now, she wanted to shout. "That's a very individual sort of thing," she said sensibly, struggling against the emotions sweeping through her, fighting the temptation in his eyes.

"Let's take you and me, for instance."

He made the suggestion in all innocence. Still, her eyes blinked wide. "What?"

"You and me," he repeated. "Purely hypothetical, of course. On the surface, you and I couldn't be more unsuited, right?"

She nodded weakly.

"But we're living here together for the time being and there's this attraction growing between us."

She tried valiantly for indignation. "Attraction?" Her voice was barely above a whisper. Instead of skepticism, however, she merely managed to convey nervousness.

"Sure. Lust. Chemistry. You know what I mean."

"We're talking hypothetical here?"

"Naturally. Now is that something that should be played out to its logical conclusion?"

"Absolutely not," she said in a rush.

"Under no circumstances?"

"None."

"Why?"

"You said it yourself. We're unsuited."

"On the surface."

"That's all we know about each other."

"And we shouldn't bother trying to dig beneath the surface? Maybe there's more we have in common than we realize. Where there's Beethoven, who knows, there could be Wagner."

She was shaking her head. "Definitely not."

"Definitely not Wagner?" he teased. "Or definitely not us?"

"Us," she said, barely getting the word past a throat gone suddenly dry.

He tilted the chair forward and touched his lips to her forehead. "Coward," he murmured softly.

And then, with a wink that made her heart flip over, he was gone again. One of these days, when she had her wits about her, she was going to have to talk to him about walking out in the middle of a conversation. It was a really lousy way to have the last word.

* * *

Super Bowl Sunday. Hank could hardly wait. He'd thought about going back to Miami to hang out with the guys, but by the time he'd finished working on Saturday it had been too damn late to tackle the drive. He considered going to a bar, which would be rowdy and filled with eager fans. But as beat as he was, nothing appealed to him more than settling down in front of the TV at home with a six-pack of beer, some chips and maybe a couple of hamburgers at halftime.

He hadn't stopped to consider that Ann would regard the entire plan as tantamount to treason.

"You want to do what?" she said when he suggested they flip the channel on the TV away from some documentary on PBS.

"Watch the game." When she stared at him blankly, he added, "The Super Bowl. You know, the big end-of-the-season matchup. This is what it's all about."

She looked appalled. And unyielding. "Only if you're a cretin," she said emphatically.

He sighed heavily. "Oh, Annie, there were such sad gaps in your education."

"There were no gaps in my education. I have my B.A., my M.A. and my Ph.D."

"But you obviously missed cheerleading."

"Thank God." She said it so fervently he had to hide a smile.

"Now, Annie, how do you expect to identify with your average American male if you know nothing about the sport that consumes most of his Sunday afternoons from late summer through winter? You owe it to yourself and the future of your practice to watch the Super Bowl."

"I prefer to identify with his poor wife, who's left to raise the children, mow the lawn and suffer in silence while the slob sits in front of a TV and stares at a bunch of grown men beating one another's brains out."

"Obviously you've missed the finer points of the game," he said dryly.

"That's okay by me."

This clearly wasn't getting them anywhere. Ann's beliefs seemed entrenched. With only ten minutes to go until game time, he didn't have a lot of time to win her over. He gazed longingly at the comfortable sofa and the thirty-four-inch television screen. "Is there another TV in the house?"

"Jason and Paul have an old tube TV in their room."

Hank felt his heartbeat screech to a halt. It would be a travesty to watch the Super Bowl on a tube TV. "I don't suppose…"

"Not on your life," she said adamantly, turning the sound back up with a quick flick of the remote control.

If he drove like hell, there was still time to get to a bar. Or he could suffer through the game on the smaller screen. Or, he decided with a certain amount of roguish delight, he could use his considerable charms to get Annie to change her mind about sharing. As skittish as she was, ten minutes ought to be just enough time for that. He dropped down on the sofa beside her, mere inches from her.

"So what are you watching?"

She regarded him warily. "It's a report on herbal medicine in China."

"Any good?"

"It's fascinating."

"Good. Tell me what's happened so far."

She gave him a sharp look. "Why?"

"So I can catch up. If this is what we're going to watch, I don't want to feel left out."

"This isn't a suspense thriller. You won't be confused if you don't know what's already happened."

"But you said what you'd seen so far was fascinating. Fascinate me."

"I thought you wanted to watch the Super Bowl."

"I did, but I'd rather spend a quiet evening right here with you." He allowed his hand to drift innocently to her thigh when he said it. He felt the muscle jerk beneath his touch, but to her credit Ann never glanced away from the television.

"Go away, Hank."

"Am I bothering you?"

"Yes."

He chuckled at her honest, heartfelt response. She turned a fierce scowl on him.

"Go away," she repeated.

"Why? I think this is cozy. I want to share your interests. If this herbal medicine thing is as good as you say it is, I'm sure I'll enjoy it just as much as a football game."

With a deep sigh, she turned and handed him the remote control. "You win. Watch the game."

"Are you sure?" He'd flipped the channel before the question was out of his mouth.

"Very sure," she said wryly, getting to her feet.

Hank grabbed her wrist and pulled her back down. "Stay and watch it with me."

"When pigs fly."

"Give it a chance. I was willing to watch the China thing with you."

"Sure you were."

"Honest."

She chuckled despite herself. "Your nose is growing, Riley."

"Okay, so it was a calculated risk. Stay and watch this with me. Football's no fun alone." He reached behind the sofa and came up with two beers. "Here you go."

To his astonishment, she took the bottle without protest and tilted it up. When she took another long swallow and then another, he began to get worried. "Maybe you should slow down," he said.

"Why? Isn't this the way you're supposed to watch the game? A beer in one hand, a bowl of chips in the other. Where are the chips, by the way? I'm sure you have them hidden away somewhere."

Still watching her warily, he reached behind the sofa again and retrieved the potato chips.

"Any dip?" she inquired as she took a handful.

"In the refrigerator," he murmured, bemused by her odd behavior. Chips? Dip? Why wasn't she yelling her head off by now? "I'll get it."

When he came back, to his amazement she hadn't switched channels. He held out the onion dip. She loaded down a chip with the sour-cream mixture, then popped it into her mouth.

"Are you okay?"

"Fine."

"But you hate all this stuff."

"But I'm a good sport. Don't forget that. Now be quiet. They're playing the national anthem."

All through the first quarter, Ann sat stoically beside him, drinking her beer and eating potato chips as if she'd been deprived of them since childhood. She did not, however, look as though she were enjoying herself. She closed her eyes every time she anticipated the players making contact, which meant she was missing most of the game.

She watched the aftermath of a particularly violent third-down defense with a sort of avid fascination, then shivered. "Brutal. What is wrong with you? How can you stand this?" she said, turning her gaze on him. She actually looked shaken.

"Annie, this isn't just a matter of brute force out there. It's not just twenty-two guys trying to see how hard they can slam into one another."

"You'll never prove that to me."

"I can if you'll keep your eyes open for a couple of plays here. Now watch this. See the receiver going out for that pass. See that leap, the way he turns his body and reaches over his shoulder for the ball. Have you ever seen a ballet dancer execute a turn any more gracefully than that?"

"What do you know about ballet?" she scoffed.

"Season ticket holder, Miami City Ballet," he retorted.

She stared in obvious astonishment. "You?"

"Me. Do you know that male dancers have almost as many injuries as football players? They wind up with bad backs, knee surgery, hip replacements. Do you wince when you see them on stage?"

She considered the argument thoughtfully. "I never thought of it like that."

"These men are just as agile in their own way. If you watch a game as an exercise in athletic skill, rather than a display of brute strength, it takes on a whole different perspective."

She glanced at the screen, then back at him. "Ballet, huh?"

"Pirouettes, leaps and all."

"I'll give it another inning."

He groaned. "Half, Annie. Another half."

Chapter 5

The last of Ann's patients had left an hour ago. She'd finished her notes, put away the files, emptied the teapot and tidied her desk. She'd even plumped every last cushion on the sofa and aligned every slat in the vertical blinds. Practically the only thing left that could possibly delay her departure for home was kneeling down and picking every piece of lint from the carpet. She glanced down consideringly, then muttered an oath that rarely crossed her lips.

She was losing it. If this wasn't proof enough, then yesterday's behavior was. She had sat in front of the television through an entire football game. She had actually caught herself cheering for one extraordinarily evasive runner. She'd only barely noticed the violent tackles that had cleared his path. She had eaten more than her share of a huge bowl of greasy potato chips slathered with sour-cream-and-onion dip. She'd allowed the kids to order pizzas for dinner. Stunned by the unexpected permission, they had asked for fat-laden pepperoni and sausage. She hadn't even blinked. She blamed it on the beer.

Worse, though she would never on pain of death admit it to another soul, she had enjoyed herself. More precisely, she had enjoyed sharing the evening with Hank. Over the past few days, she had even started looking forward to their morning runs. Now she awoke to coffee already perking and Hank waiting for her on the back porch. The five miles had started to go by all too quickly.

Which was, of course, exactly why she didn't want to go home now. Hank was going to be there. Every sexy, self-confident, increasingly intriguing inch of him. Lord only knew what temptation he had planned for her tonight. He seemed to have established himself as some sort of guiding spirit whose only purpose in life was to make her forget all of her long-held, rational beliefs. He was doing a darn good job of it. He was proof incarnate that opposites attract. She was struggling to keep in mind that it was usually disaster when they did. Maybe a review of a few of her case files would drive home the point.

When the phone rang, she grabbed it, praying for a reprieve from yet another struggle against some perverse fate that had tossed her into this emotional fray.

"Dr. Davies."

"Ann, it's Tom. How'd you like to do your civic duty tonight?"

The mayor! Perfect. The gods were listening after

all. She lifted her eyes heavenward and without asking a single question said a fervent, "Yes!"

Tom laughed. "Don't you even want to know what I'm after?"

"Well, of course, but I trust your judgment. It must be important or you wouldn't be asking."

"How come you're never that complimentary when I'm asking for a date?"

"Maybe it has something to do with knowing that I'd be competing with the entire female population of the Keys."

"I'd throw them all over for you."

"You say that, knowing you're safe. If I took you up on it, you'd develop a nervous tic. Now what exactly did you need me to do tonight?"

"There's a hearing in Key West on offshore drilling. Can you go? I'll drive. We need bodies down there."

"No brains?"

"Okay. That goes without saying. What about it?"

"Of course I'll go. Let me call home and make arrangements for the kids."

"Terrific. I'll pick you up at the office in ten minutes. Sorry about the late notice, but we just got word that the state officials were coming tonight. We'd thought it was only a preliminary strategy session."

"No problem. See you soon."

She disconnected the call, then dialed home. She knew Hank was there but she didn't want to make him feel like he had to completely take over when she wasn't home. She'd ask Tracy to cover dinner. Melissa answered. Next to overflowing bathtubs, the telephone was her favorite thing.

"Hi, sweetheart," Ann said.

"Hi." Melissa whispered the response so softly Ann could barely hear her.

"Honey, is Tracy there?"

That was greeted by a long silence, then finally a hesitant, "No."

So much for that idea. "How about Jason?"

"Uh-huh."

"Can you get him for me?"

"Okay."

Melissa hung up the phone. Ann gritted her teeth and called back.

"Hi," Melissa said cheerfully.

Ann used her sternest tone, the one that always got results. "Melissa, I want you to get Jason at once."

This time the phone clattered to the floor. She heard Melissa's footsteps receding, accompanied by choking sobs.

"Oh, Lord. Now what?" Tapping her fingers against the desktop, she waited on the off chance that Melissa would actually get Jason. She could hear the shouts of various children in the background.

"Hey," Paul yelled. "Who left the phone off the hook?"

"Paul!" she yelled back, just as the phone clicked off. She dialed again. This time Paul answered.

"Paul, it's Mom."

"Oh, hi, Mom. Have you been trying to call? The phone's been off the hook."

"I know," she said with rapidly ebbing patience. "Would you please get Jason for me?"

"Sure thing. Hey, Jason, Mom wants to talk to you. Are you coming home soon? Melissa's crying something fierce."

"She'll be okay," Ann promised just as she heard Tom's horn blow. "Is Jason coming?"

"Yeah, he's right here, but I gotta ask you something first. Is it okay if Hank takes Tommy and me to the construction site tonight?"

She couldn't imagine Hank volunteering to do that. "Is that your idea or his?"

"He said it would be okay."

She sighed. "I'm not sure that's an answer, but if he's willing, fine. Be careful, though, and do exactly what he tells you to do."

"Okay," he said quickly. "Here's Jason."

Visions of Tommy tumbling off a girder twenty feet in the sky suddenly made her shake. "Wait, Paul... Paul!"

"It's me, Jason. What's up, Mom?"

"Tell Paul to be sure to hold Tommy's hand the whole time they're at that construction site."

"I'll tell him, but how come you didn't tell him yourself?"

Ann very nearly groaned. "Just tell him, Jason. And tell him to do exactly what Hank says."

"Is that all you wanted?"

"No, it is not all I wanted!" She took a deep breath and lowered her voice. "I have to go down to Key West for a meeting. Can you make sure the kids all get their dinner? Tracy should be home soon."

"Wrong. She's staying in Key West tonight. She called a while ago."

That gave her second thoughts. Maybe she shouldn't be taking off like this. Jason was old enough to babysit, but he didn't have a lot of experience at it and he didn't get along with the little ones the way Tracy did. With him in charge, she was likely to find all of the kids still up when she got home. A thought occurred to her.

"When is Hank taking Paul and Tommy to the site?"

"I don't know." Jason's voice immediately turned surly as he sensed her lack of faith. "Besides, I don't need him. I can watch the kids."

She decided to risk it. Hank would have Paul and Tommy with him. Maybe it would be good for Jason to develop a sense of responsibility. Surely he could keep an eye on David and Melissa for a couple of hours. "Okay. Make sure they get to bed on time."

"Yeah."

She'd hung up the phone and was halfway to the door when she began reconsidering. She picked up her phone again and scrolled through the numbers, searching for Hank's cell. She found it and, after an instant's hesitation, she dialed. It rang and rang before finally his voice mail kicked in. That reassured her. It must mean that he was already on his way to the construction site. Jason would tell him where she was when he came home. There was no need to leave a message.

Relieved on all counts, including the fact that she was being saved from another close encounter with the man who'd been awakening her senses from a deep slumber, she closed the office door behind her and left for Key West.

When Hank walked into the kitchen after taking Paul and Tommy on a tour of the construction site, he found the counter littered with the makings of peanut-butter-and-jelly sandwiches. A trail of milk extended from the refrigerator to the kitchen table. Ann obviously wasn't home yet. He'd been hoping earlier that she'd be there in time to go along with him and the kids. He'd even considered waiting for her, but Paul and Tommy had been too eager to leave and he hadn't wanted to look quite so obvious about wanting to include Ann in the outing.

He was wiping off the counter when Jason came in.

"I was going to do that," he muttered defensively.

"It's no big deal. How about getting the milk off the floor before somebody slips?"

"You're so hot to clean up, do it yourself," Jason said, taking off and slamming the screen door behind him. Hank's temper kicked into overdrive.

"Jason, get back here this instant!" he ordered as he yanked open the back door and hit the porch at a run. Jason already had one foot in the yard, the other on the bottom step. He turned slowly and came back onto the porch.

"Who's gonna make me?" he said, facing Hank toe-to-toe, even though he stood barely shoulder height to him. Hank had to admire the kid's guts, if not his sense or his rotten attitude.

"You don't really need to ask that, do you? Now get back in here, mop up the milk and go to your room. While you're in there, do a little thinking about minding your manners. If I ever hear you talking to Ann the way you just sassed me, I'll tan your hide till they can use it for shoe leather."

"Real tough guy, huh? Why don't you just go back to Miami and leave us alone," Jason muttered, but he went back in and cleaned up the floor.

When Jason had stalked off to his room, Hank fixed himself a sandwich, took out a beer and sat down at the kitchen table to wait for Ann. He couldn't get his mind off Jason. The boy was trouble just begging to happen. Maybe what he needed, aside from some old-fashioned discipline, was an improved sense of self-worth. Maybe in the morning, after Jason had done a little thinking about his behavior, he'd talk to him about an after-school job. Good hard work and a little cash in his pockets might do wonders for him. He'd ask Ann about the idea tonight. If she agreed, he'd find something for him to do at the construction site.

Funny how he was starting to look forward to talking things over with her. He'd never been particularly anxious to get home after work before, but now he could barely wait to leave the office behind. It was nice having someone to share the day with, someone whose opinions he increasingly respected.

Face it, Riley, it's a hell of a lot more than that. She's getting under your skin.

All he'd been able to think about during the Super Bowl was the way her skin had burned beneath his touch, the way her cheeks had colored when he'd brushed them with his fingertips, the way her lips had parted breathlessly when he'd pressed an innocent good-night kiss against her brow. It had taken every ounce of willpower in him to keep from claiming more. He'd had to remind himself over and over that he had ruled out a casual affair with this woman days ago. His body, unfortunately, hadn't gotten the message. Even now it tightened at the vivid memories.

Where the hell was she? It was after eight and there was still no sign of her. He knew the nightly routine now. The little ones should have had their baths and been tucked in by eight. He walked into the living room and found Melissa still sitting in front of the TV, a thumb stuck in her mouth, her blanket clutched tightly in her other hand. Tommy, still wearing the hard hat Hank had given him, and Paul were racing their miniature cars around her. Despite the noise, it was obvious she could barely keep her eyes open. Someone had to take over in Ann's absence and it seemed he was elected. The unaccustomed role made him uneasy. He might be able to handle a hundred construction workers without blinking an eye, but these pint-size terrors still scared the daylights out of him.

"Okay, kids, bedtime," he announced in what he hoped was a convincing tone of voice. The boys scowled their protest, but Melissa just lifted her arms. He bent down and picked her up. Her arms circled his neck and her head rested under his chin. She smelled of baby shampoo and peanut butter. There was something about the combined scents that plunged him back more than thirty years. He wasn't crazy about that particular bit of time travel. He snapped himself back to the present, his voice rough. "Clean up the toys, Tommy, Paul. Then go get ready for bed."

"What about our baths?"

Hank groaned. How could he have forgotten the baths? Maybe they could get by without them for once. He looked at Melissa. She was as clean as she had been when Ann had helped her dress in the morning. He almost wished she were a little messier. It would have indicated that she'd played hard, instead of spending the day sitting quietly in front of the television afraid to get dirty, terrified of doing something wrong. The boys, however, were filthy from their streaked faces to their bare feet.

"You two guys go get cleaned up while I put Melissa to bed." He recalled their tendency to flood the bathroom. "And call me if you have any problems with the drain." As they started to race down the hall, he shouted one last warning. "And no water fights."

In Melissa's room, he struggled with the tiny, unfamiliar buttons on her blouse, then tugged off her shorts and searched for her pajamas.

"Where's Ann?" Melissa demanded sleepily.

"She'll be home soon," he promised. "She'll be in to give you a kiss as soon as she gets here."

"Want Ann," she protested, then stuck her thumb back in her mouth.

"I know you do, baby. She'll be here before you know it." He tried to get the pajama top on, but Melissa stubbornly refused to help. Her thumb left her mouth only long enough to ask plaintively again and again for Ann. Feeling utterly helpless, Hank awkwardly tucked her in and patted her head.

"Sleep tight, little one," he murmured, backing toward the door.

When he reached for the light switch, Melissa began to cry. "No go," she whimpered.

"I'm right here, baby," he said, turning off the light and plunging the room into darkness.

"No go!" Melissa wailed.

Responding instinctively to the genuine note of terror in her cries, he went back to the bed and sat down beside her. "Shh, little one. It's okay. I'm right here."

Melissa sniffed. As his eyes became accustomed to the dark, he saw that she was curled into a tight little ball, her whole body tense. All at once he recalled the lonely, scary nights he'd spent as a child, his mother away from home, some strange babysitter in the living room. The dark had been filled with all sorts of terrifying shadows. Ann would never let Melissa know that fear. He got up and searched the room, finally finding the tiny light plugged into a socket over the dresser. He switched it on.

"Is that better?" he murmured softly, looking down at the little girl whose body was finally relaxing. He reached out and rubbed away the last of the tears on the petal-soft cheeks. His throat tight with some overwhelming and unfamiliar emotion, he leaned down and touched a gentle kiss to that cheek. "Sweet dreams," he whispered.

Melissa wound her fingers trustingly around his thumb and sighed. Minutes later he heard the steady rise and fall of her breath. He tiptoed from the room, his heart filled to overflowing with sensations he couldn't identify, sensations that both frightened and intrigued him.

Tommy and Paul had finished their baths by the time he went to get them. The bathroom floor was under a sea of puddles. Plastic boats and toy animals were underfoot and soaked towels were scattered everywhere. For the most part, as near as he could tell, they had managed to wash off the worst of the dirt in the process of creating the watery havoc.

"Okay, guys, into bed."

"Will you come and tuck us in?"

Hugs and kisses later, the house was quiet. He knocked on David's door, poked his head in and found the boy doing his homework.

"Don't stay up too much longer."

"I won't."

"I wish you'd come with us tonight."

"It's okay. I had stuff to do here."

Hank nodded. "Maybe another time."

"Yeah, sure."

Sighing, Hank shut the door. David's aloofness saddened him, especially since he now knew the cause. He'd stayed behind tonight simply because he'd been afraid of doing something wrong. It was safer to stick with something familiar, to sit quietly in his room doing his homework. Nobody got angry at a straight-A student. Nobody got rid of a thirteen-year-old who never made any noise. Hank vowed to keep trying to include him in more activities, to give him back his boyhood.

After Hank had cleaned up the bathroom, he went outside to wait for Ann. He took a beer with him and settled down in the hammock. Rocking it to and fro with one foot, he began drifting off. Rousing himself, he glanced at the illuminated dial of his watch. It was almost ten o'clock. He sat straight up, nearly tumbling from the hammock in the process.

"What the hell? Where is she?"

Ann would not go off and leave those children alone unless it had been an emergency. Now wait, he reminded himself. They hadn't been alone exactly. Jason had been there, which explained the makeshift dinner. Still, surely she should have been home by now. What if one of the kids had gotten sick? What if Melissa had had one of her dreams and had awakened frightened and crying? Jason couldn't have coped with that. The more he thought about it, the more furious he became.

It was typical female behavior. His own mother hadn't been able to stand the loneliness of the house at night. By the time he was ten he was used to the absences, accustomed to her flighty refusal to accept parental responsibility. His father had apparently had enough of her flirtations within the first year of the marriage. He had gone before Hank had even been born. The whole experience had colored Hank's relationships with women. He enjoyed them, appreciated their beauty the way a connoisseur appreciated a fine vintage wine, but he'd never wanted to possess one in any sort of lasting way. He'd learned from the cradle on that there was no such thing as a lasting commitment when it came to a woman.

Still, everything he'd discovered about Ann ran counter to that image. She'd always seemed rock solid, dependable. She was an instinctive nurturer, one of those people who gave a part of herself to everyone she met. She adored these kids. She'd never once given him any reason to doubt her love or her commitment to them. A blinding image of her car crashing made him sick to his stomach. He began pacing. If she didn't get home in the next half hour, he'd call the police. In the meantime, he'd ask Jason what he knew about her absence. Surely she'd at least called.

He tapped on Jason's door, then heard Paul's sleepy voice. He stuck his head in. Paul was blinking at him. There was no sign of Jason. Damn that kid. He'd obviously sneaked off the minute he heard Hank go outside.

The only thing left to do was wait. He paced some more. It was nearly midnight when he finally heard the car door slam and heard Ann's voice as she called out a cheerful good-night.

"Thanks, Tom. I'm glad I went."

Tom? He'd been tucking in kids and worrying

himself sick and she'd been out on a date? He watched as she came around to the kitchen door.

"So you had a good time?" he said, his voice brimming over with sarcasm. He was furious with himself for believing that she was any different.

"Hank?"

"Who else were you expecting?"

"Is everything okay?"

"Everything is just swell. Next time you want a baby-sitter, though, I'd suggest you hire one."

Even in the dark, he could see her stiffen. Her arms folded around her waist. "What are you talking about?" she said defensively. "Jason was watching the kids."

"Wanna bet?"

"But I talked to him. He promised. Besides, I thought Paul and Tommy were going to be with you."

"They were. Once we got home, though, Jason took off without mentioning that you had a date."

"I did not have a date. I went to a meeting. I tried to call you, but you'd already left. I thought Jason would tell you where I was." A tense silence hung over them for several minutes before she finally took a deep breath and asked, "Is that the problem? You thought I had a date?" There was a note of surprise in her voice. He was too angry to acknowledge what it implied about her self-esteem.

"Why the hell should that be a problem?" he snapped. "You don't owe me anything."

"That's right, I don't. This household ran just fine before your arrival. I wasn't counting on you to look after the kids, so why are you in such a snit?"

"I am not in a snit."

"What would you call it?" she asked patiently.

Hank tried to analyze the emotions that were whirling through him. Relief at discovering that she was okay had quickly given way to anger and jealousy. "I was worried," he said finally. It was the only admission he had any intention of making. It was bad enough that she was so damn calm. He wouldn't have her laughing at him.

"I'm sorry. I really thought Jason would explain. I went to Key West for a meeting about offshore drilling. It was unexpected or I would have told you about it this morning. Next time I'll try your cell and leave a message to cover the bases."

He nodded. He figured it was about as close to an apology as he was likely to get and probably about as much as he deserved after his sarcasm.

"How about a cup of tea?" she said quietly.

Despite himself, he grinned and felt himself beginning to relax. Tea. Ann's cure for everything. The world was clearly righting itself, getting back to normal.

"I'll sit with you while you have one. I'll have a beer."

He sat down in the kitchen and tilted his chair back on two legs, watching as she made the tea. There were no wasted motions, just quiet efficiency. Her expression, even after his irrational behavior, was unperturbed. That serenity conveyed itself to him, drawing him into the aura of warmth that seemed to surround her. He felt the last of the tension draining away.

"So tell me about Jason," she suggested, sitting down opposite him.

The muscles across the back of his shoulders knotted at once. "He's gone off somewhere," he said carefully, anticipating her panic.

"Gone off?" she said without the slightest evidence of concern. "What makes you think that?"

"I sent him to his room earlier. When I checked a while ago, he was gone."

She shrugged. "He's probably down by the water. That's where he goes whenever he's upset. He'll be back in an hour or so. What happened?"

"We had a fight over his attitude, as usual."

"Don't you think maybe you're a little hard on him? He is just a kid."

"I know, and I had an idea. What would you think about my offering him a job? He could work after school, pick up a little money, maybe develop a better sense of responsibility."

Her eyes lit up. "You'd do that for him?"

"Why not?"

"I know you don't really trust him."

He didn't bother denying it. "Even so, maybe he just needs a break."

"That's exactly what he needs." She reached over and took his hand. "Thank you, Hank."

Startled by the impulsive gesture, Hank wasn't sure how to react. Ann kept him constantly off balance. With any other woman, the touch might have been an invitation. With Ann, it was nothing more than an innocent, friendly gesture of thanks. There was nothing at all innocent about his reaction, however. His pulse was hammering.

"Ann..." he began.

As if she'd guessed the change in his mood, the swift stirring of desire, she patted his hand affectionately once more, then withdrew.

"Tell me about your night," she suggested. Something

in her penetrating gaze hinted that she was after more than a rundown on his experiences in getting the kids to bed. He doubted she gave a hang about what he'd watched on TV, either.

"It was quiet," he said, intentionally evading what he suspected she wanted to know. "Paul and Tommy had a great time at the construction site. I think Tommy's going to be a construction worker. It was all I could do to keep him from taking off across those girders. He's sleeping with the hard hat I gave him."

"I'm sure he loved all the attention."

"I couldn't talk David into going."

"I'm not surprised, but thanks for trying."

All the polite chitchat was beginning to grate on Hank's nerves, even though he was the one who'd started it. "This isn't really what's on your mind, is it?" he said finally.

"No."

"Go ahead. Say it."

"Your reaction when I got home, it was more than worry, Hank. You were really angry. Tell me why."

The fact that she sounded as much like a psychologist as a concerned woman really bugged him. He didn't want to be treated like one of her patients. He wasn't interested in baring his soul.

"You been reading those textbooks again, doctor?" he said.

She waited, her gaze intent.

He shrugged finally. Holding out was pointless. Ann was better at it than he was. She did it for a living. "Okay. Maybe I was jealous. Big deal."

She smiled. "I'm flattered, but I'm not convinced."

He tried to smile back. "I'm making a big admission here and you don't believe me? What's the deal?"

"Let's just say you're not a man whose confidence is easily shaken. Assuming for a moment that you were actually interested in me, you wouldn't be the least bit thrown by the fact that I'd spent the evening with another man. You'd chalk it up as a challenge."

Oddly enough, Hank realized that her analysis had a ring of truth to it. "Uncanny," he muttered under his breath.

She chuckled. "I'm a psychologist, Hank. Not a wizard."

"Same difference, if you ask me."

"You still haven't answered my question. What I really sensed underlying your anger was resentment. Is that possible?"

Hank thought back to all those unexplained absences that had tormented his childhood. "Maybe so," he admitted finally.

Ann's compassion reached out to him. He could feel it stealing over him, easing years of pain. "What happened?" she asked in that gentle tone that might have set off desire under other circumstances. Now, for some utterly absurd reason, it merely made him want to weep. He wasn't wild about the reaction. He hadn't shed a tear in more than twenty-five years, not since he'd finally figured out that things weren't ever likely to be any different.

"Hank?"

Despite his intention to curtail any private revelations, he found himself saying, "I guess I was just remembering some stuff I thought I'd put behind me."

"And you felt betrayed again," she guessed with more

uncanny accuracy. Even without knowing the details, she'd struck on the truth.

He lifted his gaze to hers. A desire to be completely honest with her compelled him to admit it. "Maybe so. I got left behind all too often when I was a kid."

"I'm sorry."

"Hey, it was the kids you left on their own. Not me."

Ann shook her head. "They weren't alone, Hank. They had you."

"It's not the same."

"I think it's pretty darn good."

Her voice rang with quiet conviction, but he searched her face, looking for evidence of the easy comeback, the quick lie. He found sincerity. The last of his tension eased, replaced by a sudden need to hold her, to feel even closer to her. Then he was struck by a sudden and disconcerting revelation. He felt closer to Ann at this moment than he'd ever felt to any of the women he'd taken to his bed.

Could be he was growing up.

Could be he was heading for disaster.

Chapter 6

Something had changed between them. Ann noticed it at once the next morning. After reluctantly opening up to her, she had anticipated that Hank would be reserved. She had hoped for it, in fact. She desperately needed anything that would put a little distance between them. Instead, the expression in Hank's eyes was bolder than ever, more speculative. The atmosphere was as emotionally charged as if they'd made love. The edge of anticipation that teased her senses made her nervous.

Her wariness did not, however, keep her from snatching an entire box of jelly doughnuts from in front of Hank before he could swallow the first mouthful of sugar. She'd watched him devour about as many empty calories as she could without intervening. He watched the box go into the trash can with surprising equanimity. Heady with her success, she reached for his can of soda. He clamped it in a death grip.

"No way," he said. "I need this."

She decided it was only possible to wean an adult from so many bad habits at a time. She released the can.

"How about a nice bowl of oat bran?" she suggested cheerfully.

"I'd rather eat wood chips."

The grumpy remark brought forth giggles from the kids, who'd been avidly watching the contest of wills.

"Oatmeal, then?" she said, undaunted.

His injured gaze pierced her. "Is this some sort of punishment?"

"Take the oatmeal," David warned. "It's the best you're likely to get when she's on one of these health kicks. By the weekend she might loosen up enough to make pancakes."

"Not for you, you little traitor," she said, turning on David with mock ferocity and giving up the battle of wills with Hank. Let him figure out what to eat now that his doughnuts were in the garbage. "Where's Jason? Is he up?"

"I'm here," he said, skirting Hank's vicinity and dragging out the chair farthest from his nemesis. Ann could practically feel the animosity radiating from the teenager. She wondered if Hank could possibly bridge it or, for that matter, if he was even still planning to try.

"Morning, Jason," Hank said, practically willing the boy to look at him. Holding her breath, Ann waited.

Jason finally mumbled a greeting, but kept his eyes on his bowl of cereal. While the other kids chattered and began racing around to collect their books for school, Jason remained sullen and silent. The minute he'd finished, he scooted back from the table.

"Wait," Hank said.

"Gotta go."

"You have a few minutes. If you're late, I'll take you to school."

Jason shot a look at Ann that was clearly an appeal. "Sit down," she said gently. "Listen to what Hank has to say."

Grudgingly Jason sat back down, but his entire body was stiff. He clearly resented Hank and it was going to take an incredible effort to get through the barriers he'd erected.

"I got to thinking about something last night," Hank began. "A guy your age could probably use some extra cash, right?"

Ann saw the spark of interest that flared in Jason's eyes before he could hide it. Still, he gave a disinterested shrug.

"So I was wondering how you'd like to come to work for me after school and on Saturdays."

Jason's brief hint of interest vanished and with it Ann's hopes. Jason faced Hank with open hostility. "Work for you? No way I'm taking orders from you, man."

"Jason, that's no way to talk to Hank," Ann said. "Listen to him."

"Why should I? He's just trying to buy me off."

Hank, to his credit, ignored the bitter accusation. As if Jason had never spoken, he said, "You'll get a decent salary and you'll earn every penny of it. You'll be learning something new. Who knows, maybe you'll even like it enough that it'll help you decide on a career. That's something you should be starting to think about."

Jason ignored Hank and looked directly at Ann. "Do I have to?"

She glanced at Hank, who shook his head slightly. She sighed. "You don't have to, but I'd like you to think about it. A lot of kids your age would give anything for an opportunity like this. It's a chance to get some experience before you have to make a decision about college."

"Yeah," he said derisively. "I'm gonna go to Harvard on my looks, right?"

"Jason!" Hank warned.

Ann intervened. "You have good grades, Jason. Maybe we won't be able to afford an Ivy League school, but you can get a college degree if you want one badly enough. Working for Hank would be one way to begin getting some of the money you'd need. Think about this."

"That's all I'm really asking, son," Hank said. "Think about it. Talk it over with your buddies at school and see what they think. I'll bet a lot of them already have after-school jobs. You can give me your answer tonight."

His expression still sour, Jason gave a curt nod. "Okay. Now can I go?"

"Go," Ann said, exhausted by the exchange.

When he'd gone, she looked at Hank. "I see what you mean. His hostility's getting worse, instead of better. Maybe I've been blinding myself to it."

"You've just been loving him. And I've probably made it worse. Don't work yourself into a state over this. I can handle Jason," he said, drinking the last of his soda and getting to his feet.

"But you shouldn't have to. He's my responsibility."

Hank squeezed her shoulder reassuringly. "Uh-uh. He's old enough to take responsibility for himself. Have a good day, Annie."

After Hank had gone, with the warmth of his touch fading, but the memory of Jason's animosity still lingering, Ann wondered if a good day was even remotely possible. What if he was right about Jason? What if he was heading for trouble again? Was there anything she or even the two of them together could do to stop it?

That afternoon when the high school let out, Hank was waiting for Jason. He spotted him coming down the walk, books under his arm and a smile on his face. The slender, dark-haired girl beside him was laughing at something he'd said. When he spotted Hank, his expression sobered at once.

"What are you doing here?"

"I thought maybe we could finish our talk."

"I got nothing to say to you."

Hank permitted himself a slight grin. "Maybe not, but there are a few things I'd like to say to you."

"Save it for later. I'm busy."

"I'm sure your friend will forgive you," Hank said pointedly.

"It's okay, Jason," the girl said, smiling at Hank. "I gotta get home anyway."

Jason seemed about to argue, then his shoulders slumped. "I'll call you later."

"Great."

As soon as she'd gone, he whirled on Hank. "What'd you have to go and do that for? I don't need my friends thinking I've got some hard-ass truant officer breathing down my neck."

"I seriously doubt that's what she thought and

even if it was, I'm sure you can set her straight. In the meantime, I want to talk to you about Ann."

To his surprise, Jason hesitated. "Is she okay? There's nothing wrong with her, is there?" There was genuine concern in the boy's voice. It gave Hank the first hope he'd felt in days.

"She's worried about you."

"That's only because you've gotten her all stirred up. We was getting along just fine until you came."

"You *were* getting along just fine."

"That's what I said."

Hank rolled his eyes. "Get in the truck. We can talk on the way."

"On the way where?"

"To your new job."

"I told you, man. I ain't working for you."

"Aren't, Jason. Do you ever crack that grammar book you've got under your arm?"

"I know enough to pass."

"And that's good enough for you? Just passing."

"It beats what my old man did. He dropped out when he was fifteen."

"And look how he wound up," Hank pointed out.

Jason looked as though he wanted to take a punch at him. Hank held up his hand. "Sorry. That was out of line. What I'm trying to say here is that you're too smart to waste your potential the way you've been doing. Ann went out on a limb for you. Don't you think you owe it to her to try a little harder?"

"She's never complained."

"Because she loves you. Maybe a little too much. She doesn't want to put extra pressure on you, but I think you're tough enough to take it. What do you think?"

"I'm tough enough to take anything you can dish out."

"Prove it. Start that job this afternoon. You won't be answering to me, if that's what you're worried about."

Jason clearly saw the trap that had been laid out for him. He also apparently realized there was no way around being snared, unless he wanted to show himself as a quitter. "I'll try it," he finally conceded. "But if I don't like it, I'm out of there."

"Fair enough."

Hank introduced him to the site foreman, then watched as Ted put him to work. By six o'clock Jason was dirty, hot and exhausted, but some of his belligerence had dimmed. Hank offered him a lift home.

"What the hell," Jason muttered, climbing into the pickup. "We're going to the same place."

At home, Jason walked through the kitchen like a kid asleep on his feet. Ann started to stop him, but Hank waved her off. "Let him go. He'll feel better after he's had a shower and some dinner."

"He took the job?"

"With a little prodding."

"Hank, you didn't back him into a corner, did you?"

"Maybe."

"But…"

"There's a door. He can always get out, if he wants to badly enough."

She nodded as Hank went off to take his own shower.

When he'd cleaned up and changed, he came back and found Ann sitting on the floor in the living room with Tommy and Melissa. Tommy, wearing his yellow hard hat, appeared to be in charge. They were building a skyscraper out of colored blocks. It was already tilting precariously.

Hank watched them for several minutes, enjoying the expression of fierce concentration on Melissa's face, the tolerant amusement on Ann's. "You'd better put something under the southwest corner," he advised Tommy finally.

"This is our development," Ann retorted. "You've got your own."

"Mine's bigger."

She shot a baleful look at him. "Bigger isn't necessarily better."

"Maybe not, but mine will still be standing in twenty years. Yours may not make it another twenty seconds." As if to prove his point, it wobbled under the weight of a red block Tommy was trying to add to the top. He knelt down and quickly inserted a block in the foundation. "There you go, partner. Steady as the Empire State Building."

"Is that tall?" Tommy wanted to know.

"Very tall."

"Want to see it," Melissa said.

"Maybe someday we can," he told her, his gaze locking with Ann's just as she tried to tell Melissa that it was too far away.

"Want to go," Melissa repeated.

"Someday," Hank repeated firmly, his eyes never leaving Ann's face, which was coloring under the direct gaze.

"What's for dinner?" he said at last, breaking the tension.

"Oh, my gosh," she said, jumping up and knocking over the tower in the process.

Melissa wailed. Tommy began gathering all the blocks and methodically going back to work. Hank dropped down to the floor. "I'll help, while Mommy gets dinner on the table."

"If I wasn't so terrified of what you'd fix, I'd send you to the kitchen," Ann said. "Nobody but an inveterate chauvinist would assume that cooking is woman's work, while building skyscrapers can only be done by big, tough men."

"Hey, I didn't say anything of the kind," he protested, laughing at her indignation. "I suspect that Melissa here could make a mighty fine engineer one day. I may even train her to follow in my footsteps."

Again he saw that off-guard look of wistfulness on Ann's face. His references to events far in the future seemed to rattle her even more than his touches. Perhaps she was right to be wary. How serious was he? The remarks seemed to come out without conscious thought on his part, indicating some subconscious direction in which he was heading without realizing it.

He blamed it on weeks of abstinence. Maybe he just needed to recall the experience of having a possessive woman back in his life again. A few carefully veiled references to commitment would put the fear of God back into him. Meantime, he was going to have to learn to think before he spoke.

Oddly enough, though, he couldn't keep his mind off the future all evening long. As he watched Ann, a yearning began to build inside him. He wondered what it would be like to know that this was the way it would be for the rest of his life, to know that she would always be there waiting for him, that he would be enveloped in that loving generosity of spirit that made her care for all these children as if they were her own.

He also wondered again why she was every bit as wary of the future as he was. What had scarred her so deeply? She'd learned many of his secrets, but what about hers?

While she put the kids to bed, he stretched out in the hammock, staring up at the inky sky. The scattering of stars seemed so much brighter here, away from the city lights. What did they hold for the future?

He heard the creak of the back door.

"Annie?"

"Yes."

"Come join me."

She took several steps in the direction of his voice, then hesitated as if she'd just realized where he was.

"Come on. There's room enough here for two."

"I don't think so. I really should go in and do the dishes."

"They'll wait. This sky won't. It may never be exactly this way again. One of those stars may fall."

"Why, Hank Riley, I do believe you may have the soul of a poet after all."

"I've always said you didn't give me enough credit for having a soul at all. Come on, Annie. How can you be afraid of a poet?"

He heard her low chuckle as she came closer. "They're the worst kind of romantic," she retorted.

He reached out, grabbed her wrist and pulled her into the hammock. She fell half-across him, torturing him with the press of her breasts against his chest, the whisper of her breath across his cheek. She struggled for just an instant, then seemed to sigh.

"Stay, Annie," he pleaded. "Right here beside me."

After a long hesitation during which he remained absolutely still, she lifted herself up from his chest and resettled herself beside him in the wide hammock. Her head rested on his shoulder.

"Watch for a shooting star," he said softly. "Then make a wish."

"Don't tell me you believe in all that?" she scoffed, her voice amused.

"You never know. I'm a firm believer in hedging all my bets."

"Are you a gambling man, Hank?"

It was an idle, teasing question, but he took it seriously. He thought about it for several minutes before saying honestly, "I never thought I was until recently."

"What's your game? Poker? Blackjack? Horses?"

"Love."

Ann's breath caught in her throat. "That's not a game."

"I've always played it as though it was. What about you? Have you ever been in love?"

"Once. A long time ago."

"What happened?"

She was quiet for so long he was afraid she might not answer, but it was a night made for sharing secrets. It was still enough and dark enough to hold a promise of endless privacy no matter what was revealed. "He left me."

There was a lifetime of raw pain behind those three simple words. "Why would any sane man ever leave a lovely woman like you?"

"Because," she said, her voice emotionless, "he was

twenty-two and he was too young to want to be saddled with a wife and a baby."

Though there wasn't a sound besides the whisper of her voice and the occasional shriek of a gull, Hank knew she was crying. He could feel the dampness rolling from her cheeks onto his shirt, soaking it. The thought of her hurting for so many years made him ache inside. He wanted to enfold her in his embrace, to protect her from ever knowing such pain again, but he sensed that what she needed was to talk. He encouraged it by his silence.

"We were engaged," she began in a voice that was now roughened by tears. "But when I went to tell him about the baby, he got furious. He wanted to go to medical school. He had all these plans, you see. He blamed me for trying to ruin them. I tried to make him see that it would be okay, that we could manage, but he walked out. I never saw him again. The next day I lost the baby."

She laughed bitterly. "Ironic, isn't it? If he'd stuck around, we wouldn't have had anything to worry about."

"You would have been miserable with a selfish jerk like that."

"Maybe so, but at the time I thought my world had ended."

"And you've spent the rest of your life making sure that no other man could get close enough to inflict that sort of pain."

He felt her head shake.

"Yes, you have," he insisted. "Or you'd have found someone else by now. Instead, you've filled your life with all the children no one else wanted to make up for the one this man didn't want."

"Now who's playing psychologist?"

"Am I any good at it?"

"Not bad, actually."

"Ann…" he began, but she pressed a finger against his lips.

"Just because you know about my past doesn't change anything, though. Not between us."

"Are you so sure of that?" he said, kissing her gently. The taste of her tears was on her lips. He wanted to go on kissing her until the memory blurred and finally faded altogether. Instead, he held back and watched her.

"Are you sure?" he repeated.

Blue eyes, fringed by long, sooty lashes, gazed back at him expectantly and he lost track of what he'd meant to say to persuade her to let go of the past. Provocative images replaced all thoughts of idle conversation. He swallowed hard past the lump in his throat as he finally tore his gaze away.

"Maybe you ought to go get some sleep," he said finally.

She stared at him, then nodded. "Maybe so," she said softly.

For just an instant, Hank could have sworn he heard regret in her tone, but then she was on her feet and striding toward the house with that long-limbed gait that stirred him so.

It was nearly an hour later when he finally dared to follow her inside. He'd hoped she'd gone to bed, but he found her at the sink, rinsing off dinner dishes with those familiar, sure movements. She'd changed clothes. A man's wool plaid shirt hung nearly to her knees. Her legs were bare down to the bright yellow socks that had settled in folds at her ankles.

Looking at those legs was dangerous, he decided
at once. Taking a beer from the refrigerator, his eyes
locked instead on the movement of her hands, soft and
slippery against the fragile porcelain. He imagined
them sliding over his flesh with the same gentle touch,
the same deft strokes, water cascading around them,
cooling their burning flesh. His blood surged at the
image. He could hear the pounding of his heart, feel the
throbbing low in his abdomen. His grip on the bottle of
beer was so tight, he was afraid the glass would snap. If
she didn't get out of the kitchen in the next five minutes,
he was going to forget all of his honorable intentions
and take her right there.

As if she'd guessed his thoughts, she turned suddenly.
His expression must have confirmed what she'd sensed,
because the cup fell from her hands and shattered on
the tile floor. Her lips parted on a gasp of dismay and
her eyes widened at the noise, but she didn't look away
from him for even a fraction of a second. It was as if
she were waiting for him to act, daring him to, wanting
him to.

"I thought you'd gone to bed," she said shakily.

Silent, Hank moved slowly toward her, watching the
flare of excitement in her eyes.

"Do you know what you're doing to me, Annie?"
he murmured as his fingers caressed the curve of her
jaw, then tangled in her hair. She nodded. "I want you,
Annie love. Now. Tonight."

Again she nodded and Hank felt the tension inside
him shatter like the teacup. He leaned down and touched
his lips to hers again, his fingers light against the pulse
in her neck. It jerked convulsively, then ran wild. His
own senses took off at a matching gait as his tongue

invaded the sweet recesses of her mouth. He gave himself up to the kiss, exploring, tasting. Her soft cries of pleasure broke over him with the force of magnificent ocean waves.

"We'll be good together, Annie. I promise you that."

"I know," she whispered against the burning column of his neck, her fingers now wound tightly in his hair.

The swell of her breasts was evident beneath that oversize shirt. At the stroking of his fingertips, the peak hardened at once. He bent to capture it in his mouth, his hand moving on, drifting lower over her flat stomach, then finding the warm mound between her thighs. She gasped as he rubbed the flat of his palm rhythmically back and forth. Her hips arched into the strokes.

He lifted his head and watched her. Her head was thrown back, leaving her neck vulnerable to his kisses. Her lips were parted as her breathing came in increasingly rapid bursts. He lifted the hem of the shirt and ran his fingers up the inside of her thigh. Her eyes widened as his hand once again touched the heat between her legs, this time with only the most delicate silk as a barrier. He could feel her moistness and it almost drove him wild. If this kept up, he would take her here and now. The heat exploding through him demanded he do just that.

Some guardian angel with a perverse sense of timing stopped him. Or perhaps it was the fleeting look of panic that he'd caught in her eyes before she'd determinedly banished it and given herself up to his loving.

He removed his hand and allowed the shirt to glide back down. It didn't cover nearly enough of those long, slender legs.

"Hank?" she said, her expression puzzled.

He sighed heavily with regret.

"It's okay, Annie love." He pressed a chaste kiss to her forehead. "It's okay."

"But I wanted you to make love to me."

"I know you did and God knows I wanted to."

"Then why are you stopping?"

"Because it would be wrong. I can make you want me in your bed, but that's not good enough for you. After what you've been through, you're the kind of lady who deserves forever. I don't believe in it."

"I'm all grown-up, Hank. I can make my own decisions. I have no illusions anymore. There were no demands connected to this, no expectations."

He smiled. "You may not think so now, Annie, but I guarantee you in the morning, you'd have felt differently. Neither one of us would have been able to live with the guilt." He touched her swollen lips with the tips of his fingers and tried to ignore the hurt in her eyes. "Now go to bed, before I change my mind."

She turned back to the sink, her shoulders tensed.

He reached out and touched her. She shuddered visibly, which made him feel like crying.

"Go, dammit," he said, his voice gruff. "I'll finish the dishes."

"It's my house," she reminded him, with an all-too-familiar mixture of stiff-necked pride and indignation.

"Meaning?" Hank said.

A plate clattered to the floor, shattering. Ann clung to the edge of the counter so tightly, he could see the whitening of her knuckles. He bent down to pick up the shards of china as he waited for her to answer.

"Meaning you don't give the orders. If anybody goes

anywhere tonight," she said in a tight, controlled voice, "it ought to be you."

Grateful for the anger that was escalating by the second, he whirled her around, ready to lash out.

She lifted her chin and stared back. Defiant. Proud. Furious.

Want thundered through him. He held it at bay by sheer will.

"Fine," he said when he could control his voice. "If that's the way you want it, I'm out of here."

Chapter 7

It was practically the middle of the night and he was beat, but Hank couldn't get away from Ann's fast enough. Gravel flew. Dust curled up behind the pickup as he bounced over the rutted driveway and sped onto U.S. 1 heading north toward home.

Toward sanity.

And, face it, toward safety.

The last bounce, which very nearly sent his head through the roof, reminded him that he'd been meaning to fill in the potholes before Ann's car broke its axle. The fact that he was still thinking of the chores that needed to be done around her house infuriated him all over again. She was independent. She didn't need or want him around. She'd made that plain enough when she'd kicked him out just now. She sure as hell didn't need him making love to her, either. Why couldn't she see that?

And why the hell couldn't he leave well enough alone? Why had he gone and practically seduced the woman over the kitchen sink when he knew just how wrong it would be for both of them? He was no oversexed kid who didn't know how to keep his pants on. He'd never in his life allowed things to go so far with a woman who wasn't fully aware of the score. Like he'd told Ann, not only didn't she know the score, she didn't even know the name of the game.

He turned the radio on full blast, hoping to drown out his thoughts. Unfortunately he was tuned to a country station. He'd forgotten that the lyrics of half the songs out of Nashville were all too explicit about the pitfalls of loving the wrong woman. He should have switched the dial. Somehow, though, he felt he deserved the torment. By the time he'd gotten halfway back to Miami, he was thinking very seriously of just walking away, of turning the whole damn Marathon job over to Todd.

Or murdering him for sending him down there in the first place. As for Liz, he might never forgive her for suggesting this living arrangement.

He was not, therefore, in a particularly welcoming frame of mind at ten in the morning when Todd turned up on his doorstep while he was still tossing and turning and trying to get the first minute's sleep of the endless night. Yanking open the door at what seemed like dawn to find his cheerful, wide-awake partner on his doorstep set his teeth on edge. He scowled, then stomped back inside. Leaving Todd to make what he would of the irritable behavior, he climbed into the shower, turned it to its iciest temperature and stood under it for fifteen minutes. It didn't do a damn thing except make him shiver.

Tugging on a pair of well-worn jeans and an old shirt that he didn't bother to button, he went into the kitchen. He didn't even growl a thank-you for the mug of coffee Todd handed him in silence. He took a couple of swallows of the strong brew, sat the cup on the counter and began slamming pots and pans into the kitchen cupboard. Undaunted, Todd failed to heed the cues to leave.

"How's it going?" Todd asked instead, leaning nonchalantly against the doorjamb watching Hank's performance.

Deliberately misinterpreting the how's-life-in-general scope of the question, Hank said, "We're on schedule."

"No problems?"

"Not since you got that supplier straightened out."

"How's Ann?"

The question sounded innocent. Hank's reaction was not. His gut knotted the way an alcoholic's would at a casual reference to fourteen-year-old Scotch—with longing. He managed a disinterested shrug. It was the greatest acting of his life. "Fine, I suppose."

"You suppose? You see the woman every day. Don't you know for sure?"

"She's a hard woman to read."

"Oh, really? I've always thought of Ann as being the most straightforward, honest woman around. No subterfuge. No games."

"We don't sit around having conversations about her state of mind or her health," he snapped, then gave another offhand shrug. "Like I said, she seems about the same as when I arrived, so I guess that means she's fine."

Todd, damn him, laughed. "She's getting to you, isn't she?"

"Right," he retorted sarcastically. "Like poison ivy."

"Hmm."

He shot a glance at the man he'd known for most of his life. Todd was looking very smug. "Don't stand there gloating, old buddy, or you'll be down in Marathon before you can say goodbye to your wife and children. In fact, with the mood I'm in, I don't care if that sweet, innocent baby of yours doesn't see you again before she turns eighteen."

"That bad, huh?"

Despite the early hour, Hank grabbed a beer from the refrigerator, took a long, slow swallow, then sighed wearily. Further denials were pointless. Todd had always been able to guess what was going on in his head anyway. They'd bolstered each other up during crises far more devastating than this one.

"Worse," he admitted. "But hardly cataclysmic."

"Want to talk about it?"

"There's nothing to say."

"You falling for her?"

"Hell, no."

"Oh, really?"

Todd sounded incredibly skeptical. Hank resumed glowering and slamming things around. "Don't push it," he muttered.

"I don't get it. What's wrong? Ann's intelligent, attractive. You're both single. I've never known you to miss out on an opportunity to expand your dating circle."

"Ann Davies is not my type," he insisted.

"She's a woman."

"Very funny."

"Come on, give. What's not to like?"

"She's a terrific lady, okay? Is that what you wanted to hear? That doesn't mean we get along."

"I think I'm beginning to get the picture. Is she, by any chance, trying to reform you?"

"She took away my damn doughnuts," he retorted before he could stop himself.

A sound suspiciously like the beginning of a hoot of laughter was quickly smothered. "That's serious all right."

"She wants me to eat oat bran," he added indignantly. "Can you believe it? The woman does nothing but preach about cholesterol from morning to night. If I eat any more fresh vegetables, I'll grow ears like Peter Rabbit. I haven't had a decent steak in the past two weeks. Every time I sneak a cheeseburger for lunch I feel like I ought to go straight to a priest and confess."

"Just tell her how you feel. She's a reasonable woman."

Hank stared at Todd incredulously. "Are we talking about the same woman? The woman who threatened to pour all of my sodas down the drain? The woman who gets hysterical at the sight of potato chips?"

"Don't you think you're exaggerating just a little?"

"Exaggerating? If anything, I'm downplaying the way that woman is trying to run my life."

"I'm sure she's just thinking of your health."

"Maybe I should bring her a note from my doctor."

"If your doctor knew what you ate, he'd probably swear out a warrant and lock you up in a hospital for a month to wean you off all of that junk."

"You sound just like Ann."

"Well, she does have a point. You're at that age."

"What age? I'm thirty-seven. I exercise. I haven't had any complaints from the women I date about my stamina."

"Do you have a date for tonight?"

"What does that have to do with anything?"

"Do you?"

"No."

Exaggerated astonishment registered on Todd's face. "Hank Riley is back in town and doesn't have a date! Women across Dade County must be in the throes of despair."

Hank's eyes narrowed. Todd chuckled. "Why are you here, by the way? I tried to reach you in the Keys and Ted said you hadn't come in or called. Ann didn't make a lot more sense when I called there."

"You talked to Ann?" he said, suddenly wary.

"How else do you think I knew you were here?"

"How'd she sound?"

"Like Ann. Dammit, Hank, what the devil is going on between you two?"

"Nothing."

"If you hurt her, Liz will kill you. Come to think of it, I may kill you. She's been a good friend to us. Kevin, needless to say, adores her. She's turned his life around since she's been helping him with his reading problem."

"Who the hell says I hurt her? Did she say that?"

"*She* didn't say anything. Ann is the soul of discretion, in case you haven't noticed. I'm picking up all these weird vibes from you."

"Well, you've got it all wrong."

"Okay, we'll forget that for the moment and go back

to the other issue you seem to be evading. What brings you to Miami?"

Good question. Hank knew he should have anticipated it, but he hadn't. He'd been too busy running for his life. "I, um, I had some things to follow up on in the office."

"What things?"

"Things, okay?"

"Interesting."

"Don't get cute with me, buddy. I'm too damn tired to deal with your smart remarks."

The admission cost him. It said far too much about the sleepless nights he'd spent in the past couple of weeks, as well as his current state of mind. He caught the twitch of Todd's lips. It rankled.

"Have dinner with Liz and me," Todd suggested.

Hank visibly recoiled from the daunting prospect. "Oh, no. Not a chance."

"How come? Don't you want to see your godson? He could use a few pointers on his pitching. And the baby is almost crawling. You should see her."

"I have spent the past two weeks surrounded by rug rats. I do not need to see any more. Cute as yours might be," he amended, knowing exactly how touchy Todd could be over his offspring.

"We'll fix steaks on the grill."

His mouth began to water.

"And I just bought a case of cabernet sauvignon that will go perfectly with them."

He weakened. Obviously in the past couple of weeks his resistance had been shot to hell along with his nerves. It was pathetic. "What time?"

"Eight."

"Make it seven. I doubt if I'll be able to stay awake past nine and I'd hate to fall asleep before I get the first bite of steak."

"Great. See you later, pal. What time are you coming in to the office?"

"The office?" he repeated blankly.

"You did say that's why you came, didn't you?"

"Oh, right. Later."

"Later," Todd repeated, clearly amused. "Good time."

As soon as his still-smirking partner had left, Hank's thoughts whirled right back to Ann. He recalled a dozen different images, all of them tantalizing enough to set his blood on fire.

"No way," he muttered as he began to scrub the kitchen floor. It was a task he usually left to the maid. She came once a week. The floor was spotless. He didn't care. Scrubbing it kept him from pounding on walls. As he mopped, he forced himself to itemize every one of Ann's innumerable flaws aloud.

"Bossy." An image of her comforting Melissa countered it.

"Opinionated." He recalled how intently she'd listened to Tracy's problems at school, never once offering advice, only encouragement. Tracy had worked out her own solution and left for Key West with renewed confidence.

"She has no sense of style." She'd been wearing a man's wrinkled red plaid flannel shirt when he left and bright yellow socks. That shirt had barely reached to midthigh. To his astonishment, it had triggered sensations more powerful than the most seductive black lace teddy. Judging from the renewed racing of his pulse, its power hadn't dimmed over the past few hours. He tried harder to counteract the effect.

"That impossible hair!" A memory of his callused fingers tangled in the short, dark strands made his muscles go taut.

"Oh, hell!"

Ann was scrubbing pots and pans with a vengeance. She had already mopped the kitchen floor, vacuumed the house from one end to the other and dusted so thoroughly that the kids had scattered. She was considering washing all the windows next. It probably wouldn't help.

Hank Riley was the most infuriating, insensitive, nervy man she'd ever met. Last night had been…a disaster. An unmitigated disaster. What had ever made her think that she wanted that man in her bed? What had possessed her to even allow him into her house? In only a few weeks he'd done more to turn her well-ordered life upside down than any four of the children combined. Once he had gone for good, she was sure she'd feel quite capable of coping with another half-dozen kids.

"Ann?"

She turned and saw Tracy regarding her hesitantly. "What's up, kiddo? I thought you'd spent the night down in Key West."

"I did. I just thought I'd come back this morning."

"No classes?"

"It won't hurt me to skip 'em for once."

"No. Probably not," Ann said, studying her more closely. She sounded very defensive and she seemed a little pale. "Are you sure you're okay?"

"I said I'm fine," Tracy snapped, then flushed guiltily. "Sorry. Where's Hank?"

"I'm not sure. I assume he's at work."

"He's not. I checked there."

"Why?"

"I just wanted to ask him something."

"Can't you ask me?"

Tracy shook her head and Ann felt somehow betrayed. "You sure?"

"Yeah. It's about guys."

"I see." She considered pressing, but decided against it. With her track record in the past twenty-four hours, she was the last person to be giving out advice about men. "You could call his cell phone."

Tracy's expression brightened at once. "You have the number?"

"It's on the pad by the phone under Todd's name."

Tracy flung her arms around her. "Thanks, Ann."

Ann watched as she copied the number and raced to use the phone in the living room. Again that stirring of resentment nagged at her.

"This is just terrific, Ann, old girl. Now you're jealous of the man."

It was true. She'd noticed it more than once as Hank began slowly interacting with each of the children. Despite his reservations, he was really trying to reach Jason. As for Tommy and Paul, they clearly idolized him. It had hurt her the first time she'd realized how often they turned to Hank. They trailed him around the house, imitating his mannerisms. Tommy constantly wore the tiny hard hat Hank had gotten him. Now Tracy was defecting as well.

Ann shook her head and sighed. She ought to be

grateful. She analyzed the emotions that were rampaging through her. Gratitude wasn't among them. Nope. Jealousy was at the top of the list.

"Well, you'll just have to get over this in a big hurry," she muttered, pouring vinegar and water into a bucket and heading for the windows that faced the Atlantic.

Filled with trepidation, Hank approached Todd's house in Coconut Grove later that night. He knew that his encounter with Todd in the morning had been little more than polite chitchat compared to the cross-examination Liz was likely to subject him to. He wasn't sure he was up to it.

Ever since Tracy's phone call, he'd been tempted to head straight back down to the Keys. He didn't like the sound of this boy she was going out with. He guessed the kid's hormones were in overdrive and he wasn't one bit sure that all his advice had equipped Tracy to deal with him. His stomach knotted at the thought of the jerk laying a hand on that sweet, innocent kid. After the hell her old man had put her through, she deserved never again to be touched except with love and respect.

He wasn't aware that he'd been sitting in the car for some time until he heard Kevin shouting at him.

"Hey, Hank, come on! Dad said you'd help me with my pitching. It's only a little while till dinner."

Hank mustered a grin, grabbed the baseball mitt he'd thrown in the back and climbed wearily from his truck. At least it would provide a reprieve from Liz's inquisition.

"Okay, kid, let's see what you've got."

Todd came out moments later and joined them on the

wide sweep of lawn. "Sorry I missed you at the office. Feeling any better?"

"I'm great."

"Right."

Hank shot him a vicious look, then turned pointedly to Kevin. "Try a curveball. You remember where I told you to put your fingers."

The ball zipped toward him with surprising speed and accuracy, landing in his mitt with a solid thud. Kevin's grin split his freckled face. "How's that?"

"Not bad, kid. You've been practicing."

"Every night. At least when Dad gets home in time. Liz tried to catch for me one night, but she was pretty bad," he confided. His tone and his face registered his disgust. "Girls!"

Hank laughed. "Yeah, kid, I know just what you mean."

"I heard that," Liz called, poking her head out the front door. "People who make unkind remarks about the cook get steaks that are the consistency of shoe leather."

Hank immediately adopted a suitably contrite expression and jogged over to plant a kiss on Liz's forehead. "Sorry. Present company excepted, of course."

"Thank you." She glanced toward Kevin. "And you?"

Kevin grinned at his stepmother. "Sorry, Liz."

She nodded in satisfaction. "Good. Then dinner's ready."

Hank made the first cut into his thick, juicy steak with the enthusiasm of a half-starved man. He lifted the bite to his mouth, savored the aroma, then bit into it slowly. It was delicious, with just a hint of mesquite in the flavor. He swallowed and the image of Ann's disapproving expression flickered alive in his stupid brain. Guilt stole in. The second bite wasn't nearly as flavorful as the first. The third practically choked him. He determinedly ate another and then another, forcing himself to finish the entire steak.

When he looked up from his meal at last, he caught Todd and Liz exchanging an amused glance.

"Did you enjoy your steak?" Todd inquired with contrived innocence.

"Terrific."

"I have another piece in the kitchen," Liz offered sweetly.

"No, thanks. I've had plenty."

"More salad?" She held out the bowl.

Hank reached for it, then stubbornly jerked back his hand. "No."

"Are you sure? You've hardly eaten a thing."

He took a deliberate sip of the excellent full-bodied wine. "Guess I just wasn't as hungry as I thought."

"Aren't you feeling well?" Liz persisted, her eyes filled with concern.

"I'm fine. Dinner was superb."

"How about some apple pie?"

Hank was cheered by the prospect. Apples were healthy. Not even Ann could find anything to object to there.

"Maybe with some vanilla ice cream on top?" Liz suggested.

His mouth watered. "Terrif—" he began, then recalled Ann's speech about the fat content of ice cream as she'd given him a bowl of frozen yogurt. "No. I'll take it plain."

Damn. She wasn't within fifty miles and she was still ruining his appetite. Fortunately before Liz could make too much out of his refusal, the phone rang. "I'll get it," she said. "Kevin, how about bringing the dishes into the kitchen."

When the two of them had gone, Todd said quietly, "It's worse than you've admitted, isn't it?"

"Don't you dare start gloating again."

"I wouldn't dream of it. I've waited a long time to witness the fall of the mighty lecher. Are you in love with her?"

"Absolutely not. You know how I feel about love. It doesn't exist."

"Methinks thou does protest too much."

Hank glared. "Think whatever you want."

"Well, what are you going to do about it?"

"Not a damn thing," he insisted stubbornly.

"But…"

The ringing of his cell phone interrupted Todd's protest. It was Tracy.

He almost knocked over his chair as he stood and answered the phone. "Are you okay?" he asked, his voice raw with panic.

All he heard were muffled sobs.

"Tracy, where are you?"

"At a gas station."

"Where?"

"In Key Largo."

"Are you okay?" He closed his eyes and forced himself to ask gently, "He didn't hurt you, did he?"

"No, I'm just so mad." She choked back another sob. "Hank, he was just as big a creep as you said he was. Why didn't I listen to you?"

Hank's heart finally began beating again. "Because you wanted to believe in the guy. Trusting someone isn't a sin. It takes a lot of experience, though, before you can completely trust your judgment."

"I'm never dating again."

Hank grinned, thankful that Tracy couldn't see it. "I doubt you'll feel that way by next weekend. You stay put, honey. I'll come get you."

"You don't have to do that," she said bravely, but her voice was still thick with tears. "I can call Ann."

"Stay put. I'm on my way." He took down the location of the gas station and hung up, then turned to find Liz and Todd regarding him intently.

"You heard?"

They nodded.

"I have to go get her."

Liz reached out and touched his arm. Until he felt the gentle brush of her fingers, he hadn't realized how tense he was. "She'll be fine. She's just scared."

He felt himself beginning to relax. "I know."

He headed for the door, then turned back. "Thanks."

"Any time." Before he could close the door, she called out. "Hank."

He looked back.

"You'll make a wonderful father."

He shook his head, but as he climbed back into his truck and headed south, he realized that was exactly how he felt: like a father.

It scared the hell out of him.

Chapter 8

Tracy was waiting exactly where Hank had told her to wait, inside the office at the gas station. Sitting on a chair, shoulders slumped, her expression glum, she looked like an abandoned waif, rather than a beautiful young woman just emerging into adulthood. Seeing her like that scared him. He didn't have any experience at handling something like this. What if he said the wrong thing? What if he only made matters worse? How had Todd survived all the years he'd been a single parent to Kevin? How did Ann cope on her own with the steady stream of kids she'd taken into her home and heart? He wished he'd taken the time to call her for some quick advice on parenting before barreling down here, but he hadn't. He was on his own.

He opened the door to the office and stepped inside. "Tracy," he said quietly.

Her gaze shot up and her eyes filled with tears. She launched herself into his arms and clung like a frightened child. He held her tight. "It's okay, sweetheart. Everything's okay," he soothed.

He turned to the attendant. "Thanks for letting her stay inside."

"No problem, mister. I just wish more girls used their heads these days and called home when things got out of hand."

When they'd gotten into the car, Hank handed her a tissue. "He's right, you know. You did the right thing by calling. Don't ever be afraid to turn to Ann or me when you're in trouble."

Tracy fidgeted nervously. She glanced sideways at him.

"What's wrong?" he asked.

"You're not going to tell Ann, are you?"

He hesitated, torn. Finally he sighed. "Not unless you say it's okay."

"Thank you."

"Wait a minute. I think you should talk to her about it yourself."

"But she wouldn't understand."

It was the cry of teenagers about their parents from time immemorial, but still Hank stared at her in astonishment. "Ann? Sweetheart, she's the most understanding woman around. Of course she'd understand."

"But she's so perfect. She never makes any mistakes, at least not really dumb ones like this."

Hank thought of the story Ann had told him just last night about her own youthful error in judgment. If only she would share that story with Tracy. It would bring the two of them even closer, bridging the gap that even Ann was all too aware of.

"Talk to her," he urged again. "I think you could be surprised."

An hour later when they walked into the house together, Ann looked up from her book, her expression welcoming until she spotted Hank with Tracy. Alarm warred with dismay. Hank could read the entire gamut of emotions in her eyes. As always, concern for one of her kids won out over her own feelings.

"Is everything okay?" she asked, looking anxiously from one to the other.

"Fine," Tracy mumbled, not meeting her gaze directly. "I'm going to sleep. Thanks for picking me up, Hank."

When she'd gone, Ann stared hard at Hank. "Is she really okay?"

He nodded. "Just a little shaken."

"What happened? Was there an accident? Why was she with you?"

"I gave her a ride home."

"Don't be deliberately obtuse. Why?"

"Ask her."

"Dammit, Hank. She's practically my daughter. If she's in some kind of trouble, I ought to know about it."

He knelt down beside her so he could gaze directly into her worried eyes. He placed a reassuring hand on her knee, but removed it when he felt her go tense. "She's okay, Annie. I swear it, but I promised her I wouldn't talk about it. I think she'll tell you herself once she's had some time to settle down a bit."

She frowned at him, then asked furiously, "Where the hell do you get off deciding what's best for one of my kids? I'm responsible. Whatever happened, I should have been there, not you."

He recognized the frustration and guilt in her voice and wanted more than anything to put her fears to rest, but he'd made a promise and he intended to keep it. He knew enough about teenagers to understand that Tracy would never trust him again if he betrayed her now, no matter how well-intentioned he might be.

"She called me," he reminded her gently. "What was I supposed to do?"

After a long silence, she finally let out a deep breath. "I'm sorry. You're right. You had to go. I shouldn't have taken it out on you, but, Hank, I'm really worried about her. She was acting funny all day long."

"She really is fine."

"I'm not so sure. I'm not just talking about whatever happened tonight. I'm talking about how she handled it. She insisted on calling you earlier today, too. I'm sure that was part of the same thing. I think she's developing a full-scale crush on you."

The comment hit him from out of the blue. It rocked him back on his heels. "Come on, Annie. Don't be ridiculous."

"It's not ridiculous and you know it. You may well be the first man who's ever treated her with respect and tenderness. Why wouldn't she fall for it?"

"Hell, I'm old enough to be her father."

"Age is irrelevant in a situation like this. Young women who've had absent or abusive fathers often think they're in love with older men who are like the idealized fathers they never had."

He got up and started pacing. The movement only seemed to increase his agitation. Finally he sank down in a chair and ran his fingers through his hair. Ann was making a sort of twisted kind of sense, but he was convinced she was way off base. He wasn't that insensitive. He would have known if Tracy had a crush on him.

"You're wrong, Annie. She's thinking of me as her father. I'm sure that's all it is."

"Maybe. Just be careful. Whatever her feelings, if she begins to depend on you too much, she's going to be devastated when you leave."

"Who says I'm leaving?"

"Hank, be realistic," she said impatiently. "The job will be over sooner or later. You'll go back to Miami. We may all run into one another occasionally on holidays at Liz and Todd's but that will be the extent of it."

He studied her closely. Her expression was determinedly unemotional, her tone flat. Still, he had a feeling she was voicing her own fears now. "Is it Tracy you're worried about now or yourself?"

She flushed. "Leave me out of this. I'm an adult. I can handle it."

"Can you really? Look what happened last night."

"Nothing happened," she pointed out with a touch of wry humor.

"I was referring to how upset you got, but let's put that aside for a minute and deal with what's really bothering you. You know perfectly well that I stopped making love to you for all the reasons you're talking about. I probably will go back to Miami in a few months and when I go, I don't want you on my conscience."

"How very noble!" she said, her blue eyes flashing fire. "Don't do me any favors, mister."

Troubled by the hurt behind her remark, Hank tried

to sort through the mess they seemed to be in. "Do you want me to move out now? Maybe it would be better for everyone if I went before the attachments got any deeper." That went for him as well as them, though he wasn't willing to admit it.

"Maybe it would be," Ann said in a voice that was surprisingly weak considering her angry state only moments earlier.

There was a sharp ache in his gut, but Hank nodded and got to his feet. "I'll pack my things."

He was halfway across the room when he heard what sounded like a muffled sob. When he turned, Ann was hastily wiping the tears from her cheeks. He was beside her in an instant. Kneeling again, he took her hands in his. "Annie, is this really what you want?"

The broken sound she uttered was part laugh, part sob. "I don't seem to know what I want," she confessed. "For the first time in a very long time I don't have the vaguest idea what's right."

"Then I guess we're in the same boat. I don't seem to be sure of anything anymore, either. Liz and Todd seem to have this crazy idea we're meant for each other. They set us up, you know."

She nodded and smiled ruefully. "Think we should wring their necks?"

"It's crossed my mind. On the other hand, they are our best friends. They know us pretty well."

"What are you saying?"

"Maybe we should stay right where we are and play out this hand like a couple of grown-ups."

"Now that's a risky notion," she joked feebly. Tears trembled on the ends of her lashes, then spilled down her cheeks.

"Hey, I'm a gambling man, remember?"

"Maybe so, but *I've* never gambled on anything in my life."

With the pad of his thumb, he rubbed away her tears. "Who knows," he said. "Maybe you'll have beginner's luck."

The only trouble with this new game plan was that they didn't seem to know how to begin. For the next few days, they were both so wary Ann thought she would scream in frustration. Every time Hank so much as brushed accidentally against her, he apologized profusely and bolted. She was rapidly reaching the end of her patience.

Nor was she one bit sure how she felt about Hank's decision to insinuate himself into their lives more completely than ever. From her point of view, particularly after their talk about Tracy, she still thought a little caution was called for. When she told him exactly that one night after dinner, he snapped back, "You can't have it both ways. I can't stay here and back off at the same time."

"I don't see why not," she said stubbornly.

He simply stared at her.

"Okay, so it's not logical," she admitted finally. "I'm not feeling very rational."

"How are you feeling?"

"Like I'm being ripped in two."

"Me, too."

Suddenly she started laughing. The whole thing was utterly absurd. They were two supposedly mature, rational adults with advanced college degrees. Between them, surely they had sufficient brainpower to come up with a solution.

"I'm not sure I see what's so funny," Hank growled. "We've got a problem here."

"Exactly. Would you care to define it?"

"We're…" He fumbled for an explanation.

"Horny," she provided.

"Annie!" Shock registered on his face, though she could see from the look in his eyes that she'd hit the nail on the head. Hank was not a man used to going for long without a woman in his life. Ironically, he was probably equally adept at avoiding emotional intimacy. In their current situation, the tables had been turned on him.

"Well, that's the problem, isn't it? If I were any other woman, you'd have taken me to bed days ago, wouldn't you?"

"You are not any other woman."

"I suppose I should thank you for that," she said dryly. "But at the moment I'm not one bit grateful."

He chuckled. "I see your point."

They sat there staring at each other. "We could go to a movie," he suggested finally.

"It is nearly ten o'clock at night."

"We could rent one."

"And sit side by side, curled up on the sofa," she said, deliberately taunting him.

"Bad idea."

"I knew you'd see it."

"How about chess? We could play a game of chess. It's dull, hardly the stuff of erotic fantasies."

"I don't play chess."

"Checkers, then. Hell, help me out here, Annie. I'm trying."

"Okay, checkers. I think Paul has a set in his room."

"You get 'em. I'll make a bowl of popcorn."

"I should have known you'd try to sneak in junk food."

"I'll bring grapes for you."

Fifteen minutes later they had the checkerboard on the table between them, along with a bowl of buttered popcorn and a plate of grapes. Five minutes after that, Hank had won the first game.

"You're not concentrating," he accused.

"Who can concentrate? You're over there crunching away on the popcorn."

"Popcorn does not crunch. At least not a lot. It's hardly enough to distract a really good checkers player."

"I never said I was any good. Even Tommy can beat the socks off me. You're the one who wanted to play."

"I wanted to do something that would keep my mind off taking you to bed."

"Is it working?"

"No!"

"That's what I was afraid of. It's not working for me, either."

"Do you know why?"

"Physiologically or psychologically?" she inquired. He glared at her.

"It's because we're living here together, playing house, so to speak. Only we're not...you know." His voice trailed off weakly.

"See," she gloated. "You can't even talk about it."

"Do you honestly want to talk about it?"

"It's been my experience that talking usually helps."

Hank was shaking his head adamantly. "Not in this

case. Take my word for it, Annie. Talking about sex will not get our minds off it."

"It might put it into perspective."

"Right now about the only thing that would put it into perspective for me is a cold shower, which I intend to take." He got as far as the door before turning back, a wistful expression on his face. "I don't suppose…"

"I am not taking the shower with you."

He grinned. "It was worth a shot."

The next morning they were both bleary-eyed and grouchy.

"What's wrong with you two?" Paul asked when they'd both snapped over something totally inconsequential.

"Not enough sleep," Hank said, staring pointedly at Ann.

"Whose fault was that?" she retorted, slamming a teacup down in front of him and pouring him some herbal tea.

"I want my soda," he said, pushing the cup aside.

"I threw them all out."

"You did what!" he bellowed, sounding like a wounded bear.

She smiled. "Try the tea."

"I will not drink this watered-down excuse for tea. There's no caffeine in it."

"That's the point."

In midargument Ann noticed that the kids were following the battle as if they were at a tennis match, looking back and forth, back and forth, as the barbs flew.

"Enough," she said with a sigh. "Truce."

"Does that mean I get my soda?" he inquired hopefully.

"It means we're going to stop fighting about it."

"We're only going to do that if one of them turns up on this table in the next ten seconds."

"Oh, go fly a kite!" she said and stalked out of the house. Openmouthed, the kids stared after her.

"Is Mom okay?" David asked hesitantly.

"She's fine," Hank said tersely.

"Are you sure?" David persisted.

Tracy shot a knowing look at Hank. "I think she's in love."

"Mom!" The chorus of voices was incredulous. Hank could feel his skin burn.

"Tracy, I don't think this is a topic that needs to be discussed just now."

"I'm right, aren't I?"

"Not now, Tracy."

Jason stared from one to the other before finally sending his chair flying as he got to his feet, scowling fiercely at Tracy. "You think Mom's in love with him? You're crazy! She's not out of her mind."

"Just because you and Hank don't get along doesn't mean Ann can't like him," Tracy retorted. "Don't be such a jerk."

"You're the jerk." He slammed out of the house.

"If you and Ann fall in love does that mean you'll be our dad?" Paul asked. "I think that'd be neat."

Hank felt as if he'd been punched in the gut. "Whoa, everybody. Let's slow down a minute. First of all, the way Ann and I feel is nobody's business but ours."

"Hey, we live here, too," Tracy protested.

"My point is that this is something she and I have to

work out and we can't do that if you all are watching and questioning every move we make."

Tracy was nodding knowingly. Hank didn't trust that smug expression one bit. "You're in love all right."

"Tracy!"

She grinned unrepentantly. "Sorry. I got carried away. What can we do to help?"

"Keep your opinions and your guesswork to yourselves," he grumbled, knowing that was about as likely as shutting down the lurid speculation in the national tabloids. He began to have some sense of what celebrities went through when their personal lives got turned inside out in public.

As soon as the kids had all gone off to school, including Melissa, who was attending a nearby nursery school in the mornings, Hank left the house and walked slowly across the highway to Dolphin Reach, where Ann had her office. Though he knew all about the innovative treatment she was involved in there—it was where Todd had brought Kevin for help with his dyslexia—this was the first time he'd entered her professional domain.

A young receptionist looked up and smiled a harried greeting as she continued handling phone calls. When she was finally free, he asked for Ann's office.

"It's the second one on the left, but she's not there. I think she's down with the dolphins."

"Is she with a patient?"

"Nope. Her first one's not till ten."

"Thanks."

As he walked through the grounds and headed for the dock, his curiosity about her work mounted. What had ever given her the idea of using dolphins as a part of her psychological counseling? Then he spotted her at the end of a dock and thought he knew.

She was kneeling on a platform that stuck out into the protected harbor, her skirt swirling around her. A brisk wind tousled her hair. Dolphins surrounded her, their built-in smiles impossible to resist as they bobbed in the water. Seeing Ann's laughing response to their antics and knowing full well how troubled she'd been when she left the house, he began to see how the dolphins might be the perfect intermediary for a hard-to-reach patient.

"Annie."

Her laughter died at the sound of his voice and her gaze grew troubled. "Why are you here?"

"I thought we needed to talk."

"Not now. I'm busy."

"You don't have a patient scheduled for another hour. I'm booking this time."

"Sorry. I don't take clients with whom I have a personal involvement."

He grinned. "That won't work. You helped Kevin."

He saw her fighting a smile. "Okay, so I made one exception."

"Make another one."

"Why should I?"

"Because the kids just made me face up to something I've been avoiding."

Curiosity obviously overcame her reluctance to hear him out. "What's that?"

"I'm in love with you."

Ann looked stunned. And skeptical. But once the words were finally out of his mouth, Hank knew without a single lingering doubt that he meant them and that he would do anything he had to do to prove it to her. He dropped down beside her.

"Well?" he said finally.

"I don't know what to say."

"Aren't you supposed to say what you feel? That's what all those pop psychology books advise."

She searched his face for several long seconds before she finally spoke. "I think you're crazy."

"Now that's a nice professional analysis," he taunted, amused by what even he could recognize as denial. She didn't want it to be true, so therefore he was crazy.

"Don't make fun of me."

"I'm not. And, despite that panic I can see in your eyes, I'm not expecting you to admit that you're madly in love with me, either. I'm just letting you know where I stand."

"It won't work. You want to be in love with me because it would take away some of the guilt."

"What guilt? I haven't done anything to feel guilty about."

"But you want to."

"Annie, if mere lust doomed us all to hell, no one would ever get to heaven. I assure you I do not feel guilty for wanting you."

"What you really want is a short-term challenge. I can understand that. A man of your sexual appetites and past experience can hardly be blamed for following the same old predictable pattern."

Hank felt a sense of outrage building inside him. Here he was spilling his guts, admitting to an emotion he'd never expected to feel and he was getting dime-store psychoanalysis. He was tempted to pull her into his arms and kiss that silly, crooked mouth of hers until she couldn't come up with another ridiculous argument, but he had a hunch she would only see that as proving her point.

He reached over and ran his finger along her jaw, then down the pale column of her neck. He watched the pulse jump as his finger drifted onto her breast, circling and teasing until the peak was pebble hard. His eyes never left hers. Desire overcame doubts in their wary depths.

"What if this isn't a game?" he said, still caressing.

"Of course it is," she said in a choked whisper.

He leaned forward then and kissed her, very gently, holding himself back, making her want him as badly as he wanted her.

"But what if it's not, Annie?" he said when her breathing was ragged. "What then?"

With the question lingering to torment her, he stood and walked away.

Chapter 9

Love? Hank Riley, the inveterate skirt chaser, was in love with her? No way. Uh-uh. Forget it. She doubted he even knew the definition of the word. Hell, she dealt with all sorts of permutations of love every single day and even she wasn't sure she'd recognize it when it hit her, so how could he be so sure?

Despite her denials, though, Hank's unexpected proclamation reverberated through Ann's head all day long. By the end of the afternoon, her patients—even the littlest ones—were beginning to ask her if *she* was okay.

The honest answer, of course, was a resounding no. It wasn't the one she gave them. She tried to concentrate on their problems, tried to work up some enthusiasm for the small successes she was seeing in their treatment, but all she could think about was Hank's crazy, impulsive, misguided declaration of love.

It was absolutely the last thing she'd expected him to say when he'd come chasing after her that morning. She'd thought, despite his innumerable flaws, that he was too honest, too straightforward to use powerful words like that as part of an obvious seduction technique. Besides, the man had to know he could get her into his bed anytime he wanted her there. That was part of the problem. She was willing. He wasn't. He seemed to have this crazy idea that he was protecting her by maintaining his physical distance, while he closed the emotional gap. At the rate he was going he would soon have her snared so tightly she'd never escape. Then when he realized his mistake, there'd be hell to pay—for both of them.

Well, it wasn't going to happen that way, she resolved. She wasn't interested in a commitment. She liked her life just the way it was. Taking care of six unruly, troubled children was more than enough to keep her life filled to overflowing. And, for all of his crazy protestations, she knew Hank was no more seriously interested in her than he was in having tea parties with Melissa and her dolls. Right now, living in their chaotic household was a novelty, but the fascination of family life would wear off soon enough. She was going to prove it to him.

That decided, she began to feel infinitely better. In fact, by the time she had dinner on the table, she was feeling downright cheerful and on top of things again. She felt in control.

Then Hank came in, smiled and her resolve melted. Just the sight of the man curled her toes. When he dropped a casual, husbandly kiss on her forehead, her knees went weak. When he lifted the lid on the pot of soup simmering on the stove and murmured some appreciative comment, she went all mushy inside. This was far more serious than she'd realized. What was happening to them? Hank was the one supposedly in love. She was simply coming unglued.

With five speculative faces looking on—plus Jason's sullen one—dinner was an uncomfortable affair. Hank did try his best to make everything seem perfectly normal. She had to give him that. She felt suddenly tongue-tied, while he asked all the right questions about school, doled out all the right bits of praise, saw that the after-dinner cleanup was organized. For a man who only weeks ago had been frozen solid at the mere thought of dealing with a bunch of children, he was doing awfully well. In fact, he was a natural. They might actually make a pretty good team.

"Hey, Mom," David said, drawing her attention away from her own chaotic thoughts. "Is what Hank said right? Are we all going to Miami next weekend?"

She blinked and stared at him. Where had that idea come from? She looked at Hank, who seemed particularly pleased with himself.

"We'll have to talk about it," she said evasively.

"I think it'd be really neat," Tracy said. "Just think of all the stores and movies to choose from."

"And the Miami Heat," Paul said of the basketball team. "Maybe they'll have a game. Could we go to that, Hank?"

"If Ann agrees," he said with unexpected and untimely deference.

She glared at him. While she'd been woolgathering, he'd gotten their hopes up. Now he'd tossed the ball into her court. The tactics were unfair, but effective. She'd been neatly trapped.

"If Hank doesn't mind taking all of you," she began, but he deftly put a stop to her one hope for a reprieve before she could even voice it.

"We'll *all* go," he said, watching her pointedly. "We can't go off and leave you here alone." It sounded very noble.

"Yeah, Mom," David concurred. "You need a vacation, too."

"Come on, Ann. It'll be better than a zillion miles of running," Tracy said. "You're always saying that even a little break is good for reducing stress."

Ann sighed in the face of all that well-calculated concern. She was even having her own advice thrown back at her. She supposed she ought to feel flattered that Tracy had even heard her. "We'll see. We'll have to check everybody's schedules to see when it would work out."

She glimpsed the triumphant look on Hank's face just as David said, "Oh, my gosh."

"What?" Ann said.

"The schedule. I almost forgot to tell you. There's a parents' night at school." He avoided looking directly at her when he asked, "Will you come?"

"Jeez, why do you care about a dumb old parents' night?" Jason said with derision. "All it is is a chance for the teachers to shoot off their mouths."

"Jason," Hank warned in a low voice.

Ann scowled at Jason as well. "If it's important to David, that's all that matters."

"Well, excuse me," Jason said, glaring at Hank

and ignoring Ann. He took off without another word, knocking his chair into the counter in the process.

Hank looked ready to explode, but she managed to silence him with a slight shake of the head. For once, he actually listened to her. Ann vowed to have a talk with Jason later. In the meantime, though, she needed to reassure David, who was shifting in his chair, his expression embarrassed. He considered Jason to be the big brother he'd never had. Jason's criticism had obviously hurt. He looked as though he wished he'd never made the request.

"Never mind him. I'll be there," she promised, reaching for the family calendar she kept posted on the refrigerator. "When is it?"

"Day after tomorrow," he said, the enthusiasm gone from his voice.

"David!"

"I'm sorry. I forgot."

Ann knew better. He'd probably been afraid to bring it up before now. Although David had been with her a year now, he'd been shuttled through so many foster homes that he expected this one to be short-term as well. Despite her reassurances, he still wasn't convinced he had a permanent place in her heart. She ruffled his hair. "It's okay, sport. It's not a problem."

Hank stood. "Okay, guys, everybody scoot. You all have homework, I'm sure."

The kids scattered, but not before Tracy shot a knowing look at the two of them. Ann caught the thumbs-up signal she directed at Hank as she left.

"Nicely done," Ann said with an unmistakable edge of sarcasm.

He grinned unrepentantly. "Do you think they suspected I wanted to be alone with you?"

"Tracy certainly did. The others were probably just grateful that you let them off from doing the dishes."

He stared at the messy table in dismay. "Whoops. I knew there was something I'd forgotten." He stood and dropped a kiss on her cheek.

It was casual, she told herself. Perfectly meaningless.

It set off fireworks deep inside her.

"Don't worry," Hank was saying as she tried unsuccessfully to ignore the sparks he'd just ignited. "I'll get this parenthood stuff down before too long."

"Hank, we need to talk about this."

"About what?" he said with apparent innocence.

"Parenting," she said determinedly. "You and me. Trips to Miami."

"What about it?" he inquired as he ran water into the sink.

"Hank, will you pay attention to me, please?"

He gave her a wicked grin and swept her up and into his arms before she realized his intentions. "I'm delighted you finally asked."

"Hank!" she protested, trying to bite back a laugh.

"Yes?" he said, his tongue touching the shell of her ear and sending bolts of electricity shooting straight through her. Suddenly she no longer felt any desire to laugh.

"Are you ever serious?" she said with forced levity, trying to wriggle out of his embrace. If she gave in now, she had a feeling she'd be lost, that she'd never recapture her control of the situation.

"I am now," he murmured, demonstrating with a very serious, breath-stealing kiss. His lips were velvet fire against hers, persuasive. Her control slipped another notch.

"And I was this morning," he added.

She clung tenaciously to reality. "You were not. Now listen to me," she said, gasping when she felt his hands glide up and down her spine. He pressed kisses along her neck, lingering at the spots that drew tiny, unwilling gasps of pleasure.

"I am listening," he swore softly.

She brushed his hands away and backed off. "This is exactly what I mean. You're taking it for granted that I feel the same way you do."

"You do," he said with such confidence she wasn't sure whether to give in or hit him.

"I do not," she said with emphasis on each word, hoping they would penetrate that thick skull of his.

"Annie, you would not even consider going to bed with a man you didn't love. You are considering going to bed with me, ergo you're in love with me."

"You must have flunked logic."

"Actually, I did very well in it. I have a nice, tidy, scientific brain. I can reason things out with the best of them."

"This has nothing to do with reason."

"This what?"

"What we're talking about."

"You mean being in love?"

"Exactly."

"Well, I never said *that* made any sense. I just said it was a fact, a conclusion to be drawn from all the evidence."

"Go to hell."

"Annie, you're resorting to swearing again. Do you

realize how often you do that when I'm winning an argument?"

"You are not winning this argument," she shouted at the top of her lungs, all pretense of calm gone.

He smirked—quite calmly, damn him—and went back to the sink. "That's what you think," he murmured, sounding very pleased with himself.

Ann slammed the back door on her way out.

The whole world was spinning out of control. Ann tried once more to put her feet on the floor, but it rocked and her stomach lurched. The ache in her head was exceeded only by the pains in her joints. All of them, including the little tiny ones in her toes. She fell back against the pillows, wondering just how badly her very green complexion contrasted with the pale blue sheets. All in all, she felt like hell. She didn't doubt for an instant that she probably looked ten times worse.

Glancing at the bedside clock, she groaned. David's parent-teacher night at school was starting in exactly two hours. She'd come home from work early to make sure that dinner was finished and out of the way before it was time to leave. She'd never made it past the bedroom, where she'd come to change her clothes.

What on earth was she going to do? She had to be there. She'd promised and David took promises very seriously, especially since no one had ever kept them until she'd come along.

"Mom, are you getting ready?" he shouted as he raced into her bedroom. At the sight of her, he skidded to a halt, his enthusiasm wilting.

"You're in bed," he said, his voice quivering with

dismay. She saw him bravely fighting tears and her heart constricted, even as her stomach lurched.

"I'll be up in just a minute."

"But you look all funny, like you're really sick or something."

She tried not to groan at the understatement. Dying was closer to the mark, but she refused to discourage him any further. He was already looking crushed.

"You go get Tracy to iron a shirt for you and I'll be right in," she said with far more spirit than she'd ever figured to muster.

With a last skeptical look, he ran out the door, only to be replaced moments later by Hank. Ignoring his concerned expression, she struggled to her feet and promptly felt another wave of nausea wash through her.

"Oh, God," she moaned, bracing herself against the nightstand.

"Annie love, get back into bed." Hank's tone cajoled, the way it might an obstinate child.

"I can't." She did, however, compromise by sitting down on the edge. Just for a minute. Just until the room stopped spinning.

Hank strolled purposefully toward her, lifted a corner of the top sheet and pointed. "In!"

She resented the domineering tone, but arguing was beyond her. She simply shook her head.

He looked disgusted and sounded furious as he muttered something about her lousy temperament. "Hell, woman, you're a doctor. You should know better."

"I have a Ph.D. in psychology," she pointed out with another burst of contrariness. "Not an M.D."

"All the more reason for you to be using a little common sense. Even if going tonight doesn't kill you, it will spread your germs through the entire population of the Keys. I doubt anyone, including David, would thank you for that."

"But I can't let him down," she protested. She was wavering, though. What Hank said made perfect sense, but then Hank wasn't a mother. "I don't think anyone's ever gone to a parent-teacher night for him before. Can't you see how much it means?"

"Of course I can understand that. Put your head down, Annie," he tempted.

She ran her fingers over the pillow. The percale material felt very cool, very comforting. Her skin was burning up. If only...

"I'll go." Hank's announcement interrupted her mental debate.

She stared at him in openmouthed astonishment. "You?"

He grinned. "Yeah. What's so weird about that? Can't you picture me in those tiny little chairs?"

At the moment, she was having trouble picturing anything through the feverish haze of this blasted flu. Of all the times to pick up a bug. She never got sick. She was healthy as an ox. She ate oat bran and fresh vegetables and took her vitamins. Hank was the one who ought to be deathly ill.

"After all, if I'm going to be a part of this family, then it's time I took on more of the responsibilities," Hank was saying. Something in the comment alarmed her, but she couldn't think clearly enough to pinpoint it. "I'm sure David won't mind. How about it?"

"Go," she murmured finally.

With great effort, she swung her leaden legs back onto the bed and fell back against the pillows. Hank settled her more comfortably, his touch gentle as he awkwardly tucked the sheet around her and plumped the pillows. He vanished at once, only to return in what seemed like seconds with a glass of juice and a pitcher of ice water.

"They always tell you to drink plenty of fluids with this stuff," he said. He sounded very matter-of-fact, as if he'd played nursemaid to dozens of women. The idea bothered her more than she cared to admit.

"So drink," he urged.

Ann nodded. The very thought made her insides revolt. "In a minute."

"Now," he ordered, much less compassionately. He held a straw to her lips and waited until she'd swallowed several sips of the water. When she had, he placed everything within easy reach, then stood back and surveyed his handiwork, his expression troubled. "Are you going to be okay until I get back?"

She gave a weak nod.

"Tracy's taking care of the little ones. She'll feed them and get them to bed. They won't bother you. She'll check on you later and I'll be home in no time to make sure you're okay. If you need anything in the meantime, shout."

The idea amused her. She barely had enough strength to whisper. "No shouting," she murmured sleepily, wondering at the unexpected feeling of contentment that was stealing over her. No one ever fussed over her, took care of her. Not until Hank. With him, it was getting to be a habit. Again the idea was somehow troubling, but she didn't have the will to try to figure out why.

"No shouting, huh?" he said, chuckling. "That'll be

a pleasant change. I'm sorry I'm not going to be around for it."

His teasing words faded out. For an instant she was certain she felt the light brush of his beard on her cheek, the touch of his lips, but she knew she had to be wrong. Not even Hank Riley would take advantage of a woman when she was on her deathbed.

Ann awoke to sunlight streaming in the bedroom window. She lay perfectly still, testing her body, waiting for the first ache to make its presence felt. She waited several minutes. She felt...okay. Not ready for wind sprints, but intact and human.

Just as she was about to test the sensation by crawling out of bed, the door swung open and Hank came in bearing a tray.

"Well, it's about time you woke up," he said with the sort of forced cheer generally reserved for hospital rooms and uttered by nurses who thought of their patients as dimwits. It more or less suited the way Ann was feeling, slightly off kilter and out of control.

"What time is it?"

"Nearly noon."

Her eyes snapped wide and she struggled to a sitting position. "Good heavens, the kids! What about school?"

With disgustingly little effort, Hank shoved her back. "They've gone. Not a one of them was late. Their clothes could have been a little neater, but I'm lousy with an iron. Feel like some tea and toast? I fixed some earlier, but I didn't want to wake you. By now you probably need it."

She regarded him warily. In her weakened condition,

she figured a little caution was called for. "Why aren't you at work?"

"I've been. I came back to check on you."

"I'm better. You can go now."

"Here's your hat, what's your hurry," he mocked.

She flushed guiltily and fiddled with the sheet, trying unobtrusively to get it above the neckline of what she'd just realized was a practically transparent, very sexy nightgown. She didn't exactly remember getting into it. She decided it was best not to ask how it had happened or who had chosen it. She usually wore oversize T-shirts to bed. This had been one of those crazy impulse buys on a day when she'd been feeling down and had needed to remind herself of her femininity. She'd never worn it.

"Sorry," she murmured, not meeting his gaze. "I just don't want to take you away from your job when it's not necessary."

"They can manage without me for a while," he said matter-of-factly, settling down beside her on the bed. He acted as though he belonged there. She suddenly felt feverish again. He held out the cup of tea. "Drink this."

She ignored the tea. She was less successful in ignoring his proximity. "Really," she said, running her fingers through her hair. She could tell it was sticking straight out in every direction. "I can manage."

"I'm sure you can, but why don't you relax for five minutes and let me wait on you."

She met his gaze and saw something there that made her breath catch in her throat. He looked as though bringing her tea and toast was important to him in some unfathomable way. He looked every bit as confused by the need as she felt by her reaction to it. He also looked determined. She recognized that pigheaded expression and gave up the fight.

"Thanks," she said finally, her breath uneven. She took the cup and sipped. He'd made the raspberry tea. He'd even remembered to leave out the sugar. "It's wonderful."

"Now the toast," he coaxed.

"I'm not so sure…"

"Try it. You should be able to keep it down and you need something in your stomach."

She took the smallest bite possible, just to satisfy him. "How'd last night go?" she asked, hoping to get his attention away from her continued lack of appetite.

"Fine. David's teacher had nothing but good things to say about his work. She says he's improved tremendously in the time he's been with you."

"How'd you explain your presence?"

"I said we were living together."

Ann choked on the tea. "You what!" Her eyes widened in alarm.

He grinned without the slightest hint of remorse. "I tried not to leer when I said it, though."

She moaned. "Hank Riley, are you determined to ruin my reputation?"

"Annie, my love, your reputation is already well established. That's why I said it."

"I beg your pardon."

He chuckled. "You're known for taking in strays. Surely one more won't make a difference."

"Most of my strays have been under the age of twelve, at least when they arrived. Jason was a little older, but then nobody would ever think that he… None of them have been so..." She was at a loss for words that wouldn't give away exactly how he affected her.

"Decidedly masculine?" he offered with a smug expression.

She laughed, despite herself. "You never let up, do you?"

"Of course not. Why on earth would I do that, especially on a rare occasion when I have you weak and at my mercy."

"I am not weak."

"Care to prove it?" he challenged, leaning toward her.

"Go away," she muttered, shoving the tray at him with enough force to rattle the teapot.

"Ungrateful woman," he taunted, taking the tray. "We'll finish this discussion later."

"Don't count on it," she said, suddenly feeling drained.

"Ah, Annie, you really should stop fighting me. It's such a wasted effort."

"Not in this lifetime," she murmured, yawning.

She couldn't seem to keep her eyes open another second, not even when Hank whispered, "Happy Valentine's Day, sweetheart," and folded her fingers around a small package.

Once again she was almost certain she felt the gentle touch of his lips as she drifted off into a dreamless, contented sleep.

Chapter 10

It was the hard imprint of a box pressing into her cheek and the subtle crackling of paper that woke Ann later that afternoon. Opening her eyes reluctantly she found a package on her pillow. She only dimly recalled Hank putting it into her hand. Wrapped in silver paper, it had now-crushed streamers of red ribbon and clusters of tiny white hearts.

Valentine's Day.

Suddenly she remembered his whispered wish as she'd fallen asleep. Her heart thumped unsteadily as she picked the package up and studied it. The box was long and narrow and flat. There was a slight rustling sound when she shook it gently. It could be a gold pen, but somehow she doubted it. The prospect of what it might be made her very nervous. She didn't want Hank giving her jewelry. It seemed too personal, too important, too committed. Especially on Valentine's Day.

"Open it," Hank said, suddenly appearing in the doorway.

The low rasp of his voice set her ablaze. The significance of the package fanned the flames. "I'm not sure I should."

"Why not?"

"I don't think you ought to be giving me presents."

Blue eyes twinkled back, his expression a mixture of amusement and indignation. "Who made you guardian angel over my finances?"

She glared at him as desire ebbed, replaced by more familiar irritation. She hated it when he decided to be deliberately obtuse. "I am not worried about your finances. You know what I mean."

"You mean you are not in the habit of accepting gifts from men."

It sounded a little silly when he said it. It was also an understatement. The last time she'd received a Valentine's card from a male she had been in the sixth grade. "Something like that."

"Maybe you should get used to it. You deserve presents, Annie. And I intend to see that you get them. Now open this one before I have to remind you that learning to receive is as important as learning to give."

He had a point. She had been behaving ungraciously. It was only a small gift, after all. Unexpected excitement bubbled up inside her as she gently removed the ribbon. She was picking carefully at the tape, trying to prolong the anticipation, when Hank groaned and took the package from her.

"That's no way to open a present," he said. "This is how you open it."

He grabbed an edge of the paper and gave one quick rip. Grinning, he handed her the box.

"My way gives you more time to savor it," she grumbled as she caressed the velvet covering.

"Sorry. I'm not a patient man."

"So I've noticed." She snapped open the box before he could take over that as well. With trembling fingers, she lifted away the tissue paper inside. Nestled on the satin lining was a sparkling diamond heart dangling from a delicate gold chain.

Her own heart filled to overflowing with all sorts of unexpected emotions. She lifted her gaze to meet Hank's. "I've never had anything so beautiful."

He touched the diamond with a finger that seemed to shake. "It's mine, Annie," he said in a low voice that tugged at her senses. "The heart is mine and now you have it."

Tears glistened in her eyes and clogged her throat as she whispered, "Oh, Hank."

"Do you really like it?"

"I'll treasure it always," she said, fumbling with the clasp. Hank took the necklace from her and settled it around her neck. His fingers followed the chain of gold from her nape to the hollow at the base of her throat where the heart now nestled, warmed by her skin and fired by his touch.

Maybe it was just her weakened condition or maybe it was the magic of the traditional lovers' holiday, but with Hank gazing so tenderly into her eyes, Ann almost believed in love.

For the life of her, Ann couldn't remember actually agreeing to go to Miami. On Friday afternoon, though, she came home to find that each of the kids had a bag packed and that they were all in the living room waiting for her. They looked so excited, she didn't have the heart to protest. After a heated competition, Paul and Tommy won the right to ride with Hank on the trip up. Everyone else piled into her minivan.

"Now you're sure you understand the directions?" Hank asked for the tenth time as he closed the door of the car. "I don't want you getting lost."

"Hank, it is a straight drive up U.S. 1. How could I possibly get lost?"

"Okay. Just remember, if we get separated in traffic, I'll wait for you at the Suniland Shopping Center. I'll park at the north entrance. Finding my place in Coconut Grove is a little confusing. I want to lead you in from there."

"And if I get ahead of you?" she teased.

"You won't," he said with that familiar confident wink.

Before she could react, he walked away. She stared after him. As his taunt sank in, she was suddenly seized by doubts.

"Hank Riley, you be careful how you drive with my children in your truck," she shouted. He waved back cheerfully.

"What are we going to do in Miami?" Tracy asked as they pulled out onto the highway. Ann smiled at the excitement in Tracy's voice. More and more the past few days, her mood was lightening and she was allowing her natural exuberance to show. The barriers were slowly falling away. She'd even told Ann all about the date that had gone awry the night she'd called Hank in Miami. Ann knew she had Hank to thank for that. He'd been encouraging Tracy to be more open with her and Tracy was listening, as she did to everything Hank said. She clearly idolized the man, though Ann was no longer worried that Tracy might be suffering from a crush. She'd made it all too plain that she was encouraging a match between Ann and Hank.

"This is Hank's adventure," Ann told her. "We'll just have to see what he has planned when we get there."

The possibilities made her increasingly anxious. She hated the long, tedious drive, hated the faster pace of Miami, worried about the crime and wasn't crazy about allowing her children loose in that environment. She also had this nagging feeling that Hank's patience was at an end and that he was plotting something for the two of them. That very nearly panicked her. It was what she'd claimed to want, but now she felt uncertain, as if taking that next step in their relationship would commit them to a direction in which she wasn't at all prepared to go with her life.

"Well, I want to go shopping," Tracy said.

"Me, too," Melissa said.

"I've been saving up for a new outfit." Tracy looked over at Ann, suddenly sounding shy. "Would you help me pick it out? You always look so great. You have your own sense of style. You don't just follow everybody else."

Feeling as though her heart would burst at the compliment, Ann smiled back. "I'd love to help you find something really special. With your coloring, you can wear all the hot new colors that are in this year. You don't know how lucky you are."

"Who cares about shopping?" David protested. "I

want to go to the basketball game and eat a dozen hot dogs."

"Me, too," Melissa chimed in, bouncing excitedly in her car seat.

Ann chuckled. "What about you, Jason?"

"I don't see why we have to go at all."

"Aren't you excited about any of the things you could do in Miami?" she persisted.

"I've been there. It's no big deal."

"When did you ever go to Miami?" Tracy scoffed.

"Me and some guys went a couple of years ago, smart mouth."

"Sure."

"We did. It's not so hot. Just a lot of people. I like it better in the Keys."

"Well, don't let Hank hear you say that," Tracy warned. "You'll hurt his feelings."

"Nothing would hurt that guy's feelings. He's about as sensitive as a block of cement."

"Jason," Ann said very quietly, deciding things had gone far enough. "Hank wants this weekend to be special for all of you. Can't you at least try to meet him halfway?"

The request was met by silence. Ann sighed. Fortunately Melissa, Tracy and David more than made up for Jason's lack of enthusiasm. David made sporadic attempts to get Jason to talk about what he'd seen on his last trip to Miami, but eventually even he gave up and let Jason sulk.

Despite his teasing challenge about his driving speed, Hank never got too far ahead of them. She followed more closely as he led them off the highway and into Coconut Grove. Ann recognized part of the route. It was the same way she had gone to see Liz after she and Todd had married. There was something wild and seductive about the dense foliage, the spread of banyan trees and thick undergrowth. Despite their proximity, the houses maintained their privacy. Although she preferred the wide expanses of sky and water in the Keys, the intimate atmosphere here had a certain primitive appeal to it that made her blood begin to race. It stirred fantasies of jungle adventures and sensual romance.

When Hank turned into a driveway that was practically hidden, she had to swallow hard against the strong emotions that were stirring in her. She felt like the uncertain heroine in some Gothic novel first arriving at the mysterious, secluded mansion of the hero, wondering what was in store for her future. She turned off the engine and sank back in the seat, trying to regain her composure as the kids scrambled from the car.

"Annie," Hank said quietly. Her guilty gaze shot up to meet his questioning eyes. "Are you okay?"

"Just fine," she said with forced bravado, getting out of the car. "The kids were wondering what you had planned for the weekend."

"Tonight I thought we'd go for dinner and a little shopping, then to the Miami Heat game at the arena. How does that sound?"

"Busy."

He laughed, then kissed her soundly. "We'll find time just for us. I promise."

She flushed as her pulse ran wild. "That's not what I meant."

"Maybe not," he said with another of those damnable

winks. "But I meant it just the same. Now come on in and let me show you around."

The house was spectacular. Ann recognized Todd's architectural touch: clean lines, wide sweeps of glass and cool, Spanish-style tiles and stucco walls. There was a huge fireplace in the living room.

Amused, she glanced at Hank. "In Miami?"

He grinned. "It's the one thing I've always envied from northern winters. It's worth it on the few nights a year here when it's cold enough to use it." He slid his arms around her waist. "It's also very romantic, don't you think?"

Her heartbeat skipped at the seductive look in his eyes. An image of a dozen different women sipping wine in front of that fireplace made her shiver. As if he'd read her thoughts, his embrace tightened. "Never before, Annie."

She gazed up at him disbelievingly.

"I swear it," he said. "I know you think I've been quite a rake. To be perfectly honest, there's some truth to my reputation, but there's never been anyone in my life I cared about enough to bring into my home. When I come here, it's my retreat from the world."

Ann wanted very much to believe him, especially when his mouth covered hers persuasively. What began as subtle pressure quickly turned to hard, demanding hunger. All those feelings of warmth and contentment that she'd begun experiencing in the past few weeks swept through her as his tongue invaded. The deep, drugging power of the kiss claimed her, leaving her knees trembling and her head spinning. Hank's strong hands were splayed on her hips, pulling her close. Fit tightly against him, her body ached with longing. Heat flared, white-hot, all-consuming heat.

"I want you so badly, Annie. Feel what you do to me," he said, pressing her hand against him. She pulled away, but like the moth drawn inevitably toward the flame, she was drawn back, fascinated by the evidence of her power over him. When he shuddered at the gentle sweep of her touch, her eyes shot to his face in wonder.

"We're going to be good together, Annie. I know you're still afraid, but I'm going to convince you just how right this is. Before the weekend's out, I'm going to make you mine."

The vow made her knees go weak again. The unspoken *forever* behind it made her heart pound so hard against her ribs, she thought she'd die from it. How had a man so wrong for her gotten to her so completely? How had he evaded her defenses, overcome her common sense and landed smack in the middle of her heart?

Thank goodness for chaperons, she thought as the sound of running footsteps intruded on their moment of privacy. She backed out of the embrace, her cheeks flaming with color. Hank seemed unfazed by the throbbing passion that had sparked between them. She saw that ability to distance himself so rapidly as more evidence of his jaded past and it renewed her qualms. He turned to the children with a perfectly calm look on his face. One arm, however, remained tightly curved around her waist as a determined reminder of what they'd just shared.

"So did you all pick out your rooms?" he asked.

"This place is really neat," Paul said. "You gotta see it, Mom. There must be dozens and dozens of rooms."

Hank laughed at the enthusiasm. "Not quite that many, but enough for this crowd."

"There's a pool, too," David said.

"And one of those romantic hot tub things," Tracy chimed in, casting a pointed look at Ann.

Ann did not want to hear about hot tubs, not when her body was still quivering with unfulfilled expectations. She looked hurriedly at Hank. "Isn't it time we left for dinner?"

His amusement at her frantic appeal apparent, he nodded. "Okay, is everybody ready to get moving?"

He outlined the plans for the night. As she'd anticipated, they were met with wholehearted approval. The one thing he failed to mention was exactly when he intended to carry out his seduction of her. Though she was more than grateful for the omission, it left her with anticipation sizzling through her bloodstream. Visions of that hot tub danced through her head with all the dazzling temptation of Christmas sugar plums.

Anticipation, she noted with surprise. Not panic. What on earth was happening to her? Surely she couldn't actually be falling in love with the man.

But she was, she admitted candidly as she watched his enthusiasm at the basketball game. Since she had no idea what was happening on the court and didn't particularly care, she allowed herself to indulge her desire to watch Hank, to study the way he interacted with each of the children in a way that was uniquely thoughtful. He was crazy and indulgent, but he was also firm. He was interested, without fawning over them. Even with Jason, he kept his temper in check, ignoring the sullen silences and continuing to make occasional efforts to make the boy feel part of the family fun.

On the way home, the younger kids fell asleep in the car, while Tracy, David and Paul continued to chatter about the game and the plans for the next day.

"I was thinking about the Coconut Grove Art Festival," Hank said. "How does that sound?"

"Art, yuck," Paul protested.

"It's outdoors," Hank countered. "There will be music and lots of food."

"I guess that'd be okay," Paul relented.

"Sounds terrific to me," Tracy said.

"Then in the afternoon, Liz and Todd have invited us over to their house for a barbecue."

Ann gazed at him, surprised. "When did this happen?"

"I talked to them earlier in the week."

"I see," she said stiffly as they arrived at the house. Fortunately the kids took off for bed before the argument she anticipated could explode.

"What's wrong?" Hank asked the minute they were alone. He took her hand and idly drew provocative circles on her sensitive palm.

"Nothing," she snapped, trying to tug her hand away. He held tight. "Why should anything be wrong?"

"I haven't the vaguest idea, but something obviously is."

"Liz and Todd are my friends," she began, only to go silent at the justifiably amazed expression on Hank's face.

"They're my friends, too," he reminded her gently, effectively dashing her anger. He kissed her palm, his tongue hot and moist against her flesh. "Todd is my partner. Now what's this really all about?"

She sighed heavily. "I'm sorry. That was a dumb thing to say. I guess it just threw me that all these plans were made without my knowledge."

Hank drew her down on the sofa beside him and settled her against the curve of his shoulder. "Annie, you've been sick all week. I didn't want to bother you with the details. Besides, I wanted to make the plans. I wanted this to be a real vacation for you. If I know you, you'd have filled the little time we have with trips to bookstores to pick up the latest psychology books."

She managed a feeble grin. "I still plan to do exactly that," she retorted with a teasing defiance. "And I've promised Tracy a shopping trip for a new outfit. Maybe we'll take it after we leave Liz and Todd's."

Hank shook his head adamantly. "I've planned for your shopping trip. We'll stop at the mall on the way home on Monday."

"Monday? Hank, the kids have school on Monday. I have patients."

"The kids do not have school. It's the President's Day holiday. As for you, you only had one appointment on your calendar and I was able to get the receptionist over at Dolphin Reach to rearrange it."

"Dammit, Hank, you had no right," she said, pulling away from him. He was taking over her life, managing it with the same precision that he brought to his building projects. She couldn't allow it. "We're going back on Sunday."

"Annie, calm down. Why should we waste a day?"

He sounded incredibly patient. "Don't you patronize me, you muscle-bound cretin," she snapped back. "I will not calm down. And we'll go back on Sunday because I say so."

"Muscle-bound cretin? I like that," he said, chuckling. "If you really want to insist on going back on Sunday and disappointing the kids, then we'll go back on Sunday."

The ease with which he twisted things around to make her the bad guy exasperated her. His refusal to take offense only infuriated her more. She was really spoiling for a good fight and he was turning agreeable on her. She'd hoped a royal battle would take away this tension that was building inside her. Maybe it would take her mind off her desire to be in Hank's arms, in his bed.

"Damn you, Hank."

He shook his head. "Tsk, tsk. There you go again. You're swearing."

"Oh, go to hell."

"Annie, Annie, the children."

"The kids are all in bed," she mumbled, defeated by his teasing.

"And that makes it okay? I'm surprised at you, Annie."

"You are the most impossible…"

"Lovable?"

"*Impossible* man I have ever met."

"But you love me."

"I do not love you."

He pulled her into his lap and kissed her thoroughly. When she could gather her senses, she opened her eyes and met his satisfied smirk. "Liar," he whispered softly, then claimed her lips again. This time she didn't even pretend to struggle. She only sighed and whispered, mostly to herself, "If I am, then God help me."

The Coconut Grove Art Festival was not an event Ann would have expected Hank to enjoy. In fact, she had thought that even she would find the traffic jams irritating, the huge crowds tiresome and the art little more than junk. She was wrong on all counts. First of all, they were able to walk from his house, avoiding the bumper-to-bumper lines of cars. Once there, Hank clung firmly to her hand and tugged her from one display to another with all the enthusiasm of a kid in a candy store.

"Come on, Annie," he urged more than once. "You have to see this."

He pulled her to a booth filled with huge oil paintings. She studied the landscapes painted in the Everglades. They captured the barren vastness, but none of the majesty.

"Sorry. I don't like them," she said, keeping her voice low and turning away from the artist who sat nearby.

"Why not?"

"There's no emotion in them. The Everglades are unique, special. In these paintings, they look ordinary."

He stepped back and looked more closely. "You may have a point. You have a good eye."

She opened her mouth, but he touched a finger to her lips. "Don't you dare say you only know what you like."

She laughed. "I was not going to say that. I was going to tell you that I used to write an art column for my college paper."

"Oh," he said meekly.

His humble deference lasted another thirty seconds before he was touting the virtues of another craftsman a few booths away. "Look at this jewelry. What do you think?"

"It's lovely," she said distractedly, barely looking at the bold silver pieces that she normally would have loved.

"You're not even looking."

"Where are the kids?"

"Across the street, three booths down."

She looked in the direction in which he'd pointed. They were all there, every one of them. She counted just to be sure.

"I'm not going to let them get lost, Annie," he said quietly, tilting her chin up so he could look directly into her eyes. "I promise."

"Okay, so I get a little crazy."

"You're a mother."

"Yes. I am." She said it as though she was trying to make a point, but with Hank staring tenderly into her eyes, she lost track of the message she'd had in mind.

Just then they were joined by the kids. "Can we get some ice cream?" Paul pleaded.

"I want 'ade," Melissa said.

Hank turned deliberately to Jason. "You know where the food booths are, son?"

"I saw 'em."

"Then you make sure that everyone stays together," he said, handing over some money. "Meet us on the corner in a half hour."

Jason seemed startled by the gesture. Ann caught a fleeting look of pride in his eyes before he hid it behind his usual moody mask. "Come on, guys," he said, sounding put-upon.

"I'm not sure that was such a good idea," she said worriedly. "Shouldn't we go with them?"

"Tracy's with them, too, and he has to learn that we do trust him."

"But you don't," she countered. "You've said all along that he was heading for trouble."

"I know and I still think that's possible, but we've got to do everything we can to head it off. I thought the job would help, but it hasn't."

"I think it has. He won't let you see it, but he seems more self-confident. The responsibility has been good for him."

"Annie, he's not accepting the responsibility," he blurted, then immediately looked as though he wished he could retract the words. Ann's heart sank.

"At least not the way I'd hoped he would," he amended hurriedly.

"What do you mean?"

Hank sighed. "Let's talk about this later."

"We'll talk about it now."

"Annie…"

She finally lost patience and snapped, "Hank, just tell me. What's wrong?"

"He hasn't been coming in to work."

"Why on earth not? What does he say about it?"

"Ted says he's had an excuse every time. Not terribly legitimate ones, but he has been calling in, which I suppose is something."

"Haven't you confronted him about it?"

"No. He reports to Ted. For the time being, I'm staying out of it. If he gets fired as a result of his behavior, it may do him good to realize that there are consequences."

"Dammit, Hank, you should have told me about this. I would have talked to him."

"A boss doesn't go running to Mother when an employee acts up. Besides, I didn't want to upset you."

"Well, I am upset."

"Exactly." He took her by the shoulders and turned her to face him. The crowds continued to mill around them, but as far as Ann was concerned it was just the two of them—and Jason.

She sighed. What would it have been like to have met Hank at a time in her life when she was totally free of responsibilities, when she would have been free to get to know him without all the pressures they faced now? Well, she thought with a pragmatic shrug, there was no point in wondering about that. As Hank liked to remind her, this was the hand they'd been dealt. They either had to fold or play it out. Since Hank seemed unlikely to drop out, she wouldn't, either.

"We are not going to let this spoil this vacation," he insisted now. "We have three days up here..."

"Two."

"Whatever. There will be plenty of time after that to decide what to do about Jason. For now we are all going to enjoy ourselves. Understand?"

"Just like that?" she said with a skeptical snap of her fingers.

His eyes twinkled with amusement. "Just like that."

"Well, since you seem to be in charge, then I suppose we'll just have to follow orders." She caught the glint of satisfaction in his eyes and hastily amended, "For the moment."

"Your submissiveness is duly noted."

"Enjoy it while it lasts," she said dryly as the kids caught up with them.

"Oh, I intend to," he said, his gaze locking with hers.

After another hour of browsing, Hank declared it was time to move on to Liz and Todd's.

"Yes, captain," she said, giving him a jaunty salute.

He leaned down to whisper, "Watch it, lady. You can be court-martialed for that kind of disrespect to an officer."

"And the punishment?"

He slid his hand up her side until it rested just below the curve of her breast. "I have several things in mind," he said, his expression very serious. Ann's heart thumped unsteadily.

"Shall I enumerate?" he asked huskily.

Caught up by the expression in his eyes and the rasp in his voice, she could only shake her head. Hank responded with another of those slow, deliberate winks, then blithely walked off, leading the family back to the van. Ann had to jerk herself out of the sensual torpor he'd left her in.

At Liz and Todd's she was hardly aware of the food or the activity that swirled around them. She responded to Liz's curious questions with what she hoped were rational answers, but she couldn't seem to focus on anything other than Hank as he played touch football with the whole gang on the front lawn. Even David had been persuaded to join in and after an initial hesitation, he was now wholeheartedly engaged in the competition. Just more evidence of Hank's magic, she thought.

"Interesting," Liz observed, sitting down beside her on the grass.

"Hmm." She blinked and turned to her friend. "What?"

"You seem awfully absorbed in the game."

"Hmm."

"Or is it one of the players you're attracted to?"

"Hmm."

"Ann!" Liz said in exasperation.

She dragged her attention away from the sight of Hank in jeans and T-shirt sprawled on the ground under a whole gang of giggling children. They were tickling him, which she didn't recall as a traditional tactic in the game. Still, he seemed to be enjoying it thoroughly. She caught herself smiling.

"Ann!"

She dragged her attention back to Liz. "What?"

"What's going on between you and Hank?"

"Nothing."

"Oh, really. I find that difficult to believe. He's a very attractive man. You've been living under the same roof for weeks now. Surely there are sparks of some kind."

Sparks? There was a veritable forest fire. She was not ready to admit it.

"You know for a psychologist who touts the healing virtues of communication, you're awfully quiet. Do you have any idea how frustrating that is?"

She turned a baleful look on Liz. "And you, my friend, are treading on thin ice."

Liz chuckled as she got to her feet. "Gee, you seem to be in about the same state Hank was in when he was here for dinner a couple of weeks ago. I can't tell you how glad I am that it's all working out."

"Working out? Nothing is working out," she said adamantly as Liz went back inside. Ann strode

purposefully after her. She had to straighten her out
before she got some crazy notion in her head. "Did you
hear me? Nothing is working out. Do not gloat. Do not
get your hopes up. Nothing is working out."

"Hmm," Liz said.

The noncommittal reply set Ann's teeth on edge.
"Aren't you going to say anything?"

Liz returned her gaze innocently. "I think you've just
said it all."

"Oh, go to hell," she snapped, just in time for Hank
to hear her. He pulled her into a casual hug.

"There she goes again," he said to Liz. "Has she
always had this tendency to swear when she gets upset?"

"I wouldn't know. I've never seen her upset before."

"Interesting," he commented, never taking his eyes
from hers. "Very interesting."

"Leave me alone," she growled.

He shook his head. "Come with me."

"Where?" she asked suspiciously.

"Do you have to question every little thing? Just
come."

Something in his voice told her not to argue. With
a last look back at Liz, who was grinning broadly, she
went with Hank. Outside, he led her to the van and
urged her inside.

"Hank, we can't leave," she protested even as a sweet
tension began to build inside her.

"Oh, yes, we can."

"The kids…"

"Will be just fine. Liz is a teacher. She's used to
handling more kids than this."

"But they're going to think we're terribly rude."

"I assure you that is not what they're going to think."

Her eyes widened. "Hank, exactly what did you tell them?"

"The truth, that I wanted to be alone with you."

"And they went along with it?"

He gave a secretive little smile. "Let's just say they owed me one."

Ann folded her hands tightly in her lap and stared straight ahead. "Hank, I am not ready for this."

"Annie, believe me, we are both more than ready for this. Before the afternoon is out I'm going to prove it."

"But that's just it, it's afternoon."

"Late afternoon." He peered at her. "You have something against making love in the afternoon?" he teased.

Well, there it is, she thought wildly. The words were out in the open, lying there between them like a gauntlet that had been thrown down. "It all seems so calculated somehow," she retorted.

"Annie, we are living with six children. I can almost guarantee you that making love would have to be calculated under circumstances like that."

She regarded him closely. "Doesn't that bother you? Isn't spontaneity better?"

His voice dropped to a seductive murmur. "Annie, I want you in my arms. That's the only thing that matters."

She swallowed hard as he continued. "I want to kiss every single inch of you. I want to get to know your body as well as I know my own. I want to bring you alive under my fingers. If I have to do a little calculating to accomplish that, I can handle it." He turned his head toward her. "Can you?"

"I don't know," she said honestly, though her heart

was beating so hard and fast she could barely hear herself think.

He reached over and took her clenched hands in his. "Annie, once we get there, once we're inside and all alone, if this isn't right for you, we'll forget it. I promise. Okay?"

She heard the raw hunger in his voice, saw the depth of desire in his eyes and still she recognized the sincerity of the promise. Hank would be guided by her needs. What she wanted would always be uppermost in his mind.

Suddenly the last of her doubts fled, replaced by a wild, pounding urgency she'd never thought to experience. Responding to that frantic need, she lifted his hand to her lips and kissed the scarred knuckles, the callused palm. She felt the shudder that gripped him at her touch and asked softly, "Think you can drive any faster without getting caught?"

Chapter 11

One of the few advantages of winter, Ann decided, was that darkness came early. She was grateful for the rapidly dimming light because the minute they walked through the front door of Hank's house, her timidity returned. The twilight shadows helped her to hide her fears from Hank, though they did nothing to keep them from her heart.

Even though a part of her yearned desperately to be in Hank's arms, wanted to know the sheer physical pleasure of abandoning herself to his possession, another part was still holding back. She was still deeply troubled by the cold planning of it, worried even more about the long-term consequences for her emotions. The risks seemed enormous, far too great for a woman who'd only gambled on love once and lost everything.

They'd barely made it into the living room when

Hank said, "I'm a mess from the football game. I think I'll take a shower."

He said it matter-of-factly, as if there were nothing more important on his mind than washing away a little dirt and grass. The comment was so far from the romantic murmurings she'd been anticipating, Ann felt like laughing hysterically with relief. Then she felt like screaming. If they were going to make love, why couldn't they just do it and get it over with? Why this slow torture, when they'd already waited far too long? She hadn't felt this nervous the first time…the only other time.

"Hank," she began, intending to protest, only to have him take her hand and squeeze it gently.

"Come with me," he suggested softly, his gaze locked with hers.

Heat pulsed through her, quick and hard and thrilling. Excitement and that maddening, intense desire warred with caution. "I don't know…"

"You can scrub my back."

It was a light, almost innocent taunt, but the prospect of touching him, of running her fingers over his shoulders set her blood on fire. The temptation was irresistible. Further denial would have been as pointless as trying to hold back the tides.

Willing herself not to think beyond the moment, she went with him through the house to the master bedroom suite. The previous night she had avoided this end of the house, not daring to envelop herself in the intimacy of Hank's room. She'd been afraid to enter a room that was so very much his domain. Now she gazed around with rapt curiosity.

The carpeting was a thick, dark navy. The bed was

king-size, the only size large enough to accommodate a man of Hank's stature. Staring at it made her pulse race. The comforter was a rich, masculine pattern, the lines of all the furniture clean and modern. Vertical blinds let in the last of the muted afternoon light and shadowed images of the garden beyond the sliding glass doors. It was expensive, understated and very male.

She scanned the dresser and nightstand for any additional clues to Hank's personality, but found not one bit of evidence that would tell her his taste in books, his preference in after-shave or his family history. The room looked as though the decor had been completed by a disinterested professional the month before and as if it had been cleaned religiously each week since then. She might have attributed the tidiness to his absence had he not been in the room last night. There wasn't even a tossed-aside T-shirt or an empty beer bottle to indicate that he'd spent that time here, either. The bed had been remade with army boot-camp precision. She doubted there was even a dent in the pillow to indicate where his head had rested. No wonder the man had been appalled the first time he'd walked into her house. He was compulsively neat. Her professional training kicked in and she wondered what had caused it. The question was definitely untimely, but valid nonetheless.

A little bit stunned, she sank down on the side of the bed. "Hank?"

A worried frown creasing his brow, he knelt down in front of her and took her hands in his. "Second thoughts?"

"Not exactly. How do you live like this?" She gave an all-encompassing wave around the impersonal room.

Following the sweeping gesture, he stared around blankly. "I don't understand."

"It's so…sterile."

Shadows crossed his eyes, but he merely shrugged. "I guess I've never paid much attention to it."

"Don't you have any pictures of your parents? An ex-girlfriend? Something?"

He grinned at that. "You'd actually be happy to find a photograph of an ex-girlfriend by my bed?"

She reached out and ran her fingers through his hair, then touched his beard. "I actually think I might prefer it to this."

"Why?"

"This doesn't tell me anything about you. I feel as though I could be in the room of a complete stranger or even a totally impersonal hotel."

"You already know all you need to know about me." He drew her hand to his chest. "You know what's in here."

She shook her head. "I don't think so. How can I really know what's in your heart without understanding you? You told me about your mother and father, but there's more to growing up than that. Tell me about you, Hank. What were you like when you were a little boy? What subjects did you like in school? Did you always want to be an engineer?"

He touched a finger to her lips, then trailed it down along her jaw, finally moving to her breast, where he drew slow, deliberate circles around the already erect tip. Ann felt the effect of that lazy touch all the way down to her toes. As a distraction it was very effective, but she had no intention of letting him win out this time. In the long run, they'd both lose if she did. She seized his hand and held it, pressing her lips to the scarred knuckles.

"Talk to me," she pleaded.

"Now, Annie?" His voice was low, incredulous and threadbare with desire.

"Now," she said firmly, plumping up the pillows at the head of the bed and settling herself there. It was a deliberate attempt to put some distance between them without removing them entirely from the seductive atmosphere. This was a time-out, not an ending.

"I thought I was the one who was supposed to be on the couch for a session like this," he said with an edge in his voice.

She ignored the tone and patted the place beside her. "Join me."

He studied her intently. "You're really going to insist on this, aren't you?"

She nodded placidly, comfortable in the role of inquisitor as she hadn't been in the role of seductress. "I think I am."

He ran his fingers through his hair. She could see the debate raging inside him before he finally shrugged, kicked off his tennis shoes and settled himself beside her. "Okay, doc. It's the strangest sort of foreplay I've ever seen, but what do you want to know?" he asked, then peered at her closely. "I hope it's not too much, because I'm not sure how long I can stand being this close to you in this bed without touching you."

"Think of it this way," she said sweetly. "It'll put some of the spontaneity back into the afternoon."

He groaned at that and tugged her down until she was lying flat beneath him, laughing. As she recognized the look in his eyes, though, the laughter suddenly died, along with her need for immediate answers. Never before had she seen such naked longing, such open loneliness and need. How was it possible that a man who'd filled his life with so many companions could seem so desperately alone? Why had he chosen her to banish the loneliness? Could she do it with her inexperienced touches? She knew only that she had to try, that she had to share with him some small measure of the joy he had brought into her life these past few weeks. If this was all they had between them, just this moment, it would be special, it would last them forever.

She smoothed the hair off his forehead. "I do want you to make love to me, Hank." She made the admission on a sigh. "Now."

"Are you sure this time?"

She nodded. "Very sure. The talk can wait."

His mouth came down on hers then, stealing the last of her declaration. The last of her doubts fled on a wave of pure sensation as his hands began to slide over her, stroking, exploring. With fingers that actually seemed to shake, he pushed her T-shirt up to expose her breasts to the tender mercies of his lips, his beard a gentle, but oh-so-seductive irritant across the sensitive flesh.

"Don't be afraid, Annie love," he whispered, when she trembled at the intensity of the feelings sweeping through her.

"This isn't something I do every day," she managed to say.

"Neither have I lately," he said with wry humor.

"But you've had so much more experience, what if…"

He touched a finger to her lips. "Annie, this is our first time together. *Ours.* No matter what's happened in the past, we've never been together like this before. I'm every bit as nervous as you are. I want it to be perfect for you and I won't know how if you won't tell me. So, you see, we're in the same boat."

Not quite, she thought as his expert touches robbed her of further arguments. Hank made love with astonishing gentleness. He taught her the way to tease and madden. His caresses were slow, provocative follow-ups to the adoration in his eyes. And, as if to prove his point that there were no comparisons being made, he told her again and again of all the things that made her special.

"I love the way your lips are a little off center," he said, his fingertip tracing the outline.

"And your hair is so soft. It's like silk," he whispered, smoothing it back, the callused pads of his fingers gently grazing her cheek in the process.

"Do you know what your eyes remind me of? The blue is usually the same shade as those fields of wildflowers in Texas, but now..." His voice dropped even lower. "Now it's like midnight."

And on it went. He made love to her from head to toe, without hesitation, without restraint, letting her see the joy she was bringing to him, commanding her with his patient, lingering touches to share it. She was practically humming from the inside out, her body quivering with excitement, covered with a light sheen of perspiration. One by one her muscles stretched taut with expectation as he played his fingers over and inside her, kissing her with increasing urgency.

"I love *you,* Annie," he whispered with added emphasis as he held himself poised above her. "Only you."

The truth of the words was in his eyes. And the ache that had been building inside her became even more compelling. "Show me," she pleaded, willing him to dispel the last of her uncertainty. "Please, Hank."

Showing her how to help, he slipped on protection. Then he entered her, so slowly that she thought she'd go mad before knowing the sensation of being filled up by him. When he was deep inside her at last, she felt complete for the very first time in her life. And as he began more of those slow, tantalizing strokes, she began to know the meaning of magic, the rhythm of fulfillment.

"You are so beautiful," he said, his voice ragged, his muscles tense with the strain of holding back.

"Please, Hank," she cried again, rising to meet his thrusts, urging him into a more frenzied pace. His musky scent lured her. The taste of his skin only teased at her hunger. She was past the need for compliments, beyond the desire for promises. She wanted release from the wild, wonderful, awful tension that had coiled so tightly inside her that she was certain she would explode with just one more gliding touch, just one more deep, demanding kiss.

Then his tongue circled the taut peak of her breast, the hot, moist stroking almost unbearably tender. The caress was gentle, incredibly gentle, but it was that which set off the flare of rockets that ripped through her, shattering the tension and carrying him along with her.

She didn't realize she'd been crying until Hank hovered over her, his expression filled with concern. He touched a finger to the tears rolling down her cheek.

"Are you okay? Did I hurt you?" he murmured, his voice rough with anxiety.

"I didn't know…"

"What?" he pleaded. "Please, baby, you've got to tell me if I hurt you. I would never…"

She kissed him to stop the unnecessary apology. "No. I never knew it could be like that. It was beautiful." Her gaze swept over his face, memorizing the way it looked as he realized that he had made this first time so incredibly special for her. She'd never seen such a sense of wonder in a man's eyes before.

"Annie love, it's only going to get better. I promise you."

She ran her fingers over his chest, tangling them in the mat of wiry hairs, delighting in the freedom she suddenly felt, the awe he was beginning to instill in her. "You're always making promises to me."

"And I mean to keep every one of them."

She shook her head, clinging to one last shred of reality. "Hank, nothing is forever. We both know that better than anyone."

He rolled on his back and sighed. He took her hand and held it over his heart, which was thumping with a sure, steady, reassuring rhythm.

"I've always thought that, Annie," he confessed slowly.

Despite the fact that she'd been the one to say it, Ann realized that she'd been counting on a denial. Her heart sank when none came. His response hung heavily in the air between them, ruining their special moment.

As if he knew exactly what she was feeling, he reached over and lifted her until she was sitting astride him, her bare thighs clamped around his waist. "Now you listen to me," he said, his hands resting lightly on her hips, his gaze locked with hers. "That is what I used to believe, Annie. No more. What we have is forever. And if it takes me that long, I'm going to prove it to you."

For now, with the heat rising within her again, she needed him too much to argue. But the time would come, only too soon, when she knew she'd be proved right. Until then, though, they had this incredible magic.

The last gray streaks of twilight had turned to darkness when Hank woke her with a soft, sweet kiss.

"Time to go, sleeping beauty. If we don't pick the kids up soon, we really will have to explain our absence."

She ran her hand lovingly up his thigh, thrilling to the textures, the roughness of the hair, the warmth that cloaked solid strength. "It might be worth it."

He seized her fingers in midstroke. "Annie, you don't mean that."

"What if I do?"

He grinned and stripped away the sheet that covered her. "In that case," he murmured, rolling toward her, his hand already circling her breast.

Sensation swelled inside her at once, but practicality won out. Forcing a laugh, she rolled away. "Okay. Never mind. I think you're probably right."

"Tease," he grumbled. "Hurry up, before I change my mind and give Liz and Todd permanent custody of all those children of yours."

Still bathed in the warm afterglow of Hank's lovemaking, Ann felt contentment settle itself over her as they drove the mile or so back to Liz and Todd's. Even if this couldn't last forever, she would treasure it.

She had only an instant's nervousness as they walked around the house toward the patio. They could hear the kids splashing in the pool and an occasional lazy admonition from Todd.

As they were about to turn the corner of the house, Hank stopped and drew her into his arms. "Don't forget this afternoon, Annie. Don't let it slip away."

Puzzled by the intensity in his voice, she touched his lips. "Why would you say that? Of course I won't forget."

"I saw that look in your eyes just now. I just don't want you to start analyzing it to death and come up with some crazy idea that it didn't mean anything. It was important, for both of us."

"I know that. Really."

He nodded finally. "Then let's go see what we've missed."

On the patio they found Liz and Todd sprawled contentedly on chaise longues. Melissa was curled up at Liz's side, her thumb in her mouth, her blanket dragging on the red tiles.

Liz grinned up at them. "She conked out about an hour ago."

Ann immediately felt guilty. "She wasn't upset, was she?"

"No, she was not upset," Liz said firmly. "Don't you dare start feeling guilty for taking a little time off. The kids hardly noticed you were gone."

Hank groaned. "Wrong thing to say," he said. "Now she'll never let them out of her sight, for fear they'll forget all about her."

"I will not," Ann protested, though there was this tiny

twinge of guilt in the pit of her stomach that suggested there might be some truth in what he said.

"Can I get you two something to drink?" Todd said.

Hank grinned at him. "Thought you were sleeping there for a minute, pal. Did the kids wear you out?"

"Do you have any idea how much energy is in that pool right this minute? If we could harness it, we could run a power plant," he said with weary admiration.

"You just stay where you are," Hank said sympathetically. "I'll get the drinks."

As Hank went into the house, Ann walked over to the edge of the pool. She wasn't quite sure how she felt about the fact that the kids hadn't even seemed to notice her return, much less her absence. With the force of habit, she began counting heads.

Tracy was clinging to the wall at the deep end, kicking lazily. Paul, David and Todd's son, Kevin, were playing water polo, splashing exuberantly. Tommy was trying desperately to keep pace with them, but his movements were slightly hampered by his injured leg and by the water wings Todd had insisted he wear. Jason? She glanced around again. There was no sign of him. She turned back to Liz, an uneasy feeling stirring in the pit of her stomach.

"Liz? Where's Jason?" She forced herself to keep her voice calm.

"Isn't he in the pool?"

She shook her head as her heart began to beat wildly.

"He went into the house an hour or so ago," Todd said before panic could set in. "He's probably in Kevin's room playing video games."

The tension abated slightly, but didn't vanish. "I'll just go in and tell him we're back," she said casually, not wanting to admit her need to account for every one of her chicks.

"Ann..." Liz began, but Hank silenced her.

"Let her go, Liz. She won't be happy until she's made certain that they're all here and healthy."

She glared at him, but his remark didn't prevent her from going inside. She checked Kevin's room first. It was dark and deserted. Her panic returning, she dashed through the rest of the house, frantically flipping on lights, moving more and more quickly as she found each room empty.

"Hank," she called out finally, her voice trembling. "Oh, my God, Hank!"

He met her at the patio door. He took one look at her face and gathered her close, but not even the solid comfort he offered could counter the hysteria that seemed to be rising in her.

"What's wrong?"

She looked up into troubled eyes and felt tears welling up in her own as she clung to him. Her fingers dug into his shoulders as an awful emptiness crept through her.

"Annie?"

"I can't find him," she finally whispered in a voice filled with raw, unbearable pain. "Jason's gone."

Chapter 12

"If anything has happened to him, I will never forgive myself," Ann said over and over as Hank led her to the kitchen table. She felt dazed and the ache that had settled in the region of her heart was worse than anything she had ever experienced. It didn't matter that Jason was sixteen and in many ways able to take care of himself. He was still just a lost and lonely kid and she'd obviously failed him. "Why didn't I see this coming?"

She looked at Hank. "It's because we…because I was too busy."

"No," he said adamantly. "It is not because of anything you did."

"We should have been here," she said stubbornly. "If he's hurt…"

"Jason is a tough kid. Nothing's going to happen to him," Hank reassured her. Ann wanted to believe him.

She clung to the words like a lifeline, but these awful images kept creeping in.

"Drink this," Liz said, setting a cup of tea in front of her.

She pushed it away. "I don't want it. How can you even think about sitting around drinking tea when Jason is missing? We should be out looking for him, instead of wasting time like this," she lashed out accusingly.

She glared at all of them as they hovered over her. She blamed herself. She blamed Hank. Now she seemed to be including Liz in her anger. Listening to herself, she realized that her guilt was making her irrational, but she seemed unable to stop herself. Tears brimming over, she took a deep, calming breath and looked at Liz. "I'm sorry."

"You have nothing to be sorry for. Now, please, drink a little of the tea."

"Please, Annie," Hank said. "Listen to Liz. Todd and I will go look for Jason the minute I know you're all right."

"Of course I'm all right," she said impatiently. "It's Jason who's in trouble. We have to go after him. Three of us will be better than two. We can cover more territory."

"Sweetheart, it will be much better if you stay here. You don't know the area. Besides, it will only upset the other kids if all of us go racing off."

"Oh, my God!" she whispered. "I hadn't even thought about them. How am I going to tell them that he's gone?"

"There's no need to say anything yet," Hank said.

"But we have to. Maybe he said something to one of them about where he was going, what his plans were."

Hank shook his head. "He's too much of a loner. He wouldn't say anything. He'd just go. Now, please, Annie, just stay here with Liz and try to stay calm."

Calm? He was asking the impossible, but she finally admitted the wisdom in what he was suggesting. Someone had to stay with the kids and there really wasn't any point in upsetting them unnecessarily. But she felt so helpless and it wasn't a feeling she liked. She needed to do something. She needed to be part of the search for Jason. She needed to be there to talk to him, to find out why he'd gone, to hold him and remind him how much she cared.

As if she'd read her mind, Liz said, "Ann, he could come back here on his own. It'll be better if you're here waiting for him."

That was the most persuasive argument of all. Giving in finally, she sighed and buried her face in her hands.

Hank hunkered down beside her chair and took her hands and folded them tightly in his. She couldn't bring herself to meet his gaze, though.

"I'll find him, Annie," he said. "I promise."

Yet another promise. She heard the conviction in his voice, but she heard something else as well: fear. Was he more afraid for Jason than he'd admitted or was he afraid of what this would do to the two of them? Perhaps both. God knows that's how she felt. She was torn apart inside thinking about what could be happening to Jason. She also knew that things might never be the same between her and Hank if their time together had been the cause of his running away. Blame and guilt would always be there between them, eating away at the fiber of their still-new relationship.

When Hank and Todd had left, she looked over at

Liz and finally dared to speak her fears aloud. "It's my fault. I never should have left here this afternoon. I knew how much he resented Hank and I went off with him anyway."

"Don't be ridiculous. You have every right to a life of your own, Ann. You owe it to yourself to grab for whatever happiness you can find. You're long overdue."

"Not at the expense of my children."

"Spending one afternoon with Hank is not robbing your children of anything and, as much as you love them, they do not have the right to choose your friends or your lovers."

How many times had she counseled divorced parents on just that point? Living through it for the first time herself, she began to fully understand the complexities, the mine field of explosive emotions involved. Nothing was as clear-cut and easy as she'd always made it sound. "But they weren't prepared," she told Liz. "We should have talked about it."

"Do you honestly expect me to believe that you were going to sit those kids down and tell them that you wanted to go off to make love with Hank?"

Ann felt the color rise in her cheeks. "Well, I certainly wouldn't have put it like that. I could have told them that we were going out, though, instead of just sneaking away like a couple of teenagers trying to escape the watchful eyes of their parents."

Liz sighed. "Okay. I can't deny that that might have been the wise thing to do, but not doing it is hardly the end of the world. You did not behave irresponsibly. You didn't leave them alone. They were here with us. They were having a good time. There are five kids out on the patio who did not suffer any emotional harm just because you needed some time to yourself."

"But there's one who did."

"You have to stop thinking that way. You don't know that Jason's leaving had anything to do with that. He's been troubled since the day he moved in with you. Maybe he just picked today to take off because he thought he could get away with it."

When Ann started to deny Jason's ongoing behavior problems, Liz held up her hand. "Don't forget how many conversations you and I have had on just that subject."

Ann felt her shoulders sag. It was true. She had admitted more than once to Liz things she'd refused to acknowledge to Hank. It was as if she'd wanted Hank's approval of Jason so much that she'd been afraid to acknowledge to him that the boy had problems that needed correcting, problems that she'd found herself unable to address.

"For a psychologist, I've really mucked this one up royally, haven't I?"

"That's because you're a mother first and mothers sometimes make mistakes. We're not nearly as dispassionate and objective when one of our own's involved. You've spent so much time worrying about Jason's terrible past that you haven't been nearly as tough as you should have been in guiding his present. That's a very human reaction."

Seized by sudden uncertainty, Ann asked, "Do you think I can make it up to him?"

"I'm not sure you have anything to make up to Jason, if that's what you're asking. You've given that boy every chance. You've loved him as if he were your own. He's repaid you with nothing but heartache."

Ann smiled ruefully. "Actually, I wasn't talking just about Jason. I was thinking of Hank, too. I was awfully hard on him."

Liz grinned back at her. "Oh, I'm sure you can make it up to him. Hank's got a tough hide, but he's a real softie inside. I found that out when he had a heart-to-heart talk with me when I was about to walk out of Todd's life. Just make sure you tell him that you don't blame him for any of this. After all, Todd and I are the ones who let Jason get away."

"But I don't blame any of you, not really."

"I know. You only blame yourself, but there was a minute there, before Hank walked out the door, when I think everyone in this room got the idea that you did blame him."

"I'll talk to him," she vowed. "As soon as Jason is back safely…"

Left unsaid was what she would do if they didn't find Jason. Ann refused to let herself even consider the possibility. They had to find him. They had to. Her entire future with Hank might very well depend on it.

Hank had no idea how good Jason's sense of direction might be, but he was relatively certain the boy would try to make his way back to the highway so he could get back to the Keys. In fact, if he had enough of a head start, he suspected Jason would go straight to Key West. Back home. Even though it had never been much of a home to him, Key West was the one place Jason ever spoke of with genuine enthusiasm. Hank only prayed he could find him before Jason hitched a ride. Despite his reassurances for Ann's benefit, he didn't like the idea of what could happen to a kid hitchhiking.

As he drove up and down the dark, winding streets, he cursed himself for not anticipating something like this. He was the one who'd recognized Jason's increasing alienation, his obvious resentment of the place Hank was filling in Ann's life. He should have talked to the boy, instead of losing patience with his surliness. If nothing else, he'd owed it to Ann to try harder. He was the grown-up, not Jason. Maybe he wasn't father material after all. Just when he'd begun to think he had it in him to deal with family life, something like this happened to prove that he was a pretender.

His spirits sank lower and lower. By the time he finally spotted Jason walking along the side of a narrow road, half-hidden in the shadows, he was nearly out of his mind with worry and self-condemnation. Where was the kid's head, he thought furiously when he could barely pick him out alongside the darkened roadway. Wearing blue jeans and a navy-blue polo shirt while walking at night was a good way to get hit by a passing car.

Before he could make the mistake of yelling, though, he warned himself to slow down. Getting into an absurd argument over where Jason had chosen to walk and the clothes he was wearing wouldn't help anything.

"Jason," he called out, keeping his tone carefully neutral. "Hop in."

Jason kept his gaze straight ahead. His pace never faltered.

"Son," he began, only to have Jason whirl around, his expression furious.

"You are not my father!" he shouted, then took off, nearly tripping and falling in his haste to get away.

Taken aback by the anger and raw emotion, Hank

stared after him for an instant before driving slowly up beside him again. "You're right," he called out. "I'm not your father. I'm sorry."

In the blue-white glow of the headlights, he could detect the sheen of tears on Jason's cheeks and suddenly his heart turned over. For the first time he truly recognized the scared, vulnerable boy inside that tough facade. With that recognition came another blow: the person Jason most reminded him of in this world was himself some twenty years ago. He didn't like the fact that he hadn't admitted it sooner.

"Jason, let's go somewhere and talk about this," he suggested quietly, determined to find a way to make things right between them. This time it was not just for Ann's sake, but for his own.

"I got nothing to say to you."

"And what about Ann? Do you have any idea how scared she is right now?"

Jason's step faltered.

"She's back at Liz and Todd's blaming herself because you left. She thinks she failed you."

"She didn't do nothing," Jason mumbled.

"You and I both know that, but she doesn't. All she knows is that you've gone and she's convinced if she'd been there, she could have stopped you. But this is between you and me, isn't it?"

That drew Jason's gaze to him. The stark honesty of the words created a palpable tension between them and something new, Hank thought. Hope.

"Isn't it?" he persisted.

"Maybe."

"Then let's go get a soda or something and talk about it, man-to-man."

"Since when?" Jason said sarcastically. "You always treat me like some dumb kid. Until you came along, Ann always treated me like a grown-up. She depended on me."

And that, of course, was a large part of the problem that he'd never before recognized. Why hadn't he seen it before? As Jason saw it, his role in Ann's life had been usurped by a stranger. Hank had to prove to him that they both belonged, that she had more than enough love for the two of them.

"Fair enough," he said. "That's something we should talk about."

Hank thought he caught a flicker of hope in Jason's eyes before his shoulders sagged. "What's the point?" he muttered, starting to walk again.

"The point is that we both love Ann. Neither of us wants her to be unhappy, so we owe it to her to try to work out our differences," he said firmly. "Don't we?"

Jason hesitated.

"Jason? Don't we?"

"I guess," he said with obvious reluctance.

"Will you get in, then?"

Jason finally turned grudgingly and opened the door. He got into the car, but he huddled as close to the door as he could get. Hank drove to a fast-food restaurant a few blocks away and led him inside.

"Hungry?"

"I guess."

"Well, I'm starved. How about a burger, fries, something to drink?"

Jason shrugged. Hank told him to find them a table and he took the chance to phone Ann and let her know that he had found Jason and they were going to talk for a while. She wasn't happy but she agreed. He hung up his phone and placed the order, carrying it to the booth Jason had chosen once it was ready. When Jason had wolfed down his sandwich and the french fries, Hank asked him quietly, "Okay, why don't you tell me why you ran away?"

"What do you care, man? I'm just in your way. You were probably glad I was gone."

"Then why am I here?"

"Because Ann sent you."

Hank shook his head. "No, it's more than that. I never wanted you to leave, Jason. I wouldn't put Ann through this kind of pain for anything in the world. Don't you realize how very important you are to Ann? I love her, so I wanted to be a father to you, but I didn't know how. Did you ever stop to think that maybe I'm just as much afraid as you are?"

"Afraid? Right," Jason scoffed, but Hank could tell that the idea intrigued him.

"It's true. You know, I never had much of a family life myself. My dad left before I was born and my mom, well, she wasn't around a whole lot. I got pretty used to being on my own. I didn't have any brothers or sisters, so I had no idea what family life was like. Todd was the best friend I had and his family wasn't too great, either, so I've always been real careful not to get too involved with anyone. I figured that was just asking for trouble. Know what I mean?"

Jason's brown eyes were watching him with avid interest now. He nodded slowly.

"When I came to stay with Ann in the Keys, I didn't expect to like it there. It was a place to stay, that's all. I'd only met Ann once and, to tell you the truth, we hadn't gotten along all that well. As for you guys, well, the idea of a bunch of kids scared the daylights out of me. What did I know about kids? Not much. Then I started getting to know you all. Tracy and the others, they made it easy, but not you. You were just the way I was when I was your age. You'd built this wall around you and I didn't know how to get past it. Maybe that's why I've been so hard on you. Nobody made it easy for me. Nobody loved me the way Ann loves you. I figured you ought to learn to appreciate what you had. I thought maybe that job would teach you something about responsibility, about pulling your own weight."

"I just thought you wanted me out of the way," Jason finally admitted. "I figured the minute I was making some money, you'd be trying to talk me into leaving."

"Hey, I may make mistakes, some of them pretty good-size ones, but I'm not dumb. Do you know what Ann would do to me if I tried to get you out of that house?"

Jason grinned suddenly. "You mean after she chased you around with a butcher knife?"

Hank grinned back. "Yeah, after that."

"Maybe tar and feathers."

The idea seemed to appeal to him a lot. Hank tried not to wince at the enthusiasm. "Oh, I think she'd probably think even that was too good for me. She loves all you kids and she'd do anything in the world to protect you."

Jason's expression suddenly became troubled. His voice dropped to a nervous whisper. "How mad do you think she's gonna be that I ran away?"

"Oh, I think a month in your room ought to about cover it," Hank said lightly.

Jason squirmed. "I guess that's better than being tarred and feathered."

"Considerably," Hank concurred. "Ready to go back?"

"Can I ask you something else?"

Hank nodded.

"Are you and Ann gonna get married, like Tracy said?"

"If I have my way, we are. How would you feel about that?"

"It's not up to me."

"That's where you're wrong. What you think is very important to her. She'll never do anything if she thinks it would truly hurt one of you."

Jason's expression suddenly grew cocky. "So it's sort of like you need my permission, huh?"

Hank had to choke back a laugh. "Sort of."

"I guess that sort of changes things, doesn't it?"

He stood and ruffled Jason's hair. "Not that much, kid. Not that much."

Jason looked increasingly uneasy as they drew closer to Liz and Todd's. "Maybe we could just tell her that I went for a walk," he suggested hopefully.

Hank returned his look seriously. "But that would be a lie."

"So, big deal. She wouldn't worry so much, then."

"She wouldn't have worried if you'd told her that *before* you ran away. Since you didn't, the worrying is already done."

"Yeah, I guess. It was worth a shot, though."

Jason's footsteps began to lag behind as they approached the house, but Hank was already calling out. Ann came racing through the living room, Liz just a few steps behind her. Since Jason was standing perfectly still just inside the front door, she came to him and took him in her arms.

"You cost me ten years off my life," she said in a voice that was thick with emotion.

"I'm sorry," Jason said, his skinny arms going awkwardly around her.

She looked from Jason to Hank and back again. "Is everything okay?"

Hank nodded. "I think everything is going to be just fine."

She cupped Jason's face in her hands and scanned his expression closely. "What about you? What do you think?"

Hank felt his breath catch in his chest as he waited for Jason's reply. He had a feeling his future and not just Jason's hung in the balance.

"I guess it'll be okay."

Ann wrapped the embarrassed boy in another tight hug. She looked at Hank over Jason's head.

Thank you, she mouthed silently.

He nodded.

Everything was going to be just fine, he told himself repeatedly over the next few days, but it was hard to believe it. Ann never let any of the kids out of her sight for long. She also did everything she could to avoid being alone with Hank. She'd even stopped running, claiming that she had to catch up on paperwork in the mornings. They'd been back in the Keys for nearly a week before he finally called her on it.

"Okay, Annie, why are you avoiding me?" he said, lingering after the last of the kids had left the kitchen.

"I'm not avoiding you."

"No? How would I get a crazy idea like that, then?"

"Your imagination?" she suggested, inching toward the door.

He shook his head. "Nope. I think it has more to do with the fact that you have not been in a room alone with me since last Saturday afternoon."

"We're alone now."

"For how long? You have one foot out the door. The only thing that's kept you here is that you're too polite to walk out on me in midsentence."

Flustered, Ann returned his challenging gaze. He was right. She had been avoiding him. When they'd come back on Saturday night to find that Jason had taken off, she had realized anew that there were too many things standing in the way of their making any sort of future plans. She owed him an apology for blaming him for Jason's running away, but beyond that they needed to keep their distance. They certainly couldn't have a wild affair with six children in the house. And they couldn't very well go sneaking around. Just look what had happened the first time they'd tried that.

So she'd made up her mind to think of Saturday as a wonderful interlude. It had proved to her that she could still feel, that she was a woman with a passionate nature and emotions that ran deep. *Think of it as a test,* she told herself. She had passed.

Now what?

Now she had to get out of this kitchen before Hank kissed her, which was what it looked as though he had every intention of doing. She scooted through the door.

He was faster. He had one hand locked around her wrist before she could make the turn into the first hallway.

"Running, Annie?"

"I...I thought I heard one of the kids," she said nervously as her pulse leaped wildly. His mouth hovered near hers, taunting her with the reminder of its velvet softness, its moist heat, its hungry demands.

"I didn't hear a thing, except for the sound of your heart beating."

She backed up a step. The wall stopped her. She pressed hard against it anyway, as if hoping it would yield to her desire to flee. "Hank, why are you pushing this? You don't really want a relationship with me."

He stared back at her. "I don't?"

Admittedly, he did look incredulous, but she said firmly, "You don't. It's just an infatuation, a passing fancy. You know."

He pulled her tight against him. His body was solid and hard and every bit as unyielding as that wall. He smelled of the slightly spicy scent of his soap. "What I know is," he began, his breath whispering across her cheek, "you are the only thing in this life that I do want. I thought I proved that to you on Saturday."

"No," she said, ducking out of the circle of his arms. "All that proved was that there is some undeniable chemistry between us. If we ignore it, it will go away."

He brought her right back against him, where it was very clear that the chemistry was hard at work again. Her heart skittered wildly, then settled into a galloping rhythm that proved her point. Chemistry. That's all it was.

"This is not some high-school science experiment," he murmured. "I am not trying to prove some theory about opposites attracting or what happens when two incendiary devices collide in the night."

She cleared her throat. "What...what are you trying to prove?"

"That you can tell yourself from now until those dolphins of yours learn to speak fluent Italian, German and Spanish that this is nothing but a passing fancy, but I will be right here, in this house, in your bed, proving you wrong."

She shook her head, but it didn't seem to carry much conviction. She wanted to believe that fierce look of possessiveness in his eyes. She wanted to believe in the wonder of his touch. She wanted to believe so badly, she ached with it, but she wouldn't let him know that.

"Accept it, Annie," he said. His lips against her throat gave heated emphasis to the demand.

She swallowed back a gasp of pleasure and tried to rally indignation. "In your dreams," she said boldly.

He grinned, blast him all to hell and back.

"That's right," he said sweetly. "In my dreams."

And, then, with a final kiss that stole the last of her breath away, he left her to her dreams. She didn't need a textbook to figure out what they meant. The tangled sheets and aching need swelling low in her belly told her all she needed to know.

Chapter 13

Ann badly needed to run. Maybe if she ran far enough and fast enough, she could reduce the stressful effect of Hank's nonstop flirting. Her nerves were so ragged she could barely get through the day without wanting to scream.

Finally, in an act of sheer desperation, she set her alarm a half hour earlier than usual. Maybe she could sneak out of the house before he got up and put in five miles of hard running before breakfast. She spent most of the night rolling over and checking the clock, just to be sure she wouldn't sleep through the alarm. Ten minutes before it was due to go off, she hit the switch and dragged herself out of bed. She tugged on her clothes in record time, ran her fingers hastily through her hair and tiptoed through the still-dark house. She went straight through the kitchen, not even pausing to put on the coffeepot or do her warm-ups. She'd do the exercises outside, where there was less chance of Hank hearing her.

She had put one foot on the porch when she heard the creak of a rocking chair, and Hank's quiet, "Morning, Annie."

It was all she could do to keep from crying in frustration. "Why are you up?" she asked, unable to keep the annoyance from her voice.

"Waiting for you."

"But I didn't...I'm not usually..." She glared at him. "How did you know?"

"Calculated guess. Besides, I've heard you tossing and turning for the past week. I figured sooner or later you'd have to get back into your routine and work off your frustrations."

"Frustrations?" she said weakly.

He chuckled. "You know about frustration, Annie. It's what happens when a person tries to deny their feelings, especially their sexual feelings."

She could feel heat flooding her cheeks. "I am not denying my feelings."

"Then why can't you sleep?"

"I...I have a lot on my mind."

"Me?"

"Don't flatter yourself. Now leave me alone. I'm going running."

"Warm up first," he warned.

She had absolutely no intention of doing warm-ups in front of Hank Riley while he ogled her. She took off across the yard, running. Hank trotted after her. She increased her pace. With a barely perceptible output of effort, Hank kept in step.

This was not reducing her stress. This was driving her crazy.

"Hank, why are you doing this?" she asked plaintively.

"Doing what?"

"Pestering me."

"Is that what I'm doing? I thought I was keeping you company."

"I don't want company."

"You will when your muscles knot up because you didn't warm up."

"My muscles will be just fine," she said. But with a perversity she should have expected, her calf tensed painfully. She winced and tried to run through the pain. It got worse, until she was finally forced to slow down. Naturally Hank was gloating.

"Give me your leg."

"There is nothing wrong with my leg."

"Oh, for heaven's sakes, woman, sit down and let me massage your leg."

It hurt too badly to refuse. She limped over to a tree stump and sat down. Hank knelt in front of her. But the minute his strong fingers curved around her calf, every other muscle in her body tensed.

"Relax, Annie. This is not a seduction."

The reassurance was not convincing. It felt like a seduction. Only the setting seemed incongruous. With sure strokes, Hank continued to knead her leg. The muscle finally loosened. The pain eased.

"I'm okay now," she said shakily.

"As long as I'm down here, there's something I want to ask you."

She regarded him warily. "What?"

"Marry me, Annie."

Every muscle froze again. Hank unconsciously began massaging. "Well?" he said.

Her throat was so dry she couldn't squeak out a single word. Nervously she licked her lips. "That sounds more like an order than a question," she evaded.

His lips twitched. "Okay. I'll try again. Will you marry me?"

"Why?"

His fingers were sliding up and down her leg, creating more of that unbearable tension that curled low in her abdomen. "Because I love you."

The words hovered between them, the most powerful temptation on the face of the earth, next to the effect of his touch.

"Hank, face it," she said, trying desperately to cling to rational thought when she was oh-so-tempted to throw herself straight into his arms. "You and I would drive each other crazy inside of a month."

"Probably less," he concurred. "That doesn't mean it's not worth a try."

"*A try?* That's your idea of marriage?"

"Annie, I am not good with words. You know what I mean. What we have is special. It's something I never experienced growing up. I never had a father. I had a mother who didn't know the meaning of love. Now that I finally understand what it is, I don't want to let it slip away."

"Hank, you don't understand anything about love. What you're feeling is the challenge, the excitement of the chase. Once you've conquered all my reservations, once you've gotten me in front of a preacher to say all those pretty words about love and honor, it would lose its excitement. You'd be bored."

"In this household I'd have to be dead to be bored. There hasn't been a dull moment since the day I moved in."

He sounded so convincing. The look in his eyes practically scorched her with its intensity. But she knew better. He'd only been there a couple of months. The novelty hadn't worn off yet. But it would and she would not put them both through the torment of a divorce when that happened.

"No, Hank. And if you bring it up again, I'll send you packing."

If he was disappointed, he didn't show it. He simply held out his hand and helped her to her feet. "Let's go, Annie."

She was suddenly feeling oddly let down. Finishing the run would fix that, she told herself briskly, and began jogging.

"Annie?" Hank said beside her. She glanced over at him. "You can't possibly run fast enough to get away from me."

There was a deliberate taunt in his voice when he said it, but it was the glint of determination in his eyes that set her blood on fire.

Whispers. Ann had never before noticed so much whispering going on around the house. Usually she felt like wearing earmuffs to shut out the yelling. Now, though, every time she walked into a room she was greeted by sudden silence and guilty looks. They were in cahoots all right, but why? If her birthday hadn't been months away, she'd have thought they were planning a surprise party.

Whatever was going on, Hank didn't seem to be

in on it. She'd noticed that the kids were being just as secretive around him. It was beginning to get on her nerves, which were already shaky enough thanks to Hank's lingering looks and deliberately casual touches. She continued to try to avoid him, but that wasn't working one bit better than solving the mystery of the children's behavior.

She was sitting with him in the kitchen late one night, unable to think of a thing to say to combat the increasingly tense silence, when she finally said in desperation, "Have you noticed that the kids are being a little weird these days?"

"Weird?" He shook his head. "How?"

"Quiet. Secretive. What do you suppose they're up to?"

"Maybe they're planning an overthrow of the household leadership," he joked.

She scowled impatiently. "Very funny. I'm trying to be serious here. All the sneaking around has me worried."

"Forget it, Annie. Do you see any evidence that they're upset about anything?"

"No," she admitted.

"Even Jason has been on his best behavior since the trip to Miami, right?"

"I suppose so."

"And Tracy's not as moody."

"True." Tracy had, however, started offering to lend her clothes in colors she knew Hank liked. She'd even brought home a new blusher, eye shadow and a bolder shade of lipstick and left them openly on Ann's dresser. The hints were obvious and, no doubt, part of the whole plot that had her worried.

"But don't you think it's odd…" she began.

"Ann, there is nothing to worry about. Drink your tea."

He was trying to placate her. She recognized the tone. It added to her jittery state of mind. "It's so pleasant to have someone to talk things over with," she snapped irritably.

"I'm glad you feel that way," he said, deliberately misinterpreting her sarcasm. "There's something I've been meaning to talk to you about."

"Well, you can just go to hell. I have nothing to say to you."

She got up and stomped out of the room, passing Tracy and Jason in the doorway. She caught the odd look that passed between them, but she was too furious to try to interpret it. Right now all she wanted to do was get away from Hank and the emotions that seemed to get all tangled up inside her whenever she was in his presence.

She had wasted an entire afternoon in her office stretched out on her sofa trying to analyze what was happening between them. She'd viewed it as something of a private therapy session. She had toted up Hank's attributes, which were many. She had pinpointed each and every one of his flaws, also legion, and decided, on balance, that there was no rational reason to consider a future with the man. He would never be the placid, rock-solid, even-tempered man she'd always dreamed of sharing her life with. He was volatile and unpredictable on the one hand and too darned neat on the other. Even if she could get those awful doughnuts from him, she'd probably never get him to give up the rest of his junk food.

Stop being petty, some little voice had nagged. *None of that really matters.* What mattered was the fact that she knew deep down inside that Hank didn't really want to be a family man. He was kind and generous, the kind of man who'd even give a meal to a stray cat, but that didn't mean he'd keep it around for the rest of his life. He didn't want that sort of long-term commitment. He'd practically told her as much when he'd revealed the secrets of his childhood. Forget all her degrees, even an amateur psychologist could figure out the impact his mother's behavior had had on his ability to relate to women. She understood all that. She really did. Better, apparently, than he did himself.

So, she had concluded at the end of the session, she was just going to treat him casually for the few remaining weeks they were likely to have together. They would part as friends. Good friends. Caring friends.

Not lovers.

"You know, Annie," said the voice of her good, caring friend right behind her. A shiver shot down her spine and made mincemeat of her intentions.

She whipped around angrily. "Stop doing that!"

"Doing what?"

"Sneaking up on me."

"I did not sneak up on you," he said reasonably. "I walked out of the kitchen right behind you. I did nothing to hide my actions. You were just lost in thought. What were you thinking about, Annie?"

She recognized that innocently quizzical expression in his eyes. More important, she spotted the neatly set trap. He wasn't catching her in it. No, sir. "Nothing in particular," she said in a voice so cool it could have chilled champagne. "Was there something you wanted?"

Blue eyes lost their innocence at once. They captured her and pinned her right where she was with masculine intensity. Her heart skittered crazily.

"Hank," she protested weakly.

"Hmm?"

"I asked if there was something you wanted."

"Yes," he murmured, leaning toward her, his gaze fastened on her mouth.

"I meant something else," she said. Her voice sounded strangled.

"First things first."

She took a hastily drawn and very deep breath, then darted past him calling at the top of her lungs, "Melissa! Time for bed."

She heard him sigh heavily as she made her narrowest escape yet. And for just a minute, she felt a fleeting pang of regret. Then she reminded herself that what she was doing was in her own best interests and in Hank's. It was getting harder and harder to remember that, though.

Hank retreated to the backyard hammock. It was getting to be absurd. He was acting like a third grader with a crush trying to steal kisses on a playground from a reluctant classmate. That's what Ann had reduced him to with her stubborn denial that anything had changed between them on the trip to Miami. Whether she would have behaved exactly the same way had Jason not run away was a moot point. The fact remained that she was intentionally distancing herself from him. And he, despite his reputation as a ladies' man, had no idea what to do about it. He'd thought the marriage proposal would convince her, but it had only made her more skittish than ever. It left him completely at a loss.

Ann was not one bit like the women he'd been attracted to in the past. A dozen roses, a bottle of expensive wine or a box of imported chocolates would be wasted on her. She had a yard filled with rose bushes, she wasn't crazy about wine and he could just imagine what she'd have to say about the candy. He could always send her a gallon jug of apple juice or bring her a dozen oat-bran muffins, but where was the romance in that? As for taking her out to a candlelit dinner, she'd probably insist on hauling all six children along. They'd wind up taking a vote and eating pizza. It was hard to be seductive over tomato sauce. He couldn't even impress her by taking her to the ballet or the symphony. The nearest performances were in Miami and she'd never even consider going with him and staying overnight, not after what had happened last time.

He knew, despite her denials, that she was every bit as attracted to him as he was to her. In fact, if he had to put a label on what they were both feeling, he would call it love. He was the first to admit he hadn't had all that much experience with the emotion. On those rare occasions when he'd even allowed himself to believe in its existence, he'd imagined it to be more pleasurable than this, more carefree. Instead it seemed to be made up of giddy highs and astonishingly painful lows. And, in their case, instead of a simple, joyous union between two consenting adults, it seemed to involve a package deal that brought out protective instincts so deep he was shaken by them.

He wanted not just Ann's happiness, but Jason's and Tracy's and Paul's and David's and Tommy's and

Melissa's. When any one of them hurt, he hurt. He knew Ann felt the same way...about the six children. Her devotion to them was unquestioning and freely given. He was the only person she didn't trust enough to allow herself to love without hesitation. She was still terrified that he would walk out on them, leaving the kids shaken and her heart in tatters.

Their relationship needed time. He had to prove to her that he wasn't going anywhere, that his wandering days were long past. The only way to do that was to stick around. Unfortunately, his role in the Marathon project was nearing completion. In another month or so he'd be able to move back to Miami and make only occasional site visits. Unless he could dream up an excuse to stay, he was out of here by early April at the latest.

He was still trying to think of a solution to his dilemma when Tracy came out of the house.

"Hank?" she called hesitantly.

"Over here."

She walked over and settled down cross-legged on the ground beside the hammock.

"What's up?" he asked when she didn't say anything.

"Do you think it would be okay if I borrowed the car tomorrow night?"

"I'm not the person you should be asking."

"I can't ask Ann."

"Why not? She's always let you use her car before. Are you planning to go someplace she wouldn't approve of?"

"Not exactly."

"That's not an explanation."

"I know."

"And you're not going to say any more?"

He could see her shake her head. "Then I guess you're going to have to forget about the car."

"How about your truck? Could I use that?"

"Not without an explanation."

"Don't you trust me?"

Hoping she couldn't see the grin in the nighttime shadows, he said, "Not fair, young lady."

"But if you really trusted me, you'd take my word that this is really, really important and you wouldn't ask any questions."

"If you were twenty-two, I might agree, but you are barely eighteen."

"So I can't take the truck, either?"

Hank sat up in the hammock and turned until he could get a good look at Tracy's face. "Why is this so important? Can't you tell me that?"

"No. It would ruin everything."

"Ruin what?"

She jumped to her feet. "Oh, never mind. I'll think of something else."

She started across the lawn, her shoulders slumped dejectedly. Hank debated for several seconds. He knew Tracy was a good driver and she was a responsible girl.

"Tracy."

She stopped and waited.

"You can borrow the truck."

She ran back and threw her arms around him. "Thanks, Hank. You won't be sorry. I promise I'll be really, really careful."

He tilted her chin up. "You'd better be or Ann will kill both of us."

Tracy picked the truck up at the construction site

the next afternoon at three. Hank got a ride home with his foreman a couple of hours later. As he walked into the kitchen, he took one look around and came to a speechless halt.

The table was covered with a white damask cloth. Two candles had been placed in the center, along with a huge bowl of pink roses. The scent filled the room. Two places had been set with the good china, the silver and the crystal. For once, in fact, everything matched. Jason's iPod was sitting in its dock with the detachable speakers on either side of the table. Hank scanned the playlist and grinned. Someone had very romantic taste and he had a suspicion who it was. Tracy. She had plotted this. That's what all the secrecy had been about. And she had borrowed the truck to take the kids away for the evening, so he and Ann could be alone.

A setup like this called for a spectacular meal. Tracy, however, was a little shaky when it came to cooking. He could hardly wait to see what she'd left in the oven. He opened the door, leaned down and peered in. Some sort of chicken dish was simmering at the low temperature. It smelled and looked superb. Startled, he stood and looked around, chuckling when he saw the empty boxes from a gourmet grocery store. In front of the microwave he found vegetables and rice, and in the refrigerator there were bowls heaped with strawberries beside a pitcher of cream. Instead of wine, there was a chilled bottle of sparkling cider. It appeared they'd thought of everything. All this effort removed any uncertainty he might have had about how the kids would feel about a closer, more permanent involvement between him and Ann.

If they'd gone to this much trouble, the least he could

do was cooperate. He took a hurried shower, found a pair of decent slacks among the jeans he'd brought with him and a pinstriped shirt. He looked at the sports jacket hanging in the closet and shrugged. What the hell! He might as well go all out. Annie had never seen him dressed in anything more formal than jeans. Not since Liz and Todd's wedding, anyway. It hadn't made much of an impression on her then, but maybe now it would be just the thing to throw her off balance and into his arms.

When he was ready, he went back to the kitchen, chose a classical piece from the iPod, lit the candles, dimmed the lights and poured himself a glass of cider. Then he settled back to wait. As the minutes ticked by, his nerves stretched so taut he was afraid they'd snap. It was after six when he finally heard her car pull into the driveway. Feeling like a teenager on prom night, he stood and faced the door.

Ann stepped through the door and without even looking around, flipped on the lights. Hank took one look at her expression and his spirits fell. She didn't seem surprised. She didn't seem pleased. She looked as though someone had dealt a blow to her midsection from which she was still reeling.

"Annie," he said softly, taking a tentative step toward her. She looked toward him, her eyes finally focusing on his face. There was so much hurt there. Her cheeks were streaked with tears. "Annie love, what's happened? Are you okay?"

He folded his arms around her and felt a shudder sweep through her. "Please, sweetheart, you're scaring me. What's wrong?"

Her arms crept around his waist and she clung to

him, sobbing as though her heart had broken. Hank felt something tear loose inside him as he held her. "It's okay," he murmured, rubbing his hands up and down her back as if to ward off a chill. "Shh. It's okay."

"No," she said, her voice ragged from all the tears she'd shed.

"Then tell me. Let me help."

"It's Melissa."

Hank's heart began to hammer harder. Melissa, dear God, if anything had happened to their baby, if Tracy had had an accident…

"What…" he began and realized that his own throat was so thick with emotion he could barely speak.

"They called."

"Who called?" he demanded, his fingers digging into her arms. "Dammit, Ann, is she hurt? What?"

"They want to take her away from me."

Chapter 14

"Take her away?" Hank repeated in a daze. There was a huge knot in the pit of his stomach. He kept remembering the warm, tender feelings that crept over him whenever Melissa held out her chubby little arms for a hug, whenever she stared at him with those huge, innocent blue eyes. The unexpected power of those emotions had held him captive for weeks now.

"What does that mean?" he asked, studying the agonized expression in Ann's eyes and feeling his own chest constrict in pain. "Can they do that? Can they just come in here and take her?"

"They can do whatever they want," Ann said wearily. "She's a ward of the state. I'm just her foster mother."

"But why would they take her away? Can't they see how traumatic it would be for a three-year-old to be uprooted again? Explain it to them. You're more than

just a foster mother. You're a psychologist. Surely they'll
listen."

"It's not that simple. The mother has finally relin-
quished custody, which makes Melissa eligible for
adoption." Ann's bleak, uncommonly submissive tone
only heightened his dismay. Her eyes were luminous
with tears. "There's this couple, Hank. They want her."
Though she was trying to sound so brave, her voice
broke, carving a jagged path through his heart. "They
want to adopt my baby and the state thinks it would be
best for Melissa to have two parents. How can I argue?"

Hank tried to gather his composure, when what he
felt like doing was bashing his fist into a wall or better
yet into the face of whatever bureaucrat was making
this heartless decision. Couldn't they see that no one
would ever be a better parent to Melissa than Annie?

Right now, though, her vulnerability left him shaken.
She needed him to be strong. She needed him to cling
to for once. Now was no time for him to be falling apart
or charging out of here and doing something rash. They
needed to do some clear thinking. He didn't know the
ins and outs of state regulations, but surely there was a
way to block this. Melissa was theirs. She loved them.
They loved her. It was as simple—and as complex,
apparently—as that.

"We'll fight it," he said flatly. "There must be things
we can do. We'll apply to adopt her ourselves. Sit down,
I'll make you some tea and we can talk about it."

Obviously drained, Ann sank down in a chair,
folded her arms on the table and lowered her head. His
thoughts reeling, Hank put the teakettle on the stove
and tried to calm down. His outrage at the injustice of
this wouldn't help now. He poured the tea finally and

put the cup in front of her. "Drink it, Annie. It'll make you feel better."

She lifted her head and managed a trembling grin. "Don't tell me now you've finally become a convert."

"To what?" he said, staring at her blankly as he sank down in a chair across from her.

"Tea."

"Annie, I don't care what you drink. Personally, I could use a stiff shot of Scotch. The point is we have to make some decisions and I gather we don't have a lot of time."

She shook her head wearily. "Not we, Hank. Me. I have to make the decisions. I appreciate your concern, but it's my problem."

His heart hammering, Hank stood so fast his chair went spinning. It crashed into the counter. "Dammit, Annie, this isn't just some friendly concern on my part. Don't you think this matters to me, too? That little girl is mine just as much as if I'd fathered her." He slammed the chair back against the table and leaned down until he was mere inches from her. She swallowed convulsively as he said with slow, furious emphasis, "I have tucked her into bed. I have read her stories. I've bandaged her cuts and kissed away her tears. Dammit, Annie, I love her, too!" He fought to hold back tears of rage and frustration.

Looking stunned by his tirade, Ann simply stared at him. "You love her," she whispered wonderingly, touching a finger to his cheek. Her voice shook.

He hunkered down beside her and clasped her hands. "Of course I love her. What did you think?"

"I don't know. I guess I thought you'd just gotten used to her, to all of us."

"Annie, I love every crazy, troublesome, charming, infuriating person in this house and that includes you," he said fervently, cupping her chin in his hand. "If I had my way, we'd be married by tomorrow morning and we'd adopt every one of those kids and maybe even add a couple more of our own."

"But you…you've always been so…" She threw up her hands. "You know, so single."

He grinned. "So alone. That's what I've been, Annie. I've been on my own emotionally for so many years that I didn't know what it could be like to have other people in my life, to share good times and bad times, to have someone waiting for me at the end of the day. I was scared to death to enjoy it, because I was so afraid that by morning it could all be gone. I've finally accepted the fact that real love doesn't go away. It doesn't vanish in a puff of smoke. Sometimes you might have to work a little to hang on to it and it's not always magic and rainbows, but it's the best thing we're ever likely to have going for us. The tough times make the magic even more special and the rainbows even brighter."

Ann's smile trembled tentatively on her lips before finally turning bright. She curved her hand over his and held it against her cheek. Tears slid down, pooling against their clasped fingers. "You can be downright eloquent when you try, Hank Riley."

He drew her palm to his lips and kissed it. "As long as I seem to be getting through to you at last, did I mention again that I want to marry you?"

"You mentioned it, but once again you didn't ask."

"Then let me correct that at once. Will you marry me, Annie?" He gestured around the kitchen. "The kids went to all this trouble to set the scene. We wouldn't want to waste it."

Ann's heart began to beat so wildly she thought it would be impossible for her chest to contain it. For the first time she actually believed in Hank's love. She'd actually seen the devastation in his eyes when she'd told him about Melissa. It had been every bit as shattering as her own. He wasn't like the man who'd walked out of her life just because she was having a baby. Hank wasn't afraid of problems. He wanted to face them with her. An unbelievable sense of joy and relief welled up inside her. He was offering her everything she'd ever wanted, everything she'd dreamed of and never dared to expect: love, companionship, strength and family.

Marrying Hank would be a way out. Together they might be able to fight the state's decision about Melissa and adopt her themselves. She wouldn't have to give up her baby. The thought of losing Melissa had affected her more deeply than anything that had happened in the past. Though letting go of other foster children had never been easy, she'd always been able to get beyond the sharp tug of emotion to accept the decisions as being best for the child. But she'd never had Hank in her life before. She'd never felt that she, too, could offer a complete family. She had begun thinking of their relationship as permanent long before this moment and the prospect of losing Melissa had shaken the fantasy. Marrying Hank would allow her to keep it alive.

But was that the only reason she was considering his proposal? If Hank had proposed tonight under any other circumstances, would she have said yes? She couldn't be sure. Only a few days earlier she'd turned him down without hesitation. She almost laughed at the trap in which she'd caught herself. She finally knew without any lingering doubts that Hank was in love with her, was content with what they had found together. She even knew with blinding clarity that she was truly, deeply in love with him. But her motives in marrying him? They would be less than pure.

"I can't, Hank," she whispered finally. "I can't marry you. Not now."

She saw the astonishment register in his eyes, then the flash of hurt. "Why the hell not?"

If she hadn't been so miserable, she might have laughed at his purely masculine indignation. "Because it wouldn't be fair."

"Fair to whom? I love you. There's no doubt about that, right?"

She nodded, believing at last that it was true.

"And you love me? Or am I being too arrogant in assuming that?"

"No. I do," she admitted openly for the first time.

"And it could solve the problem with Melissa?"

"It might."

"Then could you explain for the benefit of my apparently simple brain why we can't get married."

"What if the only reason we're doing it is because of Melissa?"

"Didn't you hear a word I just said? We're in love, Annie. We've admitted it. No more hiding from it. People who are in love get married. They have families. They live happily ever after. It's the thing to do."

She sighed. "I know. It's the timing."

"That is the craziest, most ridiculous, dumbest bit of reasoning I have ever heard in my life," he said, dropping her hands and pacing around the kitchen, bumping into things and knocking them aside until it looked as though a war had been waged in the middle of the room.

"Hank, sit down," she said, deciding she'd better calm him down before he started breaking things.

"I don't want to sit. I want to break things," he said, voicing her fears. As if to demonstrate, he picked up a glass and hurled it across the room. It shattered against the wall. Apparently satisfied with the minimal expression of violence, he calmly walked over and cleaned it up, while Ann just stared at him.

"Feel better?" she said finally.

He dropped the shards of glass into the trash and regarded her sheepishly. "Frankly, no."

"Good. Then you won't bother to break anything else, will you?"

"Don't count on it."

An untimely chuckle emerged from somewhere deep inside her. He scowled ferociously. "I'm sorry," she said at once.

"Annie, what are we going to do about this?"

"We'll think about it. I'm sure with two well-educated brains between us we can come up with a rational decision."

"Maybe that's the problem," he said, suddenly looming over her, his expression fierce. "Maybe we've been too rational about this for too long. Maybe it's time we just acted."

Something about the hungry, determined look in his eyes made her pulse leap and then race wildly. "What do you mean?"

"This," he said, pulling her up and slanting his mouth over hers. His lips were hard and demanding, his tongue

persuasive. He backed her against the kitchen counter
and pinned her there, his body pressed tight against
hers. Ann moaned a halfhearted protest, but it was
swallowed by yet another marauding kiss as his hands
set her body on fire and melted the last of her resistance.
His arousal hard against her set off a sweet ache that
grew in intensity until it reached an almost unbearable
tension.

Hank slid a hand beneath her skirt, running his
fingers along her thigh until he reached the moist
heat at the apex. Ann felt the room spin crazily as
sensations raced through her. Raw, urgent need sprang
to life, tearing away the last shred of sanity. She began
frantically working at the buttons on his shirt. Why had
he worn the damnable thing tonight of all nights, when
she needed to be able to slide his shirt away in one easy
movement? When she needed so very badly to touch
the rippling muscles beneath? Finally she freed the shirt
from his pants. She ran her hands over his chest, then
pressed kisses on the heated flesh, finally finding the
masculine nipple that was flat and already hard with
arousal. She felt Hank tremble as she circled that nipple
with her tongue again and again.

The pain that she'd felt when she'd heard that Melissa
might be taken away began to ease, lost for the moment
in other sensations, the way his flesh came alive beneath
her fingers, the warm, musky scent of him.

"Not here, sweetheart," she heard Hank murmur as
he slid an arm beneath her knees and lifted her off the
floor. When they reached her room, he set her slowly
back on her feet, then reached behind her to lock the
door and flip on the light.

The trip through the house had restored some of

Ann's sanity. "Hank, this is crazy. There are six children in this house."

"Not at the moment."

"Where are they?"

"Out."

"Out where?" she said, then lost track of the question's importance as his lips found an especially sensitive spot behind her knee.

"Oh, my," she gasped softly, her eyes widening.

"That's good?"

"Very good."

"How about here?"

"Hmm."

"And here?"

She giggled and he laughed. "Not so good there," he said. "Okay, how about here?"

Here was…incredible, she thought with another gasp of pleasure. The laughter died and the loving became very serious indeed. Here, in his arms, she had no more doubts. Here she forgot about the past, stopped worrying about the future and lived only for the present.

She found herself letting go, allowing her body to soar, relinquishing her hard-won control without fear. Hank would never harm her. He would never take her anyplace he wouldn't go himself. And, as she felt him explode deep inside her, she believed with all her heart that he would never leave her, that their love could see them through anything. That faith sent her over the edge and, clinging tightly to him, she cried out his name in joyous surrender.

Hank propped himself up on his elbow and studied the woman lying next to him. Her cheeks were still flushed, her dark hair damp and feathered around her face. The tips of her breasts were rose-hued and puckered in the chilly air. She was so beautiful, with a radiance that began inside and left her glowing. Her skin was as smooth as ivory. Her lips had the power to tempt him beyond reason. Her slightest touch could heat his body in a way that drove him to distraction. His heart was filled to bursting with the sheer wonder of loving her.

He watched the steady rise and fall of her chest, heard the slight catch in her breath, the gentle sigh.

Her eyes still closed, a smile playing about her still-swollen lips, she said quietly, "This won't solve our problem, you know."

"If you think that, then you haven't been listening."

"Listening?" Her smile grew. "Is this your way of conversing?"

"Can you think of any more intimate form of communication?"

"No, but some people think words cover more ground and offer more clarity."

He shook his head. "Then they've never experienced the language of love." He gently cupped her breast as he gazed into her eyes, his thumb insistently grazing the sensitive peak. "What am I saying now?"

When the color rose in her cheeks and she tried to look away, he tilted her chin up until she was forced to face him.

"I'm saying I love you." He smoothed his hand over the curve of her hip. "And now?"

Ann swallowed convulsively as he continued the slow strokes.

"Well?" he prodded.

"I love you," she said hesitantly.

"Very good. You're catching on."

"Thank you, professor."

"Should I continue?"

"Please do."

He did—and no lesson had ever been more exhilarating, no discussion more thrilling.

And when they were lying tangled together, breathless from experiencing all the nuances of the language of love, he whispered, "Have I made myself clear yet?"

"Very clear."

"Then you'll marry me?"

"Yes," she said finally and without hesitation. "Yes, Hank, I'll marry you."

He grinned at her. "It's about time. I was running out of arguments."

"Somehow I doubt that." She cuddled more closely into his side.

"Annie."

"Hmm?"

"I hate to ruin a good moment, but the kids..."

"Oh, my God!" she said, sitting straight up and pulling the sheet up to her chin.

"Settle down," he soothed. "They're not in the room, but they are likely to be getting home soon and we probably should not be in here."

"Good thinking," she said, gathering up her clothes, which had been flung from one end of the bedroom to the other. "You get out. I'm taking a shower."

He grabbed her hand and pulled her back. "One last kiss."

Her lips were still warm and tasted of salt and musk. It was all he could do to relinquish her. Finally, swatting her gently on the bottom, he said, "Go. I'll meet you in the kitchen."

Fifteen minutes later, they were seated at the kitchen table with the overly done meal in front of them when the truck doors began slamming outside.

"You'd better eat fast," Hank advised. "We were supposed to eat the chicken before it turned to leather."

Ann's eyes widened. "You mean you weren't responsible for all this?"

"Nope. Your sweet, innocent children set the scene tonight for the great seduction. I think they got tired of leaving it to us."

"Are we supposed to tell them how it turned out?"

Hank glanced pointedly at Ann's glowing face and her hastily donned bathrobe. "I don't think we'll have to say a word," he said as the back door creaked open.

Tracy stuck her head in hesitantly. "Don't mind us. I just wanted you to know we're home. We'll go in the front door."

"That's not really necessary," Ann said.

"It's not?" Tracy said, her voice instantly filled with disappointment. "How come?"

"Because this is your house and you don't have to go tiptoeing around in the dark outside."

Tracy glanced at Hank hopefully. "Did you like dinner?"

"It was very special. Now why don't you just go ahead and ask what you really want to know?"

At his teasing tone, a broad grin broke over her face. "Did it work?"

He glanced over at Ann and winked. "That depends on exactly what you had in mind. I did ask Ann to marry me."

There was a barely smothered whoop from the crowd of kids huddling in the dark behind Tracy. The door opened wider and all six faces peered at Ann.

"And?" Jason demanded impatiently.

"I said yes."

"Oh, wow!" Tracy sighed dreamily.

"Fantastic!"

"We're going to be a real family?" David asked.

"A real family," Hank promised. His eyes intent on Ann's, he added, "All of us."

With Hank's promise echoing in her ears, she held out her arms to Melissa, who came running. With a lump in his throat, Hank watched the chubby-cheeked toddler crawl into Ann's lap and lay her head sleepily against Ann's breast. No matter what it took, he vowed to fight for Melissa and win. He would keep them all together.

"I think we should celebrate," Jason said, sounding very mature until his voice skidded up, then back down, in midsentence.

"Good idea," Hank and Ann concurred as Jason opened the refrigerator door, then turned to stare at them, a puzzled expression on his face. "The strawberries and stuff are still in here. What have you guys been doing all this time? We've been gone for hours."

"Jason!" Tracy said. "How dumb are you?"

He immediately blushed a fiery shade of red, then

grinned with impish enthusiasm. "I guess it worked pretty good."

"I guess it did," Hank said, reaching over to take Ann's hand. "Better than I'd ever dreamed possible."

Epilogue

The backyard was filled with pink balloons. They were tied to the backs of lawn chairs. Like bunches of colorful coconuts, they dangled from the palm trees. They floated above the redwood picnic table that was laden with brightly wrapped packages.

"Hey, Dad, what do you think?" David called as Hank rounded the corner of the house.

Hank followed the sound of David's voice and finally spotted him high up in the banyan tree. "I think you'd better get down from that tree before your mother catches you and has a heart attack."

"His mother is up here with him," Ann said, parting the branches and peering down at him. Hank's breath caught in his throat. "We're decorating."

"Ann," he began in a choked voice as his heart thumped unsteadily. The woman obviously had nerves of steel. His own had taken a decided beating over the past year.

"Don't be such a worrywart," she chided, lowering herself awkwardly from a sturdy limb to the top rung of a stepladder. "I was climbing ladders long before you came along. Who do you think painted the house?"

That was not a point he cared to discuss while his wife was dangling from a tree. He still hadn't gotten accustomed to the hodgepodge of colors. For the moment, he intended to stick to her tree-climbing activities.

"You were not six months' pregnant at the time," he reminded her, holding the ladder steady as she descended.

"I *am* a little more ungainly than usual," she admitted, patting her swollen belly. "You never answered us. How do the balloons look?"

"Plentiful. Who's blowing them up?"

"Liz. Last time I checked her lips were turning blue. You might want to relieve her."

"I don't do balloons," he said emphatically.

"What exactly do you do?" she teased. "I haven't seen you since breakfast. Have you been hiding?"

"I've been having a long talk with Tracy's new boyfriend."

Ann groaned. "Hank, you have not cross-examined that boy, have you? Tracy will kill you."

"No, she won't," he said smugly. "She gave me the list of questions."

"In that case, did he pass?"

"For a nineteen-year-old with pimples and hair longer than Tracy's, he displays remarkable maturity. If they date no more than once a month, I might consider giving them permission to marry in another five or ten years."

Ann rolled her eyes. "I'm sure she'll appreciate that. Has Jason gotten home yet?"

"He and Paul are inside putting together Melissa's new dollhouse. He's already made several modifications to the original design. Todd's so impressed, he's in there now trying to convince him to study architecture."

"Where's Melissa?"

"With Tommy. They're playing house."

Ann's eyebrows shot up. "Isn't she a little young for that?"

"Apparently not. She thinks Liz and Todd brought Amy especially to play the baby. Amy can't crawl quite fast enough to get away from them." He grinned at her. "Does that account for all of them, mother hen?"

She grinned ruefully. "I suppose so."

He reached out and took her hand. "Then come with me. I have a surprise for you."

"For me? It's Melissa's birthday."

"Just come," he said, leading her in through the front door so they wouldn't be disturbed. When he had her alone, he handed her a thick, official-looking envelope. He'd already examined the contents.

Hope and fear warred in her eyes as she took it. She fingered it nervously, but made no move to take the papers from inside. "Hank?"

"It's official. Melissa's ours."

A smile trembled on her lips and tears streamed down her cheeks. "She's really ours?"

"Really. It says so in black-and-white."

She clutched the envelope tightly, then threw her arms around him. That familiar sense of wonder filled

Hank's heart. They had it all, more than he'd ever imagined himself having.

"Hank, isn't this the most wonderful day?" Ann said with a heartfelt sigh. As she rested her head against his shoulder she placed his hand over the swell of her stomach. As if aware of his presence, their baby gave a sure, emphatic kick.

"Definitely a football player," he said with pride.

"A ballet dancer," she countered.

"Why are you fighting?" a little voice asked from the doorway.

"We're not fighting," Ann told Melissa. "We're discussing."

"Mommy tends to discuss rather forcefully," Hank explained as Ann poked him in the ribs.

"Isn't it time for my party yet?"

"It's time, short stuff," Hank concurred. "How about a ride to the backyard?"

Melissa's eyes lit up as Hank swooped her onto his shoulders, then held out his hand to help Ann to her feet.

"Let's go celebrate," he said, his gaze catching Ann's and holding. "Melissa, don't forget to make a wish before you blow out the candles on your cake."

"I already made one last year," she confided, leaning down to peer into his eyes from an upside-down angle.

"And what did you wish for?"

"I wished for a mommy and daddy, and you know what?" She tapped a tiny finger against his lips.

"What?" Hank said, exchanging a look with Ann.

"It worked," she said happily. "I got a mommy and daddy now."

Ann slid her arm around his waist as Hank said, "You

sure do, half-pint. And nobody in the whole wide world could love you any more."

Melissa tugged impatiently on his beard. "Now can I open my presents, please?"

He lowered her to the ground. "Go to it, kid."

As Melissa raced across the yard, the whole family gathered around. Ann looked up into Hank's face, her eyes shining. "No matter what's in all those packages," she said, "I don't think there's anything to compare with the gift we got."

"That's right," he agreed, lowering his lips to capture hers. "Ours is going to last a lifetime."

* * * * *

To Gail Chasan,
for helping me reach my own dreams.
Many, many thanks.

LIGHT THE STARS

USA TODAY Bestselling Author

RaeAnne Thayne

RAEANNE THAYNE

finds inspiration in the beautiful northern Utah mountains, where she lives with her husband and three children. Her books have won numerous honors, including three RITA® Award nominations from the Romance Writers of America and a Career Achievement Award from *RT Book Reviews* magazine.

RaeAnne loves to hear from readers and can be reached through her website at www.raeannethayne.com.

Chapter 1

On his thirty-sixth birthday, Wade Dalton's mother ran away.

She left him a German chocolate cake on the kitchen counter, two new paperback mysteries by a couple of his favorite authors and a short but succinct note in her loopy handwriting.

Honey,
Happy birthday. I'm sorry I couldn't be there to celebrate with you but by the time you read this we'll be in Reno and I'll be the new Mrs. Quinn Montgomery. I know you'll think I should have told you but my huggy bear thought it would be better this way. More romantic. Isn't that sweet? You'll love him, I promise! He's handsome, funny, and makes me feel like I can touch my

dreams again. Tell the children I love them and I'll see them soon.

P.S. Nat's book report is due today. Don't let her forget it!

P.P.S. Sorry to leave you in the lurch like this but I figured you, Seth and Nat could handle things without me for a week. Especially you. You can handle anything.

Don't take this wrong, son, but it doesn't hurt for you to remember your children are more important than your blasted cattle.

Be back after the honeymoon.

Wade stared at the note for a full five minutes, the only sound in the Cold Creek Ranch kitchen the ticking of the pig-shaped clock Andi had loved above the stove and the refrigerator compressor kicking to life.

What the hell was he supposed to do now?

His mother, Marjorie, and this huggy bear creature couldn't have chosen a worse time to pull their little disappearing act. Marjorie knew it, too, blast her hide. He needed her help! He had six hundred head of cattle to get to market before the snow flew, a horse show and auction in Cheyenne in a few weeks, and a national TV news crew coming in less than a week to film a feature on the future of the American cattle ranch.

He was supposed to be showing off the innovations he'd made to the ranch in the last few years, showing the Cold Creek in the best possible light.

How was he supposed to make sure everything was ready and running smoothly while he changed Cody's diapers and chased after Tanner and packed Nat's lunch?

He read the note again, anger beginning to filter through the dismayed shock. Something about what she had written seemed to thrum through his consciousness like a distant, familiar guitar chord. He was trying to figure out what when he heard the back-porch door creak and a moment later his youngest brother stumbled into the kitchen, bleary-eyed and in need of a shave.

"Coffee. I need it hot and black and I just realized I'm out down at my place."

Wade glared at him, seizing on the most readily available target for his frustration and anger. "You look like hell."

Seth shrugged. "Got in late. It was ladies' night down at the Bandito and I couldn't leave all those sweet girls shooting pool by themselves. Where's the coffee?"

"There isn't any coffee. Or breakfast, either. I don't suppose you happened to see Mom sneaking out at two in the morning when you were dragging yourself and, no doubt, one or two of those sweet girls back to the guesthouse?"

His brother blinked a couple of times to clear the remaining cobwebs from his brain. "What?"

Wade tossed the note at him and Seth scrubbed his bleary eyes before picking it up. A range of emotions flickered across his entirely too charming features—shock and confusion, then an odd pensiveness that raised Wade's hackles.

"Did you know about this?" he asked.

Seth slumped into a kitchen chair, avoiding his gaze. "Not this, precisely."

"What *precisely* did you know about what our dear mother's been up to?" Wade bit out.

"I knew she was emailing some guy she met through

that life coach she's been talking to. I didn't realize it was serious. At least not run-off-to-Reno serious."

Suddenly this whole fiasco made a grim kind of sense and Wade realized what about Marjorie's note had struck that odd, familiar chord. *By the time you read this I'll be the new Mrs. Quinn Montgomery,* she had written.

Montgomery was the surname of the crackpot his mother had shelled out a small fortune to in the last six months, all in some crazy effort to better her life.

Her "life coach"—Caroline Montgomery.

He knew the name well since he'd chewed Marjorie out plenty the last time he'd balanced her checkbook for her and had found the name written on several hefty checks.

This was all this Caroline Montgomery's fault. It had to be. She must have planted ideas in Marjorie's head about how she wasn't happy, about how she needed more out of life. Fun, excitement. Romance. Then she introduced some slick older man—a brother? An uncle?— to bring a little spice into a lonely widow's world.

What had been so wrong with Marjorie's life, anyway, that she'd needed to find some stranger to fix it?

Okay, his mother had a few odd quirks. Today was not only his birthday, it was exactly the eighteen-year anniversary of his father's death and in those years, his mother had pursued one wacky thing after another. She did yoga, she balanced her chakras instead of her checkbook, she sponsored inflammatory little book-club meetings at the Pine Gulch library where she and her cronies read every controversial female empowerment self-help book they could find.

He had tried to be understanding about it all. Marjorie's marriage to Hank Dalton hadn't exactly been a happy one. His father had treated his mother with the same cold condescension he'd wielded like a club against his children. Once his father's death had freed Marjorie from that oppressive influence, Wade couldn't blame her for taking things a little too far in the opposite direction.

Besides, when he'd needed her in those terrible, wrenching days after Andrea's death, Marjorie had come through. Without him even having to ask, she'd packed up her crystals and her yoga mat and had moved back to the ranch to help him with the kids. He would have been lost without her, a single dad with three kids under the age of six, one of them only a week old.

He knew she wasn't completely happy with her life but he'd never thought she would go this far. She wouldn't have, he thought, if it hadn't been for this scheming Caroline Montgomery and whatever male relative she was in cahoots with.

He heard a belligerent yell coming from upstairs and wanted to pound his head on the table a few times. Six-thirty in the morning and it was already starting. How the hell was he going to do this?

"Want me to get Cody?" Seth asked as the cries rose in volume. *Gramma, Gramma, Gramma.*

Wade had to admit, the offer was a tempting one, but he forced himself to refuse. They were *his* children and he was the one who would have to deal with them.

He took off his denim jacket and hung his Stetson on the hook by the door.

"I'm on it. Just go take care of the stock and then we've all got to bring in the last hay crop we cut yesterday. The weather report says rain by afternoon so we've got to get it in fast. I'll figure something out with the kids and get out there to help as soon as I can."

Seth opened his mouth to say something then must have thought better of it. He nodded. "Right. Good luck."

You're going to need it. His brother left the words unspoken but Wade heard them anyway.

He couldn't agree more.

Two hours later, Wade was rapidly coming to the grim realization that he was going to need a hell of a lot more than luck.

"Hold still," he ordered a squirmy, giggling Cody as he tried to stick on a diaper. Through the open doorway into the kitchen, he could hear Tanner and Natalie bickering.

"Daaaad," his eight-year-old daughter called out, "Tanner's flicking Cheerios at me. Make him stop! He's getting the new shirt Grandma bought me all wet and blotchy!"

"Tanner, cut it out," he hollered. "Nat, if you don't quit stalling over your breakfast, you're going to miss the bus and I don't have time to drive you today."

"You never have time for anything," he thought he heard her mutter but just then he felt an ominous warmth hit his chest. He looked down to the changing table to find Cody grinning up at him.

"Cody pee pee."

Wade ground his back teeth, looking down at the wet stain spreading across his shirt. "Yeah, kid, I kind of figured that out."

He quickly fastened the diaper and threw on the

overalls and Spider-Man shirt Cody insisted on wearing, all the while aware of a gnawing sense of inadequacy in his gut.

He wasn't any good at this. He loved his kids but it had been a whole lot easier being their father when Andrea was alive.

She'd been the one keeping their family together. The one who'd scheduled immunizations and fixed Nat's hair into cute little ponytails and played Chutes and Ladders for hours at a time. His role had been the benevolent dad who showed up at bedtime and sometimes broke away from ranch chores for Sunday brunch.

The two years since her death had only reinforced how inept he was at the whole parenting gig. If it hadn't been for Marjorie coming to his rescue, he didn't know what he would have done.

Probably flounder around cluelessly, just like he was doing now, he thought.

He started to carry Cody back to the kitchen to finish his breakfast but the toddler was having none of it. "Down, Daddy. Down," he ordered, bucking and wriggling worse than a calf on his way to an appointment with the castrator.

Wade set his feet on the ground and Cody raced toward the kitchen. "Nat, can you watch Cody for a minute?" he called. "I've got to go change my shirt."

"Can't," she hollered back. "The bus is here."

"Don't forget your book report," he remembered at the last minute, but the door slammed on his last word and he was pretty sure she hadn't heard him.

With a quick order to Tanner to please behave himself for five minutes, he carried Cody upstairs with him and grabbed his last clean shirt out of the closet. The least his mother could have done was wait until *after* laundry day to pull her disappearing act, he thought wryly. Now he was going to have to do that, too.

He grabbed Cody and headed back down the stairs. They had nearly reached the bottom when the doorbell pealed.

"I'll get it," Tanner yelled and headed for the front door, still in his pajamas.

"No, me! Me!" Not to be outdone, Cody squirmed out of Wade's arms and slid down the last few steps. Wade wasn't sure how they did it, but both boys beat him to the door, even though he'd been closer.

Tanner opened it, then turned shy at the strange woman standing before him. Wade couldn't blame him. Their visitor was lovely, he observed as he reached the door behind his sons, with warm, streaky brown hair pulled back into a smooth twisty thing, eyes the color of hot chocolate on a cold winter day and graceful, delicate features.

She wore a tailored russet jacket, tan slacks and a crisp white shirt, with a chunky bronze necklace and matching earrings, a charm bracelet on one arm and a slim gold watch on the other.

Wade had no idea who she was and she didn't seem in any hurry to introduce herself. Probably some tourist who'd taken the wrong road out of Jackson, he thought, and needed help finding her way.

Finally he spoke.

"Can I help you?"

"Oh. Yes." Color flared on those high cheekbones and she blinked a few times as if trying to compose herself. "The sign out front said the Cold Creek Ranch. Is this the right place?"

No. Not a lost tourist. As Tanner peeked around Wade's legs and Cody held his chubby little arms out to be lifted again, Wade's gaze traveled from the woman's pretty, streaky hair to her expensive leather shoes, looking for some clue as to what she might be doing on his front porch.

If she was some kind of ranch supply salesperson, she was definitely a step above the usual. He had a lowering suspicion he'd buy whatever she was selling.

"You found us."

Relief flickered across her expressive features. "Oh, I'm so glad. The directions weren't exactly clear and I stopped at two other ranches before this one. I'd like to see Marjorie Dalton, please."

Yeah, wouldn't they all like to see her right about now? "There I'm afraid you're out of luck. She's not here."

Right before his eyes, the lovely, self-assured woman on his porch seemed to fold into herself. Her shoulders sagged, her mouth drooped and she closed her eyes. When she opened them, he saw for the first time the weariness there and was uncomfortably aware of an odd urge to comfort her, to tuck her close and assure her everything would be all right.

"Can you tell me…that is, do you know where I might find her?"

He didn't want to spill his mother's whereabouts to some strange woman, no matter how she mysteriously plucked all his protective strings. "Why don't you tell me your business with her and I'll get her a message?"

"It's complicated. And personal."

"Then you'll have to come back in a week or so."

He had to hope by then Marjorie would come to her senses and be back where she belonged.

"A week?" His visitor blanched. "Oh no! I'm too late. She's not here, is she?"

"That's what I said, isn't it?"

"No, I mean she's really not here. She's not just in town shopping or something. They've run off, haven't they?"

He stared at her, wariness blooming in his gut. "Who are you and what do you want with my mother?"

The woman gave a weary sigh. "You must be Wade. I've heard a lot about you. My name is Caroline Montgomery. I've been in correspondence with Marjorie for the last six months. I don't know how to tell you this, Mr. Dalton, but I think Marjorie has run off with my father."

The big, gorgeous man standing in front of her with one cute little boy hanging off his belt loop and another in his arms didn't look at all shocked by her bombshell. No, shock definitely wasn't the emotion that hardened his mouth and tightened those stunning blue eyes into dime slots.

He brimmed with fury—toe-curling, hair-scorching anger. Caroline took an instinctive step back, until the weave of her jacket bumped against the peeled log of his porch.

"Your father!" he bit out. "I should have known. What is it they say about apples not falling far from the tree?"

Maybe if she wasn't so blasted tired from traveling all night, she might have known what he was talking about. "I'm sorry?"

"What's the matter, lady? You weren't bilking

Marjorie out of enough with your hefty life-coaching fees so you decided to go for the whole enchilada?"

She barely had time to draw a breath before he went on.

"Quite a racket you and your old man have. How many wealthy widows have you pulled this on? You drag them in, worm out all the details about their financial life, then your old man moves in for the kill."

Caroline wanted to sway from the force of the blow that hit entirely too close to home. She felt sick, hideously sick, and bitterly angry that Quinn would once more put her in this position. How else was all this supposed to look, especially given her father's shady past?

She wouldn't give this arrogant man the satisfaction of knowing he'd drawn blood, though. Instead she forced her spine to straighten, vertebra by vertebra.

"You're wrong."

"Am I?"

"Yes! I was completely shocked by this sudden romance. My father said nothing about it to me—I didn't know he and Marjorie had even met until he sent me an email last night telling me he was flying out to meet her and they were heading straight from here to Reno."

"Why should I believe you?"

"I don't care if you believe me or not! It's the truth."

How much of her life had been spent defending herself because of something Quinn had done? She had vowed she was done with it but now she wondered grimly if she ever would be.

What was Quinn up to? Just once, she wished she knew. With all her heart, she wanted to believe his sudden romance was the love match he had intimated in his email.

I never meant for this to happen. It took us both
completely by surprise. But in just a few short
months I've discovered I can't live without her.
Marjorie is my other half—the missing piece of
my life's puzzle. She knows all my mistakes, all
my blemishes, but she loves me anyway. How
lucky am I?

Caroline was romantic enough to hope Quinn's
hearts-and-flowers email was genuine. Her mother
had been dead for twenty-two years now and, as far as
she knew, her father's love life was as exciting as her
own—i.e., about as thrilling as watching paint dry.

But how could she trust his word, after years of his
schemes and swindles? Especially when the missing
piece of his life's puzzle was one of *her* clients? She
couldn't. She just *couldn't.*

What if Quinn was spinning some new scam? Something involving Marjorie Dalton—and tangentially, Caroline's reputation? She would be ruined. Everything she
had worked so hard for these last five years, her safe,
comfortable, *respectable* life, would crumble away like
a sugar castle in a hurricane.

Caroline knew what was at stake: her reputation,
which in the competitive world of life coaching was
everything. As soon as she'd read his email, she had
been struck with a familiar cold dread and knew she
would have to track him down to gauge his motives
for herself—or to talk him out of this crazy scheme
to marry a woman he had only corresponded with via
email.

Her first self-help book was being released in five
months and if her publisher caught wind of this, they

would not be happy. She'd be lucky if her book wasn't yanked right off the schedule.

That's why she had traveled all night to find herself here at nine in the morning, facing down a gorgeous rancher and his two cute little boys.

But she wasn't going to accomplish anything by antagonizing Marjorie's son, she realized. She took a deep, cleansing breath and forced her expression into a pleasant smile, her voice into the low, calming tones she used with her clients.

"Look, I'm sorry. It's been a long night. I had two connector flights from Santa Cruz and an hour's drive from Idaho Falls to get here and I'm afraid I'm not at my best. May I come in so we can discuss what's to be done about our runaway parents?"

She wasn't sure how he would have answered if the cell phone clipped to his belt hadn't suddenly bleeped.

With a grim glare—at her or at the person waiting on the other end of the line or at the world in general, she didn't know—then gestured for her to come inside.

"Yeah?" he growled into the phone as the toddler in his arms wiggled and bucked to get down. Wade Dalton let the boy down, busy on the phone discussing in increasingly heated tones what sounded like a major problem with some farm machinery. She caught a few familiar words like *stalling out* and *alternator* but the rest sounded like a foreign language.

"We don't have a choice. The baler's got to be fixed today. That hay has to come in," he snapped.

While she listened to his end of the conversation about various options for fixing the recalcitrant machine, Caroline took the opportunity to study Wade Dalton's home.

Though the ranch house had soaring ceilings and gorgeous views of the back side of the Tetons, it was anything but ostentatious. The furniture looked comfortable but worn, toys were jumbled together in one corner, and the nearest coffee table was covered in magazines. An odd assortment of circulations, too, she noticed. Everything from *O*—Marjorie's, she assumed—to *Farm & Ranch Living*.

The room they stood in obviously served as the gathering place for the Dalton family. Cartoons flickered on a big-screen TV in one corner and that's where the little blond toddler had headed after Wade had set him down. She watched him for a moment as he picked up a miniature John Deere and started plowing the carpet, one eye on the screen.

The older boy had vanished. She only had a moment to wonder where in the big house he'd gone when Wade Dalton hung up the phone.

"Sorry. Where were we?" he said.

"Discussing what's to be done about our parents, I believe."

"As I see it, we don't have too many options. It's too late to go after them. I'm assuming they left about midnight, which means they've got a nine-hour head start on us. They'd be married long before we even made it to the Nevada state line. Beyond the fact that I can't leave the ranch right now, I wouldn't know where the hell to even start looking for them in Reno since my mother's not answering her cell phone."

"Neither is Quinn," Caroline said glumly.

"I can't believe Marjorie would do something like this, just run off and leave the kids. This is your doing."

So much for their thirty-second ceasefire. "Mine?"

"You're the one who's been telling her to reach for her dreams or whatever the hell other nonsense you spout in your sessions with her."

"You don't think reaching for dreams is important?"

"Sure I do. But not when it means walking away from your responsibilities."

"Since when are *your* children your mother's responsibility?" she snapped.

Again she had to force herself not to step back from the sudden fury in his eyes. She had to admit she deserved it this time.

"That was uncalled for. I'm sorry," Caroline said quietly. "Marjorie has been caring for Nat and Cody and Tanner for two years. She doesn't see it as a burden at all."

"Right. That's why she's been paying a small fortune to some stranger so you can tell her all the things wrong with her life and how to fix them."

"That's not what I do at all," she insisted. "I try to help my clients make their lives happier and more fulfilling by pointing out some of their own self-destructive behavior and giving them concrete steps toward changing what they're unhappy about. Marjorie was never unhappy about you and your children."

Before she could continue, his phone bleeped again. He ignored it for four rings, then muttered an oath and picked it up.

This conversation was similar to the first, only Wade Dalton seemed to grow increasingly frustrated with each passing second.

"Look," he finally said angrily, "just call the tractor supply place in Rexburg and see if they've got a replacement, then you can send Drifty over to pick it up. I'll be out as soon as I can. If we put the whole crew out there this afternoon, we might still be able to get the hay in before the rain."

He hung up and then faced her again. "I don't have time to get into this with you today, Ms. Montgomery. I'm sorry you came all this way for nothing but I think we're too late to do anything about the two lovebirds. I'll warn you, though, that if your father thinks he's going to touch a penny of the income from this ranch, you're both in for one hell of a fight."

"Warning duly noted," she said tightly, wondering how a woman as fun and bubbly as Marjorie could have such an arrogant jerk for a son, no matter how gorgeous he might be.

She should cut him some slack, Caroline thought as she headed for the door. He obviously had his hands full, a widower with three active children and a busy cattle ranch.

Just as she reached the door, an acrid scent drifted from the back of the house, stopping her in her tracks.

"Do you smell something?" she asked Wade Dalton.

"It's a working ranch. We've got all kinds of smells."

"No, this is different. It smells like something's on fire."

He sniffed the air for a second, then his eyes narrowed. He looked around the gathering room, his eyes on his youngest son still playing on the carpet and the notable absence of the older boy.

"Tanner!" he suddenly roared. "What are you doing?"

"Nothing!" came a small, frightened-sounding voice from the rear of the house. "I'm not doin' anything. Anything at all. Don't come in the kitchen, Daddy, okay?"

Wade closed his eyes for half a second then took off down a hallway at a fast run.

This wasn't any of her business, she knew, but Caroline had no choice but to follow.

Chapter 2

Hot on Wade Dalton's worn boots, Caroline had a quick impression of a large, old-fashioned kitchen painted a sunny yellow with a professional-looking six-burner stove, long breakfast bar and at least eight bow-backed chairs snugged up against a massive, scarred pine table.

She imagined under other circumstances it would be a pleasant, welcoming space, but just now the room was thick with black smoke and the acrid smell of scorched paper and something sickly sweet.

Flames shot up from the stove and she quickly realized why—a roll of paper towels was ablaze next to the gas burner and already flames were scorching up the cabinets.

Even more worrisome, the older of Wade Dalton's sons was standing on a chair he must have pulled up to the stove and his pajamas were perilously close to the small fire.

"I'm sorry, Daddy," the boy sniffled.

"Get down right now!" Wade yelled in that no-argument parental tone reserved for situations like this.

Though she sensed the rancher's harshness stemmed from fear for his son's safety, his words and tone still seemed to devastate the boy into inaction. He froze on his precarious perch until his father had to lift him off the chair and set him on the floor so he could get close enough to assess the cabinets.

Wade picked up the burning mess of towels and dropped them into the sink then returned to survey the damage.

Still, the boy didn't move, standing as if he didn't quite know what was happening. He looked ill, almost shocky, and he stood directly in Wade Dalton's path.

This wasn't any of her business, Caroline reminded herself. Even as she thought it, she found herself moving toward the distraught little boy.

What was his name? Tucker? Taylor? *Tanner.* That was it. "Tanner, why don't we get out of your daddy's way and let him take care of things here, okay?"

He looked at her blankly for a moment, then slipped his hand in hers and let Caroline lead him from the room. She took him into the great room where his little brother was still busy with his trucks, unaffected by the drama playing out in the other room.

She was going to ask if he had a favorite television show she could find for him as a distraction when she noticed his left hand pressed tightly to his pajama top.

A grim suspicion seized her and she leaned down. "Tanner, can I take a look at your hand? Are you hurt?"

His chin wobbled for a moment, then he nodded slowly and pulled his hand away from his chest. He made a small sound of distress when he spread out his fingers—and no wonder.

Caroline gasped at the angry, blistering red splotch covering his palm, roughly twice the size of a quarter. "Oh, honey!"

Her reaction seemed to open the floodgates of emotion. Tears pooled in his huge blue eyes and rolled over pale cheeks. "I didn't mean to start a fire. I didn't mean to! I just wanted to roast marshmallows like me and Nat and Grandma did with Uncle Seth when we went campin'. Do you think my daddy will be mad at me?"

She thought that was a pretty good bet. Wade Dalton seemed mad at the entire world, as a matter of course. How would he treat his son, angry or not? That was the important thing.

"I'm sure he'll just be worried about you," she assured Tanner, though she wasn't at all convinced of that herself.

"He's gonna be so mad. I'm not supposed to be in the kitchen by myself." His tears were coming faster now and she knew she had to do something quick to head them off or he would soon be in hysterics. Action seemed the best antidote.

"Let's just get your hurt taken care of and then we'll worry about your dad, okay?"

He nodded and Caroline thought quickly back to her thin and purely basic knowledge of first aid.

"We need to put some cold water on that," she told Tanner, her mind trying to dredge old lessons she'd learned as a girl. "Do you think you can show me a bathroom?"

"Yeah. There's one right through those doors."

She led him there quickly and filled the sink with cold water, then grasped his wrist and immersed it in the sink, though he wasn't keen on the idea.

"I don't want to," he said, sniffling. "It hurts."

"I know, honey. I'm sorry to make you hurt more but this way we can be sure the burn stops."

"Tannoh owie?"

Caroline looked down and found the youngest one had followed them into the small bathroom. Within fifteen seconds, she wasn't sure what held more interest to him—his brother's owie or the lid of the toilet, which he repeatedly flipped up and down with a nerve-racking clatter each time.

Her repertoire of distractions was severely limited but she thought maybe she could tell him a story or something, just to keep him away from the toilet and away from his brother.

"Hey, kiddo," she began.

"His name is Cody," Tanner informed her, his sniffles momentarily subsiding. "He's two and I'm five. I just had a birthday."

"Five is a fun age," she started, but her words were cut off by a loud and angry voice from outside the room.

"Tanner Michael Dalton! Where are you? Get in here and help me clean up the mess you made!"

Caroline took an instinctive step closer to the boy. What a disagreeable man, she thought, until she remembered that he likely knew nothing about his son's injuries.

"We're in the bathroom," she called down the hall. "Do you think you could come in here for a moment?"

Silence met her request for a full five seconds, then

Wade spoke in an annoyed-sounding voice. "What is it? I'm kind of in the middle of something here."

Suddenly there he was in the doorway, two hundred pounds of angry male looking extremely put-upon, as if she'd pulled him away from saving the world to ask his opinion on what shade of lipstick to use.

This was his own son and she wouldn't let him make her feel guilty for her compassion toward the boy. Caroline tilted her chin up and faced him down.

"We're in the middle of something, too. Something I think you're going to want to see."

He squeezed into a bathroom that had barely held Caroline and two young boys. Throw in a large, gorgeous, angry rancher and the room seemed to shrink to the size of a tissue box.

"What is it?" he asked.

She pointed to Tanner's soaking hand, a vivid, angry red, and watched the boy's father blanch.

He hissed an oath, something she gauged by Tanner's surprised reaction wasn't something the boy normally heard from his father.

She had to admit, the shock and concern on Wade's features went a long way toward making her more sympathetic toward him.

"Tanner!" he exclaimed. "You burned yourself?"

"It was an accident, Daddy."

"Why didn't you say something?"

Tanner shrugged his narrow shoulders. "I was trying to be a big boy, not a b-baby."

The sympathy from his father was apparently more than Tanner's remarkable composure could withstand. The boy's sniffles suddenly turned to wails.

"I'm sorry, Daddy. I'm sorry. I won't do it again. I *won't*, I promise. It hurts a lot."

Wade picked up his son and held him against his broad, denim-covered chest. "Okay, honey. Okay. We'll take care of it, I promise. We'll find your Uncle Jake and he'll fix you right up."

Cody looked from his crying brother to their father's obvious concern and started wailing, from fear or just sympathy, Caroline wasn't sure. Soon the small bathroom echoed with loud sobs.

After a moment of that, Wade's eyes started to look panicky, like he'd just found himself trapped in a cage of snakes—except she had the feeling he would have preferred the snakes to two bawling kids.

Finally Caroline took pity on him and picked up the crying toddler. He was heavier than she expected, a solid little person in a Spider-Man shirt. "You're okay, sweetie. Your brother just has an owie."

The curly blond cherub wiped his nose with his forefinger. "Tan-noh owie."

"Yep. But he'll be okay, I promise."

"Uncle Jake will make it all better," Wade said, a kind of desperate hope in his voice. "Come on, let's go find him."

He led the way out of the room. Once free of the bathroom's confining space, Caroline could finally make her brain function again. She considered the ability to once more take a breath a nice bonus.

Wade carried Tanner toward the front door and she followed with the younger boy in her arms.

"Look, you're going to have enough on your hands at the clinic," she said. "Why don't I stay here with Cody while you take care of Tanner?"

It took a second for Wade's attention to shift from his injured son to her, something she found rather touching—until she saw suspicion bloom on his features.

"No. He can come with us to the clinic."

"Are you sure? I don't mind watching him for you."

She didn't need to hear his answer—the renewed animosity in his eyes was answer enough. "Lady, I don't know you from Adam," he snapped. "I'm not leaving my son here with you."

"Would you like me to come with you and then watch him in the clinic while you're occupied with Tanner's hand?"

He frowned, obviously annoyed by her persistence. Good heavens, did he think she was going to kidnap the child?

"No. He's fine with me. I'm sure there's somebody in Jake's office who could watch Cody while we're in the exam room."

With Tanner in one arm, he scooped up the toddler in the other and carried both boys out the door, toward a huge mud-covered silver pickup truck parked in the circular driveway.

Not sure what to do next, Caroline stood on the broad porch of the ranch house and watched as he strapped both boys into the truck. Wade seemed to have forgotten her very existence. In fact, a moment later he climbed into the driver's seat and drove away without once looking back at the house.

Now that the first adrenaline surge from the fire and dealing with Tanner's burn had passed, Caroline was aware of a bone-deep exhaustion. She had almost forgotten her long night of traveling and the worry over Quinn's whirlwind romance with one of her clients.

Now, as she stood alone on the ranch house porch with a cool October wind teasing the ends of her hair, everything came rushing back.

Since she was apparently too late to stop her father from eloping with Marjorie, she should probably just drive her rental back to the airport and catch the quickest flight to California.

On the other hand, that kitchen was still a mess, she was sure. She could scrub down the smoke-damaged kitchen while Wade was gone, perhaps even fix a warm meal for their return.

It was the least she could do, really. None of this would have happened if her father hadn't run off with Marjorie.

She wasn't breaking her vow, Caroline told herself as she walked back into the house and shut the cool fall air behind her. She wasn't cleaning up after her father's messes, something she had sworn never to do again. She was only helping out a man who had his hands full.

She tried to tell herself she wasn't splitting hairs, but even as she went back into the smoke-damaged kitchen and rolled up her sleeves, she wasn't quite convinced.

"There you go, partner. Now you've got the mummy claw of death to scare Nat with when she comes home from school."

Tanner giggled at his uncle Jake and moved his gauze-wrapped hand experimentally. "It still hurts," he complained.

"Sorry, kid." Jake squeezed his shoulder. "I can give you some medicine so it won't hurt quite so bad. But when you try to put out a fire all by yourself, sometimes you get battle scars. Next time call your dad right away."

"There won't be a next time. Right, Tanner?" Wade said sternly. "You've learned your lesson about roasting marshmallows—or anything else—by yourself."

Tanner sighed. "I guess. I don't like havin' a burn."

Jake straightened. "You were really brave while I was looking at it. I was proud of you, bud. Now you have to be a big kid and make sure you take care of it right. You can't get the bandage wet and you have to try to keep it as clean as you can, okay? Listen to your dad and do what he says."

"Okay." Tanner wiggled off the exam bench. "Can I go ask Carol for my sucker now?"

"Sure. Tell her a big brave kid like you deserves two suckers."

"And a sticker?"

Jake hammed a put-upon sigh. "I guess."

Tanner raised his bandaged hand into the air with delight then rushed out of the exam room, leaving Wade alone with his younger brother.

Unlike old Doc Jorgensen who had run the clinic when they were kids—with his gnarled hands and breath that always smelled of the spearmint toothpicks he chewed—Jake didn't wear a white lab coat in the office. The stethoscope around his neck and the shirt pocket full of tongue depressors gave him away, though.

Wade watched his brother type a few things onto a slender laptop computer—notes for Tanner's chart— and wondered how the little pest in hand-me-down boots and a too-big cowboy hat who used to follow him around the ranch when they were kids had grown into this confident, competent physician.

This wasn't a life Wade would have chosen, either for himself or for his brother, but he had always known Jake hadn't been destined to stay on the ranch. His middle brother was three years younger than he was and, as long as Wade could remember, Jake had carried big dreams inside himself.

He had always read everything he could find and had rarely been without a book in his hand. Whether they'd been waiting at the end of the long drive for the school bus or taking a five minute break from fixing fence lines, Jake had filled every spare moment with learning.

Wade had powerful memories of going on roundup more than once with Jake when his brother would look for strays with one eye and keep the other on the book he'd held.

He loved him. He just never claimed to understand him.

But there was not one second when he'd been anything less than proud of Jake for his drive and determination, for the compassion and caring he showed to the people of Pine Gulch, and for coming home instead of putting his medical skills to work somewhere more lucrative.

After another few seconds of pounding the keys, Jake closed his laptop.

"Well, I'd tell you happy birthday but it sounds like it's a little too late for that."

Wade made a face. "You can say that again. It's been a hell of a day."

"And just think, it's only noon. Who knows what other fun might be in store."

Wade sighed heavily. Noon already and he hadn't done a damn thing all day. He had a million things to do and now he had a little wounded firefighter who couldn't get his bandage dirty to think about.

His mother ought to be here, blast her. He was no good at the nurturing, sympathy thing. Did she ever stop to consider one of the kids might need her to shower kisses and sympathy?

"So what do you suggest we do about Mom?" he asked.

Jake leaned a hip against the exam table, and Wade thought again how he seemed to fit here in this medical clinic, in a way he'd never managed at the Cold Creek.

"What *can* we do? Sounds like the deed is done."

"We don't have to like it, though."

"I don't know. She's been alone a long time. It's been eighteen years since Hank died and even before that, her life with our dear departed father couldn't have been all roses. If this Montgomery guy makes her happy, I think we should stand behind her."

He stared at his brother. The finest education didn't do a man much good if he lost all common sense. "What do you mean, stand behind her? She doesn't even know the guy! How can we possibly support her eloping with a man she's only corresponded with through email and clandestine phone calls? And what kind of slimy bastard runs off with a woman he's never seen in person? He's got to be working some kind of scam. He and the daughter are in it together."

"You don't know that."

"They've got to be. She trolls for unhappy older women through this life-coaching baloney, finds a vulnerable target like Mom, and then he steps in and charms them out of everything they've got."

"You're such a romantic," Jake said dryly.

"I don't have time to be a romantic, damn it. I've got a national television crew coming to the ranch in six days. How can I possibly get ready for this shoot when I've got three kids underfoot every second?"

"You could always cancel it."

He glowered at Jake. "You're not helping."

"Why not? It's just a TV spot."

"Just a *national* TV spot I've been working toward for almost a year! This is huge publicity for the ranch. We're one of only a handful of cattle operations in the country using this high-tech data-collection technique for our stock. You know how much of an investment it was for us but it's all part of our strategy of moving the ranch onto the industry's cutting edge. To be recognized for that right now is a big step for the Cold Creek. I don't know why Mom couldn't have scheduled her big rendezvous *after* the news crew finished."

"So what will you do with the kids?"

"I'm still trying to figure that out. You're the smart one. Any suggestions?"

"You could hire a temporary nanny, just until after the video shoot is over. Didn't Mom's note say she'd be back in a week?"

He started to answer but stopped when he heard Cody wailing from the reception area, something about a "stick-oh."

Wade sighed and headed toward the sound, Jake right behind him.

"Right. A week. Let's hope I'm still sane by then."

Cody fell asleep on the six-mile drive from Jake's clinic in Pine Gulch to Cold Creek Ranch. Tanner, jacked up by the excitement of the morning and probably still running on adrenaline, kept up a steady stream of conversation that didn't give Wade a minute to think about what he was going to do.

Tanner didn't even stop his running commentary during the phone call Wade took on his cell from Seth, who informed him glumly that the shop in Rexburg wouldn't have the part they needed for the baler until the next day. Without it, they wouldn't be able to bring the hay in, which meant they might lose the whole damn crop to the rain.

"I'm almost home. I'll get the boys some lunch and then try to come down and see if we can jury-rig something until tomorrow."

The clouds continued to boil and churn overhead as he drove under the arch that read Cold Creek Land and Cattle Company, and Wade could feel bony fingers of tension dig into his shoulders.

Sometimes he hated the responsibility that came from being the one in charge. He hated knowing he held the livelihood of his own family and those of three other men in his hands, that his every decision could make or break the ranch.

He couldn't just take a week off and play Mr. Mom. Too much depended on him meeting his responsibilities, especially right now.

But who could he ask for help? His mind went through everyone he could think of among their neighbors and friends.

His wife's family had sold their ranch a year ago and her parents were serving in South America as missionaries for their church.

Viviana Cruz was the next logical choice. She owned the small ranch that adjoined the Cold Creek to the west and was his mother's best friend as well as a sort of surrogate grandmother to his kids. Unfortunately, she had left the week before to spend some time with her daughter in Arizona before Maggie's national guard unit shipped out.

He couldn't think of anyone else, off the top of his head. Everyone who came to mind was either busy with their own ranch or their own kids or already had a job.

Seth knew every female with a pulse in a fifty-mile radius. Maybe his brother could think of somebody in his vast network who might be suitable to help with the kids for a week. Though it didn't really have to be a woman, he supposed as he pulled up to the back door of the ranch house.

"Can I watch TV?" Tanner asked when Wade unhooked him from his booster seat.

"Sure. Just no soap operas."

He grinned at the wrinkled-up face Tanner made. "Yuck," the boy exclaimed. "I hate those shows. Grandma watches them sometimes but they're so *boring!*"

By that, Wade assumed he didn't have to worry about Tanner developing a deep and abiding love for drama in the afternoons.

His injury apparently forgotten for now, Tanner skipped up the steps and into the house, leaving Wade to carefully unhook the sleeping Cody and heft him to his shoulder, holding his breath that he could keep the boy asleep. Cody murmured something unintelligible then burrowed closer.

So far so good, Wade thought as he went inside and headed straight up the back stairs to Cody's bedroom.

This was always the tricky part, putting him into his

bed without disturbing him enough to wake him. He held his breath and lowered him to the crib mattress.

Cody arched a little and slid toward the top edge, where he liked to sleep, but didn't open his eyes. After a breathless moment, Wade covered him with his quilt, then returned downstairs to find Tanner and figure something out for lunch.

He found Tanner in the great room with the TV on, the volume turned low.

"Can you even hear that?" Wade asked.

Tanner answered by putting a finger to his mouth. "Quiet, Daddy. You'll wake up the lady."

Wade frowned. "What lady?"

Tanner pointed to the other couch, just out of his field of vision. Wade moved forward for a better view and stared at the sight of Caroline Montgomery curled up on his couch, her shoes off and her lovely features still and peaceful.

Looked like she had made herself right at home in his absence.

He wasn't sure why the discovery should send this hot beam of fury through him, but he couldn't stop it any more than he could control those clouds gathering outside.

Chapter 3

"Hey lady! Wake up!"

Caroline barely registered the voice, completely caught up in a perfectly lovely dream. She was riding a little paint mare up a mountain trail, the air sweet and clear, and their way shaded by fringy pines and pale quaking aspen. She'd never been on a horse in her life and might have expected the experience to be frightening, bumpy and precarious, but it wasn't. It was smooth, relaxing, moving in rhythm with a huge, powerful creature.

The mountains promised peace, a warm embrace of balance and serenity she realized she had been seeking forever.

"Lady!" the voice said louder, jerking her off the horse's back and out of the dream. "You want to tell me what you're still doing here?"

Jarred, disoriented, Caroline blinked her hazy way

back to awareness. Instead of the beautiful alpine setting and the horse's smooth gait beneath her, she was
in a large, open room gazing directly at a painting of a
horse and rider climbing a mountain trail.

Beneath the painting stood an angry man glowering
at her from beneath a black cowboy hat, and it took her
sleep-numbed brain a moment to figure out who he was.

Wade Dalton.

Marjorie Dalton's oldest son. In a flash, she remembered everything—Quinn's gushing email about his
lady love, her shocked reaction to find his lady love
was her client, then that frenzied trip to eastern Idaho
in a mad effort to stop him from doing anything rash.

She'd been too late, she remembered. Instead of Marjorie and Quinn, she had found only a surly, suspicious
Wade Dalton and his two darling, troublemaking boys.

Striving desperately for composure, she drew in a
deep, cleansing breath to clear the rest of the cobwebs
from her brain, then sat up, aware she must look an
absolute mess.

She pushed a hank of hair out of her eyes, feeling at
a distinct disadvantage that he had caught her this way.

"I'm sorry," she murmured. "I didn't mean to fall
asleep. I sat down to wait for you and must have drifted
off."

"Why?"

"Probably because I traveled all night to get here." To
her embarrassment, her words ended in a giant yawn,
but the man didn't seem to notice.

"I wasn't asking why you fell asleep. I was asking
why in the…" He looked over at his son and lowered
his voice. "Why in the *heck* would you think you had

to wait for us? As far as I'm concerned, we've said everything we needed to say."

She followed his gaze to the boy, noting the bandage on his hand. "I wanted to make sure Tanner was all right."

"He's fine," he answered. "Second-degree burn but it could have been a lot worse."

"Uncle Jake put lots of stinky stuff on it," Tanner piped up from the other couch, "and said I have to keep it wrapped up for a week 'cept at bedtime, to keep out the 'fection. This is my mummy claw of death."

He made a menacing lunge toward her with his wrapped hand and Caroline laughed, charmed by him.

"You'll have to make sure you do everything your uncle told you. You don't want to get an infection."

"I know." His sigh sounded heartfelt and put-upon. "And I can't ever roast marshmallows by myself again or Daddy will drag me behind Jupiter until my skin falls off."

"Jupiter?"

"My dad's horse. He's really big and mean, too."

Caroline winced at the image and Wade frowned at his son. "I was just kidding about the horse, kid. You know that, right? I just wanted to make sure you know there would be a punishment for playing on the stove again."

"I know. I told you I wouldn't do it again ever, ever, ever."

"Good decision," Caroline said. "Because you'd look pretty gross without all your skin."

Tanner giggled, then turned back to his television show.

Caroline shifted her attention back to the boy's father

and found him watching her closely, a strange look on his features—an expression that for some reason made her wish her hair wasn't so sleep-messed.

Silence stretched between them, awkward and uncomfortable, until she finally broke it.

"I made some soup for you and the boys. It's on the stove."

He scowled. "You what?"

"I figured you would be ready for lunch when you returned from the clinic so I found some potatoes in the pantry and threw together a nice cheesy potato soup."

She wasn't quite sure why, but her announcement turned that odd expression in his eyes into one she recognized all too well. She watched stormclouds gather in those blue depths and saw his mouth tighten with irritation.

"Funny, but I don't remember saying anything about making yourself right at home." Though his voice was low to prevent Tanner from paying them any attention, it was still hot.

"You didn't. I was only trying to help."

"My mother has apparently been stupid enough to marry your father, but that sure as hell doesn't give you free rein of the Cold Creek, lady."

She inhaled deeply, working hard to keep her emotions under control. No good would come of losing her temper with him, she reminded herself. As far as he was concerned, she had invaded his territory, and his reaction was natural and not unexpected.

At the same time, she couldn't let him minimize her, not when she had only been trying to help.

"My name is Caroline," she said calmly.

"I don't care if you're the frigging queen of England. This is my ranch and right now you're trespassing."

She raised an eyebrow, trying to hang onto her temper. "Are you going to have me thrown in jail because I had the temerity to make you and your boys some soup?"

"The idea holds considerable appeal right about now, believe me!"

Though she knew he was only posturing, dread curled through her just at the possibility of going to jail again. She had a flashing image of concrete walls, hopelessness and a humiliating lack of privacy.

She couldn't bear contemplating that brief time in her life—and couldn't even begin to imagine having to go back.

She took another deep breath, focusing on pushing all the tension out of her body.

"I was only trying to help. I thought perhaps Tanner might need something comforting and warm after his ordeal."

"I don't need your help, Ms. Montgomery. I don't need anything from you. It was the *help* you gave my mother that led to this whole mess in the first place."

Oh, this man knew how to hit her where she lived. First he threatened her with her worst nightmare, then he dredged up all the guilt she'd been trying so hard to sublimate.

Before she could summon an answer, two noises started up simultaneously—his cell phone rang and strident cries started to float down the stairs as Cody awoke.

Wade let out a heavy sigh and rubbed two fingers on his temple. Deep frustration showed on his features and she reminded herself she didn't want to be fighting with him. While she had worked to clean up the sticky, smoky mess in the kitchen, her mind had been busy trying to do the same to the mess her father had created in Wade Dalton's life.

She wanted to think she had arrived at a viable solution.

"I disagree," she said. "I think you do need help. And if you can swallow your anger at me—justified or not—and listen to me, I have a proposal for you."

His glare indicated that the only kind of proposal he wanted to hear from her concerned her plans to leave his ranch, but she refused to let him intimidate her.

He answered his phone just as he headed out of the room to get Cody, now crying in earnest.

When he returned five minutes later, she had Tanner settled at the kitchen table, eating soup with his unbandaged hand and talking her ear off about his trip to the doctor and the stickers he got from his Uncle Jake and how he heard Amber, one of his Uncle Jake's nurses, talking about how his Uncle Seth was the sexiest man in the county.

This Seth person sounded like an interesting character, she thought, then she forgot all about him when Wade walked into the kitchen with Cody on his hip. The rancher looked big and powerful and intimidating, and she thought his brother would have to be something indeed if he could possibly be more gorgeous than Wade Dalton.

Not that she noticed, she reminded herself. As far as she was concerned, he was grouchy and unreasonable and determined that everything in life had to go his way or else.

Still, there was something about seeing the sleepy-eyed toddler in his arms, one little hand flung around his father's neck and the other thumb planted firmly in his mouth, that tugged at her heart.

The boy studied her warily until she smiled, then his reserve melted and he gave her a chubby smile in return, which only seemed to deepen his father's scowl.

"Would you and Cody like some soup?" she asked.

Wade would have told her no but his stomach growled at just that moment and he had to admit the soup smelled delicious—rich and creamy, with a hint of some kind of spice he didn't quite recognize.

"I didn't put rat poison in it, I promise."

He didn't like this suspicion he had that she found him amusing somehow. He plain didn't like *her*. Caroline Montgomery was everything that turned him off in a woman. She was opinionated and bossy, and he didn't trust her motives one iota.

Trouble was, he couldn't figure out what she could be after. What kind of woman travels eight hundred miles to find her father, then, when she doesn't find him, sticks around to make soup in a stranger's house?

She took the decision out of his hands by setting a steaming bowl on the table and setting another smaller bowl on the counter to cool for Cody.

He could eat, he thought grudgingly. Breakfast had been a long time ago and he'd been too shocked over that letter from his mother to pay much attention to what he'd been eating.

He set Cody in his high chair and pulled him up to the table next to Tanner, then noticed something else about the kitchen. It gleamed in the afternoon sunlight shining in through the big windows.

The place had been a mess when he'd left to take Cody to the clinic, with scorch marks on the walls and a sticky marshmallow goo on the stove. All that was gone.

"You cleaned up." The statement came out more like an accusation than he'd intended but she only smiled in response. He noticed as she smiled that one of her eyeteeth overlapped the tooth next to it just a bit. It was a silly thing but he felt a little of his irritation with her ease at the discovery of that small imperfection.

"I figured you had enough on your hands right now. It was the least I could do anyway. If you hadn't been distracted yelling at me…" Her voice trailed off and she flashed that crooked little smile again. "Excuse me, if you hadn't been talking to me in a loud and forceful voice, you probably would have been able to keep a closer eye on Tanner and he might not have had the opportunity to injure himself."

"He would have found a way," Wade muttered. "That kid could find trouble in his sleep. He's a genius at it."

"He does have a lot of energy but he seems very sweet. They both do."

"Sure, while they're busy eating," Wade muttered, then felt like a heel complaining about his own kids.

"Which you should be doing," she pointed out.

Right. He didn't like bossy women, he reminded himself. Even if they had cute smiles and smelled like vanilla ice cream.

Still, he obediently tasted the potato soup his boys were enjoying with such relish, then had to swallow his moan of sheer pleasure. It was absolutely divine, thick and creamy, and flavored with an elusive spice he thought might be tarragon.

Tanner and Cody were carrying on one of their conversations, with Tanner yakking away about whatever he could think of and Cody responding with giggles and the occasional mimicry of whatever his brother said, and Wade listened to them while he savored the soup.

After he had eaten half the bowl in about a minute and a half, Caroline spoke up. "I know Marjorie helped you take care of your children. Do you have someone else to turn to now that she's gone?"

He swallowed a spoonful of soup that suddenly didn't taste as delectable. "Not yet. I'll figure something out."

Before she could answer, Tanner burped loudly and he and Cody erupted into hysterical laughter.

"Hey, that wasn't very polite," Wade chided, even as he saw that Caroline was hiding a smile behind her hand. "Apologize to Ms. Montgomery."

"Nat says that's how people in some places say thank you when their food is real good."

"Well, we're not *in* one of those places. On the Cold Creek, it's considered bad manners."

Cody suddenly burped, too, something Tanner apparently thought was the funniest thing in the world.

"See? Now look what you're teaching your little brother. Apologize to Ms. Montgomery."

"Sorry," Tanner said obediently, even though he didn't look the slightest bit sincere.

"Sowwy," Cody repeated.

"Can we go play now? We're all done."

Wade washed their faces and hands—well, Cody's hands and Tanner's unbandaged one—then pulled Cody down from his high chair and set him on the floor.

"Remember to be careful," he told Tanner, who

nodded absently and headed out of the kitchen after his brother.

"It doesn't look like his injury is slowing him down much," Caroline observed.

He sighed. "Not much slows that kid down."

"So what will you do with them while you work?" she asked again.

"I'll figure something out," he repeated.

She folded her hands together on the table and he noticed her nails weren't very long but they were manicured and she wore a pale pink nail polish. He wasn't sure why he picked up on that detail—and the fact that he did annoyed him, for some reason.

"I'd like to volunteer," she said after a moment.

He stared at her. "Volunteer for what?"

"To help you with your children." She smiled that crooked smile again. "I'm self-employed and my schedule is very flexible. I happen to have some free time right now and I'd like to help."

What the hell was her game? he wondered. "Let me get this straight. You're offering to babysit my kids while your father and my mother are off honeymooning in Reno."

"Yes."

"Why would you possibly think I'd take you up on it?"

She slanted him a look. "Why not?"

"Because you're a stranger. Because I don't know you and I don't trust you."

"I can understand your hesitation. I wouldn't want a stranger caring for my children, if I had any. But I can give you references. I was a nanny in Boston for two years while I finished college. I've had plenty of experience with children of all ages and with cooking and cleaning a house."

Did she actually think he would consider it? "Absolutely not."

"Just like that? You won't even think about it?"

"What's to think about? If you were the parent here, would you leave your kids in the care of a total stranger?"

"Probably not," she admitted. "But if I were in great need, I might consider it after I checked out the stranger's references."

His cell phone rang again before he could answer. One of these days he was going to throw the blasted thing out the window.

He saw Seth's number on the caller ID and sighed. "Yeah?" he answered.

"Where the hell are you? You said you'd be down." Seth sounded as frustrated as Wade felt.

"I'm working on it."

"Those clouds aren't moving on. In another hour we're going to be drenched and lose the whole crop. I was thinking I ought to call Guillermo Cruz and see if we can borrow the Luna's baler."

The Rancho de la Luna was the owned by their closest neighbor, Viviana Cruz. Though a much smaller operation than the Cold Creek, Guillermo Cruz kept his sister-in-law's equipment in tip-top shape.

It was a good solution, one he would have thought of if he wasn't so distracted with the kids. "Yeah, do that," he told Seth. "I'll be down as soon as I can. Maybe I can throw together something to fix the other one temporarily. If we can get two machines running out there, we might have a chance."

He hung up to find Caroline Montgomery watching him carefully.

"As I see it, you don't have too many other choices, Mr. Dalton," she said quietly. "Tanner is going to need pampering with that burn of his, at least for a few days, and it needs to be kept free of infection. You can't just lug him and Cody around the ranch with you where the two of them could get into all kinds of things without proper supervision. And by the sounds of it, your plate is pretty full right now."

"Overflowing," he agreed tersely. "Your father picked a hell of a time to take a bride."

She winced and for a moment there he thought she almost looked guilty before her features became serene once more. "I'm sorry. I understand you don't want me here but for the children's sake, at least let me help for a day or two until you come up with another arrangement. I've come all this way for nothing, I might as well make myself useful."

He rubbed the ache in his temple again, the weight of his responsibilities cumbersome and heavy.

What would be the harm in letting her help for a day or two? Her presence would take considerable pressure off him and it *would* be better for the boys to have more diligent supervision than he could provide.

She was a virtual stranger but, like it or not, she was connected to him now by virtue of their parents' hasty marriage.

Anyway, the work he had to do the next few days was close enough to the ranch house that he could keep an eye on her.

That might not be such a bad thing, he thought. If she and her father were cooking some kind of scam together, he might have some advantage in the long run by keeping his eyes open and knowing just who he was dealing with.

Hank Dalton had had an axiom for cases just like this. *Keep your friends close and your enemies closer.*

What better way to keep her close than by having her right here in his own home?

A stiff gust suddenly rattled the kitchen windows and he watched the clouds dance across the sky as he tried to calculate how much more they would have to pay for feed during the winter if they didn't get the hay in before that storm hit.

"You're right. I don't have too many options right now. I, uh, appreciate the offer."

The words rasped out of his throat as if they were covered in burrs, and she gave him an amused look, as if she sensed how hard they were for him to say.

He really didn't like being such a ready source of amusement for her, he decided.

"Where are your reference phone numbers?" he growled.

She looked at him for a moment, then scribbled some names and phone numbers on a memo sheet off a pad by the phone. Wondering if he was crazy, he grabbed them and stalked to his ranch office off the kitchen.

Ten minutes later he returned. He'd only been able to reach someone at one of the numbers, a woman by the name of Nancy Saunders. He knew it could be a set-up, that she could be part of the con, but at this point he didn't have any choice but to trust her words. She had raved about Caroline's care for her two children a dozen years earlier, about how they'd stayed in touch over the years and she considered Caroline one of the most responsible people she'd ever met.

He didn't want to hear any of this, he thought. He wasn't buying half of it but decided he would be close enough to the house that he could keep an eye on her.

He returned to the kitchen and found her cleaning up the few lunch dishes.

"Did I pass?"

"For now," he muttered. He grabbed his hat off the hook by the back door and shrugged back into his denim work coat.

"Natalie comes home on the bus about three-thirty and she can help you with the boys and with dinner. The freezer's full of food. I don't know what time I'll be in—probably after dark. You and the kids should go ahead and eat, but my mother usually leaves a couple of plates in the fridge for me and for Seth."

"Your brother."

"Right. He's second in command on the ranch and lives in the guesthouse out back, though he usually takes his meals here at the house with the family."

"What kind of food do you like?"

"Anything edible." He headed for the door, anxious to be gone. He stopped only long enough to scribble his cell number on the pad by the phone. "You can reach me at that number if you need anything."

He hurried for his truck, trying his best to ignore the little voice in his head warning him he would regret letting Caroline Montgomery into their lives.

Through the kitchen window, Caroline watched Wade hurry to his truck as if he were being chased by an angry herd of bison.

She still couldn't quite believe he had actually agreed to her offer. She hadn't really expected him to take her up on it, not with the animosity that had crackled and hissed between them since she'd arrived at the Cold Creek.

He must, indeed, be desperate. That's the only reason he would have agreed to leave his children in her care.

The man wasn't at all what she had expected, and she wasn't sure what to think of him. So far, he had been surly and bad tempered, but she couldn't really blame him under the circumstances.

He intrigued her, she had to admit. She couldn't help wondering what he was like when he wasn't coping with an injured child, a runaway mother and various ranch crises.

She was intrigued by him *and* attracted to him, though she couldn't quite understand why. Something about his intense blue eyes and that palpable aura of power and strength thrummed some heretofore hidden chord inside her.

Big, angry men weren't at all her cup of tea. Not that she really knew what that cup of tea might be—and heaven knew, she'd been thirsty for a long time. But her few previous relationships had been with thoughtful, introspective men. An assistant professor in the history department at the university in Santa Cruz had been the last man she'd dated and she couldn't imagine any two men more different.

Still, there was something about Wade Montgomery....

What had she gotten herself into? she wondered as she set the few dishes from lunch in a sink full of soapy water and went in search of the boys. Or more precisely, what had Quinn dragged her into?

Here she was falling back into old patterns, just hours after she'd sworn that self-destructive behavior was behind her.

She had vowed she was done trying to clean up after Quinn. The only thing she'd ever gotten for her troubles was more heartache. The worst had been those four months she'd spent in jail in Washington state after Quinn had embroiled her in one of his schemes.

Even though she'd had nothing to do with any of it, had known nothing about it until she'd been arrested, she had been the one to pay the price until she had been cleared of the charges.

Even then she couldn't bring herself to sever all ties with her father. Ironic, that, since she frequently counseled her clients to let go of harmful, destructive relationships.

Quinn wasn't really destructive, at least not on purpose. He loved her and had done his best to raise her alone after her mother had died when she was eight. But she was weak when it came to him and she felt like she had spent her entire life trailing behind him with a broom and dustpan.

This time was different, she told herself. This time, three innocent children had been affected by Quinn's heedless behavior. His impulsive elopement with Marjorie had totally upset the balance and rhythm of life here at the Cold Creek.

She knew from her coaching sessions with Marjorie that the older woman had been the primary caregiver to her three grandchildren since Wade's wife had died two years earlier.

Marjorie hadn't minded that part of her life and had loved the children, but she'd been lonely here at the ranch and hungered to find meaning beyond her duties caring for her son's children.

Though intellectually Caroline knew she wasn't responsible for Marjorie's loneliness, for Quinn's apparent flirtation that had deepened and become serious, she still felt guilty.

If not for her connection to Marjorie, the two would never have met, and Marjorie would have been home right now caring for her grandchildren.

Caroline had no choice but to help Wade in his mother's absence. It was the decent, responsible thing to do.

Chapter 4

By the time three-thirty rolled around, Caroline had no idea how Marjorie possibly kept up with these two little bundles of energy.

She was thirty years younger than her client and already felt as limp as a bowl of day-old linguine from chasing them around. Between keeping track of Cody, who never seemed to stop moving, and trying to entertain a cranky, hurting Tanner, she was quickly running out of steam and out of creative diversions to keep them occupied.

They had read dozens of stories, had built a block tower and had raced miniature cars all over the house. They'd had a contest to see who could hop on one foot the longest, they'd made a hut out of blankets stretched across the dining table and, for the last half-hour, they had been engaged in a rousing game of freeze tag.

Who needed Pilates? she thought after she'd finally caught both boys.

She had to think Tanner could use a little quiet time and, heaven knew, she could.

"Guys, why don't we make a snack for your sister when she comes home from school?"

"Can I lick the spoon?" Tanner asked.

"That depends on what we fix. How about broccoli cookies?"

Tanner made a grossed-out face that was quickly copied by his brother. They adjourned to the kitchen to study available ingredients and finally reached a unanimous agreement to make Rice Krispies squares.

They were melting the marshmallows in the microwave when the front door opened. Caroline heard a thud that sounded like a backpack being dropped, then a young girl's voice.

"Grandma. Hey Grandma! Guess what? I got the highest score in the class on my math test today! And I did my book report on *Superfudge* but I only got ninety-five out of a hundred because Ms. Brown said I talked too fast and they couldn't understand me."

That fast-talking voice drew nearer and, a moment later, a girl appeared in the doorway, her long dark hair tangled and her blue eyes narrowed suspiciously.

"Who are you? Where's my grandma?" she asked warily.

Rats. Hadn't Wade told her about Marjorie and Quinn?

"This is Care-line," Tanner announced. "She can make a block tower that's like a thousand feet high."

It was a slight exaggeration but Caroline decided to let it ride. "Hi. You must be Natalie. I'm Caroline

Montgomery. I'm helping your dad with you and your brothers for a couple of days."

"Where's my grandma?" Natalie asked again, her brows beetled together as if she suspected Caroline of doing something nefarious to Marjorie so she could take her place making Rice Krispies squares and chasing two nonstop bundles of energy until her knees buckled.

Caroline wasn't quite sure how to answer. Why hadn't Wade told her about her grandmother's marriage? Did he have some compelling reason to keep it from the girl? She didn't want to go against his wishes but she really had no idea what those wishes were.

Finally she equivocated. "Um, she went on a little trip with a friend."

"Hey look, Nat. I have the mummy claw of death," Tanner climbed down from his chair and shook his arm at her.

"What did you do this time?" Nat asked.

"I burned me when I was roasting marshmallows on the stove. I only caused a little fire, though. Uncle Jake put yucky stuff on it and wrapped it up. Do you want to see it?"

She made a face. "You're such a dork," the girl said.

Tanner stuck his tongue out at his big sister. "You are."

"No, you are."

Caroline decided to step in before the conversation degenerated further. "Would you like to help us make these? We wanted to make a snack for you. They won't take long."

Natalie frowned. "My grandma always fixes me a peanut butter and jelly sandwich after school."

The truculence in her tone had Caroline gritting her teeth. "I can make you one of those if you'd prefer."

Natalie shrugged. "I'm not really hungry. Maybe later." She paused. "What friend did my grandma go on a trip with? Señora Cruz? She lives next door on the Luna Ranch and she's her best friend."

Caroline debated how to answer and finally settled on the truth. If Wade didn't want his daughter to know her grandmother had eloped, he should have taken the time to tell that to Caroline.

"No. Um, she went with my dad."

Natalie digested that. "Is your dad named Quinn?" she asked after a moment.

Okay, so Natalie apparently knew more about her grandmother's love life than her father had. "Yes. Do you know him?"

Natalie shrugged. "Grandma talked to him a lot on the phone. I got to talk to him once. He's funny."

Oh, her father could be a real charmer, no question about that.

"Where did they go?" Natalie asked.

Here, things grew a little tricky. "You'd probably better ask your dad about that."

"Will they be back by tomorrow?"

"I doubt that."

"But I have a Girl Scout meeting after school. Grandma was supposed to take me. If she's not home by then, does that mean I can't go?"

Blast Quinn for putting her in this position, she thought again. For grabbing what he wanted without considering any of the consequences, as usual. She doubted he had spared a single thought for these motherless children and their needs when he'd charmed their grandmother into eloping with him.

"I can probably take you. We'll have to work out those details with your dad."

"I don't want to miss it," she said. "Grandma and me already bought the materials for the craft project."

"We can explain all that to your father. I'm sure there won't be a problem."

Natalie didn't look convinced but she didn't pursue the matter.

The rest of the afternoon and evening didn't go well. Tanner's pain medication started to wear off and he quickly tired of the limitations from wearing the gauze on his hand. He wanted to go outside in the sandbox, he wanted to play with Play-Doh, he even claimed he wanted to wash the dishes, that he *loved* to wash dishes, that he would die if he couldn't wash the dishes.

Caroline did her best to distract him and calm his fractious nerves, with little success. How could she blame him for his testiness? Burns could be horribly painful, especially for a child already off balance by the absence of his grandmother, his primary caregiver.

Cody, the toddler, also seemed to feel his grandmother's absence keenly as bedtime neared. He became more clingy, more whiny. Several times he wandered to the front door with a puzzled, sad look on his face and said "Gramma home?" until Caroline thought her heart would break.

Though she did help with Cody, Natalie added to the fun and enjoyment of the evening by bickering endlessly with Tanner and by correcting everything Caroline tried to do, from the way she added pasta to boiling water to how she made the crust on the apple pie she impulsively decided to make to the shade of crayons she picked to color Elmo and Cookie Monster.

By the time dinner was finished, Caroline thought she just might have to walk outside for a little scream therapy if she heard *That's not how Grandma does it* one more time.

At the same time, Caroline couldn't help but notice the girl never said anything about the way her father did things, only her grandmother. And none of the children seemed to find it unusual that they didn't see their father all evening long.

She had to wonder if this was the norm for them. Poor little lambs, if it was, to have lost a mother so suddenly and then to have a father too busy for them.

The only reference any of them made to their father came when Caroline found a cake in the refrigerator and asked Nat about it.

"Oh! That's my dad's cake. Today is his birthday and we forgot it!"

"I made a present," Tanner exclaimed. "It's in my room."

"Present. Present," Cody echoed and followed after his brother up the stairs.

"Why don't we save the pie for your dad's birthday?" Caroline suggested.

Natalie shrugged. "Okay. But grandma made the birthday cake and she makes really good cakes. He probably won't want any pie."

Caroline sighed but set her crooked-looking pie on the countertop to cool.

Despite Natalie's bossiness, she was a huge help when it came to following the boys' usual bedtime routine. She even helped Caroline tightly wrap a plastic bag on Tanner's hand so he could have a quick bath.

Her cooperative attitude disappeared quickly once the boys were tucked in their rooms, right around the time Caroline suggested it might be Natalie's bedtime, since by then it was after eight.

"I don't have a regular bedtime." Natalie focused somewhere above Caroline's left shoulder and refused to meet her gaze, a sure sign she was stretching the truth.

"Really?" Caroline asked doubtfully.

The girl shook her head, her disheveled hair swinging. "Nope. I just go to bed when I get tired. Like maybe ten, maybe eleven."

"Hmm. Is that right?"

"Yeah. My grandma doesn't care what time I go to bed. Neither does my dad. He's usually out working anyway. Sometimes I even stay up and watch TV after he comes home and goes to bed."

Natalie said this with such a sincere expression that Caroline had to hide a smile. She wasn't quite sure how to play this. She didn't want to call the girl a liar. Their relationship was tenuous enough right now. Natalie had made it plain she didn't like the way Caroline did anything, that she wanted her grandmother back. Caroline didn't want to damage what little rapport she'd worked so hard to build all evening.

On the other hand, she certainly couldn't allow the little girl to stay up all night for the sake of keeping the peace.

She pondered her options. "How about this?" she finally suggested. "I've got some great bath soap in my suitcase that smells delicious. You can use some while you take your bath and then I'll let you stay up and watch TV until nine. Does that sound like a deal?"

Natalie agreed so readily that Caroline realized she'd been conned. She could only hope Quinn didn't decide to take his new stepgrandaughter on as a protégé, the willing pupil he had always wanted. The partner in crime Caroline had always refused to become.

The storm that had threatened all afternoon had finally started around seven and Caroline discovered an odd kind of peace watching television with Natalie while the rain pattered against the window.

They hadn't been able to find anything good on TV so after her bath Natalie had put in an animated DVD— one of her grandma's favorites, she'd proclaimed.

If it gave the girl comfort, some connection to her grandmother, Caroline was fine with any movie. Before starting the DVD, Nat dug a couple of soft quilts out of an antique trunk in the corner.

"My mom made these," she said casually.

Caroline fingered the soft fabric, deep purples and blues and greens. "They're beautiful! She must have been very talented. Are you sure we're supposed to be using them?"

Nat nodded. "We use them all the time when we're watching TV. Grandma says it's like getting a hug from our mom every time we wrap up in them and it helps keep her a part of our family to use them instead of putting them away somewhere. That one you have is my dad's favorite."

Her chest ached a little to think of Wade Dalton finding some connection to his dead wife through one of the beautiful quilts she had made.

She pulled it over her and watched the movie and

listened to the rain and wondered about this family whose lives Quinn's actions had thrust her into.

She was going to kill him.

Wade glanced at the clock glowing on the microwave in the dark kitchen and mentally groaned. Ten-thirty. He had left a stranger with his children—including a cranky five-year-old with a bad burn—for more than ten hours.

He deserved whatever wrath she poured out on him. He'd had every intention of being back at the house before the kids went to sleep. But since the rain had decided to hold out until dark, they had been able to bale the entire crop, even with their busted baler, and then had had to load it and move it to the hay sheds.

Before he'd realized it, the kids' bedtime had come and gone, and here he was creeping into his own house, tired and aching and covered in hay.

At least they had been able to take care of business before the rain had hit in earnest.

Agriculture had changed tremendously with computers and handheld stock scanners and soil sensors that took most of the guesswork out of irrigating crops.

But for all the improvements, he found it humbling that he was just as dependent on the weather as his great-great-grandfather had been a hundred years ago when he'd settled the Cold Creek.

Caroline probably wouldn't understand all that, though. All she knew was that he'd virtually abandoned his children with a stranger all day.

He'd be lucky if she was still here.

Now that was an odd thought. He didn't want her there. He would have vastly preferred things if she had stayed in California where she belonged. He was unnerved whenever he thought of her in his house, with her soft brown eyes and her vanilla-ice-cream scent and the unwelcome surge of his blood when he was around her.

The kitchen sparkled and smelled like apples and cinnamon, with no trace of the charred marshmallow smell Tanner had left behind. He found a small pile of birthday presents on the table along with a crooked-looking pie that looked divine.

Wade studied the pile, guilt surging through him. The day had been so crazy he hadn't given his birthday much thought at all and certainly hadn't considered that his children might want to share it with him.

They had even made him a pie. Apple, his favorite. His stomach growled—Caroline's delicious soup had been a long time ago—and he wanted to eat the entire pie by himself.

He almost grabbed a fork but stopped himself. He had to face the music first and apologize to Caroline for dumping his kids on her all day.

He actually heard music coming from the great room. That wasn't the music he needed to face but at least it gave him a clue where to find her. He followed the sound, his shoulders knotted with tension at the confrontation he expected and deserved.

In the doorway to the room, he frowned. The menu to a Disney DVD was playing its endless loop of offerings but the room was dark except for the light from the television set. At first he didn't think anyone was in the room, but once his eyes adjusted to the dim light, he saw that both couches were occupied. Nat was stretched out on one and Caroline took the other, and both of them were sound asleep.

He studied them for a moment, noting Nat had pulled out Andrea's quilts. Did she miss her mother as much as he did? he wondered.

She stirred a little but didn't wake when he scooped her up and started to carry her back to her room. She was growing up, he thought with a pang in his chest. She was heavier even than she'd been the last time he'd carried her to bed.

It seemed like only yesterday she'd been a tiny little thing, no bigger than one of the kittens out in the barn. Now she was on her way to becoming a young lady.

Another few years and she'd be a teenager. The thought sent cold chills down his spine. How the hell was he going to deal with a teenaged daughter? He had a hard enough time with an eight-year-old.

He pulled back her comforter and laid her on her bed, then studied her there in the moonlight.

She looked so much like her mother.

The thought didn't have the scorching pain he used to have whenever he thought of Andi, taken from him so unexpectedly. That raw, sucking wound had mellowed over the last year or so until now it was a kind of dull ache. He was always aware of it throbbing there, but the pain and loss hadn't knocked him over for a while.

He turned to go but Nat's voice, gritty with sleep, stopped him by the doorway.

"Daddy?"

He paused and turned around. "Yeah. I'm home now. Go on back to bed, sunshine."

"You never call me sunshine anymore."

"I just did, didn't I?"

She gave a sleepy giggle then rolled over.

He watched for a few more moments to make sure she stayed asleep. He wasn't avoiding Caroline, he assured himself.

Finally, he forced himself to walk back down the stairs to the great room.

His houseguest was also still asleep, with her knees curled up and her hands pillowing her cheek. A lock of hair had fallen across her cheek. He almost tucked it back behind her ear but managed to stop himself just in time.

What the hell was wrong with him? he thought, appalled. It seemed wrong, somehow, to stand here watching her while she slept. She wouldn't appreciate it, would probably see it as some kind of invasion of her privacy. He imagined California life coaches were probably big on things like healthy personal space and respecting others' boundaries.

He had to wake her up, though he was loathe to do it for myriad reasons.

"Ms. Montgomery? Caroline?"

Those incredibly long lashes fluttered and she opened her eyes. She gazed at him blankly for a moment then he saw recognition click in. "You're back. What time is it?"

Here we go. Lecture time. He sighed. "Quarter to eleven."

She sat up and tucked that errant strand behind her ear without any help from him. "My word, you keep long hours."

"Show me a rancher who doesn't and I'll show you a Hollywood wannabe." He shrugged. "This is a crazy time of year, trying to bring in the last crop of hay for the season and get everything ready for snow."

"The children had a little birthday celebration planned for you. We made a pie and everything. Nat said you don't like pie as much as cake so I guess you have your choice now."

He scratched his cheek. "Did Nat happen to mention I don't like birthdays much at all? And I can't say this one is shaping up to be one of my best."

She smiled a little and he was struck by the picture she made there, with her hair messy and feet bare and her eyes all soft and sleepy.

"You've got an hour left. You should make the most of it."

He had a sudden insane image of pressing her back against that couch cushion and kissing that crooked little smile until neither of them could think straight.

Where the hell did that come from? He could feel himself color and had to hope it was too dark for her to see—and that one of her life-coaching skills didn't involve mind reading.

Wherever the thought had come from, now that he'd unleashed it, he couldn't stop wondering how she would taste, whether her skin could possibly be as soft as it looked.

He wasn't going to find out, damn it. He jerked his mind away from those forbidden waters and answered her.

"My big plans include eating most of that birthday pie and then hitting the sack."

Alone, as he'd been for the last two years.

"What about the children?"

"I guess I could save a slice or two for them."

"They were disappointed that they didn't see you before they went to bed so they could give you your presents."

Because he felt guilty, he responded more harshly than he would have otherwise. "This is a working cattle ranch. The kids understand I have responsibilities. I'll try to see them at breakfast and we can open the presents then."

She opened her mouth and he braced himself for the lecture he was sure would follow, but to his surprise, she closed it again.

"Fine."

The chill in her voice annoyed him, for some reason. He deserved it, he reminded himself, and swallowed what was left of his pride.

"I'm sorry I left you alone with them so long. I should have called or something but we had to work our tails off to get the hay in before the rain hit."

"We were fine. Tanner's hand was hurting before bed so I gave him another dose of his painkiller. I hope that's okay."

"Yeah. I, ah, appreciate your help."

"You're welcome."

"Are you sure you don't mind staying a day or two, until I figure something else out?"

"Of course not. I'm more than happy to help."

He couldn't quite understand why she was so willing to step in and help him but he was too tired and hungry now to figure it out.

"Do you have a spare room I could use while I'm here?" she asked. "I left my luggage in my car because I wasn't quite sure where to put it."

"Oh. Of course. I should have thought of that earlier.

There are two guest rooms on this floor and a couple more upstairs. Of the eight bedrooms in the house, only four are being used right now since Cody and Tanner share."

"Upstairs near the children is fine," she said.

"Go ahead and pick one and I'll go get your luggage and find you."

He came back five minutes later with a single suitcase from her trunk, a laptop case and what he guessed was a makeup bag.

He found her in the room across the hall from his own and he tried not to let his imagination get too carried away with what might happen if he crossed that hall in the night.

"Thank you," she murmured and he could tell by the exhaustion in her voice that she would be asleep in minutes.

"You're welcome. Uh, good night."

He brushed past her on his way out the door and was immediately assailed with the delectable scent of vanilla ice cream and warm, sleepy woman, and it was all he could do to keep from reaching for her.

He was definitely going to have come up with another caregiver solution until Marjorie came back. He wasn't sure he was strong enough to withstand having Caroline Montgomery in his house.

Chapter 5

Caroline had no clue what time the day started on a big cattle operation like the Cold Creek so she decided to err on the side of caution. Her travel alarm woke her at 5:00 a.m. and by 5:30 she stood in the large ranch kitchen with a spatula in one hand and a pencil in the other.

With the coffee brewing, biscuits cooking in the oven and bacon sizzling and popping on the huge commercial stove, Caroline tried to organize her thoughts and make some order out of the chaos that had suddenly become her life.

Quinn's latest escapade and her inevitable efforts to clean up the mess he left behind threatened to wreak havoc with her business. She had phone coaching sessions set up with a half-dozen clients today that she would have to reschedule and a speech she was supposed to give to a woman's meditation group over the weekend would have to be canceled.

The timing was lousy, a complication she could ill afford, but it wouldn't destroy her, either. One of the advantages of coaching—one of its big appeals to her when she found herself burning out physically and emotionally in her work counseling abused women at a shelter—was that her schedule could usually be flexible.

Sometimes that flexibility took a little creative time management, though, like now.

She glanced out the window over the sink and saw the sun beginning its slow rise above the mountains. She hadn't done her own meditations and affirmations yet this morning so she turned down the bacon, grabbed her sweater and slipped outside to the deck outside the kitchen.

This area must be Marjorie's handiwork, she thought with a fond smile for her client.

Fall-blooming flowers and herbs filled a variety of containers, from an old metal washtub to a rusted watering can. Several sets of whimsical wind chimes hung from an awning, their music gentle and sweet. Under the awning, protected from the cool breeze, a swing covered in green-striped fabric faced the mountains, a welcoming spot to greet the morning.

She sat on the wide, comfortable swing, enjoying the soft swaying, and looked around the Cold Creek.

She wasn't really sure what she thought of Wade Dalton yet, but one thing she could tell just by looking at his ranch—the man ran a tight ship.

The barns she could see from here were freshly painted, the fences near the house gleamed white in the predawn light and she couldn't see any old farm machinery or junk parts sitting around. Everything was neat and organized.

She watched a light flicker on in a small cedar house twenty yards away and wondered if that was the guest house where Wade's brother lived. She hoped she'd made enough bacon for two hungry men and three children.

The air was sharp with fall but sweet and clear, heavy with moisture from the storm the night before. She drew it deep into her lungs and closed her eyes, mentally taking a broom and dustpan to all the stress cluttering up her mind.

It took some effort this morning, as she had worried for a long time before she fell asleep about Quinn and Marjorie. That negative energy still flowed through her but she breathed in the sweet mountain air until she could feel herself moving back toward center.

When at last she opened her eyes she could see the promise of day in the pale rim above the jagged Tetons.

Though she had a vague memory of seeing those stunning mountains from the more familiar Wyoming side, she didn't think she'd ever been to Idaho before. How had she and Quinn managed to miss it in their rambling life?

She thought they'd been everywhere as they moved from town to town, her father charming and scamming his way across the country, always after the next big deal.

Please, God, not this time, she prayed silently as part of her meditation. Quinn's intentions toward Marjorie had to be just what they seemed. She couldn't bear thinking he might be cooking up another of his schemes. Her father knew how hard she had worked to build Light the Stars, how very much she cherished the career she had created for herself.

Her success meant everything to her. It was her mission in life, the one thing she had discovered she excelled at.

Knowing how much she loved it and how hard she had worked for her success, would Quinn have risked it all by exploiting her connection with Marjorie for less than altruistic motives?

She couldn't bear thinking of it, not now after working so hard to find serenity this morning. But in her deepest heart, she knew she must suspect it or she wouldn't have dropped everything to come after him. She wouldn't be in a stranger's house right now, cooking his breakfast.

She would be burning his bacon, if she didn't stop woolgathering out here, she reminded herself with a grimace, and slipped back inside the warmth of the house to turn it over.

Ten minutes later, she had a tidy pile of notes and an even bigger pile of bacon strips when Wade Dalton walked into the kitchen.

He must have come right from his shower as his hair was damp, his strong, chiseled features freshly shaved. Her insides quivered a little at the sight but she forced herself to push away the instinctive reaction and offer him a friendly smile.

"Good morning."

He headed straight for the coffeemaker. "Didn't expect to see you up this early."

"I wasn't certain what time you started your day and I wanted to be sure to have breakfast ready. How do you like your eggs?"

His eyes startled, he studied her over the rim of his cup. "Um, scrambled is fine," he said after a moment.

"But you didn't have to get up so early just to do that. I'm not completely helpless. I can usually manage to toast a couple pieces of bread."

She grabbed three eggs out of the refrigerator and started cracking them in a bowl.

"I enjoy cooking," she assured him as she poured a splash of milk into the eggs and beat them vigorously. "Besides, I wanted to catch you before you left the house anyway. I have a couple of questions for you."

As she added the eggs to the frying pan, she saw Wade shift his weight and realized he looked less than thrilled at the prospect of conversing with her. "What about?"

"Yesterday was so crazy, with Tanner's burn and everything else, that we really didn't have a great deal of time to discuss your expectations."

"My...expectations?" He seemed uncomfortable with the word, though she wasn't quite sure why.

"What you want from me, as far as the children are concerned."

"Oh. Right. As far as the children are concerned." He paused. "I don't know. Whatever you did yesterday is probably fine."

The day before she'd been flying blindly and she disliked going into a situation unprepared. "Last night before I went to bed I made a list of everything I feel I need to know about the children's schedules and their preferences and daily chores. I thought perhaps we could discuss it over breakfast."

She transferred his eggs to a plate, added several strips of the crispy bacon, a couple of the warm biscuits and some strawberry jam she'd found in the refrigerator.

She set it all on the table at one of the place mats

she'd found earlier, along with a pretty matching cloth napkin. Wade studied the place setting with a baffled kind of expression on his face but he finally sat down and took a bite of eggs.

Caroline contented herself with a biscuit, a peach yogurt and a glass of juice and sat across from him at a matching place setting.

"That's all you're having?" he asked. "It looks like you fixed enough bacon to feed the whole county."

She shrugged, a little embarrassed that she'd overestimated what was needed. "I'm not much of a breakfast eater."

The kitchen was quiet and she thought how intimate it was sitting with a man while he enjoyed his breakfast. She found the thought disconcerting and quickly spoke up to divert her attention from how very attractive Wade Dalton was.

"Do you mind if I ask you some questions while you eat?"

"I guess not," he said in a tone that plainly conveyed he didn't think her interrogation would improve his digestion.

She plunged forward anyway. "I suppose some kind of rough schedule is the first thing I need to nail down. What time does Nat need to be ready for the bus?"

He swallowed a mouthful of eggs. "Um, you'll have to ask her when she gets up. I think it's about eight or so but she can be more specific."

Caroline wrote a question mark next to bus pickup.

"And what time does the bus usual bring her home?"

"About three-thirty or so. You're probably going to want to ask her that for more specifics. I'm usually not around when she comes back."

Next to bus drop-off, she wrote 3:30 and then another question mark.

"Natalie told me she has Brownies after school today. I need to know what time she is supposed to be there, how long it lasts and directions to her troop meeting."

"I hate to sound like a broken record but you'll have to ask Nat. She'll know all that."

What do *you* know about your daughter? she wanted to ask but held her tongue. So far she wasn't very impressed by Wade's parenting skills. He had ignored his children completely the day before and now he seemed oblivious to the small routines that made up their lives.

Something of her thoughts must have showed on her face because his expression turned defensive.

"Sorry, but my mother took care of those kind of details."

"All right. I'll ask Natalie. She most likely at least has the name of the troop leader I can call."

She studied her list and wondered whether she'd be able to get *any* information from Wade at all. "I suppose that leaves the boys. It would help me to have some idea of their usual routine. Does Tanner go to preschool?"

"He goes a few days a week but, uh, right off the top of my head I'm not sure what days those are. Nat might be able to tell you that, too. Or maybe Marjorie wrote it on the calendar or something."

"I checked there. No luck."

"Well, with his burn and all, he probably ought to just stay home for a while anyway."

"You're probably right."

Wade rose from the table, deciding even if she was a great cook, the fluffy biscuits and crisp bacon weren't worth the price of this awkward conversation. "Thanks for the breakfast but I should be on my way."

"I'm not quite finished. That still leaves Cody. Can you tell me what kind of schedule Cody might be on as far as nap time? Does he nap in the morning or afternoon?"

"Um, afternoon." It was a total guess, judging by what had happened the day before, but Wade decided she didn't have to know that.

How could one small, delicate woman make him feel like such an idiot? he wondered. He didn't much like the feeling that he knew nothing about his own children.

It wasn't true anyway. He might not be up on every single detail but he knew Nat adored horses and Tanner liked helping him fix farm machinery and asked a million questions while they were doing it and Cody enjoyed snuggling with his daddy at the end of the day.

"My mother is the one who kept things running around here." Wade's guilt at his own ignorance made him testy. "She would still be keeping them running if not for you and your Don Juan of a father."

Heat flashed in those huge brown eyes but it was gone so quickly he wondered if he'd imagined it.

"We're all trying to make the best of a less-than-perfect situation, Mr. Dalton."

"You don't need to call me Mr. Dalton in that prissy, annoyed voice. You can call me Wade."

"Wade, then. I've known your children less than twenty-four hours. I know nothing of their likes and dislikes, their routines, their favorite activities. You're asking me, a total stranger, to jump right in and take care of all these details that you don't know and you're their father!"

He stared her down. "I didn't ask you to do anything. You insisted on staying."

She folded her hand together. "You didn't exactly throw me off the ranch when I offered to help."

Just because something was true didn't make it any easier to swallow. Yeah, he'd taken her help and agreed to let her stay. He hadn't had a whole lot of options. He still didn't.

"I've known *you* less than twenty-four hours but already I know you well enough to doubt you would have gone. You're like a cocklebur, lady. You stick to something and don't let go."

She opened her mouth to respond but before she could, the back door opened and Seth came inside—in search of coffee, no doubt.

He was grateful for the interruption, Wade told himself as he watched Seth spy Caroline. Seth instantly shed his typical morning grouchiness to offer her that slow smile of his that seemed to make every female within a hundred-mile radius sit up and purr.

From the cradle, it seemed as if Seth could charm any female into doing anything he wanted. Wade didn't know he did it, he had just seen it hundreds of times. From the checker at the grocery store to the eighty-year-old church organist, every woman in Pine Gulch adored Seth, probably because he adored them right back.

Usually he found his brother's fascination with the opposite sex—and their inevitable response—mostly amusing. He wasn't sure why but today it bugged the hell out of him.

"Morning. You must be Caroline." Seth aimed the full force of that killer grin in her direction.

"Yes. Hello."

Just because Wade was annoyed didn't mean he could ignore the manners Marjorie had drilled in them. "This is my brother Seth," he said stiffly. "He lives in the guesthouse out back and is the second in command on the ranch. Seth, this is Caroline Montgomery."

Seth smiled at her again. "I always wanted a baby sister. I just never expected to get a full-grown stepsister as pretty as a columbine. Welcome to the family."

Caroline blinked several times but seemed to soak in the whole load of baloney. "My goodness. Stepsister. I hadn't thought of that."

She slanted a quick look at Wade and he wondered why color was suddenly creeping across her cheeks.

He wasn't sure what annoyed him more—her blush at Seth's teasing or the idea that she might be related to him in any way, shape or form.

"What a crock of sh…sunshine. She's not a step-anything."

"Her dad married our mother. Seems to me that's clear enough."

Seth poured coffee and took a sip, then made an exaggerated sigh of delight. "That is one fine cup of coffee. Somebody who can make coffee like that is just what this family needs."

She shook her head. "It's just coffee. Nothing fancy."

"Not just coffee, trust me. I'm something of an expert and this is delicious."

"Would you like some breakfast?" Caroline asked. "I'm afraid I overdid it a little on the bacon so you can have as much as you want. There are fresh biscuits, too, and I'd be happy to scramble some eggs or make an omelet to go along with it."

Seth grinned. "Beautiful, and she cooks, too. I'd

have tried to marry Marjorie off a long time ago if I'd known about all the fringe benefits that would come from having a stepsister."

Her laugh sounded like music and Wade decided he needed to leave before he lost his breakfast.

He stomped up from the table and shoved on his Stetson. "I've got work to do," he growled.

Caroline looked startled. "But what about the rest of my questions about the children?"

"Why don't you ask Seth?" he snapped on his way out the door. "Apparently he's got nothing better to do this morning than sit around flirting with anything that moves."

He slammed the door after him, knowing they were both probably watching him like he'd lost his marbles.

The bitch of it was, he wasn't so sure they'd be wrong.

Chapter 6

Caroline's day improved considerably from its inauspicious beginning, though not at first.

Natalie nearly missed the bus since she insisted it didn't come until 8:05 and instead it showed up ten minutes earlier. She managed to make it, just barely, leaving Caroline with a cranky Tanner, who was hurting and mad at the world for it.

Cody slept in until about nine and woke with soaking wet sheets. She couldn't find anything clean to replace them, so the three of them spent the morning tackling mountains of laundry.

She didn't mind the work—it might have been pleasant except for Tanner's crankiness. He whined when she wouldn't let him have leftover pie for breakfast. He wrapped about half a roll of toilet paper around his other unburned hand so both hands would match. He threw a tantrum when she refused to let him take off his bandages to help her wash dishes.

It was all she could do to remember he was a little boy in pain and in need of comfort.

Cody was a sweetheart but he stuck to her like fly-paper and didn't seem to want to let her out of his sight. That was fine since she could always keep an eye on him, but he also managed to find something to make a mess with wherever they were—unmatched socks in the laundry room, flour and sugar in the kitchen, the rest of Tanner's roll of toilet paper that ended up stretched all the way down the stairs.

Worn out by lunchtime, she finally promised the boys a walk after they ate if Tanner agreed to wear a sock over his bandage to protect his hand and keep it clean.

Both boys were thrilled at the prospect of showing her around the ranch, so they ate their peanut-butter sandwiches quickly and even helped her straighten up the Cody mess.

Outside, they found a perfect October afternoon—sunny and pleasant, with just a hint of autumn in the cool breeze and the dusting of bronze on the trees. The storm of the day before seemed to have blown away, leaving everything fresh and clean.

Keeping close watch on Tanner racing eagerly ahead of them, she held Cody's hand and let the toddler's short legs set the pace as she enjoyed the fresh air and the beautiful mountain views.

Up close, the ranch was even more impressive than it had been in the pale early morning light. Everything she saw pointed to a well-run, well-organized operation.

Wade Dalton hadn't sacrificed aesthetics, either.

Instead of what she assumed would be more efficient and inexpensive barbed-wire fences, the ranch had gray-weathered split-rail fence that looked like something out of an old Western movie.

They walked along the fence line down the long gravel driveway toward the main road, stopping to admire a small grazing herd of horses.

"Horse, horse!" Cody exclaimed with glee.

She smiled down at him, charmed by his enthusiasm. "They're pretty, aren't they?"

"See that yellow one?" Tanner leaned on the middle slat of the fence and pointed to a small buckskin pony. "Her name is Sunshine and she used to be Nat's but now she's mine 'cause Nat has a new horse named Chance. I can ride her all by myself. Want to see?"

He started to slip through the rails but Caroline grabbed him by his belt loops. "Not a good idea, bud. At least not until your uncle Jake clears it, okay?"

"But she's my horse! Grandma taught me how to take care of her. She comes when I call her, except she's too big for me to put the saddle and bridle on. Grandma helps me with that part. We ride just about every day."

"Do you go with your dad, too?"

Tanner shrugged. "He's usually too busy."

Too busy to take his son riding? She frowned but before she could say anything, Cody pulled away from her and headed off as fast as his little legs could go. "Hi, Daddy! Hi, Daddy!" he shrieked.

She turned and found Wade coming out of the nearby barn, carrying a bale of hay in each arm like they were feather pillows. He had his jacket off and his sleeves rolled up and she saw those powerful muscles in his arms barely flex at the weight.

Caroline didn't like the realization that her mouth had completely dried up, like an Arizona streambed in the middle of the summer.

Cody collided with his father's legs at a fast run but Wade managed to stay upright. "Hey there, partner. Watch where you're going."

He dropped the bales to the ground as Cody hugged one long leg. Tanner hurried over to his father, too, and hugged the other leg. She was pleased to see he didn't look annoyed at his sons, just distracted.

"Hey Dad, guess what? We're showin' Caroline around," Tanner announced. "I showed her Sunshine and told her she's my very own horse. She is, huh, Dad, 'cause Nat rides Chance now. She says Sunshine is a baby's horse but that's not true 'cause I'm not a baby, am I, Dad?"

He opened his mouth to answer but before he could, Cody tugged on Wade's jeans and held his arms out.

"Daddy, Cody up!"

Wade picked him up and immediately Cody started trying to yank off his hat. Wade held onto his hat with one hand and the wriggling toddler with the other. "I didn't expect to see you guys outside today."

"Caroline says we all needed fresh air and she wanted to see the ranch so we're givin' her a tour. She made me wear a sock on my hand so I won't get a 'fection. That's stupid, huh, Dad?"

He looked at the sock then raised an eyebrow. She knew she shouldn't feel defensive but she couldn't seem to help it.

That instinctive reaction gave way to surprise when he shook his head. "Doesn't sound stupid to me, cowboy. I think it's a good idea. Remember what Uncle Jake said—you have to keep it clean."

"I wanted to play in the sandbox but she wouldn't let me do that, either," he complained.

"Tough, kiddo. Right now you need to listen to what she tells you. I know it's hard but it would be a whole lot harder if you don't do everything you can to keep your hand clean. If you got an infection, you might even have to have shots and stuff. Caroline is just trying to help you do what Uncle Jake told you. Instead of giving her a hard time, you ought to be thanking her for looking out for you."

She knew it was ridiculous but she still felt a soft, warm glow spread through her at his support of her, and she couldn't contain a pleased smile. He studied her for several seconds and she could almost swear he was staring at her mouth.

Color spread across her cheekbones and she was relieved when Tanner spoke up.

"Hey Dad! Can we show Caroline the kittens?"

"If you promise not to touch them. You'll have to just look today because they might have germs."

"I promise." Tanner took off running. The minute Wade set Cody down, the little boy raced after his brother and the two of them went inside the barn. Caroline followed and was surprised and pleased when Wade accompanied them.

The kittens were right inside the door, in a small pile of hay that looked warm and cozy. She had expected newborns, for some reason, and was surprised to see the half-dozen or so gray and black kittens looked at least a few weeks old.

They wriggled and mewed and climbed all over each other.

"Can Caroline hold one, Dad?" Tanner asked. "She doesn't have a sore hand."

"If she wants to."

"I do," Caroline declared, picking up a soft gray kitten with big blue eyes. "You are darling!" she exclaimed.

"She'll be a good mouser like her mother in a few months."

She made a face at Wade. "I'd prefer to enjoy her like this for now, all cute and furry, instead of imagining her with a dead mouse in her mouth, thanks."

"Whatever helps you sleep at night, I guess."

She laughed and met his gaze over the kitten. He was looking at her mouth again. She could swear it and she didn't quite know what to read into that.

"Any word from the newlyweds?" he asked.

Any glow she might have been foolish enough to briefly enjoy in his company, warm or otherwise, disappeared at his abrupt question and the sudden hard look.

"Nothing," she said. "You?"

"No. I expected them to check in by now. This isn't like Marjorie. Your father doesn't appear to be the best influence on her."

She had to bite back a sharp retort that maybe *Marjorie* was the bad influence on *Quinn.* But since she knew that was highly unlikely—that Wade was likely in the right since Quinn had spent his whole life perfecting the art of being a bad influence—she kept her mouth shut.

"I've tried to call my mother's cell phone at least a half-dozen times this morning. No answer."

"Same goes for Quinn. I guess they've turned them off."

"Probably because they know they've been selfish and irresponsible to run off in the middle of the night."

"Or maybe because they're on their honeymoon and in love and don't want to be disturbed by lecturing children."

She could only hope.

"Right." The skepticism in his voice was plain. "I've got to get back to work."

"Thank you for showing us the kittens." She set the little gray one back with its siblings. "Come on, guys. We'd better head back to the house so we can meet Natalie's bus and get her to Girl Scouts on time."

Both boys were reluctant to leave the fascinating kittens but they obediently walked out into the afternoon sunshine.

"Bye-bye, Daddy," Cody said.

"We're havin' cake and ice cream for your birthday tonight, Daddy, since we missed it yesterday," Tanner chimed in. "Don't forget, okay? We have presents and everything."

Wade looked about as thrilled by that prospect as the boys had been at leaving the kittens. "Is that really necessary?"

"Yep," Tanner said.

"See you at dinner," Caroline said, forcing a smile, then herded her small charges back toward the house.

Wade watched them go, Cody's little hand tucked in Caroline's and Tanner skipping ahead. Why did he suddenly feel so itchy and uncomfortable, like he'd broken open those hay bales and rolled around in them?

He wasn't sure he liked seeing her with his kids. After less than a day, Tanner and Cody both already seemed crazy about her. They sure didn't obey *him* so immediately.

A hundred feet away or so, she stopped abruptly and the three of them bent down to look at something in the dirt—a bug, he'd wager, since the ranch had plenty and Tanner was fascinated with them all.

He looked at those three heads all bent together: Caroline's soft sun-streaked hair, Cody's curly blond locks several shades lighter and Tanner's darker. His chest suddenly felt tight, his insides all jumbled together.

He wanted her. The grim knowledge sat on him about as comfortably as a new pair of boots.

How could he be stupid enough to hunger for a completely inappropriate woman like Caroline Montgomery? He didn't like her, he didn't trust her, but for the first time in two years he felt that undeniable surge of physical attraction to a woman.

Two years. He hadn't been with a woman since Andrea had died—before that, really, since she'd been pregnant with Cody and hadn't felt great the last trimester.

He hadn't even considered it until now, until Caroline had shown up on his doorstep.

Even thinking about this woman he barely knew in the same breath as Andi seemed terribly disloyal and he suddenly missed his wife with a deep, painful yearning.

In the two years since she'd been gone, the first wild shock of unbelievable pain had dulled to a steady, hollow ache except for moments when it flared up again like a forest fire that had never quite been extinguished.

Andi should be the one out there showing bugs to the boys and walking with Cody's little hand tucked in hers and kissing Tanner's owies all better. For a moment, the gross unfairness of it cut at him like he'd landed on a coil of barbed wire.

She'd loved being a mother and she'd been great at it. It was all she'd wanted. She used to talk about it even when they were in high school, about all the kids she would like and how she planned to get a teaching degree first, then wanted to be able to stay home and raise her children.

She'd been two years behind him in school, Andrea Simon, the prettiest girl in the sophomore class. She'd been barely sixteen when they'd gone on their first date and, from that moment, he'd known she was it for him.

He picked up the hay bales and headed for the pens, remembering how sweetly innocent she'd looked at his senior prom. They'd dated on and off while she'd finished high school, though he'd been so busy after his father had died, with all his new ranch responsibilities, he hadn't had much time for girls.

Still, he'd known he loved her from the beginning and he'd asked her to marry him when she was only twenty, on the condition that she finish her education first.

The day after her college graduation, they'd been married in a quiet ceremony in her parents' garden. Marjorie and his brothers had still been living in the ranch house, so Wade had brought his bride home to the little guesthouse out back where Seth lived now.

He could still see Andi's delight in fixing up the place that summer before she'd started teaching at the elementary school in town—sewing curtains, painting, refinishing the floors. While he'd been consumed with the ranch, she'd been building a nest for them.

He cut the twine on the bales and tossed them into the trough, then went back to the barn for a couple more, his motions abrupt as he remembered the heady joy of those early days.

His wife had been his first and only love—and his first and only lover.

Something like that would probably make him look pretty pathetic in the eyes of someone sophisticated like Caroline Montgomery, but he didn't care.

He had loved his wife and would never have dreamed of straying. Their relationship had been easy and comfortable. They had always been able to turn to each other even when hard times had come—the trio of miscarriages she'd suffered in quick succession, the surgery to correct a congenital irregularity in her uterus, then the eighteen months they'd tried without success to become pregnant.

He had lived through the most helpless feeling in the world watching the roller-coaster ride of hope and heartache she'd gone through each month when she realized she hadn't conceived.

And then, three years after they'd married, Andi had become pregnant with Natalie. They hadn't told anyone for nearly half the pregnancy, until well into the fourth month when they'd finally allowed themselves to hope this pregnancy wouldn't end in heartbreak.

Andi had never been happier than she was after Natalie had come along—though with complications— and then Tanner. She'd quit teaching, just as she had dreamed, and had spent her days coloring and singing and looking for bugs on the sidewalk.

He'd been happy because *she* had been happy and

they slipped into a comfortable, hectic routine of raising cattle and raising kids.

And then fate had taken her from him and for the last two years he'd done his best to figure a decent way to do both by himself.

He sighed. Why was he putting himself through this today, walking back down a memory lane covered with vicious thorns on every side?

Because of Caroline. Because even though it was crazy and seemed disloyal to Andi somehow, he was attracted to her.

It was only his glands, he told himself, just a normal male reaction to a beautiful woman brought on by his last two years of celibacy.

She was the first woman in two years to even tempt him. He found that vaguely terrifying. He'd had offers at cattle shows and the like, but had always declined the not-so-subtle overtures, feeling not even a spark of interest in any of those women.

Something about their heavy makeup and the wild, hungry light in their eyes turned him off, cheapened something that had always seemed beautiful and natural with his wife.

He had wondered if that part of him was frozen forever. Things had been easier when it had been. But now Caroline had him wondering what it would be like to kiss her, to touch that soft skin. To remember once more the sweet and compelling curves of a woman.

He wasn't going to find out. His mother would be back soon and everything would get back to normal, to the way it should be without strange women showing up to complicate an already stressful life.

Until then, he would just do his best to get Caroline

out of his mind. Hard, relentless work had helped him survive these last two painfully lonely years.

It could certainly help him get through a few more days.

Caroline wasn't sure what to think of a man who was forty-five minutes late for his own birthday party.

"He's not coming, is he?" The resignation in Natalie's voice just about broke her heart.

"He'll be here," Caroline promised, though even as she said the words she questioned the wisdom of raising potentially false hope in the girl.

"No he won't. He's probably too busy. He's *always* too busy."

She shrugged like it meant nothing to her but Caroline only had to look at all Nat had done since her Girl Scout meeting to know her nonchalance was a facade— the festively decorated table, the cake with its bright, crooked frosting and the coned party hats Natalie had made out of construction paper, markers and glitter all told a far different story.

Caroline wanted to find Wade Dalton wherever he was hiding out on his ranch and give the man a good, hard shake.

"I'm hungry," Natalie announced after a moment. "I don't think we should wait for my dad. We should just go ahead and eat since he's not coming."

"I'm hungry, too," Tanner announced.

"Hungry, too," Cody echoed, but whether he meant it or was just parroting his siblings, she didn't know. It didn't much matter anyway. She had three children here who needed their dinner.

"We can wait a few more minutes and then I'll call him to see how much longer he's going to be."

And maybe add a few choice words about fathers who neglect their children, while I'm at it.

The thought had barely registered when they heard the thud of boots on the steps outside and, a moment later, the door opened and a dark head poked through the opening.

A dark head that did not belong to Wade Dalton.

Caroline let out a frustrated breath but her annoyance at finding another man there instead of their father didn't seem to be shared by the children.

"Uncle Jake!"

Pique at her father apparently forgotten for the moment, Natalie shrieked and launched herself at the man. He picked her up with an affectionate hug.

This must be Marjorie's middle son, the family physician, Caroline realized. She studied him as he greeted the children with hugs all around. Jake Dalton was about the same height as Wade but perhaps not as muscular. His hair was a shade or two lighter than Wade's and not quite as wavy, but he shared the same stunning eyes, the same chiseled features.

She could only wonder at the genetics that produced three such remarkably good-looking men in one family. The Dalton gene pool certainly didn't look like a bad place to swim.

While she was studying Jake Dalton, his attention was drawn to the table with its festive decorations and the thickly frosted cake. "Wow. A party for me? You shouldn't have!"

Natalie giggled as he set her back on her feet. "It's not

for you. It's supposed to be Dad's birthday party since we forgot it yesterday. Only I bet he's not coming."

"All the more cake for me, then," Jake teased his niece, although Caroline thought for a moment there she saw just a hint of irritation flicker in his gaze.

Did he also notice his brother's careless attitude toward his children? she wondered.

He turned to her and offered a smile she somehow found calming and kind.

"Hello. You must be Caroline. I'm Jake Dalton, Wade's brother. Wade told me you offered to stay on for a few days and help him with the boys. I can't decide if you're insanely nice or just insane."

"A little of both, I guess." She smiled. "Since you're here, why don't you stay for dinner? I was just about to call your brother to see when he's going to make it back."

"I just dropped in to take a look at Tanner's hand but I could probably be convinced to stay and eat."

"And I thought the days of the house call were over."

"I give special service for five-year-old rascals in desperate need of a sucker transfusion." He pulled a lollipop from his shirt pocket and waved it like a magic wand.

She played along. "I only hope you're not too late, Doctor."

"Been that kind of a day, has it?" His expression was both sympathetic and understanding. Dr. Dalton must have a heck of a bedside manner with that calm, competent manner, she thought.

"He's a young boy in pain. A little crankiness is to be expected."

"You're an angel to put up with him. If your father's

anything like you, no wonder he swept Marjorie off her feet."

She had spent her entire life trying *not* to be like her father, charming and feckless and irresponsible, but of course she couldn't say that to another of Marjorie's concerned sons.

"He hasn't been too bad, as long as I keep him busy," she said.

"Let's have a look at it, shall we? Climb on up here, cowboy."

Tanner made a face but obeyed his uncle, scrambling up to sit on the breakfast bar.

"Caroline, if you're not too busy with dinner, can you play nurse for a moment?" Jake asked her.

"Of course. Let me wash my hands."

She scrubbed hard then helped Jake as he started unwrapping the bandage. To Caroline, the boy's injury looked red and ugly but Jake smiled. "You're doing great. Everything looks good."

"When can I stop wearing the stupid bandage?"

"Another few days. Maybe a week. You can hang on that long, can't you?"

"I guess." Tanner didn't look thrilled at the prospect, but his uncle told him a couple of knock-knock jokes to take his mind off it while he pulled some ointment from his bag and applied it with gentle care, then put a new bandage on.

While he worked, Caroline couldn't help comparing the three Dalton brothers.

Where Seth had been flirtatious and charming to her at breakfast, the kind of man who knew his own tremendous appeal and reveled in it, in just a few moments

Caroline had determined that this middle Dalton brother seemed to be the thoughtful, introspective brother.

That must make their oldest brother the grouchy, unreasonable one.

Her sudden smile drew Jake's attention. "So you're the life coach my mother's been working with."

Her smile turned wary. "Yes," she said, not at all eager for another confrontation with one of the Dalton brothers.

"You must be doing something right. The last few months Marjorie has seemed—I don't know, more centered, focused—than I've ever seen her."

"I don't know how much of that is my influence or how much is from her email romance with my father—a courtship, by the way, that I knew nothing about until yesterday."

Wade didn't believe her but for some reason she felt it important to convince at least one of the Dalton brothers of her innocence.

"A sore spot, is it?"

She hadn't realized how much her professional pride had been stung by Marjorie and Quinn's elopement until just that moment. Until the day before, she had been so pleased with Marjorie's progress in the six months she'd been working with her.

She supposed it was arrogant to think she'd been making a difference in the woman's life, but she had seen her client blossom as she'd started to break free of destructive patterns and take control of her own life.

Now she had to wonder how much of Marjorie's transformation had been due to her coaching and how much was from Quinn's attentions.

Jake was waiting for an answer, she realized. She

sighed, checking to be sure the children's attention was occupied elsewhere. Tanner was busy with his lollipop in hand and had wandered over to the refrigerator where Natalie and Cody were busy making words out of alphabet magnets. Natalie was spelling out *horse,* Caroline noted with little surprise.

"Your brother thinks my father and I are running a scam to bilk mature women out of their retirement nest eggs," she finally said.

Jake leaned against the counter and folded his arms. "Are you?"

"Of course not! I have a legitimate business. You can check my website with my complete résumé, articles I've written and dozens of client testimonials!"

"You have a masters in social work, spent five years working in the field then graduated from an accredited coaching school. You've had articles published in various women's magazines, have an active affirmation email newsgroup and will soon be publishing a book from Serenity Press on how to tap into the healing energy within. Sounds great, by the way. I'm going to want to order autographed copies since I've got plenty of patients who can use all the healing energy they can find."

She stared at him. "How do you know all that?"

He smiled as he shrugged. "I checked you out months ago when Marjorie started working with you. Wade isn't the only overprotective son in this family. You can find out all kinds of things about a person just by Googling them."

Caroline wasn't sure what to think about this middle son of Marjorie's. Part of her wanted to be offended that he had run a background check on her, but she expected her clients to fully investigate before signing up for her services. She couldn't be annoyed when their family members did the same thing.

How far back did his background check go? she wondered. Her record should have been expunged when she'd been cleared, but he might still find evidence that she'd served jail time while awaiting trial. No, he wouldn't be looking at her with such a friendly smile if he knew about that part of her past.

"You have a solid business," Jake went on, "a healthy reputation and the recommendation of many very satisfied customers. When your book hits the stands, I'm sure you'll have people knocking down your doors wanting your services."

"I've worked hard for what I've earned."

And everything would be ruined if Quinn decided to grift someone he'd found on her client list. But she couldn't let herself worry about that now.

"It shows."

"Apparently not to your brother."

"Wade will come around. He's a hard man but he's not completely unreasonable."

Her doubtful look earned a laugh from Jake but he quickly grew serious again.

"He's a hard man," he repeated. "But he's had to be. He took on the whole responsibility for running the ranch when he was eighteen years old and helped Mom finish raising Seth and me, not an easy job. These last few years since Andi died have been tough in a lot of ways. If he's abrupt and surly, he has reason to be. Don't take it personally."

"Thanks. I'll try to remember that. A doctor who

makes house calls and doles out advice, too. You must do a booming business."

"All part of the service."

He smiled and she couldn't help but return it, but before she could respond, she heard a noise and turned to find Wade standing in the doorway.

Hard, indeed. Right now the oldest Dalton brother looked tough enough to chew nails.

Chapter 7

Wade registered two things when he walked into his kitchen.

The first was the table adorned with balloons and other festive decorations and a birthday cake covered in chocolate icing. His damn birthday party, he remembered. So much for his hopes of grabbing a quick bite to eat and going back to work.

He didn't like the other thing he saw any better. His brother Jake was there, as solemnly handsome as ever. Normally he enjoyed having Jake around but he wasn't thrilled to see Caroline smiling up at his brother in a way she'd never looked at *him*.

His mood darkened further when she caught sight of him and her smile instantly melted away like icicles on a tin roof.

His reaction was irrational, he knew it, but it bugged the hell out of him that she couldn't spare him so much as a tiny smile, when she seemed to have more than enough for his brothers.

He wasn't jealous, he told himself. Just protective of his brothers. Sure, they were grown men, but he didn't need either of them to get tangled up with her until they knew what she and her old man were up to.

Somehow the rationalization rang hollow but it was the best he could come up with.

Before he could give even so much as a terse greeting, the kids caught sight of him.

"Daddy birthday!" Cody exclaimed gleefully. "Birthday, birthday, birthday!"

"You made it!"

Why did Nat have to sound completely astonished? he wondered. "Sorry I'm a little late. The vet showed up an hour ago and we had a few things to take care of."

They weren't close to being done, either. Wade had planned just to slip away for a moment to eat and say good-night to the kids, but now he wondered if he ought to tell Dave to come back in the morning.

"That's all right." Caroline's voice was calm but impersonal. "The important thing is that you're here now. The children have been so excited to celebrate your birthday."

"We made you a cake," Tanner said. "It's chocolate. I got to put on some frosting but only if I used my hand that doesn't hurt."

"I bet it's delicious."

"We're having roast beef since I told Caroline it's your favorite dinner," Natalie announced.

Was it? He liked plenty of different foods—anything

put in front of him, usually—and he wasn't quite sure why his daughter thought roast was his favorite.

"Sounds delicious," he murmured.

"We didn't make mashed potatoes, though. I told Caroline that was your favorite but she decided to do a different kind of potato. What's it called again?"

"Twice-baked," Caroline said. For some reason she looked a little embarrassed. "It's a lot like mashed potatoes, just a little fancier."

"Everything smells great. Um, just let me wash some of the dust off and then we can eat."

He would rather have just washed his hands and sat down in all his dirt but he couldn't, not with Jake sitting in there looking so suave and professional and *doctorly* in tan pants and a button-down shirt.

The thought made him wish, conversely, that he had time to shower, but he knew he didn't, not with the vet waiting, so he quickly settled for changing his shirt, combing his hat-flattened hair and washing his face and hands.

On the way back to the kitchen, he called Dave to tell him what was up and invite him for dinner.

"I ate before I came over. Linda's on swing shift this week so we ate before she left for work."

"Well, come on up for cake then," he mumbled, embarrassed all over again about the whole thing.

Dave laughed. "Thanks but I think I'll pass. I've got plenty to keep me busy until you come back down and we can finish up."

"I'll get away as soon as I can," he promised, then disconnected, squared his shoulders, and headed into the kitchen.

Once there, he discovered Seth had come in while he'd been gone, and his younger brother *had* taken time to shower, apparently.

His hair was damp and he looked his usual charming self. He and Jake were both watching Caroline bustle around the kitchen like a couple of fat toms eyeing a nice juicy canary.

He couldn't blame them for it. With that apron and her hair up in some kind of ponytail thing, she looked sexy and rumpled. Her cheeks were flushed, her eyes bright and she had a tiny smudge of what appeared to be chocolate icing on her chin, like a beauty mark.

His sudden desire to reach forward and lick it off just about had him heading right back out of the kitchen.

"Sit down, Daddy," Natalie ordered, in what Andi used to call her lady-of-the-manor tone.

He obliged, taking his place at the head of the table.

"You have to put on your birthday hat," Nat commanded. "Tanner and me made 'em ourselves."

He studied it by his plate, a spangled creation that looked like something a mad magician would wear. A shower of multicolored glitter fell off when he picked it up and he figured he would have rainbow sparkles in his hair for weeks.

Nat, Caroline and the boys all had similar but less gaudy creations on but both his brothers were looking on with bare-headed amusement.

"Why don't you have hats?" he growled.

Seth shrugged, but there was a gleeful look in his eyes that made Wade want to pound something. "You're the birthday boy."

He felt like an idiot but he couldn't disappoint his

kids. With a resigned sigh, he pulled on the creation, snapping his chin with the elastic in the process.

"Let's eat, then," he said.

Caroline had to give credit to Wade for being a good sport.

Though he looked as if he would rather be sitting in church in his underwear, he wore the birthday hat without further complaint all through dinner; he endured the off-key singing of "Happy Birthday" from his children; he suffered through his brothers' jokes on his behalf about his advancing age.

He even made a birthday wish before blowing out the candles on his sagging cake—though if she had to guess, she suspected his wish most likely involved figuring out some way to escape the unwanted attention.

If not for his frequent looks at the clock or the faint, embarrassed expression or the increasingly hard set of his jaw, she might have thought he was even enjoying himself.

He lasted nearly forty minutes before sliding his chair back and removing the birthday hat.

"This has been great, guys. Really. The best thirty-sixth birthday party I've ever had."

Nat made a "duh" kind of face. "It's the only one you've ever had!"

"Well, I'm afraid I have to go," he said. "I can't keep the vet waiting any longer."

Seth stood up. "It's your birthday celebration. Why don't you stay and I can go out and help Dave?"

Caroline saw surprise register briefly on Wade's tanned features at the offer before he shook his head.

"Not this time. We're working out the breeding schedule for next year and it's not something I can miss."

Seth's jaw worked for a moment, but he slouched back down to his seat and reached for his drink, saying nothing.

Did Wade completely miss the sudden restless light in his brother's eyes? she wondered. How could he completely shoot down his brother's offer of help, especially during his own birthday celebration with his children?

The way he ran his ranch *or* his family was absolutely none of her business, she reminded herself as he kissed his children and bid them good-night.

To her shock, before he left the kitchen, he paused beside her chair, looking big and rangy and slightly uncomfortable.

"Thank you for the nice birthday dinner. I can't remember roast beef ever tasting so good and those potatoes were wonderful. It was a lot of trouble to go to and I, um, appreciate it."

She blinked several times but before she could summon a response, he shoved on his Stetson and headed out the door.

"You're welcome," she murmured to his back.

What a complicated, contradictory male, she thought. Just when she thought she had him figured out, he threw a curveball at her, leaving her completely unsure what to expect.

He obviously still distrusted her but they'd managed an entire meal in peace. She supposed she should be grateful for that.

After Wade closed the kitchen door behind himself, Caroline turned back to the table to find Jake standing up as well. "I should go, too. I've got a patient having surgery tomorrow and I promised I'd stop by tonight to answer any of her last-minute questions."

"Really? You do that for all your patients?" She couldn't believe a doctor would go to so much trouble.

"If they need it."

"That's wonderful! It's so refreshing to find a doctor who genuinely cares for his patients as more than just a few dollar signs."

Jake made a face. "When the patient also happens to be my ninth-grade English teacher, I have to be on my best behavior. Agnes Arbuckle was a holy terror. I barely squeaked past her class as it was and I live in dread that if I don't treat her well, she'll give me a pop quiz about gerunds, and when I freeze and botch it she'll find some way to revoke my diploma."

"What's a gerund?" Natalie asked.

"Beats me." Jake winked. "I was never very good at studying."

Caroline laughed. "That was a gerund right there, Natalie. Studying. It's a verb ending in *ing* that acts as noun. Like, *I love dancing.*"

"Really?" Seth stepped into the conversation, though there was a militant light in his eyes. "We ought to go sometime. I can do a mean two-step."

She gave him a look. "Or *I dislike teasing.*"

"I wasn't teasing," he said with a smile, though she thought his heart didn't seem to be in his light flirtation. "Just say the word and I'll show you a night out on the town."

Even with his odd mood, Seth was a remarkably good-looking man. So was Jake, she thought, wondering why on earth she couldn't experience even a little sizzle of the awareness for either of them that surged through her when Wade was in the room.

"Well, hate to break up this grammar lesson but I really do have to run," Jake said. "I'll echo what Wade said. It's been a long time since I've enjoyed a meal like that. Thank you."

Seth slid his chair back. "Yeah, I've got to go, too."

"Where?" Jake asked with a mildly critical look. "The Bandito?"

"What of it?" Seth stalked to the sink, his plate in hand. "Sorry I don't have somewhere more important to go. Like maybe paying house calls to old biddies who only want the attention of a red-blooded young doc like yourself. Or the oh-so-important decision to inseminate the cows by June 1, just like we've been doing at the Cold Creek for fifty years."

The bitterness in his voice shimmered in the air and she saw Jake open his mouth, then apparently think better of whatever he was going to say. He closed it again as Seth headed for the door.

"Thanks for dinner, Caroline," the youngest Dalton brother said, with none of his customary charm, then he slammed the door behind himself.

"Sorry about that." Jake looked annoyed. "Out of all of us, Seth seemed to get most of our father's temper."

She shrugged. "It wasn't aimed at me."

In truth, she felt sorry for him. She wasn't sure why but Wade seemed to discount Seth's ability to help shoulder more of the burden of running the Cold Creek.

None of it was her business, Caroline reminded herself again as she said goodbye to Jake then helped the children through their bath routine—washing hair, finding bath toys, wrapping Tanner's arm and helping him keep it above the water.

As she went through their routine, she thought about the things she had observed that day, of the three motherless children starving for their father's attention.

They each exhibited behaviors she believed were directly linked to Wade's distracted parenting. Natalie had stepped up to mother and boss everyone around; Tanner was a bundle of energy who seemed to find trouble everywhere he went; Cody was clingy, hungry for affection.

And then there was Wade, who buried himself in work, and Seth, who would like to.

Not that she planned to jump to any rushed judgments, Caroline thought wryly.

She had only been here thirty-six hours. She couldn't expect to know and understand all the dynamics of the Dalton family in such a short time. Besides, even if she was spot-on with her assessment, none of it was her business. She was only the temporary help.

After she settled the boys in bed, she crossed the hall to tell Natalie good-night. She found the girl in her bed, her long dark hair still damp and a book propped on her knees.

Nobody walking in this room could ever doubt the girl was horse crazy, Caroline thought with a smile. The walls were covered in horse posters, a knickknack shelf that ran around the entire perimeter of the room about eighteen inches from the ceiling held dozens of horse figures in all colors and sizes, and the bedspread covering those little knees was, of course, equine in design.

"May I come in?" Caroline asked from the doorway.

"Yeah."

She sat on the edge of the bed, drawn to this little girl despite her bossiness. Something about Natalie reminded Caroline of herself, though she wasn't quite sure why.

She had been quiet, almost shy, something that certainly couldn't be said of Natalie. Heaven knows, even if Caroline had shared a similar obsession for anything like Nat's with horses, she and Quinn had never stayed in one place long enough for her to have a collection like this one.

"What are you reading?" she asked.

"Misty of Chincoteague."

"That's a great one."

Natalie shrugged. "It's okay. I've read it three times before."

"Don't you think the very best books are those you can enjoy more every time you read them?"

"I guess."

They lapsed into a not-uncomfortable silence and Caroline wondered what it would be like to have a daughter of her own. It wasn't an unreasonable idea since she had friends with children this age. Still, her mind boggled at the thought.

"The birthday party for your father was very nice. Your hats showed great creativity. I set them aside while I was cleaning up the dishes. I thought maybe we can put them away and save them for whoever's birthday is next in your family."

"That's Grandma," Natalie said. "Her birthday is in November. Mine's not until March."

"We can put them in a box for your grandmother's birthday party, then. She'll love them."

Natalie closed her book, shifting her legs under the comforter.

"My grandma's not coming back, is she?" she said after a moment.

Caroline drew in a sharp breath at the unexpected question. Where did that come from?

And wasn't this the kind of thing Wade should be discussing with his daughter? she thought, irritated at him all over again. If Natalie needed reassurance, she should be able to turn to her father for it, not to a virtual stranger.

But she was here and Wade wasn't, so it looked like she was nominated. "Oh, honey. Of course she's coming back."

The girl's hair rustled as she shook her head. "I heard Uncle Jake and Uncle Seth talking about it. They said how she eloped with your dad. Is it true?"

Caroline squirmed under Natalie's accusing look. She *had* been the one to tell the girl only that Marjorie had gone on a trip with a friend.

"Yes," she finally admitted.

Natalie nodded, her eyes solemn and sad. "So she's not coming back, then."

"Why do you say that?"

"My friend Holly's big sister eloped. She ran away to get married and she never came back. She lives in California and she's gonna have a baby. What if that happens to Grandma?"

Despite the gravity of the conversation, Caroline had to bite back a smile at the idea. "I think I can safely promise you that's not going to happen, honey."

"But what if it does? What if she doesn't come back? Who's gonna take care of me and Tanner and Cody?"

"You still have your dad," she pointed out.

"My dad's too busy with the ranch. He doesn't have time to take me to Girl Scouts or make cookies for my class when it's treat day or fix my hair in the morning. Grandma does all that stuff. If she doesn't come back, who's going to do it?"

"Your grandma's coming back. She said so."

"But what if she doesn't?" Natalie persisted.

"Well, your dad will probably hire somebody to help him."

Natalie didn't look at all thrilled by that idea. "Like a babysitter for all the time?"

"Something like that."

The girl peeked at Caroline under her lashes. "Would you do it if he hired you? You fixed my hair today and the braids looked even better than Grandma's. And your roast beef was the best we ever had, even my dad said so."

"Oh, honey," Caroline said helplessly, not sure how to answer.

"That means no, doesn't it?"

"I can't just stay here. I have a job and a house back in California."

"You could if you wanted to. You just don't want to."

"That's not true. Anyway, you don't have to worry about this, Natalie. Your grandma says she's coming back. Has she ever lied to you before?"

"Yes. She promised she would take me to Girl Scouts today and she didn't."

Okay, Nat had her there. Caroline sighed. "I know your grandma and I know she loves you very much. She said she's coming back and she will. Whatever happens, I also know your dad will make sure you have somebody nice to take care of you and your brothers."

She brushed a kiss on Natalie's forehead. "Now go to sleep and stop worrying."

Though she still looked unconvinced, Nat nodded and rolled over, her cheek pressed against yet another horse on her pillow.

Chapter 8

Wade had been working eighteen-hour days from about the time he'd hit puberty. It was a fact of life on a ranch, something he was used to. When work needed to be done, a man didn't sit around complaining about it, he knuckled down and did it.

If you put off doing what was needed, you only ended up having twice as much to do the next day.

He was used to days when he didn't have five minutes to grab a sandwich, when the minute he finished one task, a dozen more crept up to take its place on his to-do list.

Still, by the time he returned to the ranch house the evening of his birthday dinner, he was more than ready to find his bed. His muscles ached from a hard day of physical labor and his brain was weary from racing around in circles trying to work out the last-minute details before the camera crew arrived on Monday for the pre-interview shots.

He would have loved nothing better than lounging in front of ESPN with a beer and the remote right about now. But since not too many football games were played at eleven on a Thursday night, he figured he would just have to settle for a hot shower and a late-night talk show, while he gave his mind and body time to settle down.

Maybe he could find a piece of birthday cake left, he thought as he parked his pickup at the house and flicked off the headlights. It had been a mighty good cake, even though he'd been too rushed earlier to really savor each bite.

He would have to make sure he remembered to tell Nat she'd done a good job with it, even if Caroline had helped her. As he was pretty sure his daughter would still be in bed before he left in the morning, he'd probably be best to leave her a note about it.

The thought left him feeling vaguely guilty, but he pushed it aside. Another few days and the TV interview would be done. He would still be busy, but at least he wouldn't have that hanging over him, too.

The house was dark except for a small light glowing in the kitchen. It was a silly thing but somehow seeing that glow and knowing Caroline must have left it burning for him warmed him and managed to ease the ache in his muscles just a little.

The night was cool and crisp as he walked into the house, and all was quiet on the Cold Creek.

Wade hung his hat and jacket on the mudroom hook then walked into the kitchen, his mind on cake and, regrettably, on Caroline.

He found both delectable things in the kitchen, the

cake on the table and Caroline sitting at the breakfast bar with a laptop open in front of her and papers fanned neatly around her.

She looked up when he walked in, her forehead creased with concentration. Her hair was slipping free from her ponytail and a honey-brown strand lay across the curve of her jawbone, he noticed. She brushed it away, giving him a distracted smile.

In the pale glow from the laptop and the light above the stove, she looked soft and sweet and delicious, and his body instantly jumped with hunger.

"You're still up." It was a stupid thing to say, but for some reason he couldn't seem to hold a coherent thought.

She nodded. "I had some work to catch up on. This seemed a quiet time to do it."

They were alone in the kitchen, the children presumably asleep long ago. "What kind of work?"

"Notes on some of my clients to help me prepare for sessions with them when I return next week."

He almost made a derogatory crack about her work but the words caught in his throat.

He might not see the use in paying somebody else to tell you how to live your life but she was staying in his house, taking care of his kids, and it didn't feel right to give her a hard time about her career.

It was one of those clumsy moments when he couldn't say the first thing that came into his head but couldn't think of anything else to take its place, and they lapsed into an awkward silence.

He was about to excuse himself and head to bed when she finally spoke. "Are you hungry?" she asked. "There's roast beef left and plenty more cake. I could make you a sandwich if you'd like. With the roast, of course, not the cake."

His mouth watered and dinner seemed a long time ago. On the other hand, he had a funny feeling it wouldn't be exactly the smartest idea he'd ever come up with to fix a snack and sit down to eat it across from Caroline Montgomery, just the two of them in the middle of the night in a warm, cozy kitchen.

Not when he couldn't seem to shake his crazy, unwanted attraction to her.

Since he didn't see any other choice besides grabbing his cake and running away like a coyote-spooked yearling, he opted to pass on the whole thing.

"I'm good. But thanks. You, uh, did a good job with dinner."

"I only made the roast and the potatoes. Natalie did the rest. She worked very hard to give you a memorable birthday dinner."

Did that carefully bland voice hide censure or was it only his guilty conscience?

"Yeah, I was just thinking I should drop her a note about it before I took off in the morning. Tell her what a good job she did and all."

"I suppose you could do that," she said slowly.

"You have a better idea?"

He did his best to keep any trace of defensiveness out of his voice but he wasn't sure he succeeded.

"I just wonder if perhaps it would mean more to her if you could take the time to tell her in person."

A lecture from this woman would be just the thing he needed to cap off a perfect day. He braced himself. "Maybe, except I'm usually gone before she gets up for school."

"I've noticed." She carefully slid the cap onto her pen and rose from the bar stool. "You're gone before your children awake and not back until long after Natalie and the boys are in bed. I can't help wondering when you do see your children."

Here we go. By force of will, he shoved back the wall of guilt that threatened to crash over him. "I see them."

"When?" she persisted.

"I try to make sure I'm home with them at dinnertime, unless I absolutely can't break away."

"And then you go again."

"Sometimes." Most of the time, he admitted. Not that it was any of Caroline's business. "I also usually have the chance to see the boys for a couple minutes at lunchtime and take them on errands with me when I can."

"Do you think that's all they need from you?" If her voice was at all sarcastic, he would have blown up at her. But she spoke calmly, rationally, and somehow that made it seem worse.

"It's all I have to give them right now. I'm sorry if that doesn't fit your storybook image of what a perfect father ought to be but I'm a little busy here trying to provide for my family."

"You seem to be doing an excellent job of that. Your children don't lack for anything, except maybe your attention."

"Thank you for that two-second analysis, Dr. Montgomery. You'll be the first one I'll turn to if I want an opinion on how to raise my children from a total stranger who has no children of her own and who knows nothing about my situation."

She drew in a sharp breath and her soft, lovely skin seemed to pale a shade.

His guilt kicked up a notch but he shoved it back down. No. This wasn't his fault. She'd asked for it, butting in to things that weren't her concern. If she couldn't take his reaction, she shouldn't have yanked his chain.

He waited for tears or any of those other dirty tricks women used when they were challenged during an argument, but she only nodded. "Fair enough. You're right. I've only been here a day and can't pretend to know all there is know about you and your family. But let me ask you something. What does Natalie want to be when she grows up?"

Another feminine tactic—throw in a non sequitur. What the heck did one thing have to do with the other?

This he had to think about for a minute. "A nurse?" He heard the question in his voice and quickly repeated it with more confidence. "She wants to be a nurse."

"Maybe. But what she most wants to be at this moment is a barrel racer, like her mother."

Really? He hadn't even realized Nat knew of Andi's high-school rodeo days.

Before he could answer, Caroline went on. "What's her favorite color? What friend asked her to sleep over tomorrow night? What grade did she get on her math test, the one that was the highest in her class?"

He glared at her, angry at himself for not knowing the answers to her interrogation and angry with her for pushing him on this when it was none of her damn business.

Though it strained his self-control to the limit, he managed to contain his temper.

He wasn't about to engage in a shouting match with

Caroline Montgomery in his own kitchen. No good could possibly come of it. And besides, there was a very real chance he would lose, since everything she'd said was right on the money.

"I don't know," he finally said quietly. "I'm sure it just makes your day to hear me admit that. I don't know those things about my daughter. I guess that makes me the world's worst father."

To his considerable dismay, she reached out and touched his arm, and he felt the heat of it through every nerve ending. "Of course it doesn't make you a bad father. I never meant to imply such a thing. You're busy. It must be hard work running a ranch of this size. I understand that."

To his relief, she withdrew her hand and frowned. "But I'm not so sure your children do."

"They will. My brothers and I figured it out."

He didn't add that he and his brothers hadn't much minded their father being consumed by the ranch all the time as long as it had kept the son of a bitch away from them.

He couldn't be a completely lousy father—how could he be, since he wasn't anything like Hank Dalton? He was never cruel to his children; he didn't taunt them, or berate them or make them feel lower than the lowliest vermin on the ranch.

"Did you?" Her voice was soft but it still cut through his memories like a buzz saw.

"Did I what?"

"Understand about your father?"

His glare sliced at her. "What's that supposed to mean?"

She shouldn't have said anything. This wasn't at all

what she'd wanted to talk to him about tonight. She was concerned only for his children, only Nat and the boys.

Still, in the day and a half she'd been on the ranch, she had begun to wonder if anyone at the Cold Creek was truly happy. Wade certainly didn't seem to be, and this evening at dinner she had witnessed firsthand Seth's unhappiness.

She couldn't put her finger on why she thought this, but there was a kind of sadness to the ranch, a deep and profound melancholy that seemed to permeate the air.

She'd thought it was because he and his children were still grieving for the wife and mother they had lost, but now she wondered if it went deeper than that.

For a moment there after he'd mentioned his father, she had seen something in Wade's eyes, an old pain that suddenly made him seem big and lost and lonely, and that tore at her heart.

"Nothing," she murmured. "I'm sorry. None of my business."

He leaned forward suddenly and was once more the hard man she'd come to know.

"No, you started this. You might as well finish it. What did you mean by that snide little 'did you'?"

She hadn't meant it to sound snide. Obviously his father was a sore subject and she chose her words carefully.

"Marjorie told me something of your father's personality during our coaching sessions. Not much, but enough that I know he wasn't an easy man to live with."

"That's one word for it. My father was a stone-cold bastard, there's no secret about that. He figured he owned everything and everyone on the Cold Creek. We all had to walk his line or else. I used to think he invented that old phrase about my way or the highway. He sure liked to use it enough."

He shook himself a little. "But I'm not my father. I would never be deliberately cruel to my kids."

"Not deliberately, no. But they notice your absence in their lives far more than you might think. When parents are too distant and distracted, no matter what the reason, children can't help but view it as a rejection. They begin to wonder what makes them so unlovable and find themselves doing all kinds of crazy things to find that attention they need."

Like cutting off all her hair when she was twelve or getting her nose pierced the year she'd turned fourteen, all in the hopes that Quinn might look at *her* once, instead of the next deal.

Somehow Wade must have picked up on her thoughts.

"That sounds like the voice of experience." He moved forward slightly, his eyes an intense blue in the low lighting.

She forced herself not to flinch. "We're not talking about me," she said coolly, wondering how this conversation had suddenly twisted around to her.

"Maybe we should be."

"My childhood isn't very interesting and has no bearing on this discussion," she said, then mentally cringed at the cool, prim note she heard in her voice.

"I think it does. What kind of a father was Quinn Montgomery? The doting kind who adored your every move and let you get away with murder? Or the stern, authoritarian type who laid down the law and insisted you follow it?"

Neither. Quinn had been just like Wade. Distracted, distant. Disinterested. Maybe that's why it was so painful for her to watch. Her father loved her, but on his own schedule, when he could fit her in between scams. Not when she needed him most.

She certainly wasn't going to share that with Wade, though.

"I'm sorry," she said, gathering up her notes and closing up her computer. "I shouldn't have said anything. It's been a long day and we're both tired. I'll see you in the morning."

"Running away?"

Her gaze flashed to his and she wasn't sure how to read the expression there.

"No. I just…"

"You should be. It would be better for both of us."

Before she could figure out that odd statement, he stepped forward, his eyes dark and stormy, and an instant later his mouth descended to hers.

For one shocked second, she froze as his powerful arms captured her and tugged her against his unyielding strength, as his mouth moved slowly over hers.

He tasted dusty and male, a combination she somehow found irresistible, and she softened in his arms, giving in to the attraction that had been buzzing through her like an insistent hummingbird from the moment she'd arrived at the Cold Creek.

She shivered as every cell surged to awareness, to a sweet and heavy arousal, and she was lost to everything but this—the taste and scent and feel of him surrounding her with heat and strength.

What had brought them to this? She wasn't quite sure. One moment they'd been arguing, the next here they were, mouths tangled together, both breathing hard as they tasted and touched and explored.

He didn't like her and thought she was a nosy busy-body. So why was he holding her with a kind of desperation, one hand buried in her hair, the other at the small of her back drawing her close enough she could feel the hard jut of his arousal?

She was vaguely aware of the world outside their embrace, of the pig-shaped clock ticking above the stove and a sudden breeze rattling the glass panes and the hard countertop of the breakfast bar digging into her back as he pressed her against it.

But none of it mattered.

Her entire world had condensed to this moment, to this man with his solid strength and the sadness in his eyes.

"You smell so good." The low whisper in her ear was more arousing even than his touch. "Like home-made vanilla ice cream fresh from my grandma's old tin ice-cream maker."

She shivered as his mouth slowly slid down her jaw-line then found the rapid pulse in her neck.

He kissed her there, then his mouth found hers again and Caroline decided she could cheerfully die right here in the Cold Creek kitchen as long as Wade Dalton could kiss her to heaven.

One of her clients had reached a goal earlier in the year of parachuting out of an airplane for her fiftieth birthday. She'd described a free fall to Caroline as incredible, not so much a sensation of falling as flying, soaring above the earth with arms outstretched and the wind rushing to meet you.

For the first time, here in Wade's arms with his mouth hard on hers, Caroline began to understand what she'd meant by that and she never wanted this twirling, whirling free fall to stop.

One of his hands moved to her waist and slid beneath her shirt just enough to touch the bare skin above the waistband of her jeans. She moaned, her arms tight around his neck, and leaned into his slow, arousing touch, desperate for more.

She wasn't sure what sound intruded first, the scrape of a boot on the steps outside the kitchen door or the low, tuneless whistling—she only knew someone else was coming.

No. Go away, she thought, but the sounds drew nearer. She didn't know how, but at the last moment she managed to organize her scattered brain cells just enough to yank out of Wade's arms half a second before the door opened with a squeak.

Seth stood in the doorway, a basket of laundry in his arms and those heartbreakingly blue eyes wide with surprise. His gaze shifted from her to Wade and then back again, and she knew hot color was soaking her cheeks. Beside her, she could hear Wade's ragged breathing and she was mortified to see the surprise in Seth's eyes give way to speculation.

"I didn't think anybody else would be up. Sorry to interrupt."

"You didn't," Caroline said quickly, compelled for some insane reason to protect Wade from his brother's knowing look. "We were, um, talking about the children."

Not exactly a lie, she told herself. They *had* been talking about the children right before that earthshaking kiss.

"Right. Must have been a pretty heated conversation.

You're both looking a little flush. What were you doing, comparing your philosophies about corporal punishment? That's bound to get anybody a little hot. Personally—and I hope this doesn't make me sound like a cretin—I come down on the side that sometimes a little swat on the behind is the only thing you can do to get the little buggers' attention. You can give all the timeouts in the world but they won't be as effective as one well-timed hand to the tush. Don't you agree, Wade?"

"Whatever," Wade snapped, looking so completely stunned by what had just happened that Caroline wanted to die of mortification.

"Well, I was only going to throw in a load of laundry," Seth said. "But I can certainly come back later if you're not done, uh, talking."

"Leave it alone," Wade growled to his brother.

To her immense gratification, Seth held his tongue, though he did nothing to hide his amusement.

Caroline decided she had no option left but to flee. "Do your laundry," she said to Seth. "I was just heading to bed. Good night."

The last was directed to both of them but she hurried from the kitchen without daring to look at Wade.

She might never be able to look at him again, not after the way she had responded instantly in his arms as if he'd set spark to dry tinder.

Chapter 9

Wade watched Caroline rush from the kitchen and wondered if he would ever be able to taste vanilla ice cream again without remembering those incredible few moments she had burned in his arms.

"You're an idiot," he growled, though he wasn't completely sure whether his words were aimed at his brother or himself.

"That's the rumor." Seth grinned, unoffended, and headed for the laundry room just off the kitchen.

"I *am* sorry I interrupted," he called over his shoulder. "I should have knocked first. I just never expected to find my cold and passionless older brother locking lips with our beautiful new stepsister."

"She's *not* our stepsister, damn it!"

This seemed to amuse Seth even more. Grinning like a fool, he started the wash cycle.

Wade thought about going upstairs for that shower

he so desperately needed—the one that would now by necessity have to be frigid—then decided he might as well settle at least one of his hungers.

He was cutting a slice of leftover birthday cake when Seth wandered back in.

"Oooh, cake. Mind sharing a piece of that?"

He would have preferred for Seth to take that amused, knowing look and cram it. But it was hard to smirk and eat at the same time, so he gestured to the cake server with his fork. "Help yourself."

"Thanks. I worked up one hell of an appetite down at the Bandito tonight. Bunch of women from New York are staying out at the Swan Valley Dude Ranch, sort of a girls' week out, I guess. They were in the mood for a little cowboy boogie, if you know what I mean. I couldn't let them go home disappointed."

Sometimes he wondered if Seth had been born knowing how to irritate him or if he'd honed the skill through years of study and practice. His brother knew how much he disliked hearing about his exploits so, of course, he delighted in sharing at every opportunity.

He was damn sure not in the mood tonight to hear them, so he decided to change the subject.

"Do you think I'm a poor father?"

Seth froze, the fork halfway to his mouth, then he set it down like it was handblown china. "Is that what Caroline says?"

"Not in so many words."

Seth cocked his head, his eyes baffled but moderately impressed. "Okay so explain to me how a woman goes from questioning your parenting skills to swapping saliva with you?"

To his dismay, Wade could feel his ears turn red. "We were just talking," he mumbled.

"Right. That's why when I came in, her sweet little mouth was all swollen and her cheeks matched the pink of Mom's climbing roses. All that talking, huh?"

Served him right for thinking he could ever have a serious conversation with Seth. "Just drop it. Forget I said anything."

"No, you want to know if I think you're a poor father." To Wade's surprise, his brother didn't offer any more wisecracks and he even appeared to give the matter some thought. "I don't think I've ever heard you say a harsh word to Nat and the boys, unlike our own dear old dad."

"That has to count for something."

"Something," Seth agreed, taking another bite of cake. "You're not half the bastard he was."

"Gee, thanks."

"On the other hand, you do tend to leave a lot of the work to Mom, when it comes to the kids."

First Caroline now Seth. He sighed. "What else am I supposed to do? Can somebody just tell me that? I don't have much choice. The ranch won't run itself."

Seth's too-handsome features seemed to harden a little and for a moment Wade almost thought he saw bitterness flicker in his eyes. "No, it won't. But your kids won't raise themselves, either. What if Mom decides not to come back?"

"Don't think that hasn't been keeping me up at night." And now he would have memories of kissing Caroline to help do the job. "I don't know. I guess I'll have to figure something out. Hire a housekeeper or something."

"Or a ranch manager."

"Can't say I'm crazy about either one of those ideas." He sighed again and took a sip of water. "This wasn't the way things were supposed to turn out. This whole single-father thing sucks."

"Imagine your life without the kids, though," Seth pointed out.

For one brief second, Wade considered how much less stress he would have in his life right now.

Yeah, his life might be less frenzied. But it would also be bleak and miserable.

No Natalie, with her rapid chatter and her freely offered opinions, no Tanner and all that energy, no Cody to cuddle up with him on Sunday afternoons while they napped and watched fishing shows. It didn't even bear thinking about.

He loved his children but it was still tough raising them on his own, wondering if every move he made was the wrong one.

Caroline didn't help things, coming here, stirring him up, making him question himself even more.

"So while you and Caroline were, uh, talking, did she offer any advice for you?"

Not at the time, but he was willing to bet she had a few choice suggestions for him after that kiss. A few of them might even have something to do with the kids.

"I'm sure she's working up to that," he murmured. "I imagine before she goes back to California, I'll have an earful of advice. The woman's not exactly shy about expressing her opinions."

He wanted her gone, he told himself.

So why did his chest feel hollow just at the thought of it?

* * *

How could she ever face him again?

The sun hadn't yet managed its rigorous daily climb above the Tetons but Caroline was already dressed. She wasn't quite ready for the day, though, as she curled up in the window seat of her bedroom, a blanket across her knees, gazing out at the quiet, dark ranch.

Her eyes burned, gritty and tired, and she wondered if she had managed any sleep at all. Her mind couldn't seem to stop racing around and around that stunning kiss.

It was just a kiss, she reminded herself. Nothing to get so worked up about.

But that wild conflagration certainly seemed on a completely different level from your regular, everyday kiss. One moment they had been arguing about the children, the next they'd been tangled together, wild and hungry. If Seth hadn't wandered into the kitchen, she could only imagine how far they might have taken things.

Unless Wade was a better actor than she, both of them had been lost to the world, to propriety, to the sheer *insanity* of the sudden shocking heat between them.

Where had it come from? What strange command did he have over her? She had scarcely recognized herself in that needy, hungry creature in his arms the night before.

She was thirty years old, far from a giddy teenager, and though her love life wasn't exactly the stuff of legend, she'd enjoyed a few relationships she considered serious.

Each of them had been pleasant in its own way. Yes,

that was exactly the word. *Pleasant.* Calm, comfortable, easy.

The heat she and Wade generated had been something else entirely, something completely out of her experience.

It had been raw and fierce and wild, almost frightening in its intensity. She had never had any idea she could burn like that and she wasn't sure she liked it.

Perhaps because of her chaotic childhood, she preferred the comfort of order and calm in her relationships. What she'd experienced in Wade's arms the night before had been anything *but* ordered and calm.

She supposed her reaction disturbed her most because she didn't understand it. Wade was so different from the usual sort of man she dated. He was powerful, forceful, the kind of man who seemed to consume all the oxygen molecules in every room he entered. Despite that, there was also a deep loneliness about him that drew her like a magnet.

She was a sucker for anyone in need, always had been. She wanted to comfort and heal, to hold him close and absorb his pain.

What must he think of her for responding so passionately to him? She cringed just thinking about it.

He already seemed to think she had ulterior motives for coming to the ranch, that she and Quinn were part of some complex scheme to drain the Cold Creek coffers. What if he thought her response to him was another indication that she had somehow set her sights on him as part of their twisted plans?

Nothing could be further from the truth.

Yes, she was attracted to him. But that heated kiss in the kitchen was the only thing they could ever share, even if Wade was interested in more. She had coached enough people struggling through bad relationships to know that one based only on attraction would never survive. And though she'd only known the man a few days, what she had seen didn't lead her to believe he was a good fit for her, relationship-wise.

She could never let herself care for a man who ranked his own children so low on his priority list. She had lived through it herself and knew the pain firsthand.

So how did she make it through the next few days? she wondered as she yawned and stood up. She couldn't avoid the man—it was his house, after all. In a few moments, she would probably see him over breakfast, when she would have to smile and be polite and pretend nonchalance about their scalding embrace.

Though she wanted just the opposite for his children, for her own sake, she had to hope he would be even more busy the next few days as the television interview approached. With any luck, he would be too distracted by that to pay much attention to her.

And while he was busy ignoring her, she would work on shaking free of her unwanted attraction toward the man.

How hard could it be?

Her resolve to keep her distance lasted all of an hour—and then she saw him again.

She had to admit, she had been relieved not to find him in the kitchen when she finally made her way there, though Seth showed up a few moments after she started frying bacon and mixing pancake batter. She assumed Wade had already left for the morning, as someone had made a fresh pot of coffee on the coffeemaker and left a dirty cup in the sink.

The most she had to contend with before the children came down was Seth's flirtation, though it seemed more mechanical than sincere. She didn't know the youngest Dalton brother well but this was the first time she'd seen him so pensive.

The compliments he gave her were almost benign, with none of his flowery prose. He also didn't make any cracks about the scene he had to know he'd interrupted the night before.

She almost asked if he was feeling well but decided that would seem presumptuous.

The children woke soon after Seth had left with a subdued thank you for breakfast. After that, she didn't have time to worry about either Dalton brother, she was too busy taking care of the next generation.

For the next hour she ran nonstop—helping Nat find her library books, rewrapping the bandage on Tanner's burn that had slipped loose in the night, and changing and dressing Cody, who for some reason decided to cling to her like an orangutan baby while she fixed plates of pancakes and bacon for the children.

She was on the floor mopping up the second spilled orange juice of the morning due to Tanner's awkward use of his bandaged hand when she heard the door creak behind her.

Some instinct told her who had come in and she froze, mortified at being caught on her hands and knees, her rear end in the air and Cody leaning against her hip.

Grabbing Cody to keep him upright as she shifted position, she rose quickly to her feet and faced Wade.

Why did the air seem high and thin suddenly? She

couldn't seem to breathe, her mind jumping with images of the last time she had faced him here in this kitchen.

"Morning."

Wade's deep-voiced greeting encompassed the room and his progeny. He took off his hat as he walked inside but, instead of hanging it up on the customary hook, he kept it in his hands. She assumed that indicated he didn't plan to stay long.

"Hey Dad, guess what?" Tanner started in with his favorite phrase. "Caroline put a new bandage on my hand and she had to wrap it three times because I was moving too much and she said it was grosser than a whole room full of stinky socks."

"I hope you told her thanks for helping you," he said gruffly. "Not everybody would be willing to face something grosser than a room full of stinky socks first thing in the morning."

"I did."

"Good."

After an awkward pause, he shifted his hat to his other hand and finally met Caroline's gaze.

Her insides twirled and she could swear the temperature of the room had just kicked up at least ten degrees.

"Did I already miss Nat's bus?" Though he directed the question to her, he didn't maintain eye contact and she had to wonder if this encounter was as awkward for him as she was finding it.

"No. She just ran upstairs to change her shirt. Tanner spilled orange juice on the one she was wearing."

"Oh."

She was staring at his mouth, she realized, remembering in vivid detail how it had moved over hers the night before, licking and tasting and exploring....

She quickly jerked her gaze away, horrified at herself as heat soaked her cheeks.

"Um, would you like some breakfast?"

"I grabbed some bread and jam with my coffee this morning before I headed out. I don't have much time, just a few minutes, really."

Big surprise there, she thought, but before she could say anything, Nat burst back into the kitchen.

She stopped when she saw her father. "Hi, Dad! I thought you guys were bringing down the range cows from Hightop today."

"We are. We're leaving in a minute."

He rubbed the back of his neck. "I, uh, just wanted to catch you before you left for school. I didn't have a chance to talk to you much last night but I wanted you to know the birthday cake you made was great. I had another piece last night before I went to bed and so did Uncle Seth. We both said as how the second piece was even better than the first. I just wanted you to know."

He said all this without looking at Caroline and she had to admit, she was grateful. She couldn't have said anything past the lump in her throat, stunned that he took her advice about speaking to Natalie in person.

She'd forgotten that part of their conversation because of what had come after, but obviously Wade hadn't. Here he was first thing in the morning, his hat in his hands, taking time away from his busy schedule to give his daughter some of the attention she craved from him.

Caroline could swear she heard the bump and clatter of her heart tumbling to his feet at the look Wade's simple words had put on Natalie's face. The girl's smile couldn't have stretched any wider and she looked like she was ready to take flight.

"You're welcome."

Backpack forgotten, Nat ran to her father, throwing her arms around his waist. Wade returned her hug, then waited patiently while she grabbed up her jacket and her school things, talking a mile a minute.

"It wasn't hard to make," she gushed. "I just followed the recipe like Grandma showed me and Caroline helped me crack the eggs and put on the frosting. I knew you would like it. I *knew* it. Grandma says your sweet tooth is just as bad now as it was when you were Tanner's age. She said you could finish off a cake all by yourself if you put your mind to it."

"Between Seth and me, we did a pretty good job with yours," he said, though he didn't look thrilled at either his daughter or his mother for sharing that information.

"Do you want me to make you another one today? I can. I can make one anytime you want. I think I can even do the eggs by myself next time."

"Thanks, honey. I think one is enough for now but I'll let you know when I'm ready for more."

"You'd better go or you're going to miss the bus," Caroline murmured, though she was loathe to interrupt the girl's excitement.

Natalie hurried toward the door, where she paused and turned back, still glowing. "Dad, when I come home from school can I help you unload the cows? I won't get in the way, I promise. I just want to watch the hazing."

He opened his mouth and Caroline could see the refusal forming in his expression, but he surprised her by nodding after a moment. "If we're still at it, you can come down to the pens."

Natalie gave a delighted shout, then rushed out the door toward the bus stop.

"Can I help, too, Dad?" Tanner jumped down from his chair. "Hey, can I come up to the mountains with you to bring 'em down, too? I won't get in the way, either."

Caroline couldn't contain a smile at that bald-faced lie. She was learning Tanner's best skill was getting in the way.

She stepped in so Wade wouldn't have to be the one to say no. "I need your help around here. We're going to run into town and do some grocery shopping."

"Shopping's stupid. I want to help with the roundup."

"Next time, partner," Wade spoke firmly. "When your arm's all better, okay?"

"Why does Nat get to watch?"

"Because she's older—and because she doesn't have a bum hand she needs to keep clean."

"You said bum, Dad!" Tanner chortled.

"Right. And I'll smack yours if I catch you down at the pens today, you hear me? Those range cows are quick and mean. You stay clear."

Tanner pouted. "I know. I'm not a baby like Cody."

"Then you're old enough and smart enough to obey me, right?"

"I guess." Tanner looked disappointed but didn't push it as he turned back to his breakfast.

Wade stood there another second then shoved his hat back on. "I've got to run. The crew is waiting for me."

This time he met Caroline's gaze directly and she could swear she saw something fierce and hot leap into those blue eyes before he shielded them again. "I meant what I said to Tanner. We'll be bringing two hundred head down today in a couple of batches. Best if you keep the boys clear of them. They can be vicious."

"I will," she promised.

Wade turned to go but she stopped him with a hand to his arm. Heat sparked between them and she quickly dropped her fingers. "Sorry. I just...I wanted to tell you I was touched by what you just did for Nat."

He looked more than a little embarrassed. "It wasn't anything."

"Don't say that. It might have been a little thing but surely you could see it meant the world to her."

He opened his mouth to say something then seemed to change his mind. "I've got to run," he said abruptly, then hurried out of the kitchen without another word.

Chapter 10

The lovebirds finally called to check in just as Wade was following the last semitrailer full of range cows back to the ranch later that day.

He almost didn't pick up his cell phone when it rang, distracted by all he still had to do that day, and it took a moment for his mother's voice to register.

He barely recognized it. She sounded about a dozen years younger.

"Where the he—heck are you?" he asked.

"Reno, honey. Didn't you get my note?"

"Yeah, I got it. I just still can't believe you'd run off like that."

"I'm sorry, honey, but we just couldn't wait another day to be together. You understand, don't you?"

Not in the slightest, but he decided saying so would be mean so he kept his mouth shut.

"Are you coming back?" he asked instead.

"I told you I was, didn't I? Actually that's what I'm calling about. We were planning to be back Monday or Tuesday but now we're talking about driving over to the coast. We thought we'd spend a few days packing up Quinn's place in San Francisco and then drive down to see his daughter in Santa Cruz. Will you and the kids be all right for a few more days if we do that?"

Mentally, he was pounding his head against the steering wheel a couple dozen times. In reality, he just grimaced. "We'll survive. But you won't find Montgomery's daughter in California."

"Sure we will. That's where she lives."

"Not at the present. She's here."

"Who's there?"

"Caroline. She showed up the morning after you left."

"Caroline Montgomery?"

"That's what I said, isn't it?"

"Why, that was two days ago. She's still there?"

Only two days? It felt like forever. He sighed. "Yeah. She offered to stay and help with the kids."

"And you let her?"

The shock in her voice made him defensive. "You picked a hell of a time to run off, Mom. The crew from the network is showing up in three days and things here are a mess. I didn't know what else to do."

He heard silence on the line, then Marjorie's muffled voice telling someone—her huggy bear, he assumed—about Caroline. A moment later, his mother returned to the line.

"It's just like her to see you needed help and settle right in to do what she can. Isn't she wonderful?"

He was still reserving judgment on that one. "She's something, all right," he muttered.

"I just *knew* you'd like her once you met her. I'm sure Nat and the boys adore her already."

Too much. They were going to miss her when she left. "You didn't give me too many choices," he repeated.

"I'm losing the signal here, honey. I didn't quite catch that."

"You left things in a mess here, Mom," he said loudly. "What kind of example do you think that sets to the kids when they see their grandmother run off with some guy she never even met in person?"

"Sorry I can't hear you. These darn cell phones. Works fine one minute, then you feel like you're talking to yourself the next."

Marjorie still sounded giddy and he had to wonder if she really couldn't hear him or if she was faking because she didn't want to listen to any of his lectures.

"Since you've got Caroline there," she went on, "I know the kids are in good hands. I guess that means we can go to San Francisco without worrying. We'll be back by Wednesday. Thursday at the latest. Tell the kids I love them and I'll see them soon."

Before he realized it, she had severed the connection. He tossed the phone on the passenger seat, though what he really wanted was to chuck the damn thing through the windshield.

Somebody suddenly rapped on his window and he turned to find Seth on the other side. He rolled down the window.

"What's the holdup?" Seth asked.

Wade winced when he realized the crew was all lined up behind him waiting to get through and unload the cattle.

"I love that woman but sometimes, I swear she makes me absolutely crazy."

Seth looked confused. "What woman?"

"Mom. That was her on the phone. Apparently she and her Romeo are having such a wonderful time on their honeymoon they've decided to extend it."

Seth winced. "I don't even want to go there, man. It's an image I don't need in my head."

"They're not ready to come back by Sunday since they want to drive to the coast. Now it's looking like they won't be back until Wednesday or Thursday, which leaves us stuck with Caroline for a few more days, if she's up for it."

"No real hardship there. You don't often find a woman who is sweet as sugar, can cook like that and who looks great while she's doing it. I like her."

"You like anything that doesn't have a Y chromosome."

Seth grinned. "True enough. But I especially like Caroline. You have to admit, she has plenty of grit to pitch right in like she did. Most women would have taken off running the first time they caught sight of your little Dalton gang."

She did seem to be good for the kids. All three of them had taken to her immediately.

He thought of the way he'd seen her that morning when he'd walked into the kitchen, with Cody leaning on her while she worked, like the boy didn't want to let her get two feet away.

"I like having her here," Seth said again, then he grinned. "And judging by that scene in the kitchen I so rudely interrupted last night, I can't help but think you do, too."

Yeah, that was the whole problem and the reason he wanted her gone as soon as possible.

He did like her, entirely too much. He hadn't stopped thinking about her all day. Of her mouth, soft and warm and welcoming, of the soft, sexy sounds she'd made when he'd kissed her, of her small hands buried in his hair, sending shivers of pleasure down his spine.

He shifted in the seat, furious at himself for going down that road again. The night before had been a colossal mistake, one he would make sure never happened again.

"I would like having Mom back where she belongs a hell of a lot more," he muttered, then threw the truck in gear and drove through the gate, leaving his brother watching after him.

Caroline had to admit that even after five years of coaching people to break old patterns and alter old habits—years when she had seen some of her clients make remarkable changes—she found it amazing how quickly she adapted to a new way of life.

Four days after that stunning kiss, she stood at the kitchen window washing lunch dishes and looking out at a clear, beautiful October day. The trees outside the window were ablaze with color and leaves fluttered down on the breeze.

Beyond them, the jagged, snow-capped Tetons provided their magnificent backdrop to the scene and she thought how lucky the Daltons were to enjoy that view every day.

She had been at the ranch for six days and her life in Santa Cruz seemed far away.

She never would have expected to find such

contentment here. The children had already wiggled their way into her heart and she found each day with them a delight.

Over the weekend, she'd found Nat to have a funny sense of humor, a sweet girl who mothered her little brothers and who missed her own mother. Tanner was so bright and so inquisitive, he had a million questions about everything. And she adored Cody for his sweet disposition and eagerness to love.

She would miss them all when she returned to California, even Seth with his teasing flirtations and the three quiet, polite ranch hands she had met briefly.

And Wade. Would she miss Wade?

She sighed as she dried the last dish and returned it to the cupboard. Most definitely.

She already did, as she hadn't seen him for more than a few minutes at a time since that night in the kitchen.

With his impeccable timing, Tanner wandered into the kitchen just as she finished. "We're bored. There's nothing to do."

That was the biggest challenge with this one. His attention span was painfully short and keeping him entertained and occupied had been a great challenge, especially with his burned hand and the precautions they had to take because of it.

"Can we go play in the sandbox?" he asked now, his big blue eyes wearing a pleading expression that was tough to resist.

She stiffened her spine and shook her head. "Honey, you know you can't until your bandage comes off. But you only have to wait one more day, remember? That's not so bad. Your uncle Jake said everything's looking good with your burn and you won't have to have the mummy claw of death much longer."

Tanner made his trademark menacing lunge at her and she played along, shrieking and backing away as he advanced. When she couldn't go backward any more, she caught him in a quick hug, which he returned with a willingness that warmed her heart.

"You can hang on one more day, can't you?"

"I don't want to," he complained. "Why can't you just take it off now so I can go outside and play? You take it off to change it."

"Because then your uncle would be mad at me."

Tanner's expression turned crafty. "He won't spank you, though, 'cause you're a girl and my dad says boys don't hit girls."

She laughed. "Nice try. But even with that threat out of the way, I'm not going to take off your bandage, kiddo. I'm under orders."

His sigh was heavy and put-upon, and she hid a smile as she reached for Cody to keep him from dumping the garbage can.

"Care, Care," the toddler chanted, throwing his arms tightly around her neck.

"Why don't we find jackets and your hats and we'll go outside for a walk?"

"Can we go see Sunshine?" Tanner asked.

"Of course. But we have to stay out of your dad's way, right?"

Tanner nodded. "Yeah, 'cause the TV people are here."

"That's right. And this is important to your father."

The actual interview wasn't until the next day, but the network had sent an advance crew to lay the groundwork for it and to shoot visuals around the ranch of Wade and his crew working.

It was a beautiful day for a walk and for a video shoot, Caroline thought as she followed the two little bobbing cowboy hats outside. The sky was almost painfully blue, with only a few high clouds. It was cool, though, and she was grateful for her sweater.

On their way to the barn and Tanner's pony, they crunched through leaves and tried to catch them in the air as they fluttered down under the spreading branches of the big maples along the fence.

Maybe she ought to ask Wade where to find some rakes and she and the boys could spend the afternoon making piles and jumping in them.

Cody's pony nickered when he saw them and came trotting over for a treat.

"Please can I ride him, Care-line? Please? I'll forget how if I don't."

She debated it. His hand was much improved and, if he wore a glove, she didn't see the harm in allowing it. "Maybe when Nat gets home to help you saddle him, okay?"

"Yes!" Tanner made a triumphant fist in the air just as she heard adult voices.

She turned to find Wade walking around the barn with three others, two men carrying camera equipment and a young woman in jeans and new-looking boots with a clipboard and a cell phone.

She pondered how best to sneak out of their way before Wade and his companions spotted them. Before she could, though, the boys caught sight of their father.

"Daddy, Daddy!" Cody wriggled out of her hold like

a budding Houdini and raced to his father, Tanner right on his heels.

Caroline hurried after them, arriving just in time to watch Cody hold his arms out for his father to lift him up.

"Sorry," she said a little breathlessly. "They're faster than me."

Wade's features looked annoyed but he didn't say anything, only gave in to Cody's demands and picked him up.

She had to admit, they made a charming picture—the sexy cowboy and his two very cute little buckaroos in their matching cowboy hats.

Apparently, she wasn't the only one who thought so. The woman with the clipboard seemed to melt into a gushy pile right there next to the horse pasture.

"Oh my gosh, they are *so* precious. We have to include them in the shoot."

Wade blinked. "The boys?"

"Absolutely!" The woman was young and attractive and had a look in her eye that reminded Caroline of some of her clients who became so totally one-dimensional they weren't able to focus on anything but work.

If she were one of her clients, Caroline would probably tell this young woman to quickly find a hobby outside work before she burned herself up like Caroline had done at social work.

"Just thinking out loud here," the woman went on, "but maybe we could do something along the lines of building a legacy for your children's future or something, as those who make their living from the land have been doing for generations. I'll have to run it past the reporter."

She turned to Caroline suddenly, her features friendly. "I'm sorry. I'm Darci Perez, Mrs. Dalton. I'm producing the story about your husband and the Cold Creek."

Caroline froze, unexpected heat flashing through her at the idea. Her gaze collided with Wade's and she found the aghast expression on his face the height of humiliation.

"He's not my husband," Caroline said quickly—too quickly, she realized, when the producer looked surprised at her vehemence.

The woman winced. "Sorry. I should know better than to jump to conclusions like that."

"Tanner, don't touch anything," Wade broke in sharply and Caroline saw that one of the cameramen had set his equipment on a bale of hay and Tanner, of course, had homed in on it like a bee on a honeysuckle bush.

Tanner froze and Wade turned back to the conversation. "I'm a widower," he told the producer. A muscle flexed in his jaw, as if just saying the word was difficult.

Darci Perez looked even more uncomfortable. "That's probably in the background information I have about you. I should have read it more closely. I'm so sorry."

"Don't worry about it," Wade said, then glared again at Tanner, who, despite his father's warning, had sidled closer to the equipment. "What did I tell you about not touching anything?"

If Caroline hadn't survived six days with the boy, she might have been taken in by his angelic expression. "I'm just looking, Daddy. With my eyes, not my hand or my mummy claw of death."

"Keep it that way, bud."

The producer was studying her expectantly so

Caroline stepped forward, her hand outstretched. "I'm Caroline Montgomery, a friend of the family. I'm staying here for a few days to help Wade with the children while his mother is out of town."

The woman shook her hand. "That name is familiar. Have we met?"

"I don't believe so."

Darci frowned and then her expression brightened. "I know! Didn't you write an article for *Glamour* a few months ago about top ten best ways to guarantee yourself a happy, fulfilling life?"

Caroline was flattered, she had to admit. "I did. I'm shocked you remembered the byline. Most people skip right over them."

"Only because I practically have the thing memorized." The woman grinned. "I've done the exact opposite of at least half of the things on your list but I'm working on it."

Caroline smiled. "Progress is good."

"Don't you think you should be going back to the house now?" Wade asked and she saw that it was all he could do to hold onto Cody, who'd decided he wanted down now and was wriggling for all he was worth.

Darci observed the boy's struggles with interest. "He looks like a handful. That must be an interesting challenge, a single father trying to raise his young children and run a ranch of this size as well."

"*Interesting* is one word for it," Wade said.

"I'll mention that to the reporter, too. He might want to follow up on that angle."

Wade would absolutely detest discussing his personal life on camera, Caroline knew. She wondered how to help him avoid it, then remembered it was none of her business.

"Come on, boys. Let's go," she said. She took Cody from Wade and turned around for Tanner, then drew in a quick breath when she found him trying to heft the large camera off the hay bale.

"Tanner! Put that down!" Wade barked. The boy jumped at his tone and hurried to obey but the camera slid out of his bandaged hand and landed in the dirt with a heavy, sickening thud.

"Tanner! I told you not to touch anything." Wade's features looked harsh and angry. "Now look what you've done!"

Tanner's lip trembled. "I'm sorry, Daddy. I didn't mean to. It slipped out of my hand."

"You shouldn't have been messing with it in the first place. When are you ever going to learn to listen to me?"

Tanner gazed around at the circle of adults looking down at him, then at his father's glower. He let out a little distressed cry then took off running around the side of the barn.

Wade stared after him like he wasn't quite sure what to do. Exasperated, Caroline handed Cody back to him and started out after the boy.

Chapter 11

Caroline followed the upset boy around the corner of the barn, wondering how on earth his little legs could move so fast.

She assumed he was heading for the house but then he seemed to catch sight of something distracting. Suddenly, in mid-stride he switched directions and headed toward the pens to the east of the barn.

Caroline stopped dead, her blood suddenly coated in a thin, crackly layer of ice, when she saw what was inside the corral. At least a dozen range cows and their calves munched hay, their wickedly sharp horns gleaming in the afternoon sun.

She remembered Wade's warning about the range cows and what she'd learned in the few days she'd been on the Cold Creek. The cows were bred to be tough and aggressive to survive predators and weather conditions in the mountains, and she remembered Wade's warning that they could be nasty and bad tempered.

Tanner knew that. What on earth was the rascal thinking to go anywhere near them?

"Tanner, get back here," she yelled, but he either chose to ignore her or didn't hear over the cattle's lowing.

He moved closer to the corral, his attention fixed on something inside and Caroline had a sudden terrible foreboding that left her sick. He wouldn't go inside. He *couldn't*.

She held her breath as she raced after him but Tanner had at least a ten-yard head start. Even if he hadn't, she had learned during her time at the ranch that the boy could be quick and wily.

"Tanner Dalton, you get back here," she called again.

To her relief, this time he slowed a little and looked back at her.

"Stop," she called out.

Her relief was short-lived when he shook his head. "One of the kitties is in there," he called. "I have to get him."

She tried to see where he was looking but all she could see were milling, deadly looking hooves.

"No you don't! Let your dad go after him."

"He'll die in there and then the mommy kitty will be sad."

She was within ten feet of him now. "And if you go in there and get hurt, your dad is going to be sad *and* mad. You don't want that."

Bringing up Wade was apparently the wrong tack completely. Even from here she could see the sudden stubborn light in the boy's eyes.

"He's already mad at me," Tanner said as he reached the corral fence.

She was close, so close, but just as she reached out to grab his shirt, he slipped under the wooden slat and was inside the pen heading toward the tiny gray kitten she could now see trembling in the middle of the milling cattle.

"Tanner, get back here," she snapped, keeping a careful eye on the cows, who were paying them no attention for now.

"I will. Soon as I get the kitty."

Caroline stood on the other side, torn about what to do. Should she go after him or go get help? She didn't know the first thing about range cattle other than they were huge and horned and scared the stuffing out of her. But she didn't dare leave even to call for Wade's help.

She had no choice. She was going to have to go after him. Oh, she was going to have a head full of gray hair by the time she made it back to Santa Cruz, she thought, then drew in one last terrified breath and slipped through the slats of the fence.

They seemed even more huge on this side of the fence, as big as small cars, and those horns looked sharp and deadly. She moved through them carefully, as slowly as she dared, her eyes on Tanner as he finally reached the tiny kitten safely after what felt like a dozen lifetimes.

"I got you," she heard him murmur, holding the little creature in his bandaged hand and stroking him with the other. "You're okay now. Nobody's going to treat you like a big baby anymore."

Caroline wanted to scream and yell and shout Hosanna when he started toward the other side of the enclosure. She followed, doing her best to keep her body between his and the animals, who so far were paying them little heed, to her vast relief.

Twenty yards had never felt so endlessly long. Finally they were within five yards of the fence, safety almost in reach. She could taste it, feel it, even as she wondered whether she would ever be able to breathe again.

After this, she was swearing off beef forever, she decided.

They were almost there when the stupid, self-destructive kitten suddenly jumped or slipped out of Tanner's arms. He gave a cry that drew the attention of a few of the nearby animals, then went down on his hands and knees to grab it.

"Come on. We've got to get out of here," Caroline ordered.

"I know. I've almost got him. There!" he pounced on the wriggling kitten then stood up again.

Caroline grabbed for his hand—at this point she would damn well carry him *and* the blasted kitten out of here—but just as she caught his fingers, she heard a snort behind them. She turned slowly and found herself facing the beady eyes of a cow, not placid and gentle as she'd always imagined, but red-rimmed and wild and not at all happy to have them in her space.

The cow started loping toward them and Caroline's stomach dropped. "Tanner, move!" she ordered, but before the last word was out of her mouth, the cow came toward them so fast she never would have believed it if she hadn't seen it herself.

"Run!" Caroline yelled harshly and the startled boy obeyed. She half dragged him, half carried him as they headed at full speed for the corral fence and safety.

They weren't going to make it, she realized grimly. The blasted cow would get to them a split second before they reached the fence.

She didn't think about it, she just reacted totally on instinct, picking up Tanner and the kitten and shoving him in front of her, then she pushed him through the wooden slats of the fence.

She had time only to breathe a quick, frightened prayer before the cow reached her.

When Wade caught up with that kid, he was giving him a serious lecture on following orders. A ranch could be a dangerous place for children who didn't learn early to mind their parents the first time.

If they hadn't gotten that message yet, maybe he'd been too soft on Natalie and the boys in his efforts to be as unlike his own father as possible. Tanner obviously didn't understand, so he was just going to have to drill it into the kid's head that when Wade spoke, the kid had to jump. The consequences of doing otherwise could be deadly.

He didn't have time for this today, not with the TV crew there. He almost just let Caroline deal with Tanner and his tantrum. But as he had been the one to yell at his son, he also knew he needed to be the one to explain why. They had a head start on him, though. It had taken a few minutes for him to take Cody to the outbuilding they used as a machine shop, where Seth was fixing a tractor part.

He'd given the baby to a greasy-fingered Seth, had asked him to watch him for a minute, then had taken off after Caroline and Tanner.

As he rounded the corner of the barn, he heard a shout. He jerked his head around and his heart stuttered in his chest when he saw Caroline and Tanner in the middle of a small herd of range cows he'd culled to take to market first.

Inside the pen, Caroline's butter-yellow sweater was a small splash of color in the middle of a sea of huge russet bodies, and he could barely see Tanner.

What the hell were they doing? Did the woman not have a single brain cell in her head? He'd *told* her range cows were dangerous and here she was wandering through them like she and Tanner were tromping through a field of daisies.

At least they were heading out, he saw. They were moving toward the opposite side of the pen from where he was; he had just started around the perimeter when he saw Tanner bend down for something. A few seconds later, Caroline picked him up and headed fast toward the fence.

Just before they made it through, one of the cows got excited by the ruckus and headed toward them, head down.

His blood iced over and he yelled at them to move.

He vaulted the fence where he was, though he was still half the length of the corral away, and raced toward them, waving his hat and yelling to try to distract the angry cow.

She didn't even turn her big head, focused only on Caroline and Tanner, and Wade could do nothing but watch, horrified, as she charged.

As he ran through the milling cattle, he saw Caroline bend down and shove something through the slats—Tanner, he realized—but an instant later the cow reached her and tossed her into the air like she was a sack full of straw.

She landed with a hideous thud against the fence and the cow lowered her head, her nostrils flared. She snorted and bawled, looking for any excuse to charge the unwanted intruder again, and Wade didn't stop to think.

He raced in front of the cow, scooped Caroline up in one arm as gently as he could under the circumstances, and used the other to haul them both up and over the fence.

He made it over to the other side just as the huge cow slammed into the fence, shaking it hard.

He felt like *he* had been the one to take that crushing hit—every ounce of oxygen in his lungs seemed to have been sucked out and, for one horrifying minute, he felt shaky and light-headed as he lowered a limp Caroline to the ground.

With effort, he forced himself to stay calm, especially as Tanner seemed hysterical enough for the both of them, his eyes huge and scared in his pale face.

"What's wrong with Caroline, Daddy? Why are her eyes closed? Is she sleeping?"

"Something like that."

"Should I go find Uncle Seth?"

"No!" With visions of all the trouble the chaos-magnet could get into on his own, Wade spoke to him sternly. "You should sit down right there and stay put."

"But I…"

He didn't have time to deal with two crises right now, not when Caroline's eyes were still closed, but he knew his son well enough to see by the obstinate jut of his jaw that a little child psychology was in order.

"Look," he tempered his tone. "I might need your help, so it would be better for Caroline's sake if you stick close to me for now, okay?"

That seemed to do the trick. Tanner nodded and settled onto the dirt outside the pens, a kitten Wade assumed to be at the heart of this whole damn fiasco still clutched tightly in his arms.

No, *he* was at the heart of this fiasco. If he hadn't yelled at Tanner, the boy wouldn't have run off and none of this would have happened.

He pushed the guilt away for now and focused on Caroline, sick all over again to see her pale, chalky features and the blue tracery of veins in her closed eyelids.

"Come on, honey. Wake up," he ordered as he did a rapid medical assessment.

Growing up on a cattle ranch had, unfortunately, given him plenty of experience in first-triage and he quickly put those skills to work. Her pulse seemed fast but strong and he hoped she had just had the wind knocked out of her.

No bones seemed to be broken but her head had taken a pretty hard crack and it wouldn't surprise him if she had a concussion. A couple of bruised or cracked ribs weren't out of the question either.

If that was the worst of it, she'd be lucky, he thought, but when he was checking her legs for fractures, he felt something sticky at the back of her thigh. He pulled his hand away and his stomach dropped when he saw it was covered in blood.

What was it from? he wondered, not sure whether he dared turn her over to see.

His mind replayed the scene in his head, relived that sickening moment when the cow had charged, and he realized exactly what must have happened, where the blood was coming from.

The cow's horn must have caught the back of Caroline's thigh as she'd tried to get away.

He swallowed a raw oath, not wanting to scare Tanner any more than he already was, and turned her over slightly so he could see what he was dealing with.

His worst fears were confirmed at the jagged puncture wound in her thigh. Blood was already pooled underneath her and the sight made his own blood run cold.

Knowing it was vital he stop—or at least slow—the copious bleeding, he yanked off his work shirt for the relatively clean T-shirt underneath to use as a pressure bandage.

He was punching in 911 when Seth and the news crew came around the corner of the barn, probably to see what was taking him so long.

When Seth caught sight of them, of Wade without his shirt and Caroline stretched out on the ground, he hurried over, Cody in his arms.

"What happened?"

Tanner suddenly started bawling and turned to his uncle for the comfort Wade didn't have time to give.

"I went to get this k-kitty in the corral and Caroline

came after me," the boy sniffled. "One of the c-cows got mad and ran to get us and Caroline pushed me out of way but the cow hurt her and now she won't wake up and it's my fault."

Seth pulled him close. "Okay. It will be okay, bud."

Wade hoped so. With all his heart, he hoped so. The 911 operator finally answered and he recognized a woman he'd gone to high school with, one of Andrea's cousins on her mother's side.

"Hey Sharon, this is Wade Dalton. I need an ambulance up here at the Cold Creek for a thirty-year-old female who's been gored by a range cow. She's unconscious, with a possible concussion and likely a couple bruised ribs as well as a puncture wound in the back of her left thigh."

"Is she breathing?"

Wade watched the steady rise and fall of her chest and took some small comfort from that. "Yeah."

"Is she out of harm's way?"

"You think I'm going to leave her in a corral with an angry cow? Yeah, she's safe. Dammit, Sharon. Just send an ambulance fast!"

"Sorry, Wade but I have to ask the questions. Stay on the line while I call the guys."

It would be at least ten minutes before the volunteer paramedics could make it here from town, he figured. A moment later, Sharon returned to the line. "Okay, they're on their way."

"Thanks, Sharon. Call Jake at the clinic, okay? Tell him it's Caroline and have him stand by."

"Will do. Want me to stay on the line until the crew gets there?"

"No. I've got it from here."

She was waking up, he saw. She moaned a little and started to move restlessly, trying to roll from her side where he'd moved her, to her back. He held her still and he watched her eyes blink open as she tried to get her bearings.

He saw the pain and confusion in her eyes as she looked blankly at the camera crew and Seth, then she turned her head slightly, probably so she could see what was keeping her from rolling back.

The minute her gaze found him, the distress in her features eased and her body seemed to relax.

"I guess I wasn't fast enough," she murmured.

"Told you those range cows can be ornery buggers."

He was astonished at the tenderness soaking through him, though it couldn't quite crowd out all the fear.

She closed her eyes for a moment but opened them a second later and he saw they were wide and panicky. "Tanner! Where's Tanner?"

"Over there with Seth, see? All safe and sound."

She followed the direction he pointed and the relief in her eyes touched some deep chord inside him. She was battered and bloody, but her first thought was still for his son.

At the sound of his name, Tanner approached them, his cheeks tearstained. He knelt down and grabbed hold of Caroline's hand. "Are you mad at me?"

"Oh, honey. Of course not." She squeezed his fingers and Wade felt like some icy band around his heart he hadn't realized was there had started to loosen.

"I'm sorry I went inside the pens where I'm not supposed to go. I'm sorry you got hurt."

"How's the kitten?"

"Good."

He held it up for her and she sighed. "A lot of trouble for a little ball of fur. Good thing he's cute."

The T-shirt Wade was using as a bandage was soaked with blood and he could see her features were getting paler. The kids didn't need to see all this, he thought, and he had a feeling Caroline would feel more comfortable without the crowd of onlookers.

"Seth, maybe you should take the boys and our guests up to the house until the ambulance gets here."

"You sure there's nothing we can do?"

"Send somebody back with something clean I can use as a fresh bandage."

Seth nodded and herded everyone toward the house.

When they were gone, Wade folded his work shirt and tucked it under her cheek so she didn't have to lie in the dirt.

"Thank you," she murmured, her voice weak and thready.

"Hang on. The ambulance is on its way."

Her eyes fluttered open and connected with his. "Oh, is that really necessary? I don't want to be a bother."

"Honey, you've been gored by an eight-hundred-pound range cow. Trust me, it's necessary."

She blinked and the pain in her eyes tore at his heart. He would do anything to take it away, but he was completely helpless. "Gored," she murmured. "That must be why my leg feels like it's on fire."

"Afraid so."

"I thought I just went the rounds with a freight train."

"Yeah, a close encounter with a cow will do that to you."

"You sound like you speak from experience."

"A few times. You can't grow up on a ranch without your share of bumps and bruises."

"Have you been gored?"

She was talking to distract herself from the pain, he realized, and he felt another band around his heart loosen.

"Once. I was fourteen and Jake dared me to do a little bull riding. Dad had this ornery bull he was selling to one of the neighbors, so he had it penned waiting for them to come for it. Somehow we managed to chase him into a chute and I climbed on. We didn't have a rope or anything, just me being an idiot. I probably lasted half a second before I went flying into the air. I was like you, I almost made it out before he caught me."

The worst part of the whole ordeal had been Hank's fury when he'd found they had used an expensive animal for sport. He hadn't worried so much about his son as he had about the bull. Hank had even made him walk up to the house through agonizing pain, he remembered.

Marjorie had almost left the bastard over that one, he remembered, then he realized Caroline's eyes were closed again and pushed the memory away.

"Come on, honey. Hang on."

"Hurts."

He brushed her hair out of her eyes. "I know, sweetheart. But listen, there's the ambulance. Can you hear it? They'll be here in a minute to take you to Jake and he'll fix you right up. He's a hell of a doctor."

"Will you come with me?"

Her quiet words ripped out what was left of his heart. "I doubt they'll let me ride on the ambulance but I'll bring the boys and follow it to the clinic, okay?"

She nodded just as the ambulance arrived.

A moment later, the place bustled with paramedics. Wade stood up, shirtless and suddenly freezing in the cool wind.

His hands were bloody, his chest ached, and he felt like he'd aged at least ten years in the last ten minutes.

Chapter 12

Two hours later, Wade decided he'd aged more like twenty years since seeing that cow heading straight for Caroline and Tanner.

Now he sat across the desk from his brother in Jake's pathologically clean office at the clinic, where Wade had sat for the last two hours thumbing through journal articles on topics about which he had no interest or comprehension.

"So what can you tell me? Are you done with her yet? Will she have to transfer to the hospital in Idaho Falls or can I take her back to the Cold Creek?"

Jake leaned back in his chair twirling a pen in both hands with something perilously close to a smirk on his features. "I'm afraid that as you're not a blood relative of Ms. Montgomery, I'm not at liberty to give you any information about her condition unless she signs a release."

He glared. "I'm *your* relative and I can still pound your smart ass into the ground without breaking a sweat."

"Sorry, but self-preservation is not adequate justification for me to break the law. Bring it on, brother."

Wade suddenly remembered just why Jake used to drive him crazy when they were kids. "You're enjoying this, aren't you?"

"You've been pacing in here like a nervous father for the last two hours. I have to say, I haven't seen you this upset since…" His voice trailed off, along with his grin, and his mouth tightened.

"Since Andrea's illness," Wade finished for him grimly.

Compassion and regret flashed across Jake's features. "I'm sorry for giving you a hard time. I wasn't thinking about how all this must bring back memories of Andi."

"It's not the same. Andi was my wife. My life. Caroline is just…just…"

He couldn't seem to come up with the right word for the place she had filled in his life. Sometimes he wasn't even sure he liked her very much, then others he couldn't stop thinking about her, remembering that kiss they had shared, her crooked little smile that seemed to brighten the whole house, her endless patience with his kids.

Despite his protestations to Jake, he had to admit that his emotions of the last two hours had been eerily similar to those terrible, helpless days he had prowled that hospital room in Idaho Falls while his wife had tried and failed to fight off the infection that had finally claimed her life.

How could he even compare the two experiences? It made no sense and yet his worry and fear felt the same.

"Caroline's a trooper," Jake said. "No tears, no hysterics. She even made a few jokes while she was under the local and I was sewing up the puncture wound. Forty-five stitches, all told, but she's doing fine."

"I thought you couldn't talk about her condition with me."

Jake pulled a paper out of a file and tossed it on the desk, his expression a little shamefaced. "Oh, look. A release form. I must have forgotten Connie had her sign it when they were filling out her insurance papers."

Wade glared at him in disgust. "You always were a son of a bitch."

Jake smirked. "How could I be otherwise when I had such a fine example in my older brother?"

"So what can you tell me? What's the extent of her injuries?"

Jake suddenly became all doctor, no longer a teasing younger brother trying to yank his chain. "Your triage assessment was right on. The X-rays showed two cracked ribs, just as you suspected, I'm guessing from hitting the fence. From what I can piece together, the cow came at her from behind, head down, and caught her in the leg."

"Yeah, I know that part. I was there."

Just remembering it sent cold chills down his spine. He knew he would never forget that horrible moment when she'd gone flying through the air. No doubt he would relive it in his nightmares for a long time.

"Well, she was relatively lucky. It could have been much worse. As it is, she has a deep laceration in the back of her thigh. It went through the biceps femoris but missed the popliteal artery by a fraction of an inch. If it hadn't, she probably would have bled to death at the Cold Creek before you were able to summon help."

Wade felt cold, light-headed, just thinking about the idea of a world without Caroline in it.

How had she come to be so important to him in just a few days? He let out a ragged breath then covered it by coughing a little as if he were only clearing his throat.

"What kind of a recovery time is she looking at?"

Jake studied him closely and Wade hoped like hell none of his emotions were showing on his face.

"Well, I can't lie to you, she's going to hurt for several days. The ribs are going to be the worst of it but deep tissue trauma like a gore wound isn't easy to bounce back from."

"Yeah, I remember."

"That's right, I forgot you've been there, El Matador."

He narrowed his gaze. "You should be damn grateful you're a good doctor, otherwise you'd be too obnoxious to tolerate."

Jake laughed, unoffended. "We gave her a local anesthetic while I was sewing things up and she's still a little numb from that but I don't think there's any need to transfer her to Idaho Falls to the hospital. I can keep a closer eye on her here. She'll have to stay off it completely for a couple days and I've urged her not to travel for at least a week. I figured she can stay at my place until she's ready to go back to California. I can take turns checking on her throughout the day with my clinic nurses."

"Forget it. She's staying at the Cold Creek."

His vehemence seemed to surprise Jake as much as it did him.

He wasn't sure why he hated the idea of her staying

with his brother so much. It probably made more sense all around. She would certainly be able to get more rest without his kids in the way and she would be closer to expert care with Jake in the same house, but he hated the whole idea.

Jake folded his arms. "And why is that? Because, as usual, you think you're responsible for the whole world?"

"Not the whole world. Just people who are injured on *my* ranch, by one of *my* cows, while they happen to be in the process of saving *my* son's life. I'd say that gives me some responsibility to see she's cared for properly."

"You don't think she would be at my house? See that diploma on the wall? I do happen to be the doctor here, remember?"

"As if you would ever let me forget. But just because you're the one with the fancy degree doesn't automatically make you the best one to take care of Caroline," he said. "You work eighteen-hour days and she would be alone all day except for the few times you sent people to check on her. She'd be miserable."

"You're a great one to talk about working long hours! Your kids see you for five minutes a day if they're lucky."

What was it with everybody telling him what a lousy father he was, all of a sudden?

"Look," Jake went on, "I'm sure Caroline understands you're grateful to her for going after Tanner like that. But she also has to know you have your hands more than full at the Cold Creek. I haven't forgotten how crazy autumns on the ranch can be. And with Caroline on the injured list, you're back to where you were when Mom left, without anybody to help you with the kids."

Wade clenched his teeth. "I'm well aware of that, but thanks for the reminder."

"I'm only pointing out that you can't handle the load you've already got. What makes you think you can take on the care of an injured woman, too?"

"We'll manage. I'll just have to take a few days off."

Jake stared at him like a fat, wriggling trout had just popped out the top of his head. "A few days off what?"

He shrugged. "Seth can handle things around the ranch and I'll stick close to the house and take care of Caroline and the boys until she's back on her feet."

He braced himself for more arguments but whatever his brother threw at him, Wade refused to let himself be deterred. He had absolutely no intention of letting Caroline recover anywhere but at the Cold Creek.

He owed her this for what she had done for Tanner—hell, what she'd done for all of them the last six days. She had stepped up when he needed help and he couldn't do any less for her.

Something else had been bothering him these last two hours and Jake bringing up Andi's illness finally helped him crystallize it in his mind.

When his wife had been so sick, he could do nothing for her but haunt the hospital, hound the doctors and spend every spare minute on his knees praying for God not to take her.

He was a man used to doing, not sitting back and watching others, and it had been hell to stand by while his wife had grown sicker and sicker.

Here was something concrete he could handle, something he hadn't been given the chance to do for Andi. And maybe by helping to nurse Caroline, in some way, another of the scars crisscrossing his heart might heal.

"I'm taking her home," he said firmly.

To his surprise, Jake—the same one Marjorie used to say would argue with her if she said his eyes were blue—completely folded.

After another long look at Wade, he nodded. "Fine. I'll give you a list of discharge instructions before you take her back to the ranch. She's being fitted for a pair of crutches and I'll have to call in a prescription for painkillers and heavy-duty antibiotics, then after that she should be good to go."

Despite his relief at not having to engage in hand-to-hand combat with his brother over the rights to care for her, he suddenly felt a spurt of panic at the task in front of him.

"Just like that? Are you sure you don't need to keep her longer for observation or something?"

Jake seemed to be fighting a smile. "Oh, I think I've seen all I need to see."

"What's that supposed to mean?" he snapped.

"Oh, nothing." Jake stood up, stretching a little as he did. His surgical scrubs were sweat-stained and he suddenly looked as tired as if he'd spent all day in the saddle roping steers.

"Never mind," Jake said. "I'll go let the nurses know you're ready."

Ready? He wasn't sure he'd go that far. Still, he'd made his choice and he backed his words up with action.

Hours later, Caroline dragged herself out of an uneasy, pill-induced sleep to a muted bass voice, a higher-pitched whisper and pain in every single molecule of her body.

Mercy, she hurt. For several moments after she

awoke, she concentrated only on breathing past the pain until she could think straight. Even breathing hurt and she couldn't figure out why until she remembered the cracked ribs. Wade's brother had warned her they would probably hurt worse than anything else at first and she discovered he'd been telling the truth.

Her leg burned and throbbed but she could endure that. What she hated was not being able to take a deep breath into her lungs for the pain.

She did the best she could, keeping her eyes closed while she focused. Through the layers of pain, she listened to the voices—Wade and Tanner, she realized.

"If you can't remember to whisper, you'll have to leave," Wade admonished his son.

"I'll be quiet, I promise," Tanner said and Caroline almost smiled at that impossible claim. She wasn't sure Tanner could be quiet even if his mouth were taped shut.

Her eyelids were just about the only part of her that wasn't sore right about now, so she propped one up just enough to see she was alone with Wade and Tanner in a room she recognized as one of the empty bedrooms on the main floor.

Nat and Cody were nowhere in sight but Wade sat at the old-fashioned writing desk in the room with Tanner on his lap. The boy had a blueberry-colored crayon in his hand—his *unbandaged* hand, she saw with some delight, and his cute little face wore a frown of concentration, his tongue clamped between his teeth, as he peered down at what he was coloring.

"You sure you want that horse's tail to be blue?" Wade asked, his voice low.

"Do you think I should change it?"

"I guess it's your horse so you can do whatever you

want. If you want it to be pink with purple polka dots, have at it."

"It's for Caroline, not for me, and she likes blue. She told me. It reminds her of the ocean in the summer. She lives by the ocean, did you know that?"

"I did."

"I asked her if she could go swimming anytime she wants and she said the water is kind of cold where she lives but she still likes to walk on the beach and look for seashells and sand dollars and take her shoes off so she can jump over the little waves."

"That sounds fun."

"And she said we could come visit her sometime in California and she would take us to find starfish and stuff. Can we, Dad?"

"We'll see," Wade whispered, an odd look in his eyes. "Looks like you're about done there."

"Yeah. It's a get-better card. Grandma and me made one for Molly Johnson when she had the chicken pox. You think Caroline will like it?"

Before she could answer that of course she would, she saw Wade give a slow smile then kiss the top of Tanner's head. "She'll love it because you made it for her," he said in that same low voice.

As she studied those two male heads so close together, one so masculine and dark and strong, the other small and darling, Caroline's pain faded for just a moment, overwhelmed by a stunning realization.

She was in love with him.

It poured over her, through her, an inexorable, undeniable wash of emotion.

In love with Wade Dalton. Of all the idiotic things for her to do!

Her chest hurt, but she was certain the pain had nothing to do with her cracked ribs and everything to do with her cracked head. She had to be crazy to let things come to this.

What was she thinking? Why hadn't she protected herself better? Made some effort to toughen her spine, her mind, her heart?

She tried to tell herself that was just the painkiller talking, giving her all kinds of weird delusions, but she couldn't quite make herself buy that explanation.

The worst of it was realizing she'd been sliding down this precarious path a little more each moment since she'd arrived at the Cold Creek. Surely she could have switched direction at some point along the journey if only she'd been awake enough to see in front of herself.

She had ignored the signs along the way, unwilling to face the truth until she'd been literally knocked off her feet.

Oh, this was bad. Seriously bad. She was going to end up more battered and broken by loving Wade Dalton than just a few paltry cracked ribs and a gouged thigh.

She thought of the article Darci Perez had mentioned earlier in the afternoon, another lifetime ago, it seemed. "Top Ten Best Ways to Guarantee a Happy, Fulfilling Life."

She had written it several months ago and couldn't remember everything in it but she was fairly sure that nowhere in there did she mention that one of those ways to guarantee happiness was to fall head over heels for a workaholic rancher who didn't trust her, didn't like her, and who was still grieving for his late wife.

She must have made some sound of distress—she wasn't entirely sure but she must have done something to draw attention because both of the males at the writing table swiveled their heads in her direction at the same time.

"Caroline! You're awake!" Tanner beamed with delight.

Wade studied her intently and she flushed, praying her emotions weren't exposed somehow for all to see. He approached the bed and she dug her fingers into the quilt.

"Did we wake you?" he asked. "We tried to be quiet but I'm afraid that was a losing battle."

Her mouth suddenly felt as if she'd been chewing sandpaper in her sleep and she could do nothing but shake her head.

He instinctively seemed to sense her need. From the bedside table next to her, he picked up a pitcher and ice rattled as he poured a glass of water and handed it to her. She took it gratefully and sipped until she thought she might be able to squeeze out a word or two.

"Thank you," she murmured and her voice sounded rough, scratchy.

How long had she been sleeping? she wondered. It was dark and Tanner was in pajamas, so it must have been more than a few hours.

"How do you feel?" Wade asked when she lowered the glass.

"Like I should have tire tread marks somewhere on my person."

He gave a sympathetic smile. "No tread marks that I can see. Maybe a hoofprint or two."

She winced and tried to move to a more comfortable position. She realized as she moved that she was wearing her nightgown. She frowned trying to remember how she had changed out of the clothes she'd been wearing when she'd been gored, but she couldn't grab hold of it.

She had worn what was left of her clothes home from the clinic, hadn't she? Much of the afternoon felt like a big blur. Someone here at the ranch had to have helped her change into her nightgown. Wade? she wondered and flushed at the thought.

"Where are the others?" she asked to distract herself.

"Cody didn't have much of a nap so he crashed right after dinner. And Nat's in doing homework."

"What time is it?"

"Almost eight. I gave this one a few more minutes but it's just about bedtime for him, too."

Tanner walked to the side of the bed, his picture in his outstretched hand. "I made you a get-better card."

He set it carefully on the quilt and she picked it up, touched by his effort. "It's beautiful. I especially like the blue tail on the horse."

He grinned at his dad. "See? Told you she'd like it!"

Wade rubbed his hair. "So you did. Maybe Caroline would like us to tape it up somewhere that she could see it all the time. How about there by the bed?"

"Perfect," she said as Tanner rummaged in the desk and emerged triumphant with some tape. The next few minutes were spent watching him hang it crookedly on the wall.

"Thank you so much," she exclaimed when it was done. "You know what? It's working! I feel better already."

He beamed and fluttered his hands. "Hey, guess what? Uncle Jake took off my bandage when he came to check on you a while ago and he said I could leave it off since it's looking good."

"Great news!"

"Yeah, and I can get it wet and everything! I had a bath and I could play with my boats with both hands."

Wade stepped in and placed a hand on the boy's shoulder. "Okay, bud. Time to hit the sack. We've got a big day tomorrow."

Something important was happening the next day. She knew it but she couldn't seem to grab hold of what that might be.

"We're gonna play basketball and clean out the toy box and maybe make brownies if Dad can figure out how."

No, that wasn't it. She closed her eyes but still couldn't figure it out.

When she opened them, Wade was watching her, his blue eyes dark with concern.

"Go on up and find a book and I'll be up to read to you in a minute," he told his son.

The boy nodded, then smiled. "Night, Caroline."

She reached out and squeezed his fingers. "Good night."

Tanner hesitated for a moment by her bedside then, before she knew what he intended, he bent over and kissed her cheek, leaving behind the sweet smell of just-washed little boy.

"Thanks for helping me save the kitten. I would have been sad if a cow stepped on her but I'm real sorry you got hurt."

"Me, too. But I'm glad you were safe."

After Tanner left, Wade pulled his chair to her side, watching her with a strange, inscrutable expression on his face.

"You need another pain pill. I'm on strict orders to

make you eat something before you take one. I can't claim to be a great cook but Mom left some soup in the freezer and I can heat you some. Beef barley."

She didn't want to eat and she certainly didn't want another pill. But already the pain was building and she knew it would only get worse if she didn't take something for it.

"I'm sorry to be a bother," she said. "I know you have so much to do…."

Suddenly it hit her and she remembered the scene with the TV crew that had led up to her accident. "The interview. You've got the news interview tomorrow. You don't have time to babysit me."

"It's all under control," he assured her.

"How?"

"Don't worry about it. I'm going to go in and warm up some soup for you then you can take a pill and rest."

She laid back on the pillow, too weak and sore and heartsick to argue.

Chapter 13

Twenty-four hours after leaving the clinic, Caroline felt as if that blow to the head she'd taken had permanently jostled her brain.

Either that or she had somehow slipped through the rabbit hole into some alternate universe.

She studied Wade standing in the doorway with a tray of more of the ubiquitous soup and scarcely recognized him. Who was this man and what had he done with the distant, taciturn rancher she'd come to know since arriving at the Cold Creek?

Wade had been nothing but solicitous and concerned since her accident. All day he had played nursemaid, fetching and carrying and even just sitting with her.

She had awakened in the night from a terrible dream where a vast herd of cows with glowing red eyes chased her down the beach, their heads down and their horns swinging until she had no choice but to dive into the surf to evade those vicious horns.

When she jerked her eyes open, gasping for breath, she found Wade dozing in the chair, his stocking feet propped on the bed beside her and a ranching magazine open across his chest.

She found him surprisingly vulnerable in sleep, without the hard edges and harsh lines on his features during the day.

Without the burdens and cares he carried when awake, he looked young, relaxed, and she grieved for this man who had lost so much and who could only release the load of his responsibilities while he slept.

She watched him for a long time, wondering how many opportunities she would have to share this kind of quiet moment with him. Her feelings for him were a heavy ache in her chest and she wondered what she would possibly do with them after she left the Cold Creek.

Sometime during her scrutiny, his eyes opened and she was completely disarmed when his cheeks colored and he dropped his stocking feet to the carpet.

"Sorry." He rubbed a hand through his hair. "Guess I fell asleep."

"What are you doing here?" she asked.

He shrugged. "You've had a concussion. I'm supposed to check on you through the night."

"I don't think that requires an all-night vigil, do you?"

"I promised Jake I would follow orders. He said to keep an eye on you through the night, so that's what I'm doing. Or that's what I'm supposed to be doing anyway. I won't fall asleep again."

Completely astonished, she stared at him, not

knowing how to respond. "You can't stay up all night! I'm sure that's not what Jake meant. Tomorrow's a big day for you, with the TV interview and all. You need your sleep."

He closed the magazine and set it on the desk, not meeting her gaze. "Seth and I decided he would take care of the interview. He knows as much as I do about ranch operations. They shot plenty of footage of me spouting off today before your accident. I told Darci the reporter will just have to use that if he wants me included in the story."

Maybe if her brain weren't so fuzzy from the pain and the pills, she could figure this out. As it was, nothing he was saying made sense. "So you're not going to do the interview?"

"No. Seth is."

"But why? This is an important opportunity for you to showcase the Cold Creek and the improvements you've made."

"Yeah, and Seth can do that as well as I can. Better, probably. He's young, good-looking and has a hell of a lot more charm. All that will play well on camera."

She wondered if Wade had any idea that while Seth was extremely good-looking and probably flirted in his sleep, he reminded her of a young, playful pup compared to his older brother.

Wade was rugged, masculine, *compelling*. No woman who saw him on or off camera would ever be able to forget him.

Why had Wade suddenly decided to delegate the important interview to his brother?

While she tried to puzzle it out, she shifted to find a

better position and wanted to smack her forehead when the answer came to her.

Her. He was doing this because of her. "You think you need to stay here and babysit me. *That's* why you're having Seth do the interview."

"Don't worry about it. We've got everything worked out."

"I will worry about it. I can't let you make that kind of sacrifice for me. I can take care of myself, Wade."

"You can't even get out of bed by yourself right now."

"You don't have to feel responsible for me!"

"I *am* responsible for you."

"Since when?"

He met her glare with a level look. "Since you nearly died saving my son's life."

She let out a breath, embarrassed by the depth of gratitude in his eyes. "Don't be silly. You don't owe me a thing."

"I owe you *everything.*" His voice, low and intense, sent shivers down her spine. "If you hadn't been there, Tanner would have been trampled or worse in that corral."

"Wade—"

"No sense arguing about it. Seth is going to take over for me for a few days while the kids and I get you back on your feet. That includes doing the interview."

A few days? Wade Dalton was taking time off work during what she had quickly come to learn was his busiest time of the year for *her?*

"I... You can't do that."

"It's done." Suddenly he gave her a disarming smile. If she weren't already in bed, he would have knocked the pins right out from under her with it. "Besides, mother—your new stepmother—would never forgive me if I didn't take proper care of you, especially with the circumstances of how you were injured. I can hear her now lecturing me all about bad karma and all that. Now let's get you something for the pain I can tell is coming back nastier than a one-legged dog with fleas."

She hadn't known how to answer him the night before and she still didn't know what to say as she studied him in the doorway, the boys on either side of him. Tanner held a pitcher in his hand and Cody had what she assumed was an empty plastic cup.

"Lunch time." Wade smiled.

"Hi, Caroline," Tanner chirped. "We made soup and a cheese san'wich. My dad made it and everything."

Wade shrugged, his cheeks suspiciously ruddy. "I opened a can and threw a piece of cheese and bread under the broiler. Sorry, but that's about the best I can do unless I'm standing in front of a barbecue grill."

"I'm sure it will be delicious," she said.

"Sit by Care." The youngest Dalton beamed, holding his arms up for her.

"You'll have to have your dad help you up," she told Cody.

Wade set the tray on the table by the bed. "Better not. He might bump your ribs or your leg."

"Then I'll scream bloody murder and hand him back to you."

He shook his head. "It's your funeral."

He lifted the toddler up and Cody gave her a big, toothy smile like he hadn't seen her in months. He held out his arms and hugged her, tucking his head beneath her chin. It did hurt but she decided a little pain was a small price to pay to hold a sweet, loving little boy who smelled of sunshine and baby lotion.

"Hey Dad, can I sit up there with Caroline, too?" Tanner asked.

"You'd better not. You're a little bigger and tougher than your brother."

Tanner's heart didn't seem to be broken by that news. "Well, can I go back and watch TV then?"

Wade considered. "Stay by the TV, though. No wandering around outside and no going in the kitchen."

"Okay," Tanner promised and hurried out of the room with a quick wave to Caroline.

"Can you eat like that?" Wade asked.

Caroline settled the boy next to her, on the other side from her injured leg. "We'll be just fine, won't we, Cody?"

The toddler nodded and cuddled closer. To her surprise, Wade pulled up a chair while she tackled her lunch.

"You don't have to stay," she murmured, a little uncomfortable at him watching her eat.

"I'd better, just so I can keep the kid there from giving you a judo chop to the leg."

"He's fine. I think he's going to be asleep in a minute."

Sure enough, before she even tasted her soup, his eyes were half-closed and a moment later he was out for the count. He moved a little closer, bumping her leg, but she wasn't about to complain.

"He's a beautiful boy," she said with a smile. "All three of your children are. You know, I can see bits of you in Nat and Tanner but Cody is his own little man."

She paused, debating the merits of pressing forward,

then took the plunge anyway. "From what I can tell, he resembles the pictures I've seen of your late wife."

Wade said nothing for a long moment, then he nodded slowly. "He does. If you looked at baby pictures of Andrea, you would swear you're looking at Cody. She had the same brown eyes and blond hair, the same dimples, the same full bottom lip."

He paused. "And you know, their personalities are similar in a lot of ways. He's got the same sunny disposition and same easygoing attitude toward life. I'm sure you've noticed Cody is a cuddler and Andrea was happiest when we were all sprawled together on the couch watching a movie."

She smiled, touched that he would share this piece of his past with her. "What a wonderful blessing that you've been given these three beautiful children so you can remember your wife whenever you look at them. Especially this one."

"They are a blessing. Every one of them." He paused, a faraway look in his eyes. Not pain, precisely. Just memories.

When he spoke, his voice was low and she sensed instinctively he was telling her something he didn't share easily.

"I couldn't even look at Cody for a week or so after Andi's death," he said slowly. "It was such a crazy time and I was…lost inside. Totally messed up. My wife was gone and here was this bawling newborn baby who needed so much, along with Tanner who wasn't much more than a baby himself and Natalie who was old enough to know what was going on."

"She must have been devastated."

"We all were. This sounds awful," he went on, "but

I kept thinking, I hadn't wanted another one in the first place. I'd been perfectly content with Natalie and Tanner. Andi was the one who wanted another child. I guess part of me blamed Cody. It wasn't fair, I know, but I thought, if not for him, she wouldn't have caught that staph infection during the delivery. She would have been healthy and strong, ready to take on the world, like always. My other two kids would have still had their mother, I still would have had a wife. If only she hadn't pushed so hard to have another one, everything would be just fine. I don't know if I blamed God, Andi or the baby more for her death."

"Oh, Wade."

He looked at the boy and the softness in his eyes brought tears to her own.

"Thank the Lord my Mom stepped in to help because I didn't want to see him or touch him or anything. But about a week after the funeral, Mom was in taking a shower when Cody woke up howling. I almost left the house right then, I couldn't stand it, but I finally made myself go in to see what he needed."

She almost reached for his hand but she didn't want to move, to breathe, afraid any interruption might compel him to stop talking. He was giving her a rare window into his world and she was touched beyond words that he would share this with her.

"It was like something out of the movies. You know, one of those unbelievable moments." He smiled a little. "One minute he's shrieking loud enough to knock the house over, but as soon as he caught sight of me, he shut right up, stuck a little fist in his mouth and just stared at me out of Andi's eyes for the longest time."

He didn't add that when Marjorie had finally come

in to check on the quiet baby after her shower, she'd found Wade in the rocking chair clutching Cody tightly and bawling his eyes out like he hadn't been able to do since Andi's death.

He also didn't add that in those first horrible months after she'd died, the only peaceful moments he remembered—the moments he'd somehow felt closest to Andi—were when he'd been holding their baby. On nights when he couldn't sleep for the pain, he even used to sometimes go into Cody's room in the middle of the night, just so he could pick the sleeping baby up out of his crib and rock him until he could remember how to breathe again around the vast, endless grief.

He looked up from his thoughts to find Caroline watching him, a tear trickling down her cheek. Guilt swamped him. "You're in pain and I'm in here yakking your leg off. I'm sorry."

She reached out and squeezed his arm, and the simple touch almost made him feel like bawling, too, for some crazy reason.

"No. I'm fine," she insisted. "I just can't imagine what it must have been like for you."

She was crying for *him?* He wasn't exactly sure how he felt about that but he did know that when she pulled her hand away, part of him wanted to reach for it again.

"The hardest thing was the kids. It still is, really," he said. "Trying to do right by them is tough on my own, even with Marjorie's help. Whatever you might think— whatever my mom thinks—I love my kids. They're first in my heart, even if I don't always act like it. Everything I do is for them. I might not be able to give them as much time as I should, but I love them."

He heard that blasted defensiveness creep into his

voice, but he couldn't seem to help it. He wanted so much for her to understand. It seemed suddenly vitally important that she not see him as a father trying to shirk his duty by his children.

She wiped at her eyes. "I know you do. I know. It was presumptuous of me to ever imply otherwise and I'm sorry for what I said the other night. I have this bad habit of thinking I know what everyone in the entire world should be doing to improve their lives. I forget that my help isn't always wanted or needed."

"I guess that's why you're a life coach, then. So people will pay you to boss them around."

She laughed softly at that and, for some reason, it moved him that she could still laugh even when she was in pain—and at herself, no less.

"My dad always told me that if you're lucky enough to find something you're good at, you have to hang on to it with both hands and not let go no matter what the world throws at you."

He decided in the spirit of goodwill between them, he would put aside his animosity toward her father and try to understand what his mother might have seen in the guy.

"What does your father do for a living? I never thought to ask Marjorie. I guess that's something I should know if I'm to perform my son-in-law duties effectively."

What had he said to put that strange, edgy light in her eyes? he wondered.

"Oh, he's retired," she said quickly.

"From what?"

Her fingers tightened on the quilt. "A little of everything. Sales, support, research and development. I guess mostly sales, you could say."

Now that sounded like a whole lot of nothing. He wanted to push for more specifics but he could plainly tell she was uncomfortable with the subject and he didn't want to press her when she was hurting.

He didn't want their conversation to end, though, he realized, so he fished around for another subject.

"Where are you from originally? I assumed California but I just realized I never bothered to ask."

Again, he got the strange impression she was picking her words carefully. "I'm one of those unfortunate people who doesn't really have a hometown, except the one I've chosen for myself as an adult."

She smiled a little but it didn't reach as far as her eyes.

"I'm not like you, born and bred in one place like the Cold Creek. We lived in Texas for a while when I was a kid—Houston and San Antonio, mostly—and then my mother died when I was eight and after that we moved around a lot."

"Just your dad and you?"

She gave a sharp, tight-looking nod and he wondered if she was hurting. "I was an only child."

"I'm sorry."

She looked surprised at his word. "When I was a kid, other kids at school always told me how lucky I was to have my dad all to myself. But I always wanted a couple of older brothers and an older sister or two."

"My brothers drive me crazy most of the time but I can't imagine not having either of them."

"You're very lucky," she murmured. "And your children are as well. No matter what else happens, you all have each other."

"You have your dad," he pointed out.

She seemed to find that amusing in a strange sort of way. "Right. My dad."

"And according to Seth, you're now our stepsister."

He meant it as a joke to lighten her odd mood but she gave him a long, charged look that had his palms sweating.

"I don't think either one of us wants to think very seriously about that, do you?" she said quietly.

He suddenly couldn't think of anything but the kiss they had shared, of her arms wrapped around him, of the wild heat flashing between them like a summer lightning storm.

He shifted, wishing he could get those blasted images out of his head. But every time he looked at her mouth, every time she smiled, every time her soft vanilla scent drifted to him, they came flooding back.

The room instantly seemed to seethe with tension and he regretted the loss of their brief camaraderie.

He had never told anyone about Cody, probably because he was ashamed of that initial anger he'd felt toward a helpless, completely innocent little baby. Marjorie was the only one with any inkling and even she didn't know the whole of it.

He wasn't sure why he'd told Caroline, he only knew that once the words had started, he couldn't seem to hold them back.

He had learned a few things about her but he wanted more. He wanted to know everything. The name of her second-grade teacher, her favorite kind of candy bar, her happiest memory.

The realization scared the hell out of him. He had no need to know those things about Caroline Montgomery—or to share his deepest, innermost secrets with her.

That was the kind of thing a man did with a woman he was dating, a woman he thought he might have feelings for.

A woman whose kiss he couldn't get out of his head.

Wade rose abruptly. "I'd better go check on Tanner. Who knows what kind of trouble he might get into if I don't."

"Right. Good idea," she said, her voice quiet.

"Do you want me to take Cody out of your way?"

"No. Let him sleep."

Her smile looked a little strained, he thought with concern. "Are you sure he's not hurting you?"

"He's fine," she insisted, running a gentle hand over Cody's blond curls. The boy made a sound and moved closer. "I'll call if I need you to come get him."

He nodded, picked up the lunch tray and headed for the door, wondering as he went how on earth he could be so jealous of a two-year-old.

Chapter 14

By the afternoon of the second day after her injury, Caroline decided she'd had enough of pain pills that left her loopy and disconnected, and she stopped taking them, at least during the day.

Though the result was a low, throbbing ache in her ribs and stabbing pain in her leg, she decided it was worth the price to feel moderately like herself again.

She also reached the firm conclusion that if she had to spend one more moment in her room—lovely though it was—she just might have to throw one of her crutches through the window.

She nearly planted a big, juicy kiss on Jake when he came to check on her and said there was no reason she couldn't sit on one of the recliners in the great room with Wade and the children.

"Those sore ribs are going to make it tough to work

the crutches," Jake said. "I'll go get Wade so he can help you move to the other room."

Before she could ask Jake why *he* couldn't help her, he left with a peculiar smirk on his handsome features.

She hadn't seen much of Wade since their encounter the day before. She couldn't decide if he was avoiding her or simply wrapped up in the children and the ranch paperwork she knew he tried to catch up on anytime he had a spare minute.

He had brought her meals and checked every hour or so to see if she needed anything—or sent one of the kids in to check—but there had been no more opportunities for revealing conversations.

She was glad, she told herself. She was afraid she had already revealed too much about herself. Better if he left her alone so she had no more opportunity to make a fool of herself or to slide deeper and deeper in love with him.

For an instant, she regretted asking Jake if she could start getting up and around. Maybe she should stay in her room, despite the boredom, for the sake of her heart.

The decision was taken out of her hands a moment later, though, when Wade walked through the open doorway. He wore jeans and a soft gray chamois shirt, and he looked big and hard and gorgeous.

She sighed, wishing she were wearing something a little more attractive than her old nightgown and robe.

"I'm under orders to help you into the other room," he said, gazing at some point above her head.

"Jake is afraid I'm not quite ready to handle the crutches on my own because of the bruised ribs."

For some reason, she was compelled to make it clear

to him this had been entirely his brother's idea that Wade come in to help her.

Wade finally met her gaze and her stomach twirled a little at the strange expression in his eyes. She would have given just about anything right at that moment to know what was going on inside his head.

He moved toward the bed and, before she realized what he was doing, he scooped her up gingerly. Not expecting the move, or the sudden shock of finding herself held so gently in his powerful arms, she couldn't contain a quick gasp.

"Did I hurt you?" He looked aghast at the idea.

"No. I just don't think this was what Jake meant!"

A muscle flexed in his jaw. "Oh, I'm pretty sure it was, since his exact words were *go carry Caroline from her bedroom to the recliner in the great room.*"

"He should have at least warned me what the master plan was here," she said.

"Yeah, me, too," she thought she heard him mutter but it was so low she couldn't be sure.

"I can probably make it on the crutches if you'll just spot me," she said, though she wanted nothing more than to stay right here, nestled into his heat and strength.

He smelled divine, of some kind of outdoorsy after-shave, and his shirt had to be the softest material she'd ever felt as her arms slid around his neck to hang on. He was close enough that she could have drawn his head down to hers without much effort at all....

"You could have said something if you were bored in there."

She blinked, hoping he didn't notice the sudden color she could feel creeping over her features. "I didn't want to bother you. You're already doing so much for me."

"What? A few meals, that's about it. Doesn't seem like much in return for saving my son's life."

Before she could respond to that, they made their way far too quickly to the great room.

The moment they walked through the doorway, the children reacted in different ways to the sight of her in their father's arms. The boys both shrieked her name as if they hadn't seen her in months and raced to her side.

While she was greeting them with laughter, she caught sight of Natalie sitting at the table with Jake, her math book spread out in front of her. She looked stunned at the two of them together, as if she'd never considered the possibility of ever seeing another woman in her father's arms.

Caroline wanted to assure her Wade was just helping her, that there was nothing between them, that she would never take her mother's place, even if she could.

She could say nothing, though, with everyone else looking on.

Still, she was aware of Natalie's hard stare the whole time Wade carried her to the recliner then set her down as carefully as if she were fragile antique glass.

"Is that good?" he asked gruffly and Caroline shifted her gaze from the daughter to the father. His jaw looked tight and she saw his pulse jump there and she wondered if he'd been affected by their nearness as much as she had been.

"Yes. Wonderful—thank you so much. It's amazing how a simple change of scenery can lift my spirits."

"Don't overdo it," Jake warned. "You'll pay the price if you try to take on too much."

"I know, Dr. Dalton. I'll take it easy, I promise."

He rose from the table. "Sorry I can't stick around

but I've got to run to the hospital in Idaho Falls to check on one of my patients who had surgery this morning."

"What about my homework?" Natalie asked, a plaintive note in her voice. "I still have, like, ten problems to go."

Wade frowned at her. "I'm still here," he reminded her. "Uncle Jake's not the only one who knows long division, you know."

"Yeah, but he always explains it better," she muttered.

"I'll do my best to muddle through," Wade said dryly.

"Care read?"

Caroline glanced away from the homework drama to find little Cody hovering near the arm of her chair, a favorite picture book in his chubby fingers.

She smiled. "Of course."

"No, not that one," Tanner objected, not far behind. "That one's a baby book. I'll find a better one."

He raced out of the room, most likely to scour his bedroom bookshelves for something more to his liking, leaving Cody standing by her side, his picture book held out like an offering to the gods.

She smiled at him and patted her uninjured leg. "Come on up here, kiddo. Maybe we can get through this one before your brother comes back," she said.

Cody giggled as if they shared a particularly amusing secret and climbed from the footrest onto her lap.

"Is he okay?" Wade asked. The worry in his eyes warmed her even more than Cody's sturdy little body.

"Wonderful." She wedged a throw pillow between her aching ribs and the little boy, then opened the book.

They turned the last page just as Tanner skipped in, his arms loaded with at least a dozen books.

"These are better," he announced, dropping them all to the floor. "Start with this one."

He handed her a rhyming book about trucks she had already read to him at least a dozen times during her time at the Cold Creek, then he pulled an ottoman next to her recliner and perched on it with all the anticipation of a baby bird awaiting nourishment.

The next hour would live in her memory forever as one of those rare, sweet moments when all seems perfect with the world.

A soft rain clicked against the window but a fire in the huge river-rock fireplace took away any chill from the October night and lent a cozy, snug feeling to the gathering room.

While Wade and Natalie slogged their way through the intricacies of arithmetic, Caroline read story after story to the boys, repeating a few of them several times. Tanner wasn't often able to sit still through long bouts of reading but for now he seemed content to settle in next to her, trying to pick out letters he recognized.

A few times she felt the heat of someone watching her and looked up to find Wade studying her intently. As soon as she would meet his gaze, he would quickly turn his attention back to Natalie, but not before she thought she saw an odd, baffled kind of look in his eyes.

Though she knew it wasn't productive and would only lead to more heartbreak when she returned to Santa Cruz, she couldn't prevent her imagination from playing make-believe, if only for a moment. Was this how things would be if they were a family? If she belonged here at the Cold Creek with Wade, with his children?

Autumn evenings spent in front of the fire, winter nights with a soaring Christmas tree there in the corner, springtime with the windows open and the sweet smell of lilac bushes wafting in.

They would sit here, the five of them, sharing stories and memories and laughter.

And then after the children were asleep, Wade would turn to her, those blue eyes bright with need, his strong hands tender on her skin....

She blinked, stunned at herself.

The last little part of her fantasy wasn't so surprising—since that kiss and probably even before then, sexual awareness simmered between them. She couldn't manage to look at him without remembering his mouth, firm and warm on hers, and those large, powerful hands buried in her hair, at the small of her back.

But the rest of it totally took her by surprise. She had no idea such desires lived inside her.

She had made a rewarding career out of helping people discover the true dreams of their heart.

Contrary to what many of her clients thought when they first contacted her, coaching was not about telling people how to live, gleefully doling out advice to anyone who would listen.

She tried to help her clients dig deep into their psyches to discover their potential and break down all the barriers people erected to keep themselves from risking everything to touch those dreams.

How had she so completely missed this deep-seated need inside herself, then? This intense craving for home and hearth?

She thought she was fulfilled by her life in California but as she listened to the rain and the pop and hiss of the fire and studied the sweet faces of the Dalton children, she realized how much she envied Wade.

He had this all the time, this constant, unwavering love from his children and this unbreakable connection.

She wanted it all—not just the idea of children but the idea of *these* children. Tears burned in her eyes at the warm weight of Cody on her lap and Tanner leaning against her arm. She loved them, all three of them, as much as she loved Wade.

Her heart would rip apart into a thousand jagged pieces when she had to leave the ranch and the Daltons.

She couldn't think about that now. For now, she would sit here and listen to the rain and enjoy the night and these sweet children.

She must have closed her eyes for a moment. The next thing she knew was Wade's voice in her ear, low and disconcertingly close.

"How in the world did you pull that off?" he asked and she blinked her eyes open and found him standing by the recliner.

"Sorry?"

"Must have been a pretty boring story," he murmured.

It took her a moment to realize both boys were asleep—Cody nestled under her chin and Tanner with his cheek resting on her forearm. She probably had dozed off, too. "No wonder nobody complained when I stopped reading."

He smiled, drawing her gaze to his mouth. A deep, intense yearning to taste him again washed through her and she had to clench her fists to keep from reaching for him.

"Where's Natalie?" Her voice sounded hoarse and a little ragged but she had to hope he didn't notice or would attribute it to lingering sleepiness.

"We finished her homework so I sent her off to bed."

"No matter what she said, I thought you explained her homework very well."

His smile was a little lopsided and made her want to trace a finger at the corner of his mouth. "So I guess I could always be a math tutor if the whole ranch thing doesn't work out."

She could just imagine the women of Pine Gulch lining up to have him teach their children.

"What do you think my odds are of getting these guys up to bed without waking them?" he asked.

"I didn't realize you were a betting man."

"Every rancher and farmer I know is a gambler. It's part of the package. You gamble every time you plant a crop or buy an animal or take your stock to market."

"Well, I'll give you a fifty-fifty chance on the boys. I'd have to put my money on Tanner to be the one who wakes up."

"That's what you call a sucker bet." He grinned. "I'd have to be stupid to take it and I try not to be stupid more than once or twice a week. I'll get them settled and then I'll come back and help you back to bed."

"No hurry," she assured him. "I'm still enjoying the change of scenery. Would you mind if I stayed a while?"

"No. Seth is coming in a few minutes to fill me in on what went on today. We'll probably bore you to tears with all our shop talk."

"I don't mind. I enjoy learning about what goes into running a big ranch like the Cold Creek. Anyway, if I get bored, I have a magazine I can read. As long as you don't mind if I stay."

"No. That's fine."

She smiled and he looked as if he wanted to say something, then decided against it and reached down for Cody. His arm couldn't help but touch her breasts as he scooped the boy off her lap and she was suddenly hot everywhere he touched.

She had almost managed to cool down by the time he returned from carrying Cody upstairs. Her arm was asleep, with the weight of Tanner's head pressing it against the armrest of the recliner, but she hadn't wanted to risk waking him by moving.

Still, she was grateful when Wade returned for him. "One down, one to go," he said softly.

"Good luck."

"I think I'll need it with this one."

Just as he had done with Cody, he lifted Tanner into his arms, and though the boy murmured something and flung an arm across his father's chest, he didn't appear to wake up.

She watched them go, the tall, handsome rancher and his busy little son, quiet only in sleep, and pressed a hand to her heart as if she could already feel it begin to crack apart.

He would miss her when she went back to California.

It was a hard admission but Wade had never let himself shrink from things that were tough to face. He stood in Tanner's bedroom, which his mother had decorated with everything cowboy, and watched as the boy nestled into his bucking-bronco sheets, rump up in the air like a potato bug.

Focusing on Tanner didn't help him avoid looking the cold, hard truth right in the eye.

Somehow in the few days she'd been on the Cold Creek, Caroline had managed to worm her way into their lives with her softness and her sweet smile and her gentleness with the boys.

The kids adored her, even Nat—though his daughter had seemed a little on the cool side tonight. Cody and Tanner thought she was the best thing to come along since juice boxes. He had watched their eyes light up when he'd carried her into the great room, the eager way both boys had come running just to be near her.

She seemed to adore them, too. Watching her spend the evening reading to his sons had given him a weird tug in his chest. He couldn't explain it and he wasn't sure he liked it, but he couldn't deny that his children had come to love her.

Having her there seemed *right*.

He stared at the rope border Marjorie had nailed around the room. How could that be? Caroline had only been at the Cold Creek a few days but already she seemed to belong, as if she'd been there forever, and he was having a tough time imagining how things would be when she left again.

Alone.

That's how he would be. Not just alone but lonely, and that seemed far, far worse.

He had been empty these last two years since Andi had died. Hollow, joyless, cold. There was a spring on their grazing allotment in the mountains that had suddenly dried up a few years ago when a severe drought had hit the West. But when he had taken the cattle up earlier in the summer, he'd discovered that by some miracle of nature, the wet winter had suddenly revived it and now it was pumping water again just like it had done for generations, clear and pure and sweet.

Since Caroline had come to the ranch, he felt like

that spring. He had thought his life was all dried up after Andi had died, that anything good and pure was gone forever.

Now all those empty, dry places inside him seemed to be filling again.

He wasn't sure he was ready to come back to life— nor was he really thrilled about the fact that Caroline was the one who seemed to have brought about the change.

She wasn't at all the sort of woman he needed in his life. She didn't know anything about cattle, she had the same wacky New Age ideas Marjorie did about some things, and she had a busy life and career a thousand miles away.

But she seemed to love his kids, so much that she'd risked her own life to save Tanner's. She was kind and funny and she made his pulse jump every time she smiled at him.

He blew out a breath and tucked the covers closer around Tanner.

He would miss her like crazy.

Chapter 15

When Wade returned to the great room, he found his youngest brother sprawled on the same ottoman Tanner had pulled up next to Caroline's recliner earlier for story time.

Seth appeared so close, Wade was surprised he didn't have his chin perched on Caroline's arm just like Tanner had done.

He couldn't seem to control a quick spurt of jealousy. With his charm and good looks, Seth could have any woman he wanted—and he usually did. If he set his sights for Caroline, she wouldn't stand a chance.

Right now she looked like every other woman who ventured into Seth's orbit—completely charmed. She was laughing at something his brother said and she looked bright and animated and as pretty as a mountain meadow ablaze with wildflowers.

He had to admit, he was slightly gratified when she turned as soon as he entered the room and her crooked little smile actually seemed to kick up a notch or two.

"You can't be done already," she exclaimed. "Did Tanner really stay asleep?"

He shrugged, wondering what Seth would do if he shoved him off the ottoman to the floor and took his place next to her. "So far. I admit, I cheated a little."

"I knew there had to be something underhanded!"

"I didn't put him all the way in his pajamas, just traded his jeans for pajama bottoms and left him in his T-shirt."

"Sneaky," she said in an admiring tone.

"It's one of those survival skills every parent figures out early."

"You were sneaky long before the kids came along," Seth interjected. "You were the one who figured out how to rig that rope in the old maple tree so you could climb out your bedroom window, swing over to the tree and climb down the trunk. It was genius, something I used many a time after I took over your bedroom when you moved out."

"Only I used to sneak out and get in a little late-night fishing while you used it to go make out with SueAnn Crowley. Anyway, I'm sure Caroline isn't interested in this old family history."

"Oh, I am! Did either of you ever get caught?"

Seth grinned. "Nope. That rope is still probably there."

"Guess I'd better take it down before Tanner discovers it and figures out how to use it," Wade said.

He didn't want to go sit on one of the couches and

leave Seth here in close proximity to Caroline, so he opted to remain standing by the side of her recliner.

"So are you ready for me to take you to bed?"

At his abrupt question, her lips parted just a little and Seth made a sound that could have been a laugh or a cough.

It took a moment for Wade to realize what he'd said. When he did, he felt the tips of ears go hot and red.

"I meant, can I help you back to your bedroom now?" he said quickly, making a mental note to teach Seth some manners next time the opportunity arose.

"Not yet. Do you mind terribly if I just sit here a while longer? The fire is so comforting and I'm enjoying the change of scenery. I promise, you two can take care of your business and you won't even know I'm here."

Right. And maybe tomorrow his horse would suddenly recite the Pledge of Allegiance. He had no doubt whatsoever that he would be aware of every sigh, every breath, every movement.

"You'll probably be bored to tears listening to dry ranch talk."

"I told you, I find it all interesting. Seth was telling me about the TV interview before you came down. It sounds like it went well."

"He did a good job representing the ranch," Wade said. "And the producer was fine about the change in plan."

How could she be otherwise, with Seth pouring on all his charm? He wouldn't be surprised if his brother had Darci Perez's phone number tucked away right now with all his others.

"I'm still sorry you missed it, especially when you didn't have to on my account," she said.

"She said they got enough footage of me explaining things around the ranch and they'll use that."

"When does it air?" she asked.

"Two weeks from yesterday," Seth provided. "At least that's what Darci said."

"I guess I'll be back in Santa Cruz by then," she said. "I'll have to be sure to watch it."

Her casual reminder that she would be out of their lives soon put a definite damper on Wade's mood.

"It's late," he said curtly to Seth. "Let's go through the log so we can all get to bed."

They moved to the table Nat used for homework and Seth pulled out his report of the day's activities.

For the next half hour they discussed feed schedules, which animals to cull for the winter and Seth's encounter with a neighboring rancher disputing water rights.

"Sounds like you handled Simister just right. He needs to know where we stand on this. I wouldn't have done a thing differently."

"Thanks." Seth looked surprised at the comment and Wade wondered if he'd been too stingy with the praise over the years. If so, it was something he'd picked up from old Hank Dalton.

He had worked alongside his father every day until Hank had dropped dead of a heart attack. He could count on one hand the number of times Hank had offered anything to him but criticism.

Had he become like his father in other ways without realizing it? He thought of the extra work Seth had done these last few days with an eagerness that had surprised him, then made him feel guilty, especially when he realized Seth was more than capable of the job.

His brother made sound decisions, treated the ranch

hands with fairness and decency, and had clear ideas about what they were trying to accomplish at the ranch.

Wade should have been delegating to him more, especially these last few years after Andi had died, he suddenly realized. Lord knew, he could have used the help and Seth seemed willing to step in.

Wade wasn't sure why he hadn't seen it, but somehow he had fallen into the habit of thinking of Seth as the same irresponsible kid he'd been when Wade had taken over running the ranch. Maybe because his brother was still a very swinging bachelor, still running around with his friends from high school, still hanging out at the tavern in town.

He acted like he was still in college, though he'd graduated and come back to the ranch five years ago. Seth never seemed to take anything seriously and when Wade compared his brother's life to his own, full of responsibility after responsibility, Seth came out looking reckless and carefree.

Now he wondered how much of his brother's wildness stemmed from Wade's own lack of trust in him.

It was a stunning revelation for him.

Since the day his father had died, Wade had taken his responsibilities to the ranch and his family very seriously. It was tough for him to surrender that burden to someone else because he loathed the idea of anyone thinking he was shirking his duties.

But maybe by failing to delegate more to Seth, he had caused both of them harm.

"You've done a good job these last few days," he said slowly. "I'm sorry for the extra work."

Seth started gathering up the papers he'd brought. "I'm not. It's been a major learning experience. I've gotten a whole new perspective being the big hombre for a few days."

"You're a good cattleman, Seth. Maybe you ought to give some thought to running your own herd."

Where before Seth had looked astonished at Wade's appreciation, now he looked flabbergasted. His mouth sagged open and he stared for a full moment before he composed himself.

"I've thought about it some," he admitted, then paused. "What would you say if I told you I'm more interested in training horses?"

Wade couldn't say he would be surprised. Seth had been horse-mad since before he could walk. Wade and Jake both enjoyed horses, but Seth had always been passionate about them.

His brother had been a team roper on the college rodeo circuit and had even spent a couple summers on the pro circuit. It seemed like he always had a horse he was working with.

"What kind of operation?"

"Cutters." Seth said the word so fast, Wade realized his brother had indeed given this some thought. "Breeding and training them."

"I thought that was just a hobby with you."

"A hobby I'm damn good at. You know Calliope never met a cow she couldn't work and I trained her from a colt. And remember, I worked that gelding for the Stapeley kid and he got a buckle at the PRCA finals out of the deal."

"What sort of business plan have you considered?"

"Find a good stud, to start with. I've got my eye on one from over at the Diamond Harte in Star Valley. If

I could come up with the capital, I think Matt Harte would give me a good deal on it."

"The man has quality horses, that's true."

Seth went on for another ten minutes about what he would do if he ran a breeding-and-training operation, and with every word, Wade felt more and more ashamed.

He had completely undervalued his brother, had been so wrapped up building his own legacy at the Cold Creek that he hadn't seen Seth had dreams of his own.

He wouldn't make that mistake again.

A few weeks ago, he might not have seen the value in a man holding onto his dreams. But things seemed different now. He risked a glance at the recliner where Caroline sat, a magazine propped open on her lap as she gazed into the fire.

You don't think following your dreams is important? she had asked that first day she'd shown up at the ranch.

At the time, he'd thought a man would do better to focus on fulfilling his responsibilities. Now he realized that the work he did at the Cold Creek was both his responsibility *and* his dream. He loved the ranch and had poured his heart into making it a success.

How could he deny Seth the same opportunity?

"You know, you do own a quarter share of the Cold Creek," he said slowly. "Seems to me if you've got your heart set on working with horses, you ought to stop sitting around thinking about it and get serious."

Seth narrowed his gaze. "What are you saying?"

"Off the top of my head, I can think of at least two or three spots on the ranch that would make a good location for stables and an indoor training arena."

His brother had the look of a man afraid to hope. "The Cold Creek has always been about cattle."

"Well, maybe it's time we shake things up a little."

Wade and Seth talked for another half hour about the risks and the challenges of stretching the ranch in a second direction. Seth had thought things through in great detail, and Wade wondered if his brother ever would have acted on those ideas or if he would have been like Wade, so consumed with the daily minutia of running the ranch that he'd lost sight of the bigger picture along the way.

Caroline had helped him refocus, he realized. On his kids, on himself, on more than just the ranch.

The thought distracted him from the business at hand enough that he looked over at the recliner and found her asleep, her cheek resting on one hand.

Seth followed his gaze. "I guess we bored her right to sleep."

"I better take her back to bed."

"And I'll take that as my cue to get out of here. I've got plenty to think about tonight."

If his thoughts involved more than women and whiskey, Wade had to be grateful.

Seth tugged on his denim jacket but paused before putting on his Stetson, his features serious. "At the risk of having you bash my face in, can I offer some advice?"

"You might as well, since I'm pretty sure I'm not going to be able to stop you."

Seth cocked his head toward Caroline. "I don't pretend to know all there is to know about women—"

"And yet you seem to be doing your best to screw up the learning curve for the rest of us."

Seth grinned. "I do what I can."

A second later, his grin slid away as he looked at Caroline again. "Take it from a man who knows women. Caroline is different. She's funny and sweet and smart. She listens when you talk, she's not one of those people who just waits until you wind down before they launch into their own life story. She cares about people, you can tell."

Wade glared, not liking that look in his brother's eyes. "And you're telling me this because…?"

"There's something going on between the two of you. I don't pretend to understand that, either, but nobody could miss the vibes the two of you are sending out. She watches you all the time and when she's not watching you, you're watching her. It's a good thing we're into the rainy season because the two of you put out enough sparks to start a forest fire."

Wade flushed, hoping like hell she was really sleeping and not just pretending, and embarrassed that Seth had noticed the attraction he apparently hadn't been able to conceal. "You're crazy."

"Maybe. But I've got to tell you, brother, if a man is lucky enough to find a woman like that, he'd be a damn fool if he didn't hang on to her and never let go."

Before Wade could respond, Seth shoved on his hat and headed out the back door toward his place.

Wade watched him go, a weird ache in his chest as his brother's words rolled around in his head.

Hang on to her and never let go.

Suddenly he wanted desperately to do just that.

How could this have happened?

He slid down to the much-used ottoman next to Caroline and watched her sleep in the flickering glow of the firelight. How could she have come to be so important?

Looking at her always seemed to take his breath away a little.

She was like something out of a painting hanging in one of the fancy galleries over the mountains in Jackson Hole, all soft, muted colors and elegant lines.

He hated to admit it but Seth was right. Caroline was different.

She had brought laughter and light back to the ranch, had given him hope again in a future that consisted of more than just next year's yield and what interest rates the bank would charge him.

He thought of his talk with Seth and realized suddenly that it was no coincidence they had never had that kind of conversation before. It was more than just Caroline opening his eyes to the importance of having something good to hold onto.

He hadn't talked with Seth about his dreams before because Wade had been so consumed with surviving the present—with the ranch and the kids and all of his many obligations as head of the family—that he hadn't allowed himself to give much thought to the future.

He hadn't wanted to think about the future, not when the present was so bleak.

Now it was as if a door in his mind and heart had opened somehow, showing him a world of possibilities. The only question was whether he was willing to take the chance of walking through that door.

The log in the fireplace finally burned through and broke apart with a loud crackle and a shower of sparks, and the sound seemed to jerk Caroline from sleep.

She blinked her eyes open slowly, like a tiny kitten exposed to light for the first time.

At first she looked confused and he saw the dull wash of pain there before awareness crept in and she sat up a little with just a tiny wince.

"Oh, dear. I've been asleep, haven't I?"

"Yes. I should have taken you back to bed earlier. You need a pain pill, don't you?"

She made a face and looked around the room, ignoring his question. "Did Seth leave?"

"Just barely."

"Before I drifted off, I heard you talking with him about training and breeding horses."

"It's a good idea. Seth has always been a hell of a horseman and if anyone can make it work, he can."

"He was certainly excited about it. More focused than I've seen him since I've been here. It was wonderful to see."

"Well, we've got a lot of planning to do before we bring in the first horse but we'll work up a business plan and see if it's feasible."

"You'll do it even if it's not a huge moneymaker for the ranch, won't you?"

She sounded so confident of it, he flushed that she could read him so accurately. "Probably. It's always good to diversify as long as it's not a big drain on our resources. And I've suddenly realized Seth needs something to call his own. I should have seen it before. Even though he works alongside me on the ranch, his heart has never really been in it. Not like mine is, not like Jake's is with his clinic."

She reached out and touched his arm. "You're a good brother, Wade."

More than he wanted his next breath, he wanted to tug her into his arms and kiss that soft smile. But she was hurting, he reminded himself. He could see it in her eyes. "Come on. Let's get you back to bed so you can take a pill and stretch out."

She must have been hurting more than she let on because she let him scoop his arms under her to lift her carefully from the recliner.

Her arms slid around his neck for balance and she tucked her head under his chin, and it was all he could do not to bury his face in the vanilla-ice-cream scent of her hair.

"I'm sorry you have to do this," she murmured.

I'm not, he almost said, but caught himself just in time. He didn't know how many more chances he would have to be close to her like this.

Hold her close and never let go. Seth's words echoed in his mind. If only things were that easy. Yes, he had feelings for her. But that didn't mean she returned them or that she could ever be happy at the Cold Creek.

He would do well to remember that.

He carried her into her room and set her carefully on the bed. "I'll get you some water so you can take a pill."

"I don't want any more pills."

"I can understand that but you'll sleep better if you do."

"Just tonight, though, then I'm throwing the bottle away."

He poured her water from the pitcher by her bed and handed it to her. "Do you need me to, uh, help you into the bathroom or anything?" he asked after she swallowed the pill.

She shook her head, color rising on her cheeks. "I think I can make it that far on my own. Thank you, though."

He had a million things he wanted to say to her but couldn't think of the right words for any of them.

"Well, good night, then. Call if you need anything."

"I will."

He turned to leave but froze when she reached out and touched her fingers to his arm again. She often touched him to emphasize a point, he was discovering. He didn't care why she did it, he just found he liked it, that he was hungry for any kind of contact with her.

"Wade, I... Thank you so much for all you've done for me since I was injured. I know it's been hard for you to turn so much over to Seth but I'm grateful."

"I've learned some things through the experience. My kid brother can handle a whole lot more responsibility than I've been willing to give him over the years. I guess you could say your little run-in with that cow has been good for me and for my brother."

"I'm so pleased I could help you both out," she said dryly.

He laughed out loud and she gazed at him, a strange light in her eyes.

"What?" he asked, intensely aware of her hand still touching his arm.

"I've never seen you laugh before."

He stared at her, thinking back over the week she'd been at the ranch. He hadn't laughed once? It seemed impossible. "Am I really that much of a humorless curmudgeon?"

"You smile at the children sometimes but you don't laugh. And there's always a sadness in your eyes." She was quiet for a long moment, then she spoke softly. "It breaks my heart."

His heart seemed to tumble in his own chest at her low words. "Ah, Caroline."

For a moment, he was terribly afraid she was going to cry. Her mouth tightened and her eyes glistened but a moment later she smiled, though her eyes were still a little watery.

"Now that I know you have the ability to laugh, I'm going to do everything I can think of to make you do it again."

Her confident statement surprised another laugh out of him and she grinned triumphantly and squeezed his arm. "See? Whatever I'm doing is working already."

"Something is working," he murmured, then he couldn't help himself. He had to kiss her again.

As soon as their mouths tangled, reality rushed in and he froze, stunned at his impulsiveness. He would have jerked back but she slid her arms around his neck with a soft sigh he found incredibly sexy and returned his kiss with fierce intensity, as if she'd been waiting just for this.

Chapter 16

Caroline forgot about the pain digging into her ribs, the throbbing from her leg wound. She forgot about the differences between them and her inevitable heartbreak when she left the ranch.

All she could focus on was Wade touching her, tasting her, like he couldn't seem to get enough.

He murmured her name in that slow, sexy drawl she had come to adore, the one she discovered he only slipped into once in a while when he forgot himself.

She wanted him to forget. She wanted him to think only of her, not the past or the future. Just this moment.

He was bent at an awkward angle, still standing while she was stretched out on the bed, so she slid over to make room for him and tugged him down to the bed beside her.

He pulled her across his lap, supporting her weight with his arm, and his hands were breathtaking in their gentleness as he traced her chin and tilted her face for his kiss.

His mouth explored her, tasting each hollow, each curve, until she wanted to weep from the emotions pouring through her—love and longing and terrible fear that she would never know this sweet wonder again.

She couldn't speak any of those feelings so she tried to show him with her mouth and her hands what was in her heart.

She couldn't have said how long he held her. A few moments? An hour? Time seemed to have lost all meaning; the only thing that mattered to her was Wade.

Finally, when she was beginning to seriously wish they could share more than these kisses, wonderful though they were, he wrenched his mouth away. "Stop. We have to stop."

"Why?"

His laugh—that sound she adored so much—sounded hoarse, strangled. "You want that list of reasons in alphabetical order or prioritized in order of importance?"

"Neither. I don't want you to stop kissing me." With her arms around his neck, she tried to pull his face down but he was far stronger than she was. He pulled her hands free and held them in his.

"Carrie, we can't. You're just loopy from the pain pill. It's wrong for me to take advantage of you like this."

Okay, maybe she was starting to feel a little buzz. The world suddenly seemed like a beautiful, shiny place, but she didn't know how much of that was from the pain pills and how much came simply from being in Wade's arms again.

"That's ridiculous. I've been dying for you to kiss me again since the last time."

When a muscle flexed in his jaw, she smiled and traced it with her forefinger, loving the rough texture of late-night shadow against her fingertips.

"Since the first night I stayed at the ranch, I've thought about it. Dreamed about it," she whispered.

His breathing caught and she watched his Adam's apple work as he swallowed hard. "You don't know what you're saying right now. You're not yourself."

She certainly couldn't seem to make her brain work the way she wanted it to, but still she smiled softly and reached for his hand. "Here's a confession for you, Wade. I'm more myself when I'm with you than I've ever been in my entire life."

He looked stunned, so shocked she wondered if she should regret being so open with him. No. She meant her words and she wouldn't take them back. Instead, she leaned forward and kissed him. He didn't move for several seconds, then he returned the kiss with tenderness and almost unbearable sweetness.

Finally he pulled away again, resting his forehead on hers. "You make it hard to leave."

"You don't have to."

"We both know I do. You're hurting and you need to sleep and I…" He paused. "I need to think about all this."

"About what?"

He pulled away, sitting on the edge of the bed, and said nothing for a long time.

When he finally spoke, his blue eyes were solemn. "About the two of us. About where this might be heading and whether that's a journey I'm prepared to take right now."

She nodded, sensing the admission was not a comfortable one for him. She leaned back against her pillows, suddenly exhausted.

"I don't know if this will make any of that thinking easier or harder," she murmured, "but I should tell you that it would be very easy for me to have feelings for you."

"Caroline—"

"I just thought you should know, that's all."

He watched her for a long moment. "And I should tell you that while it would be very easy for me to return those feelings, I'm just not sure whether I'm ready to let myself do that."

She could be content with that, she thought as she closed her eyes and gave in to the exhaustion. It was far more than she'd ever expected.

Caroline woke the next morning with a sweet and giddy anticipation singing through her veins.

For the first few hazy moments after waking, she couldn't quite understand how it was possible to feel so happy when every inch of her body ached, and then recollection flooded back.

She settled back on the pillow and a smile blossomed as she remembered the tenderness of the night before, the intense, smoldering kisses.

Wade cared about her. He couldn't have kissed her, touched her so sweetly if he didn't.

Oh, she knew they still had much to work through and he could very well decide he wasn't ready for a new love yet. But she would wait. She had waited thirty years to discover what she really wanted out of life. She could wait a while longer for those dreams she hadn't known lived inside her to come true.

How could she ever have imagined when she'd set off on this impulsive journey to try dissuading Quinn from a hasty marriage that she would end up falling in love with a gruff rancher and his three adorable children? With the wild, harsh beauty of the Cold Creek?

She and Wade had a future together. She was sure of it. Now she just had to convince him.

But not without a shower first, she decided. She had contented herself with quick sponge baths since her accident but she needed the full deal today before she could face the day.

Wade had brought in a sturdy plastic lawn chair to give her added support in the bathroom and she maneuvered it into the shower then positioned her injured leg outside the shower curtain so the bandage wouldn't get wet.

It was tricky work and by the time she finished, her ribs ached and her head was pounding, but she was blessedly clean.

When she turned off the spray, she heard a loud banging on the door, so insistent she had to wonder how long it had been going on.

"Caroline?" The voice was low, male and furious. "Caroline, what the hell are you doing?"

She reached for a towel off the rack. "Drying off."

"You've got no business doing that on your own!"

Was he offering to help? she wondered, her stomach trembling at the thought. Still she was compelled to refuse. "I think I can handle wielding a towel by myself, thanks."

"Not that part," he growled. "I meant the shower. You're going to fall and break your neck."

"I'm done now and I handled things just fine. I'm feeling much better this morning."

It was only a little lie, she told herself. She *did* feel better, but the qualifier was perhaps a bit on the excessive side.

"Why didn't you wait for someone to help you?"

She patted her hair with a towel. "I didn't need help. Everything's under control. I'll be out in a moment."

Suddenly she remembered with chagrin that she'd left her clean clothes on the bed in the adjoining room, thinking it would be much easier to maneuver out there where she had a little more room.

Under normal circumstances, she would wrap in a towel and grab them, but she wasn't entirely sure she could manage to stay covered and work the crutches at the same time.

She finally decided she had no choice but to throw on the robe she'd been wearing. She put it on again and ran a quick comb through her hair, then picked up her crutches.

When she hobbled out, doing her best to stay covered, she found Wade standing outside the door, his arms crossed over his chest. He looked so forbidding she had to wonder if she imagined the heat of the night before, some painkiller-induced fantasy.

No. Her imagination simply wasn't productive enough to conjure up something so magical.

"Where are the kids?"

"Nat's already on the bus and Seth took the boys into town with him to get some fencing. They always love a trip to the hardware store."

They were alone in the house, she realized, and her insides seemed to shiver as she wondered if he would take this rare opportunity for privacy to kiss her again.

Not with that distant expression back on his features, she feared.

"You do look like you're getting around okay on those," he said, instead of pledging his undying love, as some silly corner of her mind had hoped he had come to do.

"I've been practicing. I'm still not proficient but I'm trying."

"Does it hurt your ribs to use them?"

"A little. But it's worth it to feel mobile again."

Okay, maybe not as mobile as she thought. The shower had sapped her energy more than she'd realized and her knees were trembling a little with the effort to stay upright, so she hobbled to the bed and lowered herself down.

"You don't have to do everything by yourself. Call me next time. That's why I'm here."

"You're sweet to worry about me but I'm fine," she insisted. "A little weak but fine."

"I'm not sweet." He said the words so harshly she blinked. "I don't want you getting the wrong idea because things have maybe been a little different these last few days. The truth is, I'm bad tempered and pigheaded and impatient. I get caught up in a project and I lose track of time. I can be thoughtless and stubborn and I've never been one for much social chitchat."

"That sounds like a disclaimer."

He focused on a spot above her left shoulder. "I just wanted to make sure you knew these last few days have been outside the norm, that's all. And anything you might have said last night about…about feelings or anything else, I didn't take it seriously."

Ah. Now his words made more sense. "I was never more serious in my life. I haven't taken any pain medicine this morning. My brain is clear and unclouded. And my feelings for you haven't changed."

If anything, she thought, they had deepened with this show of awkwardness. How could a man so big and strong and confident in matters of his ranch be tentative and uncomfortable about this? she wondered.

"Caroline—" he began, his eyes a dark, intense blue. But before he could finish the thought, they heard what sounded like the front door open, then a familiar woman's voice.

"Wade? Caroline? Kids? Anybody home?"

Her gaze locked with Wade as she recognized the voice from her coaching sessions. What horrible timing for Marjorie and Quinn to return.

The honeymoon was over.

A week ago, Wade would have been doing handstands and jumping in circles to hear his mother's voice. But now he wished she would just go away for another week.

In their crazier moments, he and his friends used to cliff dive at a reservoir a few miles away and, talking with Caroline just now, he'd had that same shaky, pulse-pounding feeling he used to experience just before soaring toward the water.

"Caroline—" he said again, not sure what he intended to say.

"Later," she murmured. "Maybe you should go out

and say hello while I finish dressing. I'll be out in a moment."

"I'll just go let them know I'm here then come back and help you out, all right?"

She nodded and he walked out in search of his run-away mother.

He found the newlyweds in the great room, looking at the display of family pictures on one wall.

Quinn Montgomery was tall, handsome and athletic looking, with a California tan and a full head of salt-and-pepper hair. He stood with a casual arm around Marjorie and, even from here, Wade could see she looked a decade younger.

She had her hair styled a different way, lighter some-how, and there was a glow about her he was sure he hadn't ever seen before.

Both of them turned when he walked into the room. Marjorie stared. "Wade! I didn't expect to find you home at this hour."

"I do live here," he reminded her dryly.

"I know, but I assumed you would be out working." She looked around. "Where are the boys?"

"Seth went to the ranch supply store in town for some fencing and they decided to ride along."

"Are you sick? Is that why you're home at this hour?"

He didn't want to launch into a complicated explana-tion about Caroline's injury until she was there so he changed the subject by looking pointedly at her new husband.

Quinn Montgomery had his daughter's eyes, he dis-covered. They were the same warm brown and right now they were scrutinizing Wade just as intensely, with curiosity and a healthy mix of amusement.

"I believe your son is waiting for an introduction, Marjie."

His mother tittered—she actually *tittered* like some kind of teenager!—and threaded her arm through Montgomery's. "I'm sorry, dear. I don't know where my manners have gone."

She then performed a polite introduction as if they were strangers meeting at a garden party.

Wade had never felt so awkward in his life. Just how was he supposed to respond to the bastard who had eloped with his mother—especially when the bastard in question happened to be the father of the woman Wade...had feelings for?

"Montgomery," he said tersely.

Quinn Montgomery's smile also looked remarkably like his daughter's. "Dalton," he responded in kind. "You have a beautiful ranch here. I'd love to have a tour."

I'll just bet you would, he thought.

"We're very proud of it," he said instead. "The Daltons have been ranching here at the Cold Creek for four generations. We're one of the biggest cattle operations in eastern Idaho."

And we're not about to let some aging, slick-eyed Lothario swindle his way into a share of it, he thought.

"I'm afraid I know next to nothing about cattle ranching, although Marjorie has done her best to give me a primer while we were driving out here. She says you've built the ranch into a real force in the beef industry."

"We're working on it."

"And succeeding, from what your mother says."

Wade scowled. Was Montgomery's interest mere curiosity or something more sinister?

Whatever it was, he didn't want to talk about the Cold Creek's success—or lack thereof—with some total stranger, even if the man was married to one of the ranch's partners.

"So what are your plans, now that the honeymoon is over?" Wade asked pointedly.

His mother giggled. "Oh, it's far from over, believe me," she said with so much gleeful enthusiasm that Wade wanted to cover his ears. He absolutely didn't want to know that much information.

"Marjie, this whole thing is no doubt tough enough on your boys," Montgomery chided gently. "You're not making things any easier."

To his surprise, for a moment, Marjorie looked taken aback, then apologetic. "You're right. I'm sorry, dear," she said to Wade. "As far as our plans, we're going to have to work out the details but I told Quinn I still intend to help you with the children as long as you need me. We were thinking about selling my house in town and building a place of our own out here. That way we're close enough to help you but would still have a little privacy."

If it meant he wouldn't have to have her new husband underfoot all the time, Wade would build the place with his own bare hands.

Montgomery smiled. "There will be time to work out all these details. No need to rush into any decisions today." He paused. "Tell me, is my daughter still here?"

"I'm right here, Dad."

Wade turned to see Caroline standing in the doorway on her crutches.

"Good Lord!" Marjorie exclaimed, her eyes wide and horrified. "What happened?"

"I had a little accident a few days ago, but I'm feeling much better now and Jake says everything is healing nicely."

"Sit down before you fall over on those things," Wade growled. "You were supposed to get dressed and wait for me to come back and get you, not come trekking in here like Sir Edmund Hillary."

"I walked twenty feet, I didn't climb Mount Everest. That may have to wait a while."

She looked wobbly to him, her features pale and her weight leaning a little too heavily on the crutches. He shook his head but hurried forward and scooped her up, then set her carefully in the recliner.

He was rewarded with a blush. "You can stop babying me anytime now, Wade. I'll never learn how to use the crutches if I don't practice. You can't carry me everywhere."

"You think I'm going to let you kill yourself when I'm standing right here to help?"

"You're not always going to be standing right there," she pointed out. "I have to figure it out on my own sometime."

She changed the subject by looking past Wade to Montgomery. "Hello, Dad." There was a reserve in her eyes Wade wasn't expecting, though he thought he saw love there, too.

Quinn stepped forward and kissed her cheek. "Hello, baby. I was surprised to learn you were here at the ranch."

"Were you?" The coolness in her voice again surprised Wade. Since she'd come to the ranch, she'd been nothing but warm and friendly to everyone, from the ranch hands to Natalie's bus driver.

"There was no reason for you to come chasing after me. I thought I explained everything sufficiently in my email. You shouldn't have been so concerned."

"When you decided to run off with one of my clients without a word to me beforehand, you really didn't have the slightest inkling that I might consider that a cause for anxiety?"

"Carrie—"

"No, tell me Dad. Why didn't you mention to me that the two of you were corresponding?"

"We knew you would be upset," Marjorie broke in. "Quinn knew he had done the wrong thing answering your work phone that day you weren't home but we had such a lovely conversation, neither of us wanted to see it end. There was nothing underhanded about it, it was just too precious to share with anyone at first, especially when we knew you wouldn't be happy about how we met."

Caroline said nothing to that, only gave her father a long look. There were undercurrents zinging between her and her father that Wade couldn't pretend to understand. He did know she looked upset, though, and for that alone he decided to step in.

Before he could, Marjorie did the job for him. "I'm starving," she said suddenly. "We've been driving all night and didn't take time for breakfast. Would anybody else like an omelet?"

Caroline shook her head but her father smiled. "An omelet sounds great. Can I help you make it?"

"No, no. Why don't you stay here and talk to your daughter? I'm sure the two of you have a great deal to say to each other. Wade, why don't you help me in the kitchen and fill me in on everything that's happened around here since I've been gone?"

That particular conversation would take far longer than the time needed to whip up a couple of omelets, but he followed Marjorie anyway, impatient to talk to his mother.

"Isn't he wonderful?" Marjorie asked as soon as they were out of earshot. "He's kind and thoughtful and by some miracle, he's as crazy about me as I am about him."

Wade shook his head. "What the hell were you thinking, to run off with a man you only knew from the internet, a man none of us had ever met? For all you knew, he could have been an ax murderer. Or worse!"

Marjorie grabbed a carton of eggs from the refrigerator. "I'm not some desperate old lady who just fell off the turnip truck, Wade. You don't think I considered that possibility?"

"But you married the bastard anyway!"

She narrowed her gaze at him. "Be careful, son. That bastard is my husband." The steel in her voice might have been coated in velvet but it was still most definitely steel.

He sighed. "Let me rephrase, then. You considered the possibility that the man you were sharing a clandestine long-distance relationship with might have a criminal past but you went ahead and married him anyway. Explain how an intelligent, progressive woman like you claim to be can make that choice."

"Because I love him," she said simply. "Quinn is a good man, honey. I knew that right away. Yes, he's had some run-ins with the law but he's paid his debt to society and moved on."

He stared at her, his blood suddenly running cold. "What do you mean, run-ins with the law?" he asked carefully.

She made a careless, dismissive gesture, an egg in her hand. "Just that. He was a little wild in his past but that's all behind him now. And before you think I was some naive old bat who let myself be charmed by a handsome face and a smooth talker, Quinn himself told me of his past the very first time we talked on the phone. He didn't have to—we were only casual acquaintances at the time—but he did."

Wade couldn't seem to think straight with the rushing in his ears and he was suddenly filled with a bone-deep foreboding. "Mother. Exactly what did he do?"

"Oh, this and that." She whipped the egg beater. "Ran a few schemes that went bad, a little grifting here and there. He was a bit of a rascal in the past and the law finally caught up with him. But I'll have you know, he's turned over a new leaf and has been a clean, productive member of society since he was released from prison four years ago."

Prison? *Prison?* Just when he thought this situation couldn't get worse. Now he had the delightful added complication of learning his mother was married to an ex-con.

He let out a long, slow breath, so angry he didn't trust himself to speak. A criminal. His new stepfather was a criminal.

Why was he just learning about this now? Caroline had been in his home for more than a week and not once had she whispered a single word about her father's dubious past.

He had a right to know, damn it. She should have told him. He had trusted her, had told her things no one else in the world knew. With all they shared, how could she have kept this part of her life a secret?

The deep ache of betrayal settled in his gut and he wasn't sure which was more powerful, that or the fury seething through him.

His instincts had been dead on. A grifter. A scam artist. In Marjorie, the bastard had found a nice, juicy widow, then he'd wooed and wed her before her family could do a thing about it.

Caroline must have been in on the whole scheme. Otherwise, wouldn't she have told him about her father's past?

His stomach hurt suddenly like he'd been sucker punched, and he had to fight to press a hand there to help him catch his breath.

"Quinn deeply regrets the wrongs he did and has worked hard to make restitution," Marjorie went on, heedless of his turmoil. "Personally, I believe it shows a great strength of character to admit to his wrongs and try to repair the harm he caused. If you give him a chance, I know you'll love him."

She smiled as she added the eggs to the frying pan. "I'm sure you and the kids already love Caroline, don't you? She's such a sweetheart and she's so much like her father."

Yeah. He was finally beginning to figure that out.

Chapter 17

By the time he returned to the great room, Wade was fairly confident he had the worst of his rage and hurt contained behind a vast wall of ice.

Even though he wanted to pick up his new stepfather and throw him through the big picture window, he forced himself to be polite.

He was also polite to his mother, even though his second impulse was to lock her in her room until she rediscovered her brain.

Caroline, he mostly ignored, even though what he most wanted was to grab her and shake her and ask her why the hell she had to go and make him feel again, just so he could bleed.

Finally, just when he thought he might explode if he had to pretend another second, Marjorie finished her omelet and smiled at her new husband. "Why don't we go bring in our luggage and then have a look around the ranch?"

Quinn agreed with alacrity, just as Wade would have expected. Eager to get an eyeful of his score, Wade thought bitterly, grateful he'd had the foresight to contact the ranch attorneys right after Marjorie's fly-by-night wedding to make sure the Cold Creek assets were protected.

Caroline and her scheming father wouldn't see a penny.

"They seem genuinely happy, don't you think?" Caroline said as soon as they left. Her tone conveyed a relief and surprise he didn't quite understand and couldn't take time to analyze.

When he didn't answer, she gave him a searching look and then her smile froze.

"You don't agree that they seem happy?"

"Oh, they seem delirious," he snapped. "It's a regular lovefest here at the Cold Creek."

Her smile slid away completely. "What's wrong?"

His fury finally managed to burn a hole in the ice covering his emotions and he couldn't stop it from seeping through, even if he wanted to.

"Were you ever going to tell me?"

At his low, bitter tone, her face paled. "Tell you… what?"

"About my new stepfather and his interesting little hobbies. Oh, and, I don't know, perhaps you might have thought to mention the time he spent behind bars."

She drew in a sharp breath and her features lost even more of their color. "Wade—"

"What? Did it slip your mind? After all, he's such a fine, upstanding citizen now."

She folded her hands in front of her and, through his howling pain, he saw they were trembling slightly.

"What do you want me to say?" she asked in a small voice.

"What's your game, Caroline? Your father is easy to read. He finds a wealthy but vulnerable widow and charms his way into her life. It's an old and familiar story but I'm afraid this time it's not going to work. My mother can't cash in her share of the ranch unless the other three shareholders agree and I can guaren-damn-tee that neither I nor my brothers will ever do that. No matter how clever he might be, your swindler of a father won't see a penny of Cold Creek money."

Her dark eyes seemed huge, bruised, in her pale face and he had a twinge of anxiety but quickly discarded it.

"Your father's role is easy to figure out. But what is your part in this little drama? What were you hoping to gain by all this? By coming here and insinuating yourself into my life, into my children's lives?"

"Nothing," she whispered.

"Oh, come on." He bit out the words and had the hollow satisfaction of seeing her flinch. "If you were purely innocent, why didn't you ever mention your father's past crimes? You hoped I would never find out, didn't you? Because you know that once I learned the truth, your little game would be over."

He wanted her to defend herself, to tell him he was crazy, to explain, but she said nothing, her mouth compressed in a tight line.

He let out a harsh breath. "If your father's half as good at the grift as you, no wonder my mother fell for him. You'll be happy to know, whatever game you were running, it worked. I fell for all of it, the whole sweet, nurturing act."

He couldn't remember ever being so angry—most of all at himself. He should have listened to his own instincts at first, his suspicions of her. If he had held on to them and protected himself a little better, he wouldn't be feeling this terrible, crushing sense that he had lost something rare and precious.

"I trusted you, Caroline. I let my children come to care for you, let *myself* care about you. For the first time in two years, the world seemed bright and shining and new. I thought you were someone good and decent, a woman I could love."

His last word came out savage and ugly and she made a small, wounded sound.

She was crying, he saw, and the sight of it arrowed right through his fury to his heart. Damn her. He couldn't let her get to him. He wouldn't fall for it, even though part of him wanted to hold her tight, to tell her he was sorry, to kiss her tears away.

She was only crying out of frustration because her plans had been ruined, he told himself.

"The tears are a nice touch," he snarled. "Too bad I've got your number now. You can shut them off anytime."

"Oh, can I?" she whispered, blinking hard.

Tears shimmered on her lashes and one more slid down the straight plane of her nose. She swiped at it with a jerky, abrupt motion, but another one quickly took its place.

Suddenly his anger washed away, leaving only a deep, yawning sense of loss and he couldn't look at her anymore, with her soft eyes and her pretty features and her lying mouth.

"The minute Jake says you can travel again, I want you off my ranch," he said quietly.

"Of course," she murmured.

He turned away, thinking of how baffled and lost his children would be when she disappeared from their lives. Though he hated to ask her for anything, he knew he had no choice, for their sakes.

"I would appreciate it if you'd stay away from Nat and the boys during the rest of your time here. They're going to be hurt enough when you leave. I don't want them to suffer more for my stupidity."

He didn't trust himself to say anything more, just turned and walked out without looking back.

She certainly wasn't going to wait for permission from any of the Dalton brothers.

As soon as the door slammed behind Wade, Caroline allowed herself only a few ragged breaths for strength, then grabbed her crutches and pulled herself to her feet, welcoming the physical pain if it would take some of this terrible ache from her chest.

By sheer force of will, she made it to her bedroom and by the time Quinn wandered in a half hour later in search of her, she was sweating and pale but her suitcases were packed and waiting on the bed.

Quinn stopped in the doorway, his gaze taking in her luggage. "What's this about?" her father asked.

Though it cost just about everything she had left, she managed to speak in a calm, even tone. "I need a ride to the airport in Idaho Falls. I'm not physically able to drive yet."

Quinn looked surprised. "Do you really think that's wise? Hate to break it to you, baby, but you're not looking so hot right now. Maybe you ought to sit down and rest. Think this through a little."

"No. I need to leave."

Something in her tone or her expression must have given away her distress. Quinn's too-handsome features dissolved into concern and he stepped closer.

"What's the matter? Come here. You look like you just lost your best shill."

He wrapped her in his arms and for an instant she leaned her weight against him, surrounded by the familiar scent of his aftershave and the cinnamon mints he was never without.

The combination of smells made her feel ten years old again, and she wondered how she could love her father so much and still carry this heavy burden of anger.

She stepped away, balancing on her crutches. "Quinn, I haven't asked you for anything. Not anything, not even that time I spent four months in jail for something we both knew I had nothing to do with. I'm asking you now, calling in every marker. I need a ride to the airport. I can't stay here another minute."

To her chagrin, her voice broke on the last word and tears burned in her eyes again.

Quinn studied her for a long moment. "Oh, baby. I've never been much of a father to you, have I? There are plenty of sins Saint Peter can pile at my feet when I reach those pearly gates, but the worst will be the harm I've done to my little girl."

He slid his thumb over her cheek. "I was given a rare

and precious gift, better than any score I could dream up, and I treated it like pigeon bait."

She couldn't deal with this. Not now.

"I need to go home. Please, Daddy."

Her tears were falling freely now and Quinn pulled her into his arms again. When he released her, he looked sad and tired and years older.

"Let me go find my keys."

Caroline wasn't sure how she survived the two weeks after she left the Cold Creek. She had little memory of the torturous plane ride home or of that first terrible night when she had wept until she'd thought for sure she must have no tears left. The intervening days all seemed to run together, a hazy blur of sorrow and loss.

Physically, she felt much better. Though her doctor in Santa Cruz still advised her not to put weight on her leg, she was moving around on her crutches with ease and the pain had abated significantly.

Her chest still ached but she wasn't sure if that was from her broken ribs or her broken heart.

She sighed now, gazing out the window at the little slice of ocean that was all she could see from her cottage.

A cold rain blew against the glass, as it had been doing nearly every day since she'd returned from the Cold Creek. She was so tired of it. If the sky would only clear, maybe she could feel warm again. She might even remember that the sun always came out again, even after the darkest night.

There was no sunshine in sight today. From here, the sea looked a churning, angry green, and the sky was heavy and dark.

In hopes of cheering herself up, she had opened a jar

of the tomato soup she'd canned with produce from her own garden. It was warming on the stove, sending out a hearty, comforting smell, and a fire burned merrily in her little fireplace, but she still felt cold, empty.

Somehow, she had to learn to go on, but the thought of a future without Wade and the children seemed unendurable.

She missed the children so much she could hardly bear it. Nat, with her rapid-fire conversation and her bossiness, Tanner and all that mischievous energy, Cody the cuddler, who was never as happy as when he was sitting on a warm lap with a book and his blanket.

And Wade.

Her finger traced a raindrop's twisting journey on the other side of the glass. She missed Wade most of all. She missed his strength and his slow smile and the sweet tenderness of his touch.

She had to snap out of this misery. Her work was suffering—it was very difficult to help others face their problems and weaknesses when her own life was such a shambles.

She'd had two sessions that morning and had to reschedule both, with great apologies to her clients, because she just hadn't been able to focus.

Tonight would be better, she told herself. She would have her soup, turn on some cheerful music, then try to finish some of the paperwork she had been neglecting since her return to California.

She had just dished up a bowl and set it on the table to cool when her office telephone rang. She waited for the answering machine to pick up but the ringing continued.

Rats. In the distracted state she seemed to permanently inhabit since leaving the Cold Creek, she must have forgotten to switch it back on.

With an exasperated sigh, she grabbed her crutches to hobble in and turn it off. The ringing stopped just as she made her slow way to her office door, but it started up again before she could reach the phone. Whoever it was had persistence going for him.

She could turn on her machine and let technology catch the call or she could pick it up.

Maybe human contact would shake her out of her melancholy, make her feel a little less alone. She lowered herself to her office chair and picked up the phone.

"Light the Stars."

A long pause met her words and she heard a burst of static, then a male voice spoke, sounding like it was coming from some distant planet.

"Yes. Hello. I'm interested in your coaching services."

She almost told him to call back in the morning during business hours. But even through the dicey connection, she thought she heard a hint of desperation in the voice.

"Have you ever used a life coach before?" she asked, trying to gauge a little background on the potential client.

"No. But I need some serious help and you come highly recommended. I understand you're the best."

Not anymore, even if that had ever been true. Right now she was a mess and she wasn't sure she could coach a mosquito to bite.

"There are many good life coaches out there. Finding the right one is always a little tricky. I always recommend that my clients talk to several before finding the one they want to work with."

"I don't want to do that. It's you or nobody else. I'm desperate here, ma'am."

She didn't need that kind of pressure—not now, when she was filled with self-doubt. But something about that staticky voice struck a chord within her.

"All right. We can set up a time for a trial session if you'd like—"

"Can't we do that now?"

She laughed a little, though it sounded hollow and tinny to her ears, and she wondered how long it had been since she'd found anything genuinely amusing.

"I'm afraid it doesn't work that way. After we schedule an initial session, I usually have my clients fill out a somewhat lengthy questionnaire on my website and email it to me so I have a little background information going into our session."

"What kind of questions?"

"Basic things, really. Name, occupation, your family dynamics. The areas of your life you're unhappy with...."

"I can tell you that one right off. My life is a mess, mostly because I've been an idiot."

Oh, I bet I've got you beat on that one, she thought.

"I've been stupid and mean to someone who didn't deserve it and in the process I threw away something that could have been wonderful. I'm miserable. The woman I love left me and I need your help trying to figure out if there's any chance I could win her back."

Caroline closed her eyes. Why couldn't his problem be something simple like a midlife crisis or dissatisfaction with his career choices? Why did it have to be a romance turned sour?

She couldn't deal with this right now, not with the shambles her own life was in.

"I don't think I can help you," she said quietly.

"You have to. Look, I'm desperate. This woman brought joy and laughter back to a cold and lonely world. She made me feel again, when I wasn't sure I ever would again. I can't face a future without her in it. I can't."

Even through the bad connection, the raw emotion in his voice came through clearly and Caroline was shocked to feel tears burn behind her eyelids. She definitely couldn't take on this client—or any client dealing with a relationship disappointment right now.

"I'm sorry," she said after a moment, "but I'm afraid you're going to have to find someone else to work with you. I can give you some referrals to some excellent coaches—"

"No. I don't want anybody else. I want you."

"I don't think I'm the right person to help you at this time."

The man gave a ragged-sounding laugh. "I'm afraid you're the only one who can help me."

"I don't—" she began but the doorbell rang before she could complete the sentence, then rang again more insistently just an instant later.

"You should probably get that," the voice on the phone said.

"Yes. I'm sorry. Could you hold on a moment?"

"As long as it takes," he responded.

Cordless phone in the crook of her shoulder, she hobbled the few steps to the door and looked out the peephole, then nearly lost her balance on her crutches.

"Wade," she breathed.

He stood on her stoop, his Stetson dripping rain, looking big and gorgeous and wonderful.

And holding a cell phone to his ear.

"Caroline," the voice on the phone murmured and she wondered how she had possibly mistaken that slow drawl for a stranger's voice.

Her heart stuttered in her chest and she could do nothing but stare at his distorted image through the peephole. He was here, not a thousand miles away on his Idaho ranch, but right here on her doorstep.

After two weeks of misery, of missing him so badly she couldn't breathe around it, he stood in front of her. She almost couldn't believe it.

"Are you still there?" he asked after a long moment.

"I...yes. I'm here."

"I'm sorry, Caroline," he said softly in her ear and she saw the truth in his eyes. "I'm so sorry. I should have trusted you. I should have trusted myself, my own instincts. In my heart, I knew you were just what you seemed but I jumped at the chance to push you away. It's a poor excuse, but I can only tell you I was scared."

"Scared?"

"When I lost Andrea, I didn't think I would survive the pain of it and I sure never dreamed I might be able to love again. And then you showed up at the Cold Creek. Somehow you started to thaw all those frozen corners of my heart and it scared the hell out of me."

"Wade—"

"It still scares me," he admitted. "But the thought of living without you scares me more."

She pressed a hand to her stomach, to the swirly, jittering emotions jumping there.

"I love you, Caroline," he said quietly. "With all my

heart. Are you going to open the door? Or will you leave me standing out in the rain for the rest of my life?"

With pounding heart and trembling hands, she worked the locks as fast as she could, dropping the phone in the process. Finally, after what felt like forever, the last bolt shot free and she jerked open the door.

It wasn't a mirage, some heartache-induced dream. He was real. And he was hers.

Using her crutches as a fulcrum, she launched herself at him, laughing and crying at the same time. He caught her, as she knew he would, and pulled her tight against him.

"Carrie," he murmured, his blue eyes bright and intense in the gloom, then his mouth found hers.

It was a kiss of redemption, of healing. Of peace and hope and joy, and she never wanted to stop.

"I love you," she said against his mouth. "I've missed you so much."

He made a low sound in his throat and kissed her fiercely, until she was dizzy from it.

"We're getting soaked," he murmured some time later.

"I don't care."

His laugh was raw. "You'll catch pneumonia, then your father will never forgive me. He's already spent two weeks telling me what an idiot I am."

She blinked. "Quinn?"

"My new stepfather is not too thrilled with me right now. Nobody on the ranch is, if you want the truth. For the last two weeks, I've been getting the cold shoulder from just about everybody. Even Cody."

She couldn't believe that. The little boy adored his father.

"The kids aren't speaking to me, my brothers only talk to me to tell me what a damn fool I am, and your father finally threatened bodily violence if I didn't get a brain in my head and come after you."

"He...he did?"

Without waiting for an invitation, Wade carried her through the door to her couch, then sat down with her in his lap. They would drip all over it, but she didn't care.

"That man might have made some mistakes where you're concerned but he loves you. He told me everything, all his years of running cons, how you used to beg him to stop but he was always after the thrill of the next deal. He told me you were the most honest person he'd ever met and would rather cut out your tongue than join him in a con."

"You believe him?"

He cupped her chin. "He told me about Washington."

She closed her eyes, mortified that he knew about her time in jail, but they opened again when he kissed her lightly.

"He told me none of it was your fault, that he dragged you into the whole mess against your will."

"I couldn't testify against him. I would have been out in a day but I couldn't do it. I'm weak when it comes to him."

"Not weak. You love him. And so does Marjorie, by the way. He seems to be crazy about her, too. After two endless weeks of living with their constant billing and cooing, I have to believe it's the real deal. Nobody could be that good an actor, even your father."

"Do you mind? About his past?"

He was quiet for a moment, his hand doing delicious things to the small of her back. "He makes her happy.

She didn't have much of that, married to my father, so I can't begrudge her this."

He made a face. "And to tell you the truth, though I hate to admit it, your dad is growing on me."

"Yes, he seems to have that effect on people," she said dryly.

"I know I hurt you and I'm sorry, sweetheart," he said after a moment. "If you can find it in your heart to forgive me, I swear I'll spend the rest of my life trying to make it up to you."

"Oh, Wade. There's nothing to forgive. Nothing! I should have told you about Quinn the moment I arrived at the ranch. That's the whole reason I came after him, I was in a panic that he might be running another con game, with Marjorie as his mark."

"He signed a prenuptial agreement. Apparently he insisted on it. Marjorie showed it to me and Quinn willingly gave up any current or future claim to any ranch assets or income."

Caroline sagged against him, as the last of the worry over Quinn's motives—the worry she hadn't even realized had been lurking inside her—seemed to seep away, leaving a vast relief.

"I guess it takes a man in love to recognize another one, and I think what Quinn and Marjorie have is the real deal."

"Oh, that's wonderful."

He smiled, then kissed her softly. "I love you. On behalf of everybody on the Cold Creek—but especially for the sake of this lonely, miserable shell of a man—I'm asking you to come back. The kids miss you. I miss you and I need you more than life, Caroline. You showed me how to dream again and I don't want to give that up. Will you come back to the Cold Creek and to me?"

She touched his face, this gorgeous strong man who was looking at her with such tenderness, then she smiled and pressed her mouth to his. "There's nowhere on earth I'd rather be."

* * * * *